Until That Good Day

THOMAS DUNNE BOOKS

St. Martin's Press ✿ New York

THOMAS DUNNE BOOKS.
An imprint of St. Martin's Press.

www.stmartins.com

Design by Kathryn Parise

LIBRARY OF CONGRESS CATALOGING-IN-PUBLICATION DATA

Kemper, Marjorie.
    Until that good day / Marjorie Kemper.—1st ed.
        p. cm.
    ISBN 0-312-29079-9
    1. Traveling sales personnel—Fiction. 2. Racially mixed children—
Fiction. 3. African American women—Fiction. 4. Fathers and
daughters—Fiction. 5. Illegitimate children—Fiction. 6. Depres-
sions—Fiction. 7. Mistresses—Fiction. 8. Louisiana—Fiction.
I. Title.
PS3611.E53 U5 2003
813'.6—dc21
                                                              2002035310

First Edition: July 2003

10 9 8 7 6 5 4 3 2 1

To the memory of my parents,
Burton and Mary Louise Anderson

Until
That
Good Day

Prelude

It is still early morning. Meadowlarks punctuate the air with their rapid, dancing flight, and red-winged blackbirds alight on the rushes in the ditches to both sides of the road. The blackbirds are singing their hearts out.

John Washington is driving this road. It is a road so familiar to him, he could drive it in his sleep. He is thinking about the dream he was dreaming when he awoke. He tries again to see the face of the woman in the dream. (Was it her?)

There's never been a morning so new or so fresh as this day that John drives through; there's never been a road so wide, so beckoning. He shares it with men and mules on their way to the fields. The men smile and wave him past with grand sweeps of battered hats.

John Washington is behind the wheel of his red Essex, traveling north toward Jackson. He considers himself the most fortunate of men. If you knew John Washington you would know that he's taking full credit for this beautiful morning—as though he himself had brought it into creation—and he takes full credit, too, for his own privileged place in it. His mother raised him to this arrogance. She may have meant well. The sleeping woman John kissed good-bye, only half an hour ago, in the green town that he's driven resolutely away from, you won't be surprised to learn, ceased to exist for John as soon as he reached the open road and hit his speed.

It is not given to John Washington, any more than it is to you or to me, to see into the future. His eyes are fixed on the road. And this particular road, this delta road, is straight as a die. The long years that will turn the dross of John's life into the silver cloth of the family myth I tell here are hidden from him. Until that far-off day when the myth will take over from him, John regards himself as the sole author of his life. Till that good day, then, he, like the rest of us, will write confidently toward his *own* ending—the inevitable triteness of which we may rely upon a stern Fate to edit.

Now John is driving south down the same road that was so heart-stoppingly beautiful back in spring. But it's December now. And it's late in the day, a day that began for John with an early morning phone call to his hotel room in Memphis. John Washington has been summoned home.

The light is failing and the air is cold. But John Washington is parched, and water feels like sand in his throat. He is drinking from a flask of whiskey. There has been a tragedy. And though it was expected, and long in coming, it still seems sudden, as tragedies always will. Despite the speed with which John takes this memorized road, the speed for which he is justly famous, he will arrive too late.

Chapter 1

The coffin was in the living room. It rested across two sawhorses that had been draped in black velvet, and it was blanketed with narcissi and tuberoses. There were standing white wicker baskets of gladioli and carnations—red and white—at each corner.

The piano had been moved back into the bay of the front window, and the sofa and wing chairs had been removed to the attic to make room for the folding chairs for the wake.

It is our living room, Vivian thought, like always; only now it isn't. Because everything had changed, and it had done so very suddenly. Vivian knew that Mother was in the coffin. Daddy had made the man shut the lid.

"I won't have people gawking at her," John Washington had shouted in an argument with his wife's older sister while the man from Thomas Brothers & Sons stood silently by, looking at his shoes.

So the man screwed down the lid. Vivian watched him do it. Now she would never see Mother again in this world. She knew because her older sister, Clara, told her so. Daddy had been sitting in one of the straight chairs that had been brought from the funeral home, with his head on the coffin, crying for three hours straight now, sobbing out Mother's name over and over: "Della, Della, Della." It sounded to Vivian like a very sad song with only one lyric.

But, Clara had whispered to Vivian, there was no sense at all in Daddy doing this because Mother couldn't hear him. She wouldn't hear anything at all, ever again. When Clara said that, Vivian stopped whispering to Mother—as she had been doing for two days. She had been saying, "Don't worry, precious little mother; our Blessed Lord and His Blessed Mother will take very good care of you." And other such phrases meant to soothe Mother because she had had such a worried look on her dead face when Daddy held Vivian up so that she might look at her. Daddy said she must memorize Mother's face, and never, never, never forget it. Vivian had already forgotten it.

Vivian sat on one of the chairs the men had brought in and rocked it back and forth experimentally. She went on talking to Mother silently, careful now not to move her lips so Clara would not know, and she watched her father, who was finally sitting up and blowing his nose into a big white handkerchief—for the moment, even his prodigious tears were exhausted.

When Della died, John Washington had been on the road. He sold wares to the little stores up and down the lower Mississippi Valley for a wholesale grocer in New Orleans. He made his living on the road. Still, Della's sisters were angry that he hadn't been present at the exact moment their precious Della had departed the earth. Bessie wasn't speaking to him; she had Leticia relay all her remarks, including the one that Bessie and her husband, Lamar, intended to take Della's children and raise them as their own. They would fight John in court, if need be. Yes, they would! She wouldn't give away Della's precious babies to a common drunk. Why, they'd take him to the Supreme Court if necessary.

John Washington said they would do it over his dead body. Vivian had heard him use this expression many times before, but now, with Mother's dead body right there where the sofa should be, it didn't seem nice to say. Vivian did not want another dead body in the house. Where would they even put it? Dead bodies took up whole rooms to themselves. Her father continued to sit and blow his nose. Vivian got out of her chair and walked softly up to him. "Daddy?"

"What, sweetheart?"

"I'll take care of you."

Vivian was five.

"I thank you for that. But I need a lot of taking care of. I don't think a little thing like you could do it."

John Washington stared at his youngest child. He'd been on the road since she was born five years ago, and when he had been home, Della's illness (and the whiskey he drank to be able to stand it) had blocked out everything; he scarcely knew this small child. When he'd driven up to the house, when he had been summoned home, John Washington had at first taken her for a neighbor's child. She had been sitting on the front porch, twisting a strand of hair around one finger, waiting for him.

She'd had one desperate hope, and that was that when Daddy got home he could make things go back right. He would, she'd thought, never stand for Mother being dead. But though he'd cried and raged and cursed the Living God, just as Vivian had expected him to, nothing changed. Vivian understood now that nothing would.

"Oh, yes," Vivian said. "I can take care of you."

The man clutched the little girl to him, lifting her toes off the floor, so that she lost her balance, and she had to steady herself with one hand on her mother's casket.

"I'm sad, too," Vivian said urgently. But her father made no answer; his own sadness had expanded to take up all the room in the world, and there was none left in it to accommodate his children's grief. Not under the roof, not even under the low winter sky that lay over the town of Myrtle like a lid on a pot.

People began entering the room, and John Washington got up unsteadily from his chair. Vivian turned and looked at the not-living room and saw the neighbors and people from church filing in. The aroma of the tuberoses was so strong that it was visible; it was, Vivian decided, yellow. The aunts had come into the room. The silk drapes with the pink roses were drawn against the afternoon sun, but they did not quite meet, and Vivian could see little specks dancing there in the slanting light. She thought maybe the specks were fairies, like the ones hidden in the garlands that decorated each page of her *Fairy Book*. She hoped they were. She hoped that the fairies were coming to help them. It seemed that no one else could.

❦

Shortly after the funeral—which neither Clara nor Vivian attended because the spots the aunts had declared to be a nervous rash turned into measles instead—the girls and their father moved across town to Grandmother's house. Grandmother was Daddy's mother, but she did not like children, and she did not come out of her bedroom except for meals, when she sat at the head of the table and watched the girls like a hawk, criticizing their dress, correcting their manners and their grammar. Sometimes when they were in their rooms napping or in bed for the night, she came downstairs to play the piano, but she always vanished back to her room before they got up. Because Vivian never saw her actually seated at the piano, she thought the piano played itself as her Aunt Leticia's did.

Grandmother's house was dark. She kept the shades down and the drapes drawn, and had ever since Grandfather's death. It always felt, even at high noon, like the middle of the night on La Salle Avenue. Grandmother's cook, Cassie, looked after the girls and made their meals, but she didn't like children any better than Grandmother did.

After the New Year, when John Washington fled back to the road and Clara went back to school, Vivian spent her days wandering the house—her father had forbidden her to play outside for fear Bessie and Lamar would make good their threat. She tried to make friends with Jupiter, Grandmother's big black cat, but he scratched her when she tried to pick him up, and thereafter hid from her. She pored over pictures in the old books that had belonged to her grandfather. She felt a strong attachment to Grandfather because he'd died the day she was born. Much had been made by adults of this coincidence. After a few weeks Vivian began cutting pictures from these priceless old leather-bound volumes, the ones containing large color plates of Indian chiefs. She worked patiently and carefully with shears she'd taken from Cassie's sewing basket to make paper dolls from the chiefs' portraits. She cut out the backgrounds, too, the forests and clearings, and the swamps and rivers that these old chiefs had ruled over. These she propped up, and she moved the dolls around in the landscapes. She'd cut out horses and dogs and canoes and long houses and wigwams and burial mounds. She disappeared into her Indian world for hours at a time. She would have been in a great deal of trouble had anyone known what she was doing.

And then Grandmother stopped coming out of her room to preside at the table or to play the piano, and the doctor came every day, as he had used to come every day at home, and he held hushed consultations with Cassie in the hall at the bottom of the stairs, and Daddy was again sent for, and then, before the year was out, there was another coffin in another living room.

And Daddy cried even more inconsolably over this coffin than he had the last. And there was yet another funeral that the girls did not attend. This time they had the chicken pox and were quarantined. The doctor nailed a yellow sign on the front door.

It seemed to Vivian as she lay in the dark bedroom, picking at the scabs on her arms and chest, that she was going to pass her entire life in the dark, in curtained houses with coffins and itchy diseases and uncelebrated Christmases.

After Grandmother died, Cassie took charge, and their father came home even more rarely than before. Grandmother's yard-man, Gilbert, who formerly slept in a room over the carriage house, moved into Cassie's room. Something that Grandmother would not have allowed, Clara said, and that perhaps John Washington would not have allowed either, had he known—which he didn't. But at least Cassie and Gilbert had raised the shades and opened the drapes, and sunshine came into the house and spilled onto the floors and over Mrs. Washington's English rugs.

It pooled first thing every morning in the music room and moved next to the study. Vivian followed the sun around the house during the day as though it were a friend or a pet from which she could not bear to be parted. She stared out the tall French windows at a world that lay outside the house like a rare and beautiful painting. She longed to enter it; and she did so in her imagination: spending most of her time in the thicket of bamboo by the fishpond or climbing to the top of the oak in the side yard, from which she could see all of the town to the bayou—even their old house, where she and Clara had played outdoors every afternoon and where they'd had a sandbox and a swing set and a bull terrier named Rex. (Daddy had sent Rex to live in the country when Mother died.) Where every night they'd been brought inside and bathed and fed and were then presented to their mother in her bedroom, where she kissed them and smoothed their hair with her long thin fingers and told them what precious, precious little girls they were and how much God loved them. (He loved them better than the very stars he'd set in the sky. That's what Mother had said. Poor stars, Vivian thought now, as God's love for her continued to play itself out.) From her imaginary perch in the real tree, Vivian watched these scenes from her former life. Over and over.

Cassie found the cut-up books, but she said nothing. The children's daddy was out of his head even when he was sober, and crazy as a tick when he was drunk—which was most of the time he was home. It wasn't like he was going to sit himself down in the library and read books. Instead Cassie took logical steps; she took away the scissors and taught the girl her alphabet so she might read the books instead of cutting them up. This was all the reading lesson Cassie herself had had; and it sufficed for Vivian, as well.

Clara, being three years older, got out of the dark house to school, where Aunt Bessie haunted the grounds with gifts of fudge and divinity—which she spent frenzied nights alone in her kitchen cooking especially for her nieces, her hot tears salting the boiling candy. She of course meant these gifts for Vivian, as well, but Clara shared them with school friends and never mentioned them to her sister.

While Clara was at school, Vivian watched the sun creep

across the long-board, cypress floors and the rugs, and she sat at the kitchen table and studied her letters, and later, she read. In the daytime Cassie and Gilbert stayed mostly in their room. Vivian had to be very quiet because Gilbert got mad if she made noise.

Vivian had come to regard her life as a long, pointless dream, from which she was patiently waiting to be awakened. She reassured herself from time to time that it was only a dream, and that it could not last always. But another Christmas went by before her father, finally emerging from his own bad dream, arranged for her to join Clara at Saint Clare's Academy.

At first Vivian was shy of all the strange children, but as it turned out she had learned a great deal from Grandfather's books—those she'd not cut up before she'd learned to read. She was ahead of her class in almost everything. She knew the names of the continents and the seas and how many there were of each, and all the kings and queens of England—in order. Humility visited her only once a day, during Arithmetic, this hitherto unknown world formed entirely of numbers came as such a surprise to her that she could not even begin to think about it. She was also surprised to learn how small a part the history of Indian chiefs played at Saint Clare's, but she assumed the nuns were saving this subject for later. Vivian had been afraid that the other children would think she was stupid and wouldn't like her, but instead it turned out they thought she was smart. And they didn't like her. It was being something they called a "pet" that led to Vivian's fights with her classmates that called so much attention to her, and in so doing, provoked and mortified Clara. Vivian was confused. Why, if you were supposed to know the answers to Sister's questions, and you did, and you said them aloud, was everyone *mad* at you? And why were people so proud of being dumb?

The principal, Sister Mary Imelda, had to take Vivian aside to tell her that nice young ladies did not fight in the school yard. In fact, Sister confided, they did not fight at all, and perhaps, she suggested, it was not altogether charitable to laugh at the wrong answers some children gave in class. Everyone had not had Vivian's advantages. That's what Sister Imelda said. Vivian was left to herself to ponder what her "advantages" had been.

That school year Daddy began spending more time at home between road trips. Cassie had to make real meals, had real laundry to do; she became, briefly, so busy actually getting the house running to speed again that she had little time for Gilbert—who had moved back into the carriage house and fallen into a very evil mood, such an evil mood that Vivian went to any amount of trouble never to be alone with him.

That winter, Daddy brought home a big radio from New Orleans, and as soon as supper was over everybody gathered in the living room to listen to it. At night after the children were in bed, John listened to music programs from famous hotel ballrooms all over America, and sang along to all the sad songs—whose every lyric he had by heart.

Sometimes after Clara fell asleep, Vivian crept back downstairs and sat next to him on the sofa. He would put an arm around her and go on singing. Vivian pretended to sleep, leaning up against her father, smelling his smell of tobacco and bourbon and lavender water—with which he scented his handkerchiefs—and listening to his heart beat. This was her favorite sound. Even more than the sound of rain on the gallery's tin roof, even more than Aunt Leticia's player piano. More than train whistles.

The sisters shared a bedroom, but little else. Clara, Vivian thought, was a lot like Jupiter. She spent her time preening and thinking her secret thoughts that she would never tell. And like the cat, she didn't like to be played with—you daren't touch Clara either.

For her part, Clara felt stuck with Vivian—who would always

remain, in Clara's mind, "the baby." She remembered Mother telling her about the baby that God was sending them; the baby who was to keep Clara company and be a friend to her for the rest of her life—like Mother was friends with Bessie and Leticia. The baby was to be Clara's Christmas present.

But it hadn't turned out the way Mother said. Mother was sick because of the baby, and even after the baby was born, Mother didn't get better; in fact, she got worse and worse. Clara still had faint memories of an earlier Mother and Daddy—happy as kings and queens, laughing and playing like children themselves. She'd seen them dancing in the living room at night; she'd seen them holding hands and talking on the sofa. She always associated the two of them with music, for Mother loved music and she played the piano, and when she wasn't playing the piano, she was playing the phonograph or singing. Sometimes she sang whole songs to Daddy.

Those pre-baby parents had played with Clara; they read to her; they dressed her up and showed her off; they took her to grown-up parties, where elegantly attired adults declared Clara to be the cutest little thing ever seen. But after the baby came, everything changed. And gradually the baby had turned into Vivian—loud old forgetful, rude, always jumping-around, always showing-off Vivian! And now Mother was dead, and Daddy was different, and would stay that way, Clara knew, and all Clara had to show for it was this sister—her friend for life. It sounded like a sentence handed out to a convict. But what had she done?

When Vivian began school she'd naturally sought Clara out at recess and lunch, but Clara scarcely spoke to her, and later, at home, she told Vivian to stay away from her at school. She said Vivian embarrassed her in front of her friends by jumping around, and braying like a jackass.

Vivian accepted this; she supposed it was even true—ever since

she'd escaped Grandmother's dark house she had been excitable
and, quite probably, loud. So she left her sister alone, though she
often stood behind a forsythia and watched her. Clara did have
many friends. They sat under the trees in front of school, talking
about movies and songs, and becoming nuns, and about who
among them was the prettiest. Clara was, Vivian knew.

Clara looked like the pictures of Mother the aunts had kept on
their crowded mantels with the seashells from the Gulf, and the
dried flowers from the home place in Mississippi where they'd
come from. A place that wasn't there anymore. Had it burned
down? Vivian asked once. No, the aunts said, it was just gone.
How could a house be gone if it hadn't burned down? It was lost,
they amplified. Gone for taxes, Leticia said once, but that upset
Bessie, and she said, No, indeed not! Vivian gave up. The aunts
didn't seem to know what had happened to their family's own
house, which was strange, but Vivian understood that sometimes
in this life you unaccountably lost things. She, after all, had lost
her mother.

Then there came a change. Daddy began going out in the eve-
nings. He whistled songs that weren't even sad! In the mornings
he joked with Cassie and teased his girls. He said he was looking
forward to the beginning of the baseball season. He read aloud
from the newspaper. He parted his hair on the wrong side of his
head, and his face went red when Vivian pointed it out. He
changed dry cleaners and had his hat blocked. He was, Clara told
Vivian, in love. Vivian thought Clara was making a joke; she
laughed.

It was during baseball season, that interminable stretch of the
year between Easter and Halloween when the marvelous radio
played nothing but Cardinals games, that John Washington

brought Antoinette Malone home to meet his children for the first time. Vivian and Clara had been playing Monopoly, Vivian was winning, having bought up the railroads and the public utilities while Clara plunged heedlessly round the board trying to land on Park Place or Boardwalk. They heard their father's car in the drive and continued the game, but then they heard the tripping sound of high-heeled shoes on the veranda steps. This was something they'd not heard in a very long time, and they ran to the window to see who it could be.

"Who is she?" Vivian whispered.

"A Malone," Clara said.

Vivian could tell that Clara did not think a Malone was a very fine thing. Clara smoothed her skirt down and pulled her anklets up. Vivian ran to the door and threw it open, skidding in front of Cassie on the polished floors in her stocking feet.

"Hey!" She shouted, and dived at her father as she always did. But instead of sweeping her up and carrying her inside, he took her by the elbow and propelled her gently back into the hall while he made a half-turn to the Malone and helped her across the threshold like he was helping her up onto a high stoop.

When the couple were inside and Cassie had taken their wraps, John escorted the Malone into the living room, and then standing by the mantel, he turned and said, "Miss Malone, I'd like to present my girls, Clara and Vivian."

"How do you do?" Miss Malone said. She had a little voice, which was only natural because she was a little woman, no bigger, and not much older than a girl—only five feet tall in her high heels. Her gloved hands were smaller than Vivian's. She was dressed all in white. Even her face was white except for the scarlet lipstick that accentuated the Cupid's bow mouth—so popular in that decade. She wore a gardenia in her jet-black marcelled hair.

"How do you do?" Clara replied.

Vivian, ignoring the woman said, "Daddy, you *said* you'd take us downtown for ice cream tonight. That's what you said. This morning. At breakfast, you said that, so let's *go!*"

John Washington ignored her; he and Miss Malone sat down on the sofa. Vivian pushed her way between them. But her father said, "Don't crowd us, darling."

Clara sat demurely on a hassock. Vivian backed away from the sofa and slumped down on the rug beside her sister; she traced one of the rug's vines with her index finger to cover her anger and embarrassment. Daddy had a new *us*.

"Now, what grades are you children in?" Miss Malone asked in her little, silly, high voice.

⸙

"I cannot believe she asked us what *grades* we were in," Vivian said when Daddy had gone to take Miss Malone home and the girls were in bed.

"Why? Everybody asks that," Clara said.

"That's what I *mean*," Vivian said. "I didn't think Daddy would pick somebody like everybody. I thought he'd pick somebody completely special. Like the people do in the songs."

"This isn't a song," Clara said.

"Do you like her?"

Clara shrugged. "It doesn't matter. Try to understand that, Viv. You may as well decide to like her."

"What if I don't?"

"It won't matter."

Vivian thought about this while she pointed one bare foot. She was trying to build up her arches by rolling her feet over a Coke bottle every night. Gilbert had remarked that her feet were flat as boards. So far this technique, which Cassie had told her about, didn't seem to be working.

"I don't like her and I don't not like her, really. I mean I never saw her before in my whole goddamned life."

Clara was brushing her hair. "I've seen her at church. Her little brother Willie is about your age and in Sister Mary Angelica's class."

"That goddamned little albino?" Vivian shrieked.

"He's not a real albino, he's just pale."

"Jesus Christ!" Vivian said.

"Vivian!"

Vivian had taken to swearing with a vengeance, in joyous imitation of her father. But though imitation is well known to be the sincerest form of flattery, John Washington had not taken it as a compliment. However Vivian felt that if her father swore—and John Washington swore the way other people breathed—it could not be exactly wrong. Also, she enjoyed watching the expressions that came across people's faces when she swore. It was plain as day that just for a moment they didn't know what to do with her. Vivian was willing to pay any price to see these expressions visit the faces of her elders.

The girls heard their father's car come back into the drive. Then they heard the car door slam shut and his steps on the porch. They waited for him to come upstairs to say good night, but instead they heard him switch the radio back on. He didn't come upstairs that night. At all. He was asleep on the sofa, in his clothes, when they came down in the morning.

⁂

Now John Washington went out most every night. He came in late and he left early. He took Miss Malone down to New Orleans to "night spots," where they danced to "hot bands." He announced he was a new man. He looked the same to Vivian.

School let out, something Vivian had been dreading because

she did not think she could bear being imprisoned inside the house again, but her father changed the rules and let the girls play outdoors. This improvement in their lives had been brought about by their Aunt Leticia. She, who had always secretly felt sorry for the young widower, had assured him that Bessie's Lamar had no intention whatsoever of raising John Washington's children. So now that John had made his way back to the land of the living, he was willing to allow his children to follow—if they could.

Like Clara, Cassie saw the handwriting on the wall: John Washington would marry Antoinette Malone sure as the world, and he would do it soon, for John Washington in a good mood was a reckless, impetuous man. Oh, while he'd been in mourning for his wife and his mother—that queen of the she-devils!—he'd seemed to have the patience of Job, but that was just because he was worn out and confused in his thinking. It wasn't patience. The man didn't know what patience was. Now it was, "Cassie, where are my shirts? Have you ironed my handkerchiefs? Let me see that bill from the drapers. . . ." Oh, he poked his nose into all the business of the house!

Never mind she'd been running it for nearly two years with no help from anyone, taking care of his bad-tempered old mother, and then his children that he was too drunk (or too gone) to know were alive or dead. Another thing Cassie knew for an absolute fact was that Antoinette Malone would never in a hundred million years move into Mrs. Washington's house. It was too old and too dark, with its big shade trees and the azaleas and the bamboo and Mrs. Washington's prize camellia bushes pressing up so close all around it. Cassie and Gilbert had talked about this already, and soon as Mr. Washington announced his engagement, they meant to give notice. Cassie pitied the woman who was going to work for Antoinette Malone. Cassie went so far as to warn off her own friends ahead of time.

One evening toward the end of summer, John Washington came home—it was still early, and the light outside was fine as thread. He turned off the radio in the living room and called Cassie in.

"Cassie, girls," he said, "I have asked Miss Malone to marry me tonight, and she has said yes."

Clara wore a sweet little smile on her face the way she might have worn a flower in her hair. Vivian studied the rug and kicked her heels against the base of the sofa. Hard, enjoying the thudding noise it made.

"Goddamn it, Vivian, stop that!" John Washington stopped to light a cigarette before he continued. "You know how lonesome and sad I've been since your mother and your grandmother died. Miss Malone has made me happy again. And I'm going to marry her."

"I thought *we* made you happy," Vivian said reproachfully.

"You do, but not in the same way."

"We hope you'll be very happy always, Daddy," Clara said.

"Thank you, darling. Thank you for that."

Vivian knew this was her cue to say the same thing, but she was damned if she would. Because as it had turned out, she didn't like Antoinette. Not at all. She didn't like her little face or her little hands or her little feet with their high, high arches or even her little scratchy high voice. She couldn't think of one thing she liked about her.

"Vivian?" Daddy said. "Aren't you going to wish me well?"

"Sure," Vivian said.

"Is that all you can say?"

"Will we still live here?"

"We haven't decided all that yet," John Washington said.

"When will the wedding be, Daddy?" Clara asked.

"Christmastime. Antoinette wants a Christmas wedding."

"A goddamn midget-stepmother for Christmas," Vivian said. "Finally I get a present, and look what it is!"

And she ran outside, letting the screen slam hard behind her, streaking across the yard until she got to the fishpond. She burrowed into the bamboo so no one could see her—but where she could see back into the living room. Daddy didn't come after her. He and Clara went on talking. Cassie left the room; she probably went back to the kitchen to finish the supper dishes. Cassie never had and never would go after anybody in her life. Not even Gilbert. Vivian admired that.

Vivian would have liked to cry, but of course she didn't. Daddy had ruined crying. He'd cried so much since Mother died there didn't seem to be any sense in anyone else even bothering. Vivian knew that she couldn't have cried as long or as loud, and she could never have looked quite so pitiful doing it as Daddy had, so she'd stopped altogether.

Daddy was going to take his wonderful beating heart away from her forever and give it to Antoinette for a Christmas present to keep the rest of her life. Just why was Vivian supposed to be happy about *that*?

She sat by the pond until the lights went out downstairs; she intended to spend the whole night outside until Daddy got so worried he came looking for her to apologize, but this didn't happen, and eventually the mosquitoes drove her inside. She climbed the stairs slowly. Clara was reading in bed when Vivian came in.

"Now you've done it," Clara said, not looking up from her book.

"Now I've done what?"

"Hurt Daddy's feelings."

"What about my feelings?" Vivian said, and she peered at her bare legs and scratched at a bite until she broke the skin and her leg bled. She dipped her finger in the blood and sucked it off her finger.

"Don't do that. It could get infected, and you could die of septicemia like Uncle Garrison."

"I'm not going to die ever—you can't make me," Vivian said. "It's too completely disgusting. You couldn't pay me to die."

"Maybe you should tell Daddy that you're sorry," Clara said. "In the morning," she added, leaving the question of Vivian's mortality for another time.

"I'm not sorry," Vivian said.

"You could at least take your clothes off and put on your pajamas. And you should really wash that bite and put some Merthiolate on it."

But Vivian wouldn't even do that.

Chapter 2

So Antoinette married John. Across town, Antoinette's family was not much happier about this union than Vivian was. Parents do not line up around the block to see their daughters marry widowers nearly twice their age. Particularly when the widower comes trailing two school-age children and a semifamous drinking habit.

"Our daughter," Mrs. Malone lamented to her husband as they dressed for the wedding, "has not really thought this through. You know our Antoinette."

Which was giving Mr. Malone more credit than he deserved. He was a civil engineer who worked on dam and levee sites and was away from home ten months out of twelve. He didn't really know any of his children. He often mixed up their names.

Mrs. Malone continued: "She's much too high-strung and far too young to deal with a dead woman's children."

"Is she, now?" Mr. Malone said. "Well, you would be the

authority on that, my dear. Can't this man hire help to care for the children?"

"His name is John, and if Antoinette is too high-strung to handle children, she's certainly too high-strung to handle help," Mrs. Malone said, pitying her husband his naïveté. "I've decided that they'll send the older girl to the Ursulines in New Orleans, and we'll take the youngest, that's Vivian, to live with us. For the time being, so long as that is all right with you, dear."

"I'm sure you know best," Mr. Malone said. He employed this phrase frequently and to good effect whenever he came home. He was working out a math problem in his head having to do with cubic feet of gravel, and he was trying to attach his cummerbund—and was not having much success with the latter. His wife had to help him.

When he'd gotten Mrs. Malone's letter with the news of the impending nuptials, he'd sat on the edge of his cot in his tent on a levee site in Tennessee and tried to remember which of them Antoinette was. He thought she was the little one who'd fainted at her First Holy Communion, and he hoped that she wasn't going to pull anything like that during the wedding ceremony. But, it turned out, he had Antoinette confused with Margaret. The wedding went off without incident.

᷿

"Oh, you have to be crazy, Mama," Willie, Mrs. Malone's youngest, said when he learned that his mother was moving yet another person into what he already called "the Mad House."

"Why, no, Willie, I don't think so." But Mrs. Malone's voice was vague, and Willie saw his mother was examining this possibility in her earnest way.

"Of course you are," Willie said severely. "Where is she going to sleep? Tell me that."

"At the head of the stairs, behind the banister by the stained-glass window. There's room to put in a bed in there."

"Why stop there? Why not fill the cellar and the attic? Why not pitch tents in the yard? Put a big sign in front of the house that says "Orphanage"? Willie tugged at his hair and rubbed at his sore eyes.

His mother ignored him. "I want you to be nice to her. We are her family now. I want you to be her special friend."

"I can't believe you're saying this to me," Willie said. "I think I shall go mad."

Willie had the distinctive look of the last child of a prodigious breeder. His skin had a peeled, pink appearance. His hair had been white when he was born and stayed that way. His system lacked even the vitality to introduce a color. His temperament was what Mrs. Malone called "uncertain."

She, on the other hand, had a philosophical nature. She was a firm believer in the will of God, and her life attested amply to its capriciousness. Kathleen Maguire Malone had begun life in a tiny fishing village in the west of Ireland, and had been "small enough to throw back," as her father was fond of saying. Who would have thought she'd end up the mother of eight, living in America, in Myrtle, Louisiana?

But the will of God, working in mysterious and complicated ways, had seen to it, going to quite a bit of trouble to bring it off: the collapse of the Irish economy, the great emigration of the Irish to America, the general fecklessness of Mr. Maguire himself, as well as the glacial resignation of Mrs. Maguire—who had taken to her bed for the last ten years of her life. Not sick, just everlastingly tired. Too tired to stir foot.

By then, Kathleen had been old enough to run the house and watch the younger children. Mr. Maguire worked in the icehouse by the freight station; he came home late, and left early.

Not surprisingly, Kathleen had married at her earliest opportunity. She was seventeen when she met Mr. Malone, a civil engineer—also born in Ireland—who'd come up from New Orleans to
inspect a bridge near Myrtle. They moved to a house on the far
side of town. And immediately began their own family. The Malones' first child was a girl whom they named Mary after Kathleen's mother. That Mary Maguire was unmoved by her first
grandchild, and all subsequent grandchildren, should not have
surprised anyone. She'd had enough of children; she'd had quite
enough of everything, as she thought she'd made abundantly clear
when she'd gone to bed and pulled the covers to her chin.

As Vivian prepared to join the Malones, Willie was the youngest child in residence, though he had a sister a year older than
Clara, and another in high school; and his brother Jim lived at
home. The children's grandfather, William Maguire, provided the
constant male presence—or what passed for it. (His wife had died
in her relentless sleep some years before. She'd been dead some
few hours before anyone noticed the transition.)

"He's no trouble," Mrs. Malone often said of her father, and he
wasn't; a heavy drinker and an inveterate gambler, he came home
only to sleep off a bender or to hide from his creditors. He had a
tiny room under the kitchen stairs, which had been meant as a
storage area for rain boots, mops, and other unsightly but necessary objects of daily life. There he had a cot and a bureau. He was
content. The Malone dogs, who had previously occupied this
space, stayed on. Nobody bothered Mr. Maguire in his lair. It
was the only privacy he'd ever known, and he was grateful to his
daughter Kathleen for providing it.

But Willie was not philosophical. Nor was he a fan of the will
of God. He felt unconnected to the tumultuous life of the family
he was a part of, and was in total sympathy with his late grandmother. He kept her photograph on his dresser.

"Poor baby," Mrs. Malone would say to Willie, stopping in the course of her awesome household duties to pull his head up against her breast and ruffle his white hair. "I know we're loud, darling. Do you have one of your headaches?"

Willie nearly always had "one of his headaches." For a time he'd thought they were a symptom of a fatal disease that might carry him off and away from the infernal racket of the Malones at their work and play, but as time wore on, his headaches proved to be a thing in and of themselves, and not a harbinger of the peace of death. This would prove true also of the nervous seizures from which he suffered on occasion and the indigestion that afflicted him all his days. None of these things was ever to kill him.

"You're like me," his grandfather told him. "Ain't nothing can kill you. You're here for the duration." And the old man would peer sorrowfully at the miserable child and shake his own head of white hair. At least his, Willie thought enviously, had had a color once.

"I could kill myself," Willie said, showing a little spunk.

"You could for a fact," his grandfather said kindly, not wanting to take from his grandson that hope, however wicked.

When Vivian arrived at the Malones with nothing but what could be packed in one of her mother's old suitcases, she was heartbroken and mad as a hornet. Her father had sent her to the Malones alone in a cab like a stranger that had to be got to a train. When Mrs. Malone met her at the door, took the suitcase, and led her upstairs to her makeshift room, Vivian scarcely noticed her surroundings. She was still too busy replaying in her mind her leave-taking. How she'd turned in the cab to wave good-bye, only to see Daddy turned away from her, kissing Antoinette. Not even looking in her *direction*, as she, his own daughter, disappeared out of his life in a hired car. How could this have happened?

Mrs. Malone left Vivian to put away her belongings in a cedar chest and to arrange her emotions, which Mrs. Malone, with her practiced mother's eye, could tell were in considerable disarray. Willie watched Vivian from behind a door on the landing for a while before coming out into the open.

"Hi."

It's the goddamn Malone albino, Vivian thought, but she was too dispirited to say it.

"I am William James. Your stepmother's baby brother, Willie."

"I know," Vivian said. "Are you sick or something?" Vivian threw herself onto the bed on her stomach, keeping her black eyes on Willie.

"Indeed I am," Willie said, unoffended and grateful that somebody had looked closely enough at him to see his pitiable state.

He walked around the banister and joined her on the bed. "I'm sorry about your mother and everything." He took out a big handkerchief and blew his pink nose. "But at least you have lived in a normal family with normal people for some *part* of your life. Probably with people who didn't talk every minute of the day and night. You'll find that people here never shut up. Sometimes I think I shall go mad with all the commotion. All these people yammering away." He looked over at Vivian, who had turned over on her back and was studying the stained-glass window over her bed. It was a replication of *The Gleaners*.

"I don't hear anybody yammering but you."

"Just wait. Right now nobody's home but us and Mama and my sister Masie. She's in her room reading a book. One on the Index."

"Really?"

Willie nodded solemnly.

"Does your mama know?"

"Mama knows everything."

"How many of you are there, anyway?" Vivian asked, sighing.

"Well, there's me and Masie. And Maureen. She's going to be a famous pianist. She *thinks*."

"I can play 'Chopsticks,'" Vivian said.

"Who can't?"

"Who else is there?"

"Jim. He works at the newspaper. Then there's my grandfather, of course."

"Where is your daddy?"

"Papa's in Tennessee. He's building a dam. Then there's Antoinette, but you know *her*, and my sisters Mary and Margaret—they're married, too, and Mary has children, which makes me an uncle. She lives in Memphis. Then there's my brother Michael; he went to Texas. That's it. My grandmother is dead. She took to her bed and died within ten years. So who do you have?"

"If I had anybody, I wouldn't be here," Vivian said. "My mother died, then Grandmother died, and then Daddy married your goddamn sister, who sent *my* sister away to a creepy school in New Orleans run by the meanest nuns in all of creation and made Daddy give me away, like I was a damn cat, to a house of crazy strangers."

"I'm not crazy, *yet*," Willie corrected her gravely when she paused for breath. "Although I do feel that I may go mad. At some *point*."

Mrs. Malone came up the stairs and stopped when her head was even with the landing. "I've fixed you children a nice lunch. Come down and eat it." Then she padded away again. She was wearing carpet slippers.

"Remember that," Willie whispered, "you can never hear her coming."

"Duly noted," Vivian said. It was a phrase that Daddy used in response to most unsolicited comment and all complaint.

"Pass me the syrup, please, Vivian," Willie reached his arm toward her. They were at the breakfast table. Now Vivian had her chance to see what Willie meant about "constant yammering." The night before at supper there had been a reduced contingent of Malones, owing to a late shift at the newspaper, a piano rehearsal, a drinking bout, and Masie's absorption in the forbidden book. But this morning everyone was home except for Mr. Malone.

Mrs. Malone sat at the foot of the table, and old Mr. Maguire sat at the head. Margaret had come home sometime in the middle of the night after a fight with her husband, Bob. So there were Jim, Margaret, Masie, Maureen, Willie, Vivian, Mrs. Malone, and Mr. Maguire. Two dogs, Rufus and Lucy, patrolled the kitchen on the lookout for fallen food, of which there was more than might normally be supposed—Mr. Maguire had the shakes, and every other forkful missed his mouth entirely. Two fat tabby cats resided on the windowsill above the kitchen sink.

"He has another think coming if he thinks I'll be crawling home any time soon," Margaret was saying to the table at large.

"I know he must be so worried about you," her mother said. "I wish you'd just call him over the telephone and let him know where you are."

"Let him call me. I doubt sincerely he's even awake."

"I never liked him," Masie said.

Maureen, the only blond-haired person at the table, looked, Vivian thought, like a fairy princess. Her manners were extremely refined. So refined she didn't eat, just sat drinking tea and flashing a blue sapphire ring. She kept her head bent over a piano score.

Jim, the one who worked at the newspaper, pushed back his chair and said, "Papa, would you like a ride uptown?"

Mr. Maguire wiped his mouth—actually his entire face—and rose up on his spindly little legs. "Please and thank you."

"Papa," Mrs. Malone hastened to say, "Someone can run you to town later. Surely there's no great rush."

"Thank you, daughter, but I've business."

Willie whispered to Vivian, "He's got no more business than a cat." But Vivian pretended not to hear. She was sorry Mr. Maguire was leaving. He'd provided a quiet presence at the table that had been physically pleasant to her.

Maureen and Margaret began clearing the table. Mrs. Malone sat on and enjoyed a cup of coffee, as she watched Willie and Vivian finish their breakfasts. Masie had gone back upstairs with her book, the dogs had thrown themselves down under the table, and the cats had jumped down and were taking little mincing, circular steps around Maureen's and Margaret's legs. The sun was lying on the linoleum in a wide swath, a bluebottle fly was butting furiously against the window glass. Maureen and Margaret were chatting, their words drowned in the running water as they did the dishes. Vivian felt sleepy.

Willie asked to be excused and said, "I'm going to show Vivian the garden."

"That's nice," Mrs. Malone said. She looked sleepy, too, as indeed she was; she'd been up for four hours and was starting even then to think about supper. "Take Rufus and Lucy with you, please."

The Malone property was a haphazard, rambling affair. Willie took Vivian out to an arbor covered in small pink roses.

"These are Florentines," Willie said proudly.

"They smell divine."

Willie wrinkled his pug, pink nose. "I can't smell anything because of my allergies."

"My sister has allergies," Vivian said. "Once a bee bit her on the lip, and even her eyes swole shut."

"Were a bee to bite me, I would die." Willie stated calmly and with a certain quiet pride.

"By rights you should be dead. I've been bit hundreds of times."

Vivian sat down on the grass under the rose arbor. Willie perched on the arm of a lawn chair. "Do you read much?" he asked hopefully.

"All the time."

"Me, too. I would have gone mad ages ago if it weren't for books."

"Me, too," Vivian said. Actually despite all the many ways she'd felt in her short life, she'd never felt for a minute that she "might go mad," but Willie seemed to set a store in madness, and she didn't want to appear rude.

"I'm reading a book about the Civil War right now. Called *Gray Ghost*. It's wonderful. I've always felt I was born too late."

"For what?"

Willie threw his arms out to his sides. "For the war. For romance and adventure."

"You'd have just been alive to lose or to die like a dog. So what would have been the point? Anyway, your people weren't even here during the war. My mother's whole family was ruined by it. They even lost their house. And there were those awful clothes the girls had to wear! We're lucky to have missed it."

Willie was not pleased to have it pointed out that his ancestors had not fought in the Civil War—a painful fact that he preferred not to dwell upon. "In any event," he said, "The Irish have a glorious history which goes back thousands of years. I'm probably descended from kings."

Vivian said that there were many chiefs and Indian princesses in her family tree, among them, Pocahontas, and the famous Seminole chief, Osceola, for whom her father was actually named—though he went by his middle name, John. "It looks like we're both blue bloods, or blue-red-bloods." Vivian could ill afford to compete with this strange boy whose friendship she could see she would need.

"I'll show you Mama's peacocks," Willie offered, mollified.

So Vivian was enfolded into the life of the Malone house. Whereas Grandmother's house had been so dark that Vivian had pursued the sun from room to room, the Malone house, which sat on a little rise facing south, was so bright that at first Vivian found herself seeking out dark corners. Instead of Grandmother's heavy draperies, Mrs. Malone's windows were hung with lace curtains. All the rooms were bright, and in dizzying turn, sunny. In the beginning, Vivian felt like a mole suddenly turned out of its tunnel.

Of course, the other great difference between Grandmother's and the Malones' was people. Willie had been right; the Malones *could* yammer you to death—all but Papa Maguire. He was a drunkard and a wastrel, and made no bones about it, but he had a sympathetic way about him. He was, when he was home, invariably kind and mercifully quiet. Vivian wondered why he should drink so much. She asked Willie.

"Because he's Irish."

"Your father's Irish, and he doesn't drink. The rest of you don't lie up in a broom closet with a bottle from morning to night, so being Irish can't explain it."

"I suppose you should ask him," Willie said. He was trying to finish *Twenty Thousand Leagues Under the Sea* before supper and was impatient with Vivian's interruptions.

Of course, Vivian knew better than to do something so patently personal, so prospectively dangerous as to ask a drunkard his reasons for drinking. She would never have asked her father about his drinking, but there was a laissez-faire existent in the Malone house that made such indiscretion not only possible but logical, as well. She went into the kitchen and knocked at Papa Maguire's little rounded door.

He was reclining on his cot, one dog lying across his feet and the other asleep on the floor beside him.

"Who's there?"

"Vivian."

Papa Maguire rarely turned on his little lamp. He neither read nor wrote, and he preferred the darkness. "Ah, little Vivian. Come in, sit yourself down."

She sat down in a faded boudoir chair tucked in under the sloping ceiling.

When Vivian was sitting down, Papa turned the lamp back off, so that the only light came from the coal at the end of his cheroot.

"I've come to ask you something."

"Indeed."

"Well, what I want to know is, is how come you drink?"

The cheroot glowed, illuminating the old man's features for a moment, and then died back. He didn't answer at once.

Vivian said, "It *is* a rude question, I know, but I thought you might tell me if I asked. I really want to know."

"And why do you really want to know?"

"Because grown-ups do so many queer things, and we aren't supposed to wonder why, and we're not allowed to ask, so life just keeps on getting stranger and stranger instead of making more sense the way I thought it would. But I think you are different and will tell me the truth. It could be the *key* to how grown-ups think and why they do what they do." And what they might do next, she thought, but did not say.

"And I will tell you the truth, girl, but it won't tell you nothing about anybody but me. Grown-ups are not alike. *That's* the secret you need to know, right there. I drink because I like to. I like the way the drink tastes. I like the way it takes time off of the clock and puts it back loose in the world where it belongs. And because it gives me something to do, and, not least of all, it gives other people a way of thinking about me. When they do, God bless them."

"Are you sad?" Vivian asked.

"Aye. I've always been sad. It's my nature."

"Do you think it's my nature?"

"No. No, I don't, girl."

"Don't you mind people calling you a drunkard?"

"Why would I mind? It's what I am."

"You're not ashamed?"

"I did my duty to my wife and to my children so far as I was able. I brought them into the world and into their faith, and sustained them until they could do for themselves. Now my children do their duty to me. I'm just a common sinner, no better or worse than I ought to be."

And though Vivian sat on in the chair another five minutes, Papa Maguire offered nothing else on this subject, or any other. He finished smoking his cheroot, and when he stubbed it out in a chipped saucer, Vivian got up to leave.

"Thank you for telling me," she said, ducking her head to go out the little door and allowing a dog to precede her.

"You're welcome, girl. Come again."

⚘

By the time that Willie and Vivian were nine, the Malones considered Vivian one of their own. Vivian tried for a time to insist on her separateness—her Washingtonioness, if you will. She spoke often of her dead mother—her memory "beat out like a kitchen fire," in Vivian's memorable phrase. But the Malones, who were softhearted, and Irish after all, cried whenever Vivian talked about her mother, and fell to lamenting the deaths of other mothers, in so mournful and heartrending a fashion that Vivian felt outclassed and stopped bringing up the subject.

Her father—in his new role as Antoinette's husband—had become a visitor in her life, but as the Malones' father was essentially a visitor in theirs, this did not serve to set her apart. John Washington and Antoinette were often there for holidays and other family occasions such as birthdays. Vivian, who was at first sickened by the sight of her father following the tiny Antoinette around like a big dog, had given up her brief but savage campaign to sabotage the marriage. She could make no headway, and she became afraid of losing the attenuated affection her father still bore her. Not to mention the hurt it caused the Malones, who were as a group protective of Antoinette—because though Antoinette was extraordinarily beautiful, she was, Vivian soon learned, exceedingly stupid. This combination of characteristics had made the Malones, from Antoinette's adolescence, guard her closely.

Clara, ensconced in her boarding school in New Orleans, the one with the fierce nuns, faced the future more realistically—as indeed she always had. Vivian wrote Clara incendiary letters about the horrible Antoinette, but Clara deftly sidestepped the topic and responded with newsy letters about her life among the Ursulines.

Clara had always known that their mother's death had effectively ended their childhoods. She had tried while they still lived at Grandmother's house to make Vivian see this—to tell Vivian in ways she might understand that Daddy was not a man who could sustain a thing so fragile, so abstract, so difficult as family life alone, but Vivian had not understood.

There remained many things that Clara understood that Vivian hadn't the maturity—and would never have the temperament—to grasp. An instance—that Antoinette's allure for John had been as much her stupidity as her beauty. Clara knew instinctively that Daddy's feelings would never run as deep for a person like Antoinette as they had for their mother. Daddy, Clara had understood, was protecting himself. Clara also recognized that with Grandmother so recently dead, Daddy had been as attracted to Antoinette's family as he had been to Antoinette herself.

And this was so. Mrs. Malone was all mother. Unlike John's mother, who had been in equal parts aristocratic, demanding, proud, and censorious. Oh, Mrs. Washington had loved her son, loved him to distraction. She'd brought him up like a little prince; and she'd stood by him when his wife got sick and died, but often in her last years Grandmother seemed to be doing it against her better judgment. John had flung himself gratefully into the less critical family life of the Malone household.

As time passed, John, without knowing that he did it, began to think of Vivian as a Malone. That this hurt and dismayed his daughter past all reckoning, John was too busy with his own life and with Antoinette and their frenetic new life together to notice.

Antoinette had to have the latest fashions, the newest phonograph records, the sportiest car, the best and most current of everything. And Cassie had been right: Antoinette spurned John's mother's house. But though she was stupid, she was no fool, she had waited until after the wedding to do it. Then she had explained to John that she was a *modern* girl who had to have modern things. (Her hair was short and marcelled, her skirts were short and drop-waisted, her tiny feet required a veritable fleet of tiny, smart shoes.)

John Washington, who'd spent the last years in a vain effort to buy Della something, anything that might for even a moment give her happiness, glutted himself with the pleasure, the incalculable luxury of purchasing happiness for another human being. Now, it seemed, he valued frivolity above practically everything, and in Antoinette he'd found the queen of frivolity. Or so it seemed in those early days.

Vivian, to preserve her pride, gave up vying for her father's affections, and she took what came her way. A pat on the head, a doll—selected by Antoinette—the smell of her father when he embraced her at the door; only sometimes, at night, just before she fell asleep, did she allow herself to remember those nights when she lay with her head against his chest as he sang along to the sad songs on the radio.

Willie, as his mother had hoped, had become Vivian's "special friend," and he knew Vivian's true feelings. He had never shared the rest of his family's infatuation with his sister Antoinette. Willie knew that she lacked even the scant ability of his other siblings to imagine the plight of another soul. Antoinette was Antoinette the way a rock is a rock. Insensibly. Willie had never been too young to understand how dangerous such a person is.

When Antoinette had rejected the idea of living in John's mother's house, John had wanted to buy a house nearby it, but Antoinette had wanted to build. She was adamant that they "start from scratch." She declared she couldn't have a "hand-me-down house."

This was a notion so sweetly novel to John, raised up in his mother's cult of ancestor worship, that he found it irresistible. Damn right cute. It tickled him about to death. So they built a new bungalow with three bedrooms, and a maid's room, and a double garage complete with a room for a chauffeur. The house was at the east edge of town and included a pecan grove that sloped down almost to the bayou.

Antoinette had filled it with new furniture, and it teemed with venetian blinds and draperies. Antoinette had spent a small fortune on these "window treatments" as the decorator called them.

It was the decorator's bill that was the last straw for John. It very nearly sent him through his expensive new roof. This, then, was when Antoinette suggested that the children should come home to live. She gave John to understand that she'd gone overboard on their house, not for herself, or even for him, but because she wanted to make a *real* home for his children. John was so touched by this regard for his beloved Della's children, that he forgave Antoinette her financial indiscretions.

For her part, Antoinette felt that the inconvenience of having the children underfoot was a small price to pay for a reprieve from the bad temper that she'd so recently discovered John Washington possessed.

How difficult could the children be? Of course, she would hire a maid, the girls would be at school all day, they'd come home and do their homework and eat supper and go to bed. People fussed too much about children. Made them the center of the universe. The way Mama had. There was no need for that. Heavens, she'd felt smothered alive at home. All she'd *ever* wanted was to get off by herself. These children would have their own room. Why, she and John would scarcely know they were in the house. Antoinette was able to go on believing this because it was a secret and so she never spoke of it; consequently, no one ever said, "Are you out of your mind?"

So, at the beginning of the Christmas season of 1931, Mama Malone told Vivian that she and Clara were to spend Christmas with their father and Antoinette. It was to be a resumption of family life on a trial basis, she explained, and if everyone got along, the arrangement would be permanent.

𝒶𝓁

When John and Antoinette arrived for Christmas Eve at the Malones'—they'd stopped first to pick up Clara from the train station—Vivian's suitcase was packed and placed behind the front door. Vivian, who'd become more of a Malone than she knew, was excited about seeing Clara, but Clara presented Vivian with a cool cheek to kiss. She was preoccupied with her rabbit muff, which had been, she told her sister, a gift from a school friend. But Vivian had no time for hurt feelings, and no quiet for conversation, for it was a Malone Christmas Celebration.

Mr. Malone was home from his current dam site; the grown children were all home, including Mary with her children. Mr. Maguire was relatively sober—earlier in the day Mama had coaxed him into the bathtub, grabbed his clothes while he was so indisposed, and laundered them. Of all his familiar stinks, he was left with only his cheap cheroot to proclaim his presence. He was feeling some reduced as a consequence, and this made him seem older.

It was Papa Maguire that Vivian felt she would miss most. Papa's company could be enjoyed only at firsthand. So she stuck close to him, sitting on the arm of his chair in the living room while Maureen played the piano and they plunged through all the verses of all the Christmas carols in the Christian world.

Mama liked a sing-song as she called it, and had memorized all the verses of all the carols in her youth, and she would not be denied; even if everyone else had to mumble and retard a note right through every song—which everyone but Maureen, who had the music in front of her, did. At the end, Mama was flushed with exertion and pleasure.

When they left the house for midnight Mass, Vivian's suitcase was put in her father's red Essex, though she rode in Jim's car with Papa Maguire. Jim was going on to the newspaper office after Mass. She snuggled up against Papa, seeking his smell beneath that of Mrs. Malone's powerful laundry soap.

"We'll miss ye, little girl."

"I'm not sure I want to go, Papa."

"Aye. Well, you're always welcome in my part of the house. Provided you don't grow so big you can't fit through that little door."

At the end of the Mass, Willie whispered, "One for all, and all for one," and Vivian, who was much taken with the Crusaders that year, whispered back, *"Deus vult."* Then Mama smothered Vivian in a good-bye hug and said, "I'll always feel like you're one of my own." And that was that.

Vivian and Clara followed their father and Antoinette up the center aisle and out of Saint Clare's.

It was a cold, clear night. Light from inside the church spilled out like a mantle onto the steps. As their father and Antoinette exchanged greetings with people at the curb, the children got into the car, and Vivian, watching out the window, saw Papa Maguire half in the shadows of the church's portico, lighting his cheroot. She waved. But he didn't see her.

❧

The house smelled new. It smelled like varnish and paint, and wool from the new rugs. There was still a woodsy smell from the lumber that had been so recently piled up in the yard while the house took shape. But it was cold. The gas grates had not been lit before John and Antoinette started out for the train station and the Malones'. John Washington went from room to room lighting them, while Clara and Vivian and Antoinette stood huddled in the kitchen, warming themselves at the stove after Antoinette lit all the burners with her chic red enamel cigarette lighter.

The Malone house had been alive with the muffled sounds of living twenty-four hours a day. There had been squirrels in the attic, mice in the walls, lost voices in the high-ceilinged rooms. The sycamores, which touched the roof, sighed and fretted in the wind. Papa's cough rang out through the night like the chiming of the house's many clocks. It was never silent. This new house echoed the voices of all who spoke, but there were no mysterious sounds. Each voice—each sound—had a harsh, resounding clarity.

"It should warm up soon now," John Washington said when he rejoined them in the kitchen. They were all still in their overcoats, and Clara had her hands jammed in her muff, now anything but ornamental.

Vivian thought, If we were home, Mama Malone would make hot cocoa and put bread in the oven for toast, and we would be warm before we knew it.

But Antoinette made no such domestic moves. While waiting for the heat she had turned on the radio to a dance band and sat down in the breakfast nook to smoke and flick through a decorating magazine. For her own part, she was chilled to the bone, and tired to *death*. Already, she'd noticed that two children could not be rendered invisible. And John seemed different. Like a stranger.

John, seeing his bride looking small and unhappy, sent the girls off to bed.

Clara and Vivian shared a room again. A big room with canopied twin beds, abloom with rose chintz ruffles and skirted vanities. "A young ladies' room," the decorator had called it. Antoinette, who at home had shared a very small room under the eaves with Margaret and Masie, thought it beautiful and had often come to stand in its doorway and gaze at the decorator's idyllic dream of girlhood. But when shown into it, the girls made no comment—except for Vivian, who remarked that it was even colder in here than in the kitchen.

Antoinette could see plainly, from that moment, that ingratitude was to be her portion, and with this bitter thought, she retired.

Vivian opened her suitcase and found her nightgown and got into her bed. Clara unpacked her suitcase; she hung up her dresses in the closet and put her other things away in her bureau. Only then did she put on her nightclothes, in the bathroom, and brushed her teeth and washed her face.

It had never occurred to Vivian to do any of this. As Clara came back in the room she was brushing her heavy black hair with a silver-backed brush. She sat down on her bed and continued to brush her hair.

"Do you still brush it a hundred strokes?" Vivian asked.

"Of course," Clara said. "Mother always did."

Clara loosed the phantom of their mother with two syllables— the phantom that Vivian had been powerless to summon at the Malones—and who now, seemed to be gently prowling the unlit edges of the cold room.

"I don't remember that," Vivian said.

"I don't know why not; we were both there. In her room every night when she brushed it." Clara gazed at her sister's face, searching it for this lost memory.

"What color was her hair?"

"Auburn. Don't tell me you've forgotten what Mother looked like!"

"I knew her hair was red," Vivian lied. "I just couldn't think what shade to call it."

"Auburn," Clara repeated, getting into bed. She turned out the light.

Vivian lay in the darkness, but she was not trying to picture her mother, as her sister assumed. Vivian was instead willfully summoning the cast of characters of the Malone house to keep her mother's ghost from gathering too near. Where, she asked it silently, were you when I needed you? But Vivian knew now where it had been. It was attached to Clara; it went where she went. Even had it been free, the poor ghost would never have appeared to someone who did not even remember the color of its beautiful hair. Vivian felt guilty for forgetting so much, and she felt sorry for Mother's ghost; but what could she do about it? She looked over at Clara's bed. Something small and white was curled at the foot; it looked like a white feather boa. Clara moved her feet, and it disappeared. Vivian pulled the covers up over her head.

It was cold. And it was Christmas Eve, but it didn't feel like it anymore. Even in Vivian's experience, which sadly had combined Christmas with death and itchy diseases twice, she hadn't known it was possible for Christmas Eve not to feel like Christmas Eve at all. But it was.

And Christmas morning did not feel like Christmas morning either, Vivian discovered when she awoke early. The bedroom windows faced east, and the sun came streaming in through the sheers between the swags of chintz. The room was icy. Clara was still sleeping.

At the Malones', Papa would be up. Smoking the first cheroot of the day in the kitchen while water boiled in a saucepan on the stove for his tea. He always made his own tea when he got up. The cats would be on the prowl; the dogs would be under the table. Vivian, who was an early riser, had usually joined Papa for a cup of tea, and she remembered the way the sun came in at the back door, and the fresh stink of Papa's cheroot mixing with the steam from the saucepan. It had been her task to pour milk into saucers for the cats. So Papa could watch them lap it up. He said it made him feel completely calm to see cats lap milk. He said it was as good as three drinks; *and* it kept the cats tame.

"They're beasties, don't forget, little girl. You have to tame them every day if you don't want them going back to their old ways."

But these memories—of what was really only the day before—had now acquired such a quality of distance that it was as though Vivian were remembering something from a previous age, a long-ago lifetime. She slipped out of her bed and into her clothes from the night before. She walked down the hall, past shut doors, to the kitchen. The room still held the smell of Antoinette's cigarette. Vivian opened a cupboard and found a box of tea; she put a saucepan on the stove. She'd never seen such a clean kitchen.

Kitchens in her experience had been the domain of black cooks or Mama Malone. None of whom had had the inclination or the luxury of time to keep a spotless kitchen. But this kitchen had yet to see any real use, even the stove was still pristine, like the ones in the magazines Antoinette had piled on every table in the house.

When her tea was ready, Vivian went outside to look at the yard. There were no arbors of Florentines, no grapes, no wisteria, no black walnut tree, no sycamores. No borders choked with chickweed and aspiring bulbs. What there was were exactly three fruit trees, saplings, lashed to stakes with lengths of rubber hose—like the Christian martyrs in Rome, Vivian thought—and a struggling lawn.

But beyond the fence there was an old pecan grove, now in winter, stark against the sky. And beyond that, woods sloping down to an arm of the bayou that bordered Myrtle to the east. A cardinal alit on a fence post and sang his song. Then he flew away, west, in the direction of the Malones' house. Where there were arbors and branches and the toast crumbs that Papa would be flinging out in the yard for Mama Malone's peacocks and the wild birds who flocked to the bounty of that house. Vivian, who'd never before regretted more bitterly her lack of wings, went back inside.

‑ℓℓ

The Washingtons had no Christmas tree. John Washington associated them with the deaths of his wife and his mother, and he wouldn't have one in the house. Antoinette didn't mind; she hadn't wanted pine needles tramped into her new rugs, anyway. An "artistic" and expensive crèche was displayed on the mantel instead. But Vivian did not think it as nice as the one at the Malones'. Antoinette's crèche was white. The Holy Family, the Magi, even the donkey—everything and everyone—was white. Antoinette said not to touch it, for the pieces were carved from pure alabaster. The only other indication of the season was the wreath on the front door—which Clara, in a whisper to Vivian, declared "showy."

Because Antoinette did not know how to cook anything but macaroni and cheese, the Washingtons went to the dining room of Myrtle's best hotel for Christmas dinner. They had, of course, been invited to the Malones', but they wanted, Daddy explained, to begin their *own* tradition.

Part of Daddy's new tradition, it seemed, was to drink cups and cups of eggnog until they left for the hotel. Vivian asked if she could have some, and was told that she could not.

And what a tradition it promises to be, Vivian thought, sitting in Banks' Hotel, picking at her shrimp cocktail in a room full of commercial travelers and ladies so old they had outlived absolutely everybody, up to and including grand-nieces.

Even the December that Mother died, the aunts had made

Christmas dinner, Vivian remembered as she fussed with the napkin in her lap. And there had been stockings tied to their beds with oranges and nuts and ribbon candy. Were Daddy and Antoinette so busy they couldn't do that much?

Daddy, who seemed to have fallen into a bad mood once they were seated in the dining room, fidgeted with the salt and pepper shakers. Vivian, seated on his left, could smell whiskey, so now she knew why he hadn't let her have any eggnog. No one talked. Everyone, even Clara—whom Vivian counted on to always know the correct thing to say and do—seemed uneasy. When the food came, they ate silently. The other people in the dining room were just as quiet, since for the most part they were eating alone. Vivian could hear ice tinkling in water glasses and the pings of forks on plates.

When they finally rose to leave, Daddy, who'd scarcely eaten anything, stumbled and then caught his balance on the tabletop, knocking over a glass of water. As they walked from the dining room, he was noticeably weaving.

Clara, mortified, kept her hands in her muff and looked straight ahead as they marched out; but Vivian watched the other people watching them. She wanted to turn and yell, "So, he's drunk as a skunk on Christmas Day, so goddamn what?" She didn't; but she scuffed her shoes and glared fiercely at the other diners as she passed them. Who did they think they were? If they'd been who they *thought* they were, they wouldn't be eating their Christmas dinners at Banks'.

Antoinette, who preceded John from the room, naturally assumed everyone was looking at her. She was, after all, wearing a new, beautiful, white-beaded dress and her green shoes with the silver buckles. She was pleased with their new Christmas "tradition." At least they hadn't had to get up at six for seven o' clock Mass and listen to old Father Ryan wheeze on about the *real* meaning of the Magi's gifts. And they weren't all crammed into Mama and Papa's house, with a small child banging on Mama's piano. She hadn't had to watch Papa Maguire spill his food down his shirtfront; she hadn't had to kick away dogs clustered at her feet under the table. All things considered, this was, in Antoinette's opinion, quite possibly the best Christmas she had ever spent.

Chapter 3

After Christmas, John Washington went back to the road—about which, more later—Clara rejoined Vivian at Saint Clare's Academy, and Antoinette began interviewing help.

The first two applicants didn't understand Antoinette's modern appliances; in fact, as she told her mother on the telephone, they seemed totally mystified by running water!

But Antoinette went on bravely interviewing women, even though the process brought on headaches so severe she had to lie down in a dark room at the end of each day, a cold cloth pressed to her temples. At these times, even a faucet dripping in the bathroom sounded like a gong, and a pair of mourning doves singing their repetitive song to one another on a wire drove her very nearly insane.

But at bottom, there was a more intractable problem than suitability. No matter how subdued, no matter how reticent the black women applying for the position were—(which in the early thirties in a rural southern state, was very subdued and very reticent indeed)—Antoinette found them all unsuitable, all of them— what? Insolent? Certainly. Dangerous? Something. She could not exactly say.

Antoinette finally turned to her mother for help. Hardly surprised, as Mrs. Malone had predicted just this to her husband the very day of Antoinette's wedding, she showed up to interview the last of the prospects. Antoinette sat in the breakfast nook, holding a newspaper open in front of her face and occasionally peeking over its edge.

One was too young, one was too countrified, another had a withered arm—which, though it engaged Mrs. Malone's ready sympathy, did not recommend her to that good woman who knew what hard work was. Mrs. Kathleen Malone, after all, was perhaps the only white woman of any means in Myrtle to do her *own* work—offering it up, of course, to the greater glory of God.

However, the last applicant, a certain Emmy Clegern seemed, to Mrs. Malone at least, entirely satisfactory. She asked her to wait in the kitchen for a moment and took Antoinette into the living room.

"Mama, she's a harelip! She's a *freak,* for heaven's sake!"

"Harelips scarcely qualify as freaks. Why, just think, Mrs. O'Brien's youngest has a little harelip; no one notices it. Hardly anyone. Anyway, I don't think that she is a *real* harelip; I think she just stutters. You only have to listen a little more carefully than you like to, Antoinette, to understand her. And she seems gentle and honest and able. You'll not do better."

"She's so ugly!"

Antoinette felt trapped; suddenly all the air emptied from the room. The light dimmed and then turned bright blue. She blinked. She had spent more than a year, and most of John's money (according to him), creating this beautiful, beautiful house;

she had had it perfectly appointed by an artist (Maurice Rich) of interior decorating, known north to Memphis and south to New Orleans, and after all this, her mother wanted to mar its beauty with blatant ugliness in the form of this freakish colored woman! Antoinette did not think it possible to bear it.

Her mother sighed.

"I wish I could hire a white woman," Antoinette said in a whisper.

"You'd make yourself ridiculous. It's not done."

Kathleen Malone regarded her daughter quietly for a moment. Antoinette had had this unreasoning fear of the blacks from childhood. Kathleen's own mother had been the same way. But that, Kathleen always thought, was because Mother had come from Ireland and was deathly afraid of anything strange. Her poor mother! Leaving Ireland and coming to a country where everything and everybody was strange had made her life so untenable, it had sent her to her bed—to await something familiar and known, and Irish: death.

In the kitchen Emmy leaned against the white and gleaming counter and waited. The older lady was nice, but if she got the job, she'd be working for the little jumpy young one. She needed the job, though, because Grandpa had passed, and with him their claim on a sharecropper cabin they'd lived in all Emmy's life. And jobs were hard to come by now. Lots of white ladies had been letting their help go since that big old crash. Emmy wasn't exactly sure what had crashed into what; she only knew there had been some kind of a big crash—she assumed out on the highway to Jackson—and since this crash that everybody talked about, there were more poor people than ever. White ones, even.

She put her hand over her mouth; it was a gesture so old, so automatic, she didn't know she did it. She hoped that the white ladies had understood her when she'd answered the questions. People could understand her, she knew they could, but seemed like once they saw her twisted mouth they thought they didn't have to bother, and many didn't.

If Emmy could have had one wish, it would be never to hear another person speak the word "What?"

Mrs. Malone came back in alone. "I think you will work out fine, Emmy. Mrs. Washington has a headache and had to lie down, so you and I will work out the details."

Antoinette lay across her beautiful bed with the pale ivory satin coverlet and embroidered pillow shams, weeping. She could take no comfort even from her pretty bed because now she visualized in her mind's eye the freak in the kitchen making it up. That image, the image of black hands on the ivory satin, caused Antoinette to scream into her pillow. To literally scream aloud.

No matter how hard she tried to make everything beautiful, it seemed something or somebody came along to ruin it. It *always* happened. Even her wedding, which had been so white—she had carried white roses and narcissi—and so beautiful had been marred, when, standing poised for her new life on the steps of Saint Clare's for the photographer, she had glimpsed that terrible old colored ragman wheeling his cart up the avenue, crying out his garbled song. She began to sob more softly. But at least, she thought, opening her eyes and looking at the clock on the bedside table, I won't have to watch John every minute. Not with a freak. There was that.

❧

So when John next came home from the road, Emmy was ensconced in the maid's room, and the kitchen had begun to show signs of use. There were smells besides the smell of new lumber and paint in the house. Good smells: biscuits and cobblers baking, bacon and chicken frying, grits and greens boiling smells. John was surprised and happy.

"Look how my darling has brought this house to life while I was gone," he said, picking up Antoinette in the living room and swinging her in the air.

"Put me down, John!"

"Never," he declared. "Where are my other girls?"

"The *children* are in their room, doing their homework. They'll join us at supper."

"They'll join us now. I want to see them."

"John, I have made some rules so that our house will run smoothly; one of the rules is that the children go to their rooms after school and work on their studies until dinner."

John, who wanted Antoinette's good mood above everything right at that moment, let it drop. "I've married a taskmaster," he said, smiling down into her green eyes, running a finger down her nose, and then placing it on the dimple beside her red lips.

Antoinette smiled.

That night they sat down to a properly cooked meal as a family for the first time. John took the opportunity to address a problem that Antoinette had brought to his attention. What would the children call her?

She was not their mother, she was too young to be their mother, and she could not and did not want to be so called. Obviously she could not be called by her first name, so how then should the children address her? John decided a pet name would make a good compromise. He himself called Antoinette "little bit," or more indiscriminately, "darling," but these monikers did not seem appropriate to the purpose. He suggested that she might be called Candy.

Clara looked up from her plate and said in her clear voice, which held the exact inflections of John's mother, "I beg your pardon?"

Vivian was thrilled that Clara dared to challenge their father's ridiculous suggestion, and in Grandmother's ringing tones, too.

"I think we should call her *Mrs.* Candy," Vivian added, to show her solidarity and admiration.

"No more backchat, please," Daddy said automatically, and changed the subject. But Antoinette stared at the girls for a long moment before she went back to eating. She would be ever after addressed, to her face, as Candy, though between themselves the girls fell into the convention of referring to her as She.

Once Emmy was engaged to care for the girls, John and Antoinette went on with their lives much as they had done before. Just as Antoinette had intended. When John came home from the road, the two of them took off for New Orleans, or occasionally Memphis, often staying over several nights.

Antoinette liked New Orleans best; it combined familiarity with anonymity. In New Orleans she could wear her fashionable clothes without hearing later which of her mother's friends had disapproved of them and exactly how much, and why. She enjoyed the crowds and the fast pace of people on the street—none of whom would be in front *or* behind her for confession come Saturday. She even liked the cathedral (filled with priests who had not come from Ireland, had never set foot there, and didn't pine to go back). These priests did not know her grandfather or her parents or her brothers or her sisters. And they did not know her—or even *one* of her sins.

In New Orleans Antoinette could be Antoinette. She had no

clear idea of who that might be, nor was she at all interested. She hated definitions and all self-appointed definers. It seemed to Antoinette that people had been trying to define—which was to say, in Antoinette's mind, belittle her—all her life. She was the Malones' third youngest daughter; she was Irish; she was Willie (you know, the one with the problem) Maguire's granddaughter; she was Catholic—a grievous sinner and a child of God. She looked like her grandmother; she was not as smart as Jim or Masie. . . . Oh, it just went on and on.

John, thank God, never defined her as anything but his adorable little wife. The first was a definition even Antoinette could live with, the second was obvious, and the third desirable. Anyway, John was not much of a talker. (Antoinette would have been very much surprised to know that John and Della had talked whole nights away.) This was what had caused Antoinette to love him in the first place. She had had more than her share of what Willie called yammering at home. She was proud that as Washingtons, John and she did not talk. Washingtons went; Washingtons did.

They went to horse races, they went to nightspots in the Quarter and out by the lake, they went to movies. They danced; they went to restaurants where Antoinette ordered things Mama couldn't have pronounced the names of, much less cooked or eaten. And John drank drinks that required special glasses named after the drinks themselves—not like Papa Maguire, who lapped up his nasty brown whiskey from milk glasses or teacups, or whatever was clean or handy. Why, she'd seen him drink straight from the bottle, so unashamed that he'd winked at her while he screwed the lid back on!

But this idyll did not continue long. By early spring of that year, John began to spend more and more time on the road, and when he came home, he often claimed to be too tired to go to

New Orleans. He said he'd been on the road for days and the last thing he wanted was to get back on it, even for fun. He harped on money. Even money for groceries and running the house. The word *Depression* came into his vocabulary. It seemed to Antoinette that he used it in every other sentence. He blamed absolutely everything on this depression; staying at home, not letting her buy new clothes, his worsening moods, the increasingly ugly scenes he provoked. He said he was working twice as hard to make the same money as he had earned the year before.

Antoinette supposed this might be so, though she couldn't see how. Her father still got paid the same. But shortly Margaret's Bob's insurance business fell way off, and Marie's husband lost his job at the bank in Memphis. Other people began using this word *depression,* and they talked incessantly about what they called the "hard times." Well, it just bored Antoinette to tears! But she put up with it. She listened to them—her eyes opened wide and her chin tilted just a little to the right—and she said things like "Oh, dear," and "Oh, my," and "Imagine!"

What more could she do? *She* hadn't caused it.

John Washington's territory extended north through Mississippi to Memphis, west to Little Rock then south to Texarkana and back through Shreveport to Alexandria and home, and he knew every improved and unimproved mile of it—dirt, gravel, asphalt, and concrete. His territory was his true home, and not even Della, on her best day, had been able to compete with it. Nowadays, the tiny Antoinette disappeared from his mind seconds after he got behind the wheel.

For when John Washington lived nowhere, he finally belonged everywhere. In fact, the only time John felt like a stranger was when he came home. And this had always been so.

John had been a determined traveler even as a young boy in New Orleans. In the summers he rode streetcars randomly around the city just to be on the move and to see different people and new places. He went down to the docks to see the ships that had sailed upriver from exotic ports, and he went to the train station to watch people arriving and departing. He always identified with the passengers who were leaving—leaning from the train to catch last words of farewell; John Washington was born to wave good-bye.

He had no aptitude for being still or for staying in one place. Which was why he had quit college. The notion of living in one place, seeing the same people day after day for four years had made him so wild that he'd left Tulane in his sophomore year— infuriating and estranging his father.

Even now, standing, talking to a customer, John shifted his weight, swiveled his neck, and rattled the change in his pockets. All his gestures were overlarge. He swept his hat from his head; he turned his neck to see what he might easily have seen from the corner of his eye. He made the sort of fuss smoking a cigarette Toscanini made conducting *Tannhäuser*. Why a man this restless wound up living in a poky town like Myrtle was a mystery to people who met him. But the truth was, he didn't really live in Myrtle, and he never had.

It was only when his father's health failed that the Washingtons had moved across Lake Pontchartrain to live in John's mother's family home in Myrtle. By then, John Washington had been living on his own for some time—in a hotel in the Quarter, upscale enough to offer room service, and seedy enough for "sisters" to call on "brothers" every night, all night long—and he was already traveling for Kraemer Brothers, Wholesalers. But while visiting his parents in Myrtle, John met Della Wilcox and fell in love. They married that same year. John, who had never given a damn where he hung his hat, hung it in Myrtle.

The road, particularly in the mornings, stretched out before John Washington like the promise of Life Everlasting. The road was everything to him—his work, his pleasure, his religion even. The road was all the church he'd ever wanted. What, he often wondered as he sped through a spring or summer's day, did people want with dark, close buildings filled with garlic-eaters and mumbling men in skirts? Slowing for small towns huddled around church spires—as if these could protect them from the vengeful and wrathful God they spent their Sundays appeasing, a God who visited them, if at all, in the guise of floods, tornadoes, and scarlet fever—John idly wondered how those obedient servants of the Lord, went on fooling themselves. John Washington had never had any use for the church (not the One True Church that claimed him—or any other).

The priests who had used to gather around his mother's dining table in New Orleans, discreetly waiting for handouts and tidbits while they listened with feigned interest to their hostess orate on the moral rot that afflicted the poor, had only amused him.

"Christ-bitten sons of bitches," his father had called them— occasionally to their faces. Why, his father hadn't set foot in church after John's christening until the old man had been carried back inside frumpy little Saint Clare's in his mahogany coffin.

The only time John ever felt a tug was when he drove past country AME churches on summer Sundays—churches that very nearly rocked off their concrete-block foundations with song and a kind of glad fussing that spilled out into the road and thrilled something inside John. He liked seeing the little girls strutting in their Sunday finery down the side of the road to services, their white anklets already slipping down into their Mary Janes, their mothers walking imperiously before them with heads high, their fathers bringing up the rear in their best clothes, laughing and joking with one another. Had things been different, he wouldn't have minded following little girls and pretty women into a church where there was singing. Sometimes he even stopped for gas he didn't need or a bottle of Coca-Cola he didn't want, to be close to all this. But that was as far as it went. In reality, Washington men were born into the church, they married in the church and were buried from the church, in between those set appointments they lived what John and his father had always called "full lives." And that is what John was living even now. A very full life indeed, including as it did his children, any number of female friends, and now two wives—though only Antoinette was legally entitled to this designation. And, John Washington reflected, a full life doesn't come cheap. There is a price to be paid, and only a part of it could be paid off in cash money. For the rest, John was finding, you had to pay with your life's blood.

The house had been organized around the schedule of its breadwinner, but now that John Washington came home only every ten days and stayed no longer, often less, than five, this became increasingly difficult to do. When John was gone, Antoinette was at a complete loss over what to do with herself—because of all the "economies" John had made her agree to.

She had used to spend the time John was gone first in decorating the house and later in readying for the trips they would make when he came home. Making hotel reservations, going over her wardrobe and choosing which clothes to pack, and in buying special clothes for particular jaunts. Having her hair and nails done, and making countless lists. Antoinette loved a list, and she never felt so grown up as when she was making one.

But now she was thrown back on her own resources. Of which she had very few. She had no close friends and no outside interests save her house and her clothes—and subordinate to these, John.

Her sisters had never succeeded in teaching her to play bridge or even hearts; Antoinette couldn't seem to remember the rules for five minutes, and she could not sit still long enough to be the dummy. She couldn't shop because she had promised John she would "be careful." And it would be absolutely years before she could redecorate. She solved her problem the way her late grandmother had solved hers. She slept. But when she slept, she dreamed.

Antoinette's dreams were, and always had been, populated entirely by black people. Her every sleeping step was dogged by a familiar black face—the ragman or Emmy, or the old woman who sold flowers outside of the Maison Blanche on Canal Street in New Orleans. Besides these faces, recognizable from real life, legions of faceless black people crowded around Antoinette's bed. And they all wanted something.

In these dreams no one ever spoke aloud. Not even Antoinette. Lips moved, but no sound issued. First she tried to get rid of them by offering them food or money, but they wanted Antoinette's prettiest things, the very things she most wanted for herself—her clothes, her jewelry, the silver services. They asked for them. Outright. When Antoinette refused, they moved forward, all together, their feet making a shuffling, muffled noise like Mama's felt carpet slippers on the stairs at home. They pressed up against her, holding out beseeching, empty hands, as their faces got larger and larger and became distorted with anger.

When she moved backwards, soundlessly moving her mouth to say she had nothing to give them, they became angry with her and began snatching at her clothes and the precious things Antoinette clutched in her arms to her breast. They regularly seized her treasures from her by force, leaving her, at the end of the dream, in possession of exactly nothing. Antoinette visualized this nothing as the color blue. The dreams ended in a cascade of blue like the last fireworks on July Fourth.

Antoinette awoke frightened and desperate; even the light in the room she'd fallen asleep in would be blue, and remain blue for a long time. Sometimes it was twenty minutes before she fully understood the dream was over, that she was awake. Even then she continued to feel forlorn and insubstantial—sometimes for hours. She would spend this time cataloging her closets and inventorying the house's furnishings, until, with the passing of time, she began to feel more herself and the blueness drained from the air.

When the girls came home from school, Emmy would meet them at the front door and shush them.

"Be quiet, be quiet," she would say, rushing to get the words out of her twisted mouth in time, "Your Candy is sleeping in her bed."

If Mrs. Washington were awakened suddenly, the rest of the day turned into a screaming match in one quick hurry. Sleeping did something to that woman's nervous system; she woke up mean as snakes in a sack. Then she prowled through the house on the hunt for things to criticize. And she found them, too. Careful as Emmy and the girls were, there would always be something: a sweater hung over a chair maybe, a jar lid on the counter, an invisible ring, God save them, on a cherry wood end table.

And Mrs. Washington would accuse Emmy of stealing! Many, many times she went through Emmy's little room looking for the things she thought she'd took. Of course, she never found anything in Emmy's room that didn't belong to her. But as Emmy watched Mrs. Washington tear through her clothes and all that she had, Emmy was always afraid that something belonging to

Mrs. Washington would suddenly turn up. Crept in on its own feet. These things, Emmy suspected, could happen.

Emmy conceived a strategy to avoid as many of these incidents as was possible. She had the girls enter through the kitchen, where she waited to tell them where Mrs. Washington was sleeping—because sometimes she slept in her bedroom, but other times she fell asleep on the sofa or the daybed in the sunroom; she even catnapped sitting up in chairs. If she'd just fallen asleep and was awakened, things were not too bad, but if she'd been asleep for any longer time, and something brought her back awake, a body couldn't get far enough away to be safe.

Mrs. Washington turned the whole natural world upside down—she slept half the day, and she prowled the house nights. Emmy never knew when she might want something done when everyone else was sleeping—same as if it were broad daylight. One night Antoinette had woken Emmy from a sound sleep saying how she had to reiron one of her blouses. Like she was going to wear it out the door right then! Of course, Emmy had done it.

Fact was, the woman was flat-out crazy, and Emmy had known it inside of a week, but seemed like nobody *did* know it but her—and the little girls. Emmy could see in their eyes that they knew it. But Emmy didn't think it proper to discuss such with them. Even if Mrs. Washington was just a stepmother, she was the only mother these children had. The husband, when he was home, he *sure* didn't know it! Sad to say the husband was a secret drinker. Always prancing out to the little room in the garage for something and coming back fortified. Emmy couldn't exactly blame him; she could have used a drink herself. But she could never put one hand to her brow, like she longed to, rock back on her heels, and say, "Lord God, that woman crazy as a spotted pup in spring," because there was no one to say it to.

And this interested Emmy, how after a while, a body just longed to say what was true. Even if it couldn't change anything. If Grandpa were still alive, she could have said the truth to him. She could just see his face and the way he'd have leaned back his chair, laughing, and then brought his chair back up and come out with some smart saying that they would have quoted back and forth to one another for weeks—and laughed every time. The oddest thing was that the longer her grandpa was gone, the more Emmy missed him—when, seemed like, it would go the other way. Oh, but they'd had some times! They'd lived kind of rough, but they'd laughed a whole bunch more on any night than these people in their brand-new house did week to week.

On her days off Emmy went uptown since she didn't have any place of her own to go; all her people were gone now, even old Auntie Vidalia, Grandpa's sister. And the Lord knew you was hard up for kin when you went to missing a woman like Auntie, who'd looked just exactly like a snapping turtle, and always had, Grandpa'd said, even when she was a little girl.

The kind of men who'd took up with Emmy in the past had proved too mean to be fooling with just for some company. It wasn't like they'd really talk to her, anyway. Or listen. Emmy had concluded that life was hard enough without getting in line for no-account men. Which seemed like the only sort of man she ever got any kind of chance at.

So she looked in store windows, and she ate barbecue at The Lucky Pig; she went down to the river and sat on the levee to see the river pass her by. Like it seemed all of life was going to do—pass her right on by. Sometimes she talked to herself. Leastwise, as she remarked to herself more than once, I understand me when I talks.

The girls were prisoners of Antoinette's sleep. They couldn't play the radio; they scarcely were safe talking to one another in whispers. They prayed constantly that the phone wouldn't ring. (Even Clara—who would rather have talked on the phone than gone to France.) As it was Antoinette's rule that Clara and Vivian go to their room when they got home from school and stay there until dinner, whenever she did wake up, she came running in to see that they were complying.

"It's a goddamned chintz cage," Vivian whispered to Clara between clenched teeth one afternoon.

"I know."

"I thought it was bad when Daddy wouldn't let me play outside at Grandmother's, but this is worse. At Grandmother's at least there were lots of books and lots of rooms." Vivian was sitting in the window seat looking out at the pecan grove framed in swags of lilac chintz. As she had when she was younger and staring out the windows of Grandmother's house, in her imagination she ran through the grove at breakneck speed. She could almost, but not quite, feel the stitch in her side that she would have had, had it been her legs and not her mind doing the running. Her eyes were drawn to the sloping tree line of the woods beyond the pecan trees.

Clara sat at her desk, an algebra text opened to her homework. She was chewing a pencil.

"We can't live this way, you know." Vivian stated.

Clara said, "We can't, but we do."

Vivian tugged at her knee-high socks and retied her saddle shoes. "We don't *have* to, we could burn this damn house down. Tell Emmy she's got the day off, then hide in the grove and roast Sleeping Beauty in her satin bed. Tell Daddy if *he* ever bothers coming home that Candy just went up in flames, sitting in a chair. Spontaneous combustion." Vivian threw up her arms. "Whoosh!"

Clara turned toward her sister. "What can we really do?"

"I just said."

"I didn't hear you," Clara said.

The next Saturday, Antoinette went to the movies with Margaret, and Clara took the opportunity to sneak over to see Susan Seine. Emmy was in her room sleeping because the night before Antoinette had been up and at it, demanding that the silver she had set Emmy to polish that day wasn't done to her satisfaction, and that there was an iced-tea spoon missing. So Emmy had gotten up at two in the morning and repolished it. All the iced-tea spoons were in the box in their little slots. But Mrs. Washington counted them three separate times just the same.

Vivian took off by herself for the trees she'd been staring at out her window for weeks. First she barreled through the grove, just as she'd imagined doing. The sensation of speed was delicious; even the side ache she had anticipated was glorious. Vivian threw herself down on the grass, clutching her side and looked up at the sky and watched the clouds scud by. When I grow up, she thought, I will be a champion runner. I will be the first person to run around the world, and they will put my picture on stamps.

Then she got up and went on her way. Just the other side of the grove it was mixed pine and hardwood forest, cut-over and scrappy, but as Vivian walked farther in, old-growth trees blocked out the sky, and the light was so dim it was almost like being back inside Grandmother's house. The soil was loamy and fragrant. Vivian followed a faint footpath that twisted down to the murky water of the bayou, where she sat down with her back against a cypress that sent its roots into the water.

She had found her way to another planet at last. A private planet with superior air. She thought she might just stay there and live out her life, like Mowgli in *The Jungle Book.*

Except for the time she'd lived with the Malones, Vivian had been close-confined. Even her dreams took place inside rooms inside houses. Now she saw the pictures in her grandfather's books come to life. Not genteel, southern, small-town prettiness, either. Not fishponds and bamboo, sandboxes and school yards and chinaberries. Not shade trees and camellias, forsythia and rose of Sharon, but Nature. Wilderness, as depicted in the books the younger Vivian had cut up. A place like those the Indian chiefs had lived when the artists, still respectful of New World royalty, came to paint their portraits.

A blue jay alit on low limb and squawked at her. Vivian squawked back. The jay cocked his head and peered narrowly at her; then he lifted one wing and searched out a mite. A woodpecker drilled away at the top of the cypress. Vivian tried picturing Antoinette in her white satin high heels and her white beaded dress here. Mercifully, it was not even possible. The jay skittered up to a higher branch. A crow cawed, and then another and another. Turtles sunned themselves on half-submerged logs and then quietly slipped back into the water. An egret picked his way along the shore, snacking on crayfish.

Vivian stayed until it was nearly dark. Walking back through the grove, feeling lighter than she had in months, she saw that only the kitchen light had been turned on in the house. Antoinette would not be home. She decided not to tell Clara about this. She would, however, tell Willie.

It had proved more difficult for Vivian and Willie to stay in touch than either of them had anticipated. Antoinette did not often visit her family, being at pains to show them that she hadn't been too young to marry, as her mother had implied at the time, and that she was perfectly capable of running her own house. And now with John gone so much, she did not want her mother to know how often or how long John was gone, or how at sea she was. And she didn't allow Vivian or Clara to go on their own, as she was afraid the girls might broadcast too much of the Washington family business. Vivian must learn to wait until she was invited, she'd said, knowing full well Malones never issued invitations.

At school, girls never came into unsupervised contact with boys. The little street that ran in front of the church and the school served no other purpose that Vivian could see but to separate the two playgrounds. One for the girls and the other for the boys. To talk face-to-face, Willie and Vivian both had to slip away, evading the notice of a nun on the girls' side and the curate on the boys' side. Still, they managed it as often as they could.

They met in the statuary garden behind the convent, which was meant strictly for the private prayer and contemplation of the nuns. But during the school day it was deserted, except for one old nun who was wheeled out by Sister Regina—the convent's cook and housekeeper—and parked in the sun by the back door in a wicker wheelchair. The children met behind the statue of the Blessed Virgin in a tangle of ivy up against the convent's back fence.

There, Willie kept Vivian abreast of Malone business—his halting progress on his road to madness, and his all important reading—and passed on to Vivian the books he'd most recently finished.

These were very welcome, for there were no books in Antoinette's house. When Daddy had tried to move Grandfather's books in, She had protested that there was not room for them, and that shelves would have to be built first, and that with all John's economizing, she couldn't see how they could do *that*. So for books that were not to be found in the library of a parochial school or the children's section of a small town library, Vivian was dependent upon Willie. She was slowly but surely catching up to Willie on the subject of the War.

Willie had been recently romanced away from General Lee and into the camp of Stonewall Jackson. It put him, he said, on the horns of a moral dilemma, as General Lee was, Willie felt, more admirable generally, certainly less crazy, and more concerned for the well-being of his troops. But the siren song of Stonewall's daring and his maniacal belief in God and by implication, himself, had been, in the end, Willie confessed, irresistible. Still, he told Vivian, he felt disloyal.

"Not to mention stupid," Vivian said, peeling a banana. "Since Lee survived and Jackson didn't."

"He died for the Cause."

"Some son of a bitch shot him down in the dark. It was a colossal blunder."

"Blunders count in wartime," Willie said earnestly. "He died on the field of battle."

"On the field of blunders, you mean. How's Papa Maguire?"

"Mostly drunk, like always."

"Besides that."

"He's okay, I'd say. He always says to say hello to you."

"Say hello to him from me, too," Vivian said. "I wish I could see him. But as at least *you* know we're being held captive. Couldn't you ask Mama to call up and invite us? Then Antoinette would have to let us come."

"I tried that, but Mama's afraid your daddy will think she's meddling."

The old nun in the wheelchair was staring up at the statue.

"You don't think she can see us, do you?" Willie whispered.

"She can't even see the *statue*. I doubt sincerely she even knows she's alive." Vivian gave the nun an insolent stare and tossed her banana peel into the ivy.

Sister Mary Alphonse saw and heard perfectly. She'd been speechless since her stroke—this enforced silence was, all told, a great relief to her, and she considered it a special and a particular blessing from God. However, now watching the bad little girl, had she been able she might have smiled. She looked forward to eavesdropping on Vivian and Willie's conversations, which were far more interesting than the radio serials that Sister Regina subjected her to in the kitchen. But the old nun worried about Vivian. She believed somebody might, indeed, be holding the girl captive. Parenthetically, she felt Willie had made a grave error— though a predictable one—in switching his allegiance from Lee to Jackson. That man had been a religious fanatic! Sister Mary Alphonse had no use for fanatics. Now less than ever before.

Daddy was home. It was Easter. They'd gone to Mass and then to the Malones for Easter dinner, and were back home again and it was still afternoon. Daddy had turned on the radio, but he was restless; he was smoking one cigarette after another and rattling the pages of his newspaper.

The girls had gorged themselves at the Malones, for Antoinette had insisted on extreme, penitential Lenten menus, and it had been a long time since Vivian or Clara had felt really full. Emmy herself was surprised everybody hadn't wasted completely away. She'd had to spend a good bit of her wages at The Lucky Pig, stoking up against the starvation meals she was preparing the Washingtons. The only time Mrs. Washington had permitted her to cook a decent meal was when Mr. Washington was home.

Now the girls were stuffed to the gills. They were also enjoying being in the living room, for they saw it only when Daddy was home. It was red and yellow. Red rug, yellow chintz sofa with red poppies, yellow silk drapes with the poppy motif repeated. It was a very pretty room, though it seemed to Vivian more like a showroom in Hodge's Furniture Store than a real room because it saw such rare use.

Antoinette had gone directly to her bedroom when they got home to lie down. She had a headache and was exhausted from the Malone holiday celebration—riding home, she had gone on at some length about the day—the noise, the untidiness, the heavy food, the dogs and cats. . . . She had summed it up as she got out of the car. "It was unspeakable!" she pronounced, heading for the blessed darkness of her room.

Everyone sat mute in the car for a moment as Antoinette rushed on ahead into the house. "Who would think it could take so long to describe something unspeakable?" Daddy said, opening his door. Vivian laughed. Even Clara smiled.

Vivian wanted so much to take Daddy by the hand and lead him through the grove to the camp she'd built from palmetto leaves and sticks by the bayou where she spent her afternoons now. (Both Clara and Antoinette thought she was staying late at school for Religion classes.) But she didn't. Because if Daddy knew something, it would not be long before Antoinette knew it, too.

Vivian happened to know that Antoinette was keeping secrets from Daddy—like the clothes she was charging at Goldman's and hiding in the spare bedroom closets—but it did not seem to have occurred to Daddy to keep any from her.

Or so Vivian thought.

Actually, as we know, John Washington was keeping many secrets from his wife. But they were not the kind of secrets that Vivian would have guessed at. One secret he was keeping from everyone was how much he was drinking. Just prior to his marriage to Antoinette he'd tapered off, very nearly quit, but it was gaining on him again now. When at home he was careful never to be seen taking a third drink. For third, and subsequent drinks, he went out to the garage; where he had appropriated the empty chauffeur's room for his own. He kept his whiskey in the trunk of his car.

"You know what we need," he said now, lolling in his chair by the radio table, staring distractedly out the picture window. There was nothing much for the window to frame but yard and a single pecan tree left to shade the front windows, and beyond that the road. John missed his mother's house with all its old plantings. He even missed his mother; it had come to that. "We need a dog."

"Yes!" Vivian said.

"But Candy doesn't like dogs," Clara said uneasily.

"Everybody likes dogs." John stated flatly.

"Everybody," Vivian echoed, giving Clara a fierce look.

"I saw a man selling off a litter by the bridge out of town. Let's say we run out there and see if he's got any left."

"Candy won't like it," Clara said. "Because of the rugs, Daddy, really. And the furniture. I think you should probably ask her first."

But John Washington did not need a woman's permission to buy a dog.

The man was still at the bridge, holding his own one-man farmers' market. There at the end of Easter Sunday, he had a peck of green beans, a lug of strawberries, and two pups left. A white and a black one.

"Which will it be?" John Washington was feeling expansive; he'd had two drinks in the garage before he brought the car around for the girls. He felt so expansive he was willing to give this peckerwood a buck apiece for pups that hadn't cost him one thin dime and, John knew, he would drown for nothing if he didn't sell them come dark.

"The black one," Vivian said. "We can name it Rex."

"Not Rex, for Christ's sake," John said. "It's bad luck to name one dog after another."

Vivian turned and looked at him. "But it's not like Rex is dead. He just lives in the country."

"It's the same goddamned thing." John lit one Chesterfield from another. "In the end."

Which in this case it certainly was because John Washington had shot Rex in a blind fury two days after Della's funeral.

The dog had been barking in a mournful fashion for days— ever since he'd been locked in a garden shed to keep him out of the way—but John had it in his mind that the dog was mourning his mistress, and he decided that since no one could put *him* out of his own misery, he at least could put the dog out of his. In actuality, and really he knew it himself, John was in a mood to shoot something and had decided to make a start with the dog.

It had infuriated him to see life going on as usual when Della was dead and buried, along with John's heart, in the hard winter ground. For Christ's sweet sake, he'd had to pay the grave diggers extra to dig her grave, because they had complained that the ground was nearly frozen. In the week after the funeral, every living thing he saw seemed to John Washington an affront to his wife's memory, as well as a personal and calculated affront to him, Osceola John Washington. Widower.

So the widower took the dog out into the country. Rex who had always loved rides in the car, hung his head out the window, lapping at the cold air, all the way. And when John stopped and let the dog out, Rex ran in happy circles. It was then that John shot him. Without compunction one, with the .38 pistol he always carried in his suit-jacket pocket. Afterwards he'd whirled and shot at a chattering squirrel who'd unwisely stopped overhead on a tree limb to view the proceedings. John would have liked very much to go right on shooting things, but he was by that time too drunk to take true aim. He sat down instead on the wet ground beside Rex's body, where he stayed, stroking the dead dog's stiffening fur and weeping, until it was dark.

Clara knelt to pet the white pup. Vivian was holding the black one tightly. The look in Vivian's eyes said plainly, I am keeping this—John Washington had seen this expression in his father's eyes. It had been, as a matter of record, his father's customary expression—just as barely concealed irritation had been his mother's. John who could not choose between his two daughters, cursed and bought both dogs. And the strawberries.

Driving home, Vivian asked what kind of dogs he thought they were. "Mongrels." he said. "Curs," he added with emphasis. He was no longer feeling expansive.

"I think they're maybe chow chows," Clara said, who had seen a movie in which Myrna Loy led a chow chow on a jeweled lead. She held the white pup on her lap.

"Chow chows!" Daddy shouted. "Not for a buck a throw, they're not." He looked at the dogs speculatively a moment. "A collie-terrier mix; that's the most you could hope for. You can be damn sure if they were good for anything Farmer McDonald wouldn't have been selling them. You girls are going to have to take care of them yourselves, now. Don't you all make Candy do your work for you. I don't want to hear about these damn dogs when I come home next."

"We will, Daddy," Clara said.

Vivian wondered if it would really be bad luck to name her dog Rex. Just to be on the safe side, she decided to pick another name.

She named him Gilbert. For the pleasure of saying aloud, "*You,* hush, Gilbert!"

When the girls got out of the car with their dogs, Emmy who was standing on the kitchen porch, could not believe her eyes. "Sweet Jesus," she said to herself, "That man got to be the biggest fool in the wide world."

Chapter 4

John had been driving all day; he had left Arkansas that afternoon and was now taking a gravel state road south from Shreveport. Two hours out of Shreveport, John reached the crossroads that was Sylvan—a cluster of shacks and Hank Stewart's store—the Dixie Home. Sylvan was an island bounded on three sides by cotton, and on the fourth by piney woods.

John had known Hank for years; they were friends of a sort, the sort that men like John and Hank allowed themselves. John often stayed over with Hank a couple of days before continuing on his way home. Fall and winter they did some bird hunting, spring and summer they talked of going fishing, but mostly they sat on Hank's back porch and drank.

When John pulled up in front of the store, the Essex was no longer candy-apple red; its sheen and color had been dimmed to a rusty pink by a thick layer of road dust from days of driving back roads. Even so, it was the best-looking car that anybody in Sylvan would see until next time John Washington came through.

As he stopped in front of Dixie Home and swung his long legs to the ground, a flock of small boys ran at the car. Had he been a stranger, they would have formed an appreciative and admiring circle around it, but he was not a stranger. He was John Washington, and they had been waiting there for him since noon. They'd been thinking about his coming since the day before the day before—which was how time was reckoned in Sylvan by boys. This was a ritual. By the time John Washington strode to the porch, they were already teeming over the Essex like wasps over a possum carcass; several had begun washing it, and others were coming along behind with rags to dry it and hand-polish it. Afterwards there would be Coca-Colas and gingersnaps for all of them—courtesy of John Washington.

For these boys, mere proximity to and familiarity with such a magnificent machine lifted them for a brief time out of their day-before-the-day-before lives and awakened in them the notion that they, too, might someday journey beyond Sylvan. To places where things reckoned almost divine in nature—such as John Washington's Essex—might be purchased.

Dixie Home, like most of the stores that John sold to, did most of its business with black sharecroppers. John was popular with these patrons because he made it his business to find out what they needed the stores to carry, and also because he told them what they hadn't known they wanted—and how bad they wanted it. Advertisers had little access to these folk without radios to hoo-rah the products every hour on the hour; so John did it himself. He talked up new cookies, crackers, and soft drinks and what-all, and then he convinced the store owners to carry them. Single-handedly, and with no help from Jack Benny, John Washington brought the wonders of Jell-O to one small corner of America.

"Look here, Roy," he'd say, leaning on a dusty counter in a store that stocked one brand of lard, dried beans, and rice, sugar, corn-meal, and coffee and little else. "You got people just a hungering for Cheez Doodles, but they can't buy them from you if you don't have them. And since you're out here on the far side of yonder, they can't buy them from anybody else. Course, if you're a non-profit outfit, go on ahead like you been doing. Anybody can see it's working out."

Roy would reluctantly order a case of Cheez Doodles on John Washington's say-so, because John knew his business. (If he didn't, he wouldn't be driving that car or wearing those clothes, would he?) And people bought them. John himself was an enthu-siast for Cheez Doodles—and Moon Pies and just about anything else you could stick in a box or wrap up in cellophane.

A good salesman, he enjoyed creating desire as much, if not more, than fulfilling it. Desire, after all, was the creative end of his business. Sometimes he felt a little bad about romancing poor people into buying snacks when they couldn't afford staples, but not all that bad, because for his own part, he'd as soon eat about anything you could sit on a Ritz than the meals available on the road—at any price.

🌿

The bell atop the door jangled when John stepped inside, and Hank came out from behind the curtain.

"Hank! Goddamn, what happened to you?"

Hank was hobbling forward on crutches, one bare, taped foot stuck out in front of him. "I'm going to let you guess, John. Get it in three, and I'll buy."

"You shot yourself in the foot to get out of going to church Easter Sunday with Irene?"

"Wrenched my ankle in a gopher hole. And I went to church

with Irene just the same, stuck my crutch straight out into the aisle and hoped somebody would trip over it on their way up to salvation, but my luck's shot all to hell!"

John and Hank leaned up against the counter at the back of the store. "You got them pickaninnies of mine washing your buggy?"

"Couldn't stop 'em with a gun, Hank." John turned and struck a match on the counter and lit a cigarette.

"You spoil 'em—then you drive away and leave me stuck with 'em. They're going to make you an honorary nigger, John, before you die."

"I accept all honors and gifts of money," John said. "It's a policy I got."

"I swear to God, sometimes I think I'm running a damn kindergarten for them kids. Let's go in the back. I got to keep this foot up."

They passed through the curtains into Hank's kitchen.

"Where's Irene?"

"She's gone over to her sister's in Vernon to look after her kids while she has some operation. Don't ask me what it is—nobody would tell me. Anyway, Irene stormed out of here, hollering I was too mean to live. She seemed right glad to be leaving, so I reckon I probably am a little mean, but nothing *you'd* notice. Man, this foot is killing me."

They went out on the screened porch at the back of the store where they had the shade of a black walnut tree and some privacy, and John poured Hank and himself a stiff drink from his pocket flask. "Well, that's all fine and good, but what are we going to eat for supper now you chased Irene off?"

"She left me a mess of fried chicken and potato salad. Don't worry about that."

"Well, then," John said, sitting down and putting his feet up on the porch railing, "We got us the perfect situation, don't we?"

"Pretty near," Hank said. "Course, it could be improved on some if we could get some women over here to put the food on the plates and bring 'em out here to us. Maybe fetch us a cold beer now and again to chase this cat piss you're pawning off on me and calling whiskey. Cool my fevered brow. Who do you think we could get to do that?"

"I don't know who *you* could get. I ain't no whoremaster, and I wasn't the one chased his wife out of her house, but I could probably get Odessa to come over here and wait on me."

"Couldn't she wait on the both of us?" Hank said.

"No," John Washington said. "She couldn't."

The first time John had seen her, Odessa was a nine-year-old girl hanging on to her mother's skirt; and the first thing he bought her was a grape soda. In the twelve years since, he'd bought her sardines, soda crackers, Oh Henry! bars, lipsticks, clothes, jewelry, and furniture—pretty much everything Odessa ever notified him that she wanted. Last Christmas he'd brought her the windup Victrola that had belonged to his mother, along with a wooden crate of records to go with it—grand opera, for that was the music his mother had claimed to love. He would have been happy to buy Odessa a modern phonograph or a radio so they could listen to music John liked, but there was no electricity to her cabin.

From the start, Odessa had called him John. Her mother had yanked her ear for her good, the first time she did it, but John Washington had said never mind, a baby cute as *that* could call him anything she wanted.

Now she called him a good many things, not all of them complimentary; John had to admit that the woman had a mouth on her. Of course, she'd learned most of her language from John, so he wasn't in a position to say much. She sure as hell hadn't learned it from her mama, who was one of those churchy niggers who made John's teeth hurt. But her mama had up and died last spring. Finally. John finished his drink, poured another for Hank, and then ambled back through the store to the front to inspect his car.

It gleamed now, it's color true again—brighter if anything. The boys had the hood up and were staring in at the powerful motor. One little boy, about four, Billy Jefferson, was hunched up on his knees behind the wheel pretending to steer.

"Go on in and help yourselves to your prizes now," John said. "I'll settle up with Mr. Stewart. And nobody'd better take anything but snaps and Coca-Colas, mind?"

There was a stampede up the porch, and John collared one boy and flipped him a nickel. "Go over and tell Odessa John Washington's over here at the store, and tell her to move her black ass, because he's tired and in no mood."

The boy pocketed the coin and took off running toward the line of shacks across the road on the edge of the pines.

John went back in the store, surveyed the scene, and put a dollar in Hank's till to cover the damage. "Soon as you get what's yours, get back outside. Mr. Stewart don't want you all milling around inside here. You know what they make gingersnaps out of, don't you?"

The children grinned and shook their heads.

"Nights when they sweep up the floor at the bakery? They take what they've swept up, throw some ginger in it, and then the night crew makes it into gingersnaps for the likes of you all."

The boys looked from the cookies in their hands to John Washington's face and laughed. "It's the God's truth," John said, but he was smiling. He took hold of Billy Jefferson's suspenders and snapped them smartly. Then he put a stern look on his face and shouted, "This is a place of business, for Christ's sake. It ain't no place for monkeys like you to run wild in. Go on, get out of here."

In less than a minute the boys were gone and the store empty, and when John walked back to the porch, Hank was snoring in his chair, his hand still wrapped around his empty glass. John sat down in a battered rocker and poured himself another drink.

The boys had gone down to the river; he could hear their laughter and splashing and yelling off in the distance. It was a happy noise, and it soothed his nerves. Closer up there was just Hank's snoring and Irene's chickens clucking at one another beyond the walnut in their pen. John hoped that Hank had a good supply of beer stowed away someplace cold. He was about to fall asleep himself when the boy he'd sent to Odessa's came around to the backyard and called up to him.

"Odessa say for you come to her 'cause she ain't in no mood either."

"Is that what she said?" John said, laughing, getting up and stretching his long frame. The only thing he didn't like about the road was how stiff he got.

The boy nodded solemnly. "She say she giving a free concert. Just for you, if you come now."

"Well, you can go on down to the river, that's where the rest of them went off to. I'll go see about Miss Odessa myself. But I ain't in no mood for a damnable concert!"

John opened the back screen and walked around the house and store. He crossed the road and walked past the houses that fronted it. There was nobody around; everybody was in the fields but for one old woman, sitting on her rickety porch. John lifted his hat to her, but as he got closer, he saw she was asleep, and put it back on his head. Odessa's place was at the back of the others, and into the woods about fifty feet. He could have been blind and still found it, because she was playing a record of *Madame Butterfly*, and he could hear the squalling and screeching all the way to the damn road.

Jesus H. Christ, John thought as he went up her wooden stairs that were like to fall in on themselves. "Odessa!" He shouted over the music. "Goddamn it, Odessa, cut that infernal machine off."

In answer, Odessa turned the volume up as high as it would go. Across the highway, beyond Dixie Home, field workers who were putting in the cotton looked up and said, "John Washington's back."

John pulled the needle off the record the moment he was inside the Odessa's dim one-room house. She was standing beside the Victrola, looking into the full-length mirror John had bought for her in Memphis and dragged all the way down here—just about herniated himself, too—and she was singing full-out. When John came in she went right on singing, really singing, singing Madame Butterfly's part, every foreign-born word of it. She'd memorized the aria in the time John had been gone—and she didn't stop when he shut the music off, or when he took her in his arms. She went on singing right at him, right *to* him, like he was a character in the opera, too, while they moved toward the bed in the corner of the room, in an improvised dance.

John could have stopped her singing with a kiss, but he didn't. Because the singing excited him, and because Odessa's voice was so strong and so pure. And because he'd never made love to a woman in a shack in the pines on an island in a sea of cotton, who was singing her heart out in Italian. John Washington thought he might want to try that.

&

"Christ Almighty, Odessa," John said. "Someday you are going to kill me, sure."

"That's all you want," she said. "You really want to die, you just afraid to suffer."

They lay a long time in bed. Odessa now quietly humming the aria, while John twined and untwined their fingers. Hers were mahogany, his a deep olive. The fingernails of both hands were a pearly pink, and their palms were both a dusty rose. John was thinking how to tell her he wouldn't be back for a while, because he was going to have to dig in with Antoinette for a spell. His wife was getting a mean, pinched look to her face that didn't bode well. It wasn't easy keeping women happy; seemed like one of them was always unhappy, and the girls, too. Clara was okay, but Vivian, he just didn't know about Vivian. Sometimes everybody was unhappy, himself included, and that's where they were at right now.

Odessa looked down at their entwined hands and said out of the blue, "I still don't know how you and your family's done it. 'Cause I'll tell you, you never fooled me; not even when I was little, not with all your swanky suits and your big cars and Mr. Stewart throwing his arm around you, like you was his brother home from the war! Facts of the matter was always plain to *me*."

"People mostly see what they expect to see," John said. "*You* were naturally expecting to see something for your own greedy self, so you bound to see the part of me that matches up with you." He took her chin in his hands and kissed her. "And I don't know why you always say I want to die," he said when the kiss was over, staring into her eyes now, the eyes he'd hidden in for months like they were his own secret cave. "It's not true, and I wish you wouldn't say it. All I want is to lie in your arms until God pulls the curtain down on this whole sorry mess. Is that so much to ask?"

A breeze had come up through the screenless window over the bed. "Is it?" Odessa asked. "You tell me. You free, you over twenty-one, and you and yours been *passing* for white since before the Flood. If you wanted to just lie in my arms, seems like you could find a way to do it."

"That part has nothing to do with it. I'm married, damn it, Odessa. You've known that from the start," John said. How he hated *this* particular subject.

"You married *and* married. There for a while you *wasn't* married, but I never noticed it made a difference." Odessa sat up and raked her hair back from her forehead. "You pleasing yourself is what you doing. Like always. And you only pleasing me some of the time. When it suit you. What I'm saying, John, is I got to start looking to my future."

"You've got a beautiful future, darling," John said, holding her wrist in a light grip, feeling her lively pulse. "And you always asking me how do I get away with it. Well, one thing I have to do, Odessa, think about it, is act normal.

"Now a normal man is going to remarry when his wife dies young, to give his children a mother. People expect it. I can't afford talk. I had to marry somebody so Della's sisters would climb down off of my back; and my somebodies have to be white as snow, 'cause Washingtons *have* to marry light, so their children will be light enough to scrape by, and darling, you and I *know,* I married the whitest woman God ever let live."

Odessa laughed in spite of herself.

"But all that's nothing to do with us," John went on, laughing now, too. "As long as I'm alive you got a future. Don't you ever worry about that. Now. What do you want me to bring you next time I come?"

"A gun," Odessa said, staring out the window at the tops of the pines, no longer laughing.

"Hush." John said. "Don't talk that way. I got to get back to Hank's—he's probably awake. I want you to come over and serve us our supper, and stick around for the evening. You know Hank; he'll go to sleep early."

"I know Hank. Did you ever ask yourself how good?"

"Hell, I know how he'd like to know you, but Hank knows *me*. Face it, darling, I'm your fate; you're looking at your damn destiny! Anyway, after me, I'm afraid Hank would be a very big disappointment to you."

John had sat up on the edge of the bed and started pulling on his pants and shirt and snapping his suspenders over his shoulders.

"Now Mama's dead, I ain't tied here to Sylvan, you know, Mr. Destiny."

"Come over and put the supper out."

"I don't like to go over there when Mrs. Stewart gone."

"Emily Post isn't going to hear about it from me or Hank either."

Odessa got up and stalked the room on her long legs, brushing at her wild hair. "If you won't get me a gun, get me a kimono, like the Butterfly wears, and one of them Japanese screens, and a fancy fan for me to use to act out this music with. And some of them records is broke. So find me a new copy, because otherwise I'll never know how this turns out."

"Will we ever get to the end of what Odessa wants?" John said, looping his tie around his collar.

"You better hope not."

John looked at her a moment. "I'll always want you."

"So you say."

"I always have, haven't I?"

"Always," Odessa said, pulling on her dress and pushing her feet into her shoes.

John caught her and held her hard up against him. He buried

his face in her hair and thought, Dear Jesus, nothing smells as good as this woman. Nothing in the whole wide, damn world can touch this magic woman.

Odessa gave him a little push. "I'll see you over at Dixie. Home. I don't want people to see us walking together."

"Great God Almighty, Odessa, everybody in Sylvan knows about us. You know Hank does. And anyway, everybody but us is in the fields."

"Mrs. Stewart don't know."

"And she never will. Irene gets five everytime she puts two and two together," John said, tying his shoes.

"I like to do this thing right."

"Oh, I see, so naturally you play that damn Victrola at top volume and make noises like a cat in heat every time I come over here. I never knew you were so damn discreet. I've got to go."

"I'll come in through the store. And I'd appreciate if you could act normal toward me in front of Stewart. It wouldn't kill you, John. You'd do it if I was white."

"Fine. You won't know we were ever introduced."

John stood on Odessa's porch, tucking in his shirt and then combing his black hair. The clouds had come over the sun, and the breeze had picked up in the top of the pines, causing them to sway and sift needles down to the ground. It would rain soon. He could hear Odessa stirring around in the room behind him—fussing with her hair, so he called out, "Looks like rain."

"It always looking like rain to you, John. You a natural-born rain man."

"What do you mean, rain man? I'm your sunshine, darling."

"You was never *anybody's* sunshine. Put that notion directly out of your mind. 'Cause clouds follow you around just to rain on you. Sometimes I wonder if I ought to stand so close, on account of when I do it going to rain on me, too. You *trouble*, John." Odessa came out on the porch with him, laughing now, and she put her arm around his waist, and they both looked out at the fields across the way and saw the clouds bunching up. They stood there like an old married couple regarding the sky that arched over them. Comfortable.

"I never been trouble to you," John said. "I been a big old Santy Claus to *you*, little girl. Before I'm trouble to women, seems like I got to marry them. So see, you're lucky, and just didn't know it."

"Yeah, I'm lucky," Odessa said, pressing her face against John's shirt, inhaling its starchy smell. "But I worry about *your* luck. I worry about you driving all over hell in that devil-car of yours, and I worry about your drinking, and I worry about your secrets. I flat worry about what would happen if you got turned overnight into a nigger. Because that would be *one* something you couldn't get in that car of yours and outrun."

John lit two cigarettes, one for her and one for him. He had to shelter the match behind his palm because the breeze that had been playing up at the top of the pines was moving down to the ground now. "Nobody's going to turn me into anything but what I am. Osceola John Washington. Period. And that includes you, Miss Odessa. If you're really worried—and not just jealous, which is what is really true—I got Indian blood to account for what people sometimes *think* they see. Not that that's a hell of a lot better," he added. "But some. Thank God for the Godforsaken Seminoles." He shook out the match.

"Seminoles, my black foot!"

Why couldn't she drop this subject? John went down the stairs, holding his jacket over his shoulder; he didn't look back at her when he spoke. "I'll see you over at Dixie Home. Bring your parasol, Miss Odessa, because my Indian blood tells me it's fixing to rain."

And it was. Thunder rumbled, and the people in the fields began moving for the shelter of the trees.

Odessa watched John Washington walk through the cluttered yards of the houses and across the road. Just when he got to the steps of Dixie Home, the skies opened up. She went inside and put the record on again, turned it up high to drown out the thunder, which she hated, but she didn't sing along. She sat on the bed and smoked the cigarette John had left her; she watched the rain lashing down and listened to the voices twining around each other like vines.

She shouldn't have told John he was a rain man. Though he was. What he didn't know was that he didn't just draw the rain to the people he loved, which was the part that scared him, she knew, but that he drew it to his own self. John didn't seem to know that. Probably it was best he didn't.

First time she saw John Washington, Odessa knew he was hers. He'd known it, too. But because of how young she was at the time, neither of them could tell anybody, not even each other. The years she was turning from a girl to a woman, the whole while she was becoming so beautiful, she'd felt she was doing it just for him. It was like she was her own prize flower that she was growing for John Washington, and when it was at the height of its perfection she'd plucked it and presented it to him. He hadn't been surprised. He'd known it would happen, too. He'd been waiting.

She'd stood by him when his wife died and afterwards, when he'd gone so crazy. He might have stayed that way, too, if it hadn't been for her. Crazy, and mean as the world, hitting out at anything that moved. But she'd tempted him back to the land of the living; she'd lured him back with her youth and her beauty. And for what? So he could marry a white woman with all the sense

God gave chickens! Who didn't know the first thing about how to please a man like John Washington and never would.

When she'd made John show her a picture of Antoinette, she had looked at it for a moment and then just broke down laughing.

John had been mad. But not until after *he'd* stopped laughing.

Chapter 5

It was the dogs that pushed Antoinette over the edge. Easter Sunday, when she was laid out flat with a sick headache, John had taken those girls of his out and bought them puppies! Not even breed dogs, but mongrels. Two of them! What had he been thinking? And when she'd demanded he get rid of them, he'd been angry with *her*. What, could anybody tell her, had *she* done? There'd been a scene. She'd put her foot right down.

Antoinette had put her foot down to good effect on quite a few occasions, or thought she had. In actuality, the issues she'd chosen to make her stands on had been of little or no importance to John, and he had simply let her have her way. Now Antoinette was learning that it was pointless to insist upon anything with John Washington—once his mind was made up. The dogs were a constant reminder of this. She hated the dogs.

Holy Week had already stretched Antoinette's nerves to the breaking point. She'd had, as she always did, to summon up all her courage to go to confession so she could be seen, along with every other Catholic in good standing in Myrtle, to receive Holy Communion on Easter morning. Antoinette secretly abominated the Sacrament of Confession. She did not like to think about her sins; she resented bitterly being made to think about them, and she purely hated telling them to Father Ryan. But she was afraid not to, or even to leave any of them out—altogether—because of her lively and abiding dread of Hell. Hell was as real to Antoinette as Myrtle itself. In fact, in her mind, it *was* Myrtle—it was Myrtle on fire, with its citizens running blindly through the fiery streets, their mouths gaping open in soundless screams. They ran past the familiar buildings downtown, past stores and shops, past the movie theater, and the churches, down all the side streets past the burning houses. They tried to run to the bayou and to the river, but the bayou was a lake of fire, and the river ran with fire in both directions.

Sometimes when Antoinette was downtown she could see all this happening, and she would have to pinch herself hard, blink twice and take three deep breaths to make the pictures go away. It was this Hell that Antoinette envisioned for herself if death were to find her unconfessed.

Hell was a fact, and everyone knew about it. What Antoinette could not understand was how so many people seemed able to forget about it from week to week. She knew Mama didn't worry unduly about Hell. Of course, Mama was not likely to wind up there either, but take Papa Maguire—now he was a terrible old sinner, and so far as she could tell, he'd never worried about it a day in his bad life.

But the more afraid Antoinette became of the consequences of her sins, the more of them she committed. And it was steadily getting worse. Every Sunday, when she stood to recite the creed, she professed to believe in the Forgiveness of Sins. But even then, right there, standing up in Saint Clare's, she was lying (another sin). Because she didn't believe anything of the sort. The sins her mama confessed to, possibly, but not hers. And because she could not fully believe in this credo, she was forced to rearrange her sins when she did confess them, leaving out the particulars whenever she could, and lying about the circumstances that surrounded them, if she couldn't.

And what about *that* sin? Lying to a priest in the confessional? Unforgivable. How could she tell Father Ryan that she had sinned right inside the confessional itself? Why he'd probably burst out of the box, shake her by the shoulders, and declare her damned in front of everyone. During Lent she had thought long and hard about this, and she had decided to go to New Orleans as soon as she could get John to take her. She meant to confess to one of those faceless priests at the cathedral. She would confess she had been lying to her own priest. That just might work. It would at least bring her even. If she could make herself do it. If John ever took her to New Orleans again.

And now she had this new and extremely terrible sin on her head, and she didn't know what to do. It really hadn't been her fault, but on the other hand, it hadn't been exactly anybody else's fault, hard as she'd tried to make it seem that way.

It concerned Emmy. Really you could say it was Mama's fault; she was the one who'd made her hire the vile creature in the first place. But Mama had not been the one to lock Emmy out of the house in the rain to catch what probably had been pneumonia. But she hadn't died! Thank a merciful God, and her mama again, for that—and Antoinette did, three times a day getting down on her knees beside her bed and bitterly expressing, from between clenched teeth, thanks that Emmy wasn't dead.

What had happened was this: Vivian and Clara had been invited to spend Easter Monday at the Malones. John was gone, of course, free as a bird—as usual—leaving her with his children to keep track of, and now two dogs! The day began nicely, Antoinette had Emmy do the washing, and supervised her hanging it out, but by late afternoon the weather turned chilly. Antoinette told Emmy that she would have to watch the dogs, for Antoinette was still headachy, and was going to have to lie down. Emmy had said Yes, ma'am, she could do that, and Antoinette had gone to bed. She had several new magazines. After she'd been reading for a while it began to rain, and she decided to go out to the dining room and get the box of chocolates that Mama had given her for Easter. And what had she found?

The dogs had dragged the chocolates off the buffet, and they'd eaten every last one of them—except for the caramels, which Antoinette didn't like anyway, and these they'd left on the living room rug. When Antoinette discovered all this, the dogs were asleep on the poppy sofa. Emmy was nowhere in sight.

Antoinette had lashed out at the dogs with the belt of her dressing gown, and they'd run from her and out the kitchen door as Emmy opened it to come in.

"Where have you been?" Antoinette screamed.

"Why, I had to get the clothes off the line, Mrs. Washington—it starting to rain."

"I told you to watch these dogs," and as Antoinette said this the dogs tried to come back in, only now, on top of everything else, they were wet. Antoinette kicked at them, and they ran back outside.

"Yes, ma'am, but I had to get the clothes, you see," Emmy said, trying to come forward into the warm kitchen with the clothes basket. But Antoinette, who was in a fury—now the dogs had tracked mud into the kitchen, too—wrenched the clothes basket from the woman and shoved her back outside.

"You can just stay out *there* and watch them," she yelled, and slammed and locked the door.

Emmy knocked on the door. "Mrs. Washington, it cold and wet out here. Them puppies might get the distemper. Mrs. Washington, it nearly dark!"

But Antoinette ran back to her bedroom and got under all the covers and shut her eyes tight. The rain came down harder. She knew she should open the door, but how could she? If she let Emmy in now, she'd look foolish, wouldn't she? That nigger might even expect her to apologize!

Emmy tapped at her window. Antoinette burrowed deeper into the bed. As always, when she was this upset, she fell asleep. Almost at once.

Emmy, trailed by the dogs, tapped at all the windows and then sat huddled by the back door under an eave. Antoinette's modern house did not have a proper porch, just an ornamental overhang with a struggling climber rose that Mrs. Malone had transplanted from her yard. When Emmy finally understood that Mrs. Washington was really not going to let her in, that she wasn't just playing with her, she set off on foot for Mrs. Malone's house. It was across town, but leastways, Emmy knew if she knocked at that door it would be opened.

❧

Willie and Vivian were sitting in the kitchen eating ham sandwiches when they heard scratching at the door.

"Lucy must be out," Willie said, and got up to let her in.

The pups ran through the door first, followed by a bedraggled and soaking wet Emmy.

"Mama!" Willie shouted.

Mrs. Malone toweled Emmy dry and got her into one of her own nightgowns and put her to bed in Papa Maguire's little room—fortuitously empty, Papa being off on his annual Easter bender.

"I think she may be having some kind of fit, Mrs. Malone," Emmy stuttered through chattering teeth, apologizing for her employer. "I think them headaches of hers has sent her off her head."

"Very likely," Mrs. Malone said. "And very charitable of you to say so."

After she'd tucked Emmy into bed, Mrs. Malone went to the phone and called her daughter's house. There was no answer. She then called Jim at the newspaper and asked him to go over to Antoinette's and fetch her home, bodily, if necessary.

"Poor Jim," Willie whispered to Vivian—who, though not exactly surprised by this turn of events, was nevertheless chilled, as if it had been she and not Emmy who had been locked out in the weather. She held Gilbert tightly. Clara's dog, Snow-Ball, had run upstairs to Maureen's room and his mistress.

"I've been telling you she's crazy," Vivian said to Willie. "I hope you believe me now."

Willie didn't answer. Then Mama sent them upstairs. She did not want the children there when Jim brought Antoinette home.

Hank was awake when John got back.

"You been over to Odessa's?"

"Yeah. She's coming over in a while, going to wait on us hand and foot." John sat back down in the rocker and poured a little something in Hank's glass and in his.

"Suits me. I wasn't expecting this rain," Hank said. "But we can use it."

"You can maybe use it—it sure as hell makes my life harder than it needs to be, turns the roads into chute the chutes. Slows me way down, costs me cash money."

"I reckon," Hank said. "I never thought about it."

"When did you ever think about anything, Hank? Goddamn, but when the roads are bad they tear up my fine automobile, *and* they ruin my good shoes!" John raised up his feet to admire his shoes, made for him in New Orleans by the same man who'd made his father's shoes.

"Sounds mighty rough. I guess Ole Huey looking after your interests then. You got more decent roads to drive on than you used to."

Though John Washington was not a fan of Huey Long's, he was nevertheless quick to agree. Since John Washington was presumed to belong to that class that despised Long vociferously, it was imperative for him to join in Long tirades when moving in those circles, which he easily did. But here on the road, where the opposite was to his advantage, John represented himself as a Long man. Privately, he felt in no way in the debt of Huey Long. It takes a pitchman to know a pitchman.

"Yes, sir," Hank added, feeling mellower than he had in some time, what with John's whiskey killing the pain in his ankle, his little nap, and his wife's blessed absence. "Huey is changing the face of this state. He's getting us some respect in the rest of the country, too."

The rain was settling in, like spring rains sometimes do, for the night. Spring peepers were adding their voices to the crickets.

John heard the tinkle of the store's door and the slap of Odessa's shoes on the floorboards in the kitchen, but Hank, who was drunker, was surprised when he turned to see her standing in the door to the kitchen.

"Great God Almighty, Odessa! You scared me creeping in like that."

"Sorry, Mr. Stewart. I thought you heard the bell on the door. I just come to see about your supper, like Mr. Washington asked me."

"Well, I wish you would," Hank said. "We're too far gone to do it ourselves."

"Don't you have a radio, Hank?" John asked.

"Course I got a radio. Do I look like a caveman? It's in the kitchen."

"Mind if I find us some music on it?"

"Be my guest."

John went into the kitchen where Odessa was slicing yellow squash to cook to go with the chicken and potato salad Irene had left in the icebox. "You happy now? I didn't even say hello to you."

Odessa stepped out from under the arm he'd laid across her shoulder. "I'm happy. Don't make a fool of me or you, and I'll stay that way." She ran some water in the pan and put it on the stove. "Is this going to be enough for you all?"

"I reckon. But I don't really like Irene's potato salad. She puts too much mustard in it."

"You got a real pitiful life, you know that, John?"

"I know. Not many could stand it." He was twisting the radio knob, looking for something besides static. He settled on a station that was delivering dance band music. "This good with you, Hank?" He shouted over the music.

"Fine. All I ask is don't play none of that opera that Odessa's, so crazy about. She's like to driven me out of my own house with that racket she's been playing. You can hear it all over Sylvan.

Now, Odessa, honey, don't get me wrong, but I don't think that's any kind of music for a gal like you. Why, hell, it ain't even any kind of music for my Irene, and she's white! People should stick to what they're used to. Now your mama didn't raise you up on no grand opera. I know that for a fact."

"No, sir, Mr. Stewart, she didn't. Mama didn't hold with music at all except it was church music. You want me to make you some biscuits or some corn bread or something to go with this mostly cold supper?"

"Some biscuits would be mighty nice, thank you, Odessa."

"What's he going to say when you get your Madame Butterfly outfit and start really belting it out?" John was nuzzling the back of Odessa's neck with his chin.

"In the first place, I don't give a good goddamn what that ignorant son of a bitch says about any subject you can name, and in the second place, back off, and while we're at it, don't you ever shave?"

John backed off and rubbed his chin. "It's not old Hank's fault he's ignorant."

"No, but I'm happy to say it's my own fault I'm not," Odessa said, rolling out biscuit dough. John started singing along to the song on the radio and doing a soft-shoe. "Me and my shadow, all alone and feeling blue. Me and my shadow, not a soul to tell my troubles, to. And when it's . . ." He swept Odessa, rolling pin and all, up in his arms and began to fox-trot around the kitchen.

"John, I'm warning you. Stop this."

"I climb the stairs, but nobody's there . . ."

Hank heard a clunking sound. "Don't be breaking anything in Irene's kitchen, now. I don't want to have to answer for that!"

"I'm not breaking anything belongs to Mrs. Stewart," Odessa said. She was back at the counter with the biscuit dough, and John Washington was holding his hand to the back of his head.

"Jesus H. Christ, Odessa! You are systematically trying to kill me."

"I ask you over and over to behave, and you don't. Learn to listen, John."

John left the kitchen and went out on the porch. "You got any beer, Hank?"

"I do, but I'd have to get up to get it."

"Well, that ain't going to kill you, is it?"

"It ain't going to do me any good either. It's out in the spring house. Irene don't like it in the house, you know that."

"I'll get it. I forgot for a minute about your foot."

"I wish I could forget about it even that long," Hank said mournfully.

After supper, and three beers, Hank was feeling more cheerful. "What about a couple of hands of poker?"

"With just two of us it wouldn't be much of a game."

"Odessa could sit in with us."

"I don't think so," John said. "I don't think she even knows how."

"Odessa!" Hank shouted.

Two hours later, Odessa had taken the pot, and Hank had hobbled off to bed. "You know where you belong," he told John as he went. Meaning the sofa in the parlor. A room used only when John or Irene's relatives visited.

"Thank you, Hank. I'm going to see if I can win some of my money back here before I go to sleep."

"Win back some of mine while you're at it. Good night."

When he heard Hank's door close, John said, "I thought your

mama didn't allow no card playing." He put his feet up on the railing and tipped back his chair.

Odessa who was rocking in the rocker said, "You in a position to know that Mama never knew everything I was doing."

The rain had slackened off but was still dripping steadily from the canopy of the big walnut. When the clouds would move just right and let it peek through, the moon looked to be snared up in its branches. Finally John brought his chair back upright with a heavy sigh.

"I'll walk you home. You carrying too much cash to go on your own." He smiled and extended a hand to her. She took it and rose easily from the low chair.

"I got to wonder what Irene would think if she knew what went on in her house when she gone," Odessa laughed as they walked across the road. Everyone was inside because of the rain, and because cultivating cotton is hard work, and those who spend their days doing it spend their nights sleeping.

"Thinking wouldn't come into it," John Washington said. "Thinking isn't done all that often about any of this. You know that. All you do is put a nickel in the slot, and out it comes."

"How you can be friends with Hank Stewart I'll never understand. You know he doesn't even think of me as being a human being. I'm just what he calls a nigger-gal. And if he knew about you, you'd be less than that."

"Well, he doesn't know. And never will, unless *you* tell him, and even then he wouldn't believe you, 'cause, like you said, you're just a nigger-gal. And why I like him is, Hank's easy."

"Easy! Hank Stewart ain't in any way, *easy!*"

"Oh, yes, he is, darling. You don't meet all the people I do. You don't know how many of them are just itching to start something—from a rumor to a fistfight. They're always kind of leaning-in, you know? They're hoping you'll say something to give offense; they're hoping your car won't start or your suit gets splashed with mud—any little thing to put you at a disadvantage. And when it happens, then they see how far they can push it. That's the way people pretty much are, but not our Hank—he can't be troubled with all that. Hank's like a big old bear. You bring him some honey, he just sits down and eats it out of the jar. You bring him enough he's likely to ask if you want some, too."

"All you describing is a lazy man with a taste for whiskey."

"If he weren't a lazy man with a taste for whiskey, you and me wouldn't be taking this midnight stroll, now, would we?" They were to the bottom of Odessa's stairs. "Are you going to let me come in? Or are we sparing your neighbors' tender sensibilities tonight?"

"Oh, please, just shut up," she said, taking his hand and pulling him inside. She stuck her head out the door and checked for witnesses; seeing none, she shut the door gently.

❦

It was late afternoon when John got back to Myrtle, but when he drove up to the house there wasn't a soul to greet him. He'd just bought two dogs, for Christ's sweet sake—seemed like to him *that* should have guaranteed him some joyful commotion when he drove into his own damn driveway. It was hot and still. The shells crunched loudly underfoot as he walked from the garage to the back door; there was a palpable air of desertion to the house when he opened the door.

On the kitchen table he found a note from Mrs. Malone, and throwing his hat on a chair, he scanned it anxiously: Antoinette and Emmy had been taken sick. Mrs. Malone had brought everyone to her house—dogs, too—to look after them. John was not to worry; she had added, it wasn't "serious." Call.

John sat down at the table and took a long drink from his flask and then put his head in his hands and rubbed his eyes—tired from staring at the road's center line. This was what he'd been afraid of. This was all he goddamn needed. Sickness creeping into one more house.

One of the reasons he'd agreed to building was to be able to sit in memory-neutral rooms where the walls had not yet absorbed the pain or despair of even one person—alive or dead. And though this house had lacked so much of what he associated with home—family mementos, the dark portraits of his mother's ancestors, and in the yard, ancient beds of day lilies and wisteria vines as thick as his arm—it also had, until this very moment, lacked everything else he associated with home: the unease, the sickening pretense that all was well, and most of all, that most human of stinks: resignation. Antoinette's house had been like a new car in a showroom. Now it had a scratch. Damnation, now there was a dent in the fender! For all he knew the whole front-end was smashed in. Whatever had happened, the spell was definitely broken; all bets were off, and John knew that the stale air and stark afternoon light in the house buffered him not at all from the next disaster waiting, invisible and patient, for John to trip it with the toe of a long, custom-made shoe.

Not serious, the note said. John picked up the piece of paper and stared at it. That was how it always began. When the first salvo is fired across the bow, somebody always laughs and says, Not serious.

He thought of Odessa and her dim, bare shack, where she'd never spent one sick day. He wanted more than anything to get in the Essex and drive back; he wanted no speaking role in the drama he sensed massing in the empty house. Instead, wearily, he picked up the phone and called his mother-in-law.

John felt better after he spoke to Mrs. Malone. Her lilting voice, her acceptance of life's large and small difficulties—distinct and separate from the Washington brand of resignation—managed to nearly cheer him. Antoinette was fine, Mrs. Malone assured him. She'd had a migraine, and Emmy had accidentally locked herself out of the house in the rain while Antoinette was asleep and had caught a heavy cold. The girls were fine. They were at school. The dogs were fine! They were absolutely adorable! John should come over and pick up Antoinette and Emmy, and she'd send the children along when they came home from school.

When he drove up to the Malones', Antoinette was waiting for him on the front porch in the swing. As she had used to when they were courting. She looked even smaller than usual, but in fact, she did not look ill.

"It's ridiculous," she said later, on the way home in the car. "Such a fuss, and over nothing! I'm sorry *you* were worried with it. I wanted Jim to bring us home last night. But no, Mama absolutely insisted I stay until you got back. Honestly, she treats me as if I were nine."

Emmy rode in the backseat with the dogs and her racking cough—which seemed quite separate and big enough to require a seat of its own. Mrs. Washington and she had not spoken of what happened; they had not spoken at all.

When John Washington had telephoned, Emmy was sitting at Mrs. Malone's kitchen table, and as she listened to Mrs. Malone's explanation of events, it sounded nearly plausible. Mrs. Malone, Emmy noted, was careful not to lie outright. And looked at in one way, you could say it had been an accident. If somebody being crazy could be said to be an accident, which in a manner of speaking, she supposed it was. God couldn't have never *meant* any of his children to be crazy.

Mrs. Malone had set her daughter down and talked to her a

good long while, that Emmy knew. From her cot in the little room next to the kitchen she'd been able to hear Mrs. Malone's voice murmuring, and she'd heard Antoinette's voice first raised in defiant argument, and then, hushed and crying. Later, Mrs. Malone told Emmy she'd understand if she quit, that she'd even help find her a new place, but she hoped she'd stay on, because she was so worried about her daughter. She'd said how Mrs. Washington wasn't the kind of person who knew how to be alone, and what a shame it was she'd married a traveling man—nice as he was. And about how young Mrs. Washington was, really, to take on Mr. Washington's half-grown children. And about what a tribulation those headaches of hers were.

In Mrs. Malone's big, sunny kitchen (drinking tea with cream and sugar in it!) Emmy nearly forgot how she'd felt sitting outside in the dark and the rain with the dogs; she almost forgot the hateful look in Mrs. Washington's eyes when she'd slammed the door in her face. Emmy's heart had been purely touched by Mrs. Malone's plain and patent love for her daughter. Emmy had no memories of her own mother, who had died soon after Emmy was born. Grandpa had not even had a picture of her.

Mrs. Malone was appealing to what she called Emmy's better nature. Asking straight-out for help. Person to person. Emmy had never had a white person do this. She'd never had anybody do it. And this worked in with the dream she'd been having over and over since she'd been sick, in the funny little room that Mrs. Malone's old daddy usually slept in: In the dream Emmy was giving speeches, not in her own halting, spitting way either. She was speaking in Mrs. Franklin D. Roosevelt's peculiar, high voice—never hesitating once. In the dream, Emmy went round the country talking to people who were suffering adversity to encourage them. She told them to take heart, to remember how much everybody loved them, that they were praying for them every day. And these speeches were greeted with wild applause and genuine out-pourings of love that brought tears to Emmy's eyes that in the dream flowed unchecked down her cheeks. At the end, a man appearing from the crowd would take her by the elbow and walk her back to the train she was riding around the country on. Then he would say to her, "Miss Clegern, we are in your debt."

Mrs. Malone had used this very expression when she talked to her. She'd said if Emmy stayed, she would be "in her debt." It was like the dream had been a sign to her. Emmy could not say no; Mrs. Roosevelt never would. Which was why Emmy was riding back to the Washingtons' house, in the backseat of Mr. Washington's car with the dogs. Because many are called, but few are chosen.

Emmy had, at last, been chosen. She had a mission.

Chapter 6

John Washington did not leave after three days this time, for which his daughters, though he didn't notice, were extremely grateful. He told them the next morning at breakfast that he couldn't trust them anymore, not since coming home to an empty house, his whole family at the Malones—sick as cats. He said he'd have to stay until they could get themselves straight. He pretended to be angry.

So for two weeks the girls could sit in the living room, listen to the radio and the phonograph, play at the piano, talk on the phone, and come and go as they pleased. Clara was off with her friends much of the time, but Vivian stuck close to her father. John got the sense that she had something she wanted to tell him, but though she talked constantly she never seemed to say anything. Clara, John Washington thought, was the most like Della, who had been a social creature, too; she had loved people and parties and good times. Vivian was the odd one. She had the strangest interests for a girl. Of course, she'd spent all that time with the Malone boy. Sometimes John Washington was as glad he hadn't had a son. What if he'd had one who turned out like Willie Malone? What would he have done? Drowned him in a sack like an unlooked-for litter of kittens was what he would have been inclined to do, but he didn't suppose anyone felt that way about their own flesh and blood. Vivian was difficult enough, with her questions about his family's experience in what she persisted in calling "the War."

"Do you mean World War One?" He'd asked her, though he knew exactly which war she meant. "Because I didn't go because of my weak lungs, and your grandfather didn't go because he was already too old."

"No, Daddy, the War. The War Between the States, the Civil War. I know Mother's grandfather ate rats at Vicksburg, but I don't know what the people on your side of the family did."

"Minded their own business," John said shortly.

"Nobody fought?"

"And nobody ate rats," he said. "Washingtons don't eat rats."

"Even if they are starving?"

"If we're starving we eat Vienna sausage," John said.

"Oh, Daddy." Vivian said in frustration, but she dropped the subject.

❦

One Saturday morning, a truck from Cochran's nursery drove up to the house and men began unloading bedding plants, shrubs, and even trees. John Washington showed them where everything was to go; he stalked around the yard imperiously pointing here and there and talking with them earnestly, his head inclined toward them as if he were Cheops explaining how he wanted the pyramids laid out. The men listened with their heads tilted respectfully to one side, and then began digging holes.

John convinced Antoinette to help with some of the flowers, and they planted a few of them together. After, that is, the men from Cochran's had hoed-out beds in the lawn, for Washingtons prided themselves on never doing manual labor; and John had no intention of breaking with that family tradition. But setting out pansies and petunias and impatiens was gardening, distinct, in John's mind, from work. Even his mother had turned her hand to a trowel upon rare occasion. He wasn't exactly planting cotton!

Antoinette gingerly placed a few pansies in their beds like dolls in a doll-crib, before putting a hand to her head to signal the approach of a headache. But in truth, with or without a headache, she had no great enthusiasm for the project. Antoinette liked her flowers wrapped in green tissue paper and delivered to the back door by the florist. And another thing, she did not have the right clothes for gardening. Obviously, if John were going to persist in this new enthusiasm, she would have to buy some. Occasionally in her magazines there were photographs of ladies out in their gardens; so she knew there was a right and a wrong thing to wear out of doors in one's yard in the spring and summer. A large hat to shade her face was the first thing she must get. Antoinette was vain of her white, white skin, but it actually tanned readily. Why, she would look like a field hand if she stayed out in this sun another twenty minutes!

But on this day she tried to be a sport because she still felt herself at a disadvantage on account of what had happened to Emmy. She knew Mama hadn't said anything to John that would implicate her, but she did not trust Emmy or the girls not to mention the incident.

Vivian and Clara followed the workmen around as they

planted the trees and shrubs in the locations that Daddy had pointed out to them.

"Do you see what he's doing?" Vivian asked her sister.

"What?"

"He's recreating Grandmother's yard. See? They're planting the bamboo in a half-circle around the fishpond we don't have. But I wouldn't be surprised to see one there quite soon. And the azaleas are going in under the living-room windows. Everything he's bought was in Grandmother's yard, and he's having them plant them in all the same places, or as close as he can come."

"So?"

"So, it's interesting, Clara, I don't think he even knows he's doing it."

"If he's doing it, I'm sure he knows it," Clara said.

Vivian did not think so. She watched as men planted a rather large young magnolia tree to the back of Daddy and Antoinette's bedroom, just where the old magnolia had been in relationship to Grandmother's bedroom. She was not surprised when a wisteria vine went in beneath it.

❧

Throughout that afternoon John Washington was almost cheerful, and this without making any trips to the garage—though John Washington's drinking ruses were plain to Vivian and Emmy, both Antoinette and Clara were deceived, and to some extent, John Washington himself was deceived.

John had been particularly and uncharacteristically solicitous of Emmy. Though he believed it had been accidental, it genuinely distressed him that someone had come to harm in his employ and under—or as it had been in this instance, not under—his roof. He paid for her cough medicine prescription, and he gave her stacks of sample boxes of Smith Brothers cough drops to appease the cough that dogged her long after she seemed otherwise well, and which sounded like it was issuing from a person twice her size. For weeks it woke everyone in the night, who, according to their private fears, first imagined it to be burglars, or wolves or ghosts, before recognizing it to be Emmy's cough, and rolling over and going back to sleep.

John had realized he could not afford to let this house slip away from him. To become a place he could not bear to return to, as Della's house had become after her death. That was when it had occurred to him to call the nurserymen and begin to put his own mark on it. He'd given Antoinette free rein with the building and the interior decoration; he'd stayed out of it except to complain of the expense. This, he sensed now, had been a mistake. Granted, he was not a homebody, but this *was* his address. This was the place the telegram would come were he killed on the road. He decided he would have some things to suit him.

Also Antoinette's mother had taken him aside to tell him what he'd already learned, that Antoinette wasn't the sort of woman who could keep up her own spirits. She'd asked John to spend some time at home, at least until Antoinette was more at ease with his children. Mrs. Malone was certain Antoinette would adjust faster if she had him home to lean on. John liked his mother-in-law; she'd never asked him for thing-one—hell, *he'd* done all the asking. She'd taken Vivian into her own house. He was resolved to make a genuine effort. And while he was so engaged he had no time to think of Odessa.

The night after the nurserymen had reconstituted his mother's yard, John asked Antoinette if she'd like to go to New Orleans. "Just you and me, little bit," he said. "See how much damage we can do in two nights."

"Can we afford it?" she asked nastily. How much had John

spent at Cochran's? More than the price of a dress at Ellen's Tog Shop, of that she was certain.

"I'm looking at it like a past-due bill. I'll tell *you* something now that you've been trying to tell me for a long time, and that's that I'm getting too goddamn cautious in my old age. Two nights in New Orleans won't break the bank—I forget sometimes that I've got such a beautiful young wife. I can't afford for you to be dissatisfied, not when I'm gone so much."

Antoinette was lying on her chaise longue, a decorating magazine open on her chest. "John, really," she said. "But," she added, "we haven't been away in a long time, and now Lent is over, it would be nice to get away. To go someplace for a change." She smiled up at John, who was standing over her, jingling the change in his pockets.

"I'll call the hotel tomorrow," Antoinette said, "I need an appointment at the beauty salon, and . . ."

"You have exactly one day. Anything that doesn't get done here can be done in New Orleans." He sat down beside her and took her hands in his.

He looked at the huge solitaire diamond in its antique setting, which had been his mother's. The ring his father had insisted she wear whenever they went out or had people in, though she had never liked it. She'd thought it made her fingers look stumpy; and she preferred the emerald her own sainted mother had left her. But it was the diamond that had signified to Winston Washington—who had noticed that when his wife wore the ring many things could be left unsaid, and many difficult topics were never raised. It was the ring Winston Washington had gotten from his own father—who had taken it from the dead hand of the woman whose husband had bought and sold him. The "family" ring, John's father had always called it, savoring the irony.

John held and kissed Antoinette's white, blue-veined hands with their perfectly oval red nails, and as he did so, he remembered Della's hands—strong, almost ruddy, with their blunt cut nails. Della's hands, which in memory, as in life, were always occupied; striding up and down piano keys, holding babies, pens, or books. Or John. When Della spoke, her hands had flown around her face like moths around a Chinese lantern, drawing pictures in the air. (For everything in Della's world lay just beyond words and lived in that realm where only music can effectively break the silence we are born into and bear with patiently, or in Della's case, impatiently, all our lives.)

John had first seen Della in a cinema, playing the piano. He sat in the dark, studying her profile and listening to her play her heart out for an hour. When the movie was over, he walked up to the front of the theater, leaned on the piano, and proposed to her. She had laughed. But before he had taken her home to her aunts' house, at dawn, she'd said yes.

John drew a deep breath. All his grieving had failed to bring Della back, had in fact, only forced her memory further and further away, so that now she existed at the back of a long dark tunnel of space and time in John's mind, accessible to him only in these brief involuntary bursts triggered by an association.

Nor could he bring Odessa forth, as he would have liked to, into his world—the white world his father had constructed for him with such audacity and boldness and such, John fully understood now, infinite cunning.

There was nothing for it but that he find a way to love Antoinette Washington née Malone. He didn't know, as Clara had from the start, that he had married the one woman he could never fall in love with. Pulling Antoinette into his embrace, he still thought he could will it so.

Antoinette had early adopted Claudette Colbert's kissing

style—which she'd attentively studied in the dark at the Ritz Theater. After a kiss, Antoinette always raised her eyebrows the way Miss Colbert did and widened her eyes to indicate mild surprise and to show that she had been deeply stirred. She was neither.

For Antoinette, sex had exactly one purpose: to bring children into the world, children who would love God and serve him. Prior to her marriage, her allure, as Antoinette preferred to think of what people were then calling *it,* had served her own purposes— to attract a handsome and, what she had *thought* was a, well-off husband.

Hating them as she did, Antoinette did not think she could possibly bear and raise children. And yet she knew that in all likelihood, someday she would. It was a stark fact. Like someday you would be dead. And there was very little to choose between these two facts, to Antoinette's way of thinking. So despite her loneliness, she was glad John traveled so much, and was secretly relieved whenever he was taken with those bouts of restlessness that caused him to troop back and forth from the garage, because in those restless moods, when he did finally come to bed he fell almost immediately asleep.

And when they traveled she was usually safe, too. For then they were out all day, came back to the hotel to bathe and change, and then were gone again far into the night. Usually by the time they got back to the hotel, often just as the sun was coming up, they were so exhausted, and John frequently so drunk, that they collapsed into bed without a thought for anything but sleep. It was, however, nights exactly like this one that made her nervous. When John suddenly came out of himself and wanted to talk. That was when he was most likely to take her to bed, and she couldn't say she had a headache tonight because she'd said that so much lately, and he was getting cross about her headaches, which she could not afford, because more often than not she *did* have a headache, an excruciating headache, which could cause her to literally forget her own name. In the throes of which she looked at John's children and couldn't think whose children they were, or what they were doing in her house, and the despised Emmy had two heads and two faces—both as ugly as original sin.

But John, who was still shaky from the sudden vision of Della's hands, felt he'd done well enough for one night, and they retired quietly to bed to sleep.

Clara had been reluctant to accept Vivian's account of what had happened to Emmy. Willie had witnessed to its veracity, but Clara did not like Willie, and she simply chose to accept Mrs. Malone's account. "I know that it happened," she said. "But I'm sure Candy didn't mean for it to happen."

"I'm sure God made the world," Vivian mocked, "but he probably didn't *intend* it to be *round*. Jesus H. Christ, Clara!"

"You don't know what really happened either, Vivian. You've decided to take Emmy's word. I have decided to take Mrs. Malone's. Tell me what possible difference it could make which account either of us chooses to believe. It's over and done with. And it makes much more sense to accept Mrs. Malone's version."

Vivian didn't say anything.

"And another thing," Clara added, emboldened by Vivian's uncharacteristic silence. "If what you and Willie say is true, why would Emmy come back to us?"

"Because she has to eat," Vivian said.

"You can't eat if you're dead," Clara said. "Emmy knows that." Which was true.

⁂

In the cotton, in Sylvan, Odessa was hoeing. She did not look up, because she did not want to see the rows stretching out before her. She didn't want to see the hours of her day strung like pearls on a necklace that belonged to somebody else. So she trained her eyes on the ground at her feet, and she sang. Sometimes only three measures of music at a time, over and over. For one at a time, she was learning and memorizing Cho Cho San's arias. She wished there was a man to take the men's parts, for the duets were the most beautiful of all the songs in the opera, to her mind. But circumstances had always decreed that Odessa sing alone.

Japan, she thought, could not possibly be more isolated than Sylvan, even in those olden times when Madame Butterfly had lived. The Japanese prints that had been reproduced on the frontispiece of the libretto showed a spit of land lapped at by white waves. In another two months, the cotton would lap at the pines and the road here. It seemed every bit as much a miracle that John Washington had found her in Sylvan as that Lieutenant Pinkerton had found the Butterfly. This was how Odessa thought of her—not as Madame Butterfly or even Cho Cho San, but simply, the Butterfly.

Odessa was herself a butterfly. Her mama had discouraged this notion with all her might while she lived, but she had done so in vain, and had known it herself. Cassandra had known what her daughter did not, and that was what all too frequently happened to butterflies. They were collected and stunned, then killed and displayed. As objects of beauty, true, but the beauty, however artfully shown, remained dead. Other times butterflies attracted a stray, roving, and murderous eye, and were killed simply for the offense of standing out in a worn-out and sorry-looking world. Cassandra would have protected her daughter from this sort of special notice. Safety, she knew, lay in fitting in. In passing unnoticed. But her efforts had been preordained to failure, for Odessa could no more go unnoticed than the hunter's moon. Odessa had been born special, and special she had remained, despite everything Cassandra had done to hide the fact.

Of course, Odessa never understood why her mother had been determined to keep her down—as she always thought of it. She'd thought her mama was jealous of John Washington's attentions to her. And Cassandra had been willing to endure her daughter's bad opinion; she had thought if she could just keep Odessa under wraps till she was grown, that then perhaps her butterfly could fly away. To New Orleans or maybe even New York City. But all her efforts—the drab colors she dressed her in, the pigtails plaited so tightly they slanted the child's eyes—had been to no avail.

Instead John Washington had driven up in his fancy car, had seen her (still in caterpillar form, but, oh, he had seen straight through that!), and what had been worse, Odessa had seen him, and she'd not seen what Cassandra saw. She hadn't seen a traveling salesman, a dandy whose skin was a little too dark, who was too ready to have a drink, and whose own future was as uncertain as March weather. No, Odessa had seen a cavalier. He became the pinnacle of her ambition. It had been a sad thing for a mother to see and to watch. And there had been nothing she could do. At the end she was even relieved that John was there, to protect Odessa from Hank Stewart and worse. At least John understood Odessa was special, even if he misunderstood the nature of her specialness. Cassandra had certainly hoped for more. But she accepted what she had gotten. She died knowing that her only child would be a man's plaything. At that, it was a happier fate than most Sylvan girls would meet. Cassandra trusted in her Lord, and she left the scene without a fuss, succumbing at last to the TB her body had harbored for years.

The future that Odessa had spoken of to John Washington last time he'd been there took many forms in her mind. The best one was perhaps the one in which she and John got in his red car and headed West, free as birds. That was the future in which they got married and lived in California. Where nobody knew them, and where they could reinvent their lives to suit themselves, and live in a pink house with orange trees instead of pine trees in the yard.

Then there was the future in which Antoinette died, and John Washington moved to Sylvan and took over Dixie Home. In that one Odessa took Irene's place, and became Queen of Sylvan. As such she dispensed justice and ruled beneficently, for the most part, over the Cotton Kingdom where she had been so little appreciated.

In reserve, for when she was mad at John, she kept the future in which she left Sylvan and went on the opera stage in Europe. In this future John followed *her* and sat every night in the front row, presenting her with huge bouquets of red roses every night. Sometimes she took one rose from the bunch and threw it back to him. And he was lucky to get that.

Odessa required a goodly number of these futures to unreel behind her eyes as she worked her way down the rows between the cotton. How the others managed to keep on hoeing with no future at all but the one that the world had slapped together for them like a bologna sandwich, Odessa really did not know. She could no more imagine being them than they could imagine being her. Which was to say, not at all. Butterflies are much misunderstood.

It was hot, and it would get hotter. Odessa picked another future, the one where she and John moved to Alaska. There John could do what he was always saying he could do: sell ice to Eskimos.

-❧-

When John and Antoinette went to New Orleans, Vivian and Clara went to stay with the Malones. Willie and Vivian camped up in Willie's room, talking and laughing, plotting the overthrow of practically everyone and everything. Clara, who in many ways shared Antoinette's opinion of the quality of life at the Malones, spent her time with Maureen, who was practicing for a piano recital she would give in late June. Clara, who read music and played passably well, due to her time with the Ursulines, served as her page turner and most devoted fan.

Clara thought Maureen truly beautiful. With her gold, fairy hair and her pale pink complexion, she resembled amazingly a doll that Clara had when she was little, in the happy, pre-Vivian days of her real childhood.

The dogs were staying at the Malones', as well, for both girls were now so attached to them that they could scarcely bear to leave them long enough to go to school. Snow-Ball, who in fact did look rather like a chow chow but was more likely a spitz-mix, sat by Clara's feet when she sat and walked by her heel when she walked, and never, never jumped up on furniture or whined or barked. He was an exemplary dog—everybody but Antoinette said so—and he was devoted to Clara. Gilbert the dog, on the other hand, bore not even a passing resemblance to any known breed, and he neither came when called, nor did he sit—or anything else—on command. He was hell on furniture and had a deep and ferocious bark that was the equal of Emmy's cough for waking the sleeping and the dead. He was most generally to be found with Vivian, but he also took notions of his own and wandered or dallied. The Malone dogs, Rufus and Lucy, ignored both interlopers; they holed up under the kitchen table and defended that small space with determination and surprising ferocity for dogs of such advanced years.

Vivian and Clara shared Vivian's old bed at the top of the stairs. The first night of their stay, Vivian woke up from a dream in which she was perishing of thirst, lost in the trackless Sahara. When she sat up she found herself under a mound of blankets nearly a foot high. Clara was asleep beside her, shivering so hard that she shook the old bed's frame.

"Clara! Wake up!"

Clara sat up and opened her eyes, trying to think where she was; then, remembering that they were at the Malones', she lay back down. She had stopped shivering.

"Do you think you're sick? Should I wake up Mama Malone?" Vivian asked. She put her hand on Clara's forehead, but it was as cool as ever.

"No. I'm fine. It was my dream."

"What dream?"

"The Snow Dream," Clara said, closing her eyes.

"What happens in it?" Vivian asked, really wanting to know. It intrigued her that Clara had a dream so particular that it had a title: "The Snow Dream!"

"Nothing *happens*. It's just cold."

Vivian watched Clara narrowly. "*What's* just cold? "Where are you?" she persisted.

"I'm nowhere. And it's cold. It's snowing and it goes on snowing and I get colder and colder. That's the whole dream."

"And it's always the same? Because I have a dream that is always the same, too. In my dream . . ."

"I don't want to hear your dream, Vivian. I want to go back to sleep."

"Where did you get all these blankets?"

"They were in the chest at the bottom of the bed. I put them on after you went to sleep, in case I had it, the Snow Dream, I mean."

"You even know when you're going to have it?"

"I don't *know*, Vivian, but if anything is different or mixed up or upset, I'm more likely to have it, so then I put on extra blankets."

"Well, you about *cooked* me," Vivian said.

"I'm sorry. Now can we go back to sleep?"

Clara turned her back to Vivian. Vivian got up to get a drink of water from the bathroom and came back to bed and lay thinking about dreams.

Her own dream was about Mother. She'd never thought of giving it a title like a book, the way Clara had hers. In her dream she was in the bamboo at Grandmother's house. She was hiding from something. Something extremely bad, but in the dream she never knew who or what the bad thing was. She held her breath so that it would not hear her. The bad thing could hear through doors and walls and could hear a little girl breathing miles away. Then she heard Mother's voice calling her. But she was afraid to answer, for if she did, the bad thing would hear, too. Then she heard Mother crying—crying and crying because Vivian did not know her. But though the crying was horrible and broke Vivian's heart, she made no answer. It might be a trick, not Mother at all, but the bad thing using Mother's voice. Then she woke up. What could you call that dream? While she wondered, she fell asleep.

Beside her, Clara shivered in the snow. The snow she had never seen except in pictures and movies and Christmas cards. The snow, that in fact, she would never see. Except at night, in the Snow Dream. When Clara was an old lady in a convalescent hospital on a wide, treeless street, attendants piled blankets on her bed until you could barely make out the old woman's form beneath them. Clara, even then, was dreaming the Snow Dream.

The dogs slept on the girls' bed. Snow-Ball slept at the foot, but Gilbert had worked himself up nearly to the top, and he was lying with his head next to Vivian's on the pillow. Gilbert did not like to sleep at the foot of the bed because of it. It was white and cold, and it curled around Clara's feet. Snow-Ball made room for it. But Gilbert gave it a wide berth. It had no scent, and it was cold like ice cream. Even in the daytime it was never far from

Clara. Like a draft of cold air at ankle height it wafted along beside her. Lucy and Rufus growled at it. Gilbert ignored it. Snow-Ball sometimes let it ride on his back.

⚜

"I asked Daddy what his family had done in the War," Vivian said to Willie. They were out under the Florentines. "And all he said was that they minded their own business!"

"He didn't know what they'd done?" Willie asked. If he had been lucky enough to have had a relative in the Rebellion, as he was now calling it, he would know each and every one of his accomplishments—even if it had existed exclusively of his death from dysentery. Anything suffered for the Cause, after all, was holy. Had his ancestors so much as marched out into the road and got blisters from ill-fitting boots, he would have known their names and every fact about them! People didn't appreciate what they had. That much became clearer to Willie every day.

"Well," Vivian said, chewing on a grass stem, "He won't say. Maybe they didn't fight so he doesn't want to talk about it. Maybe they were too valuable, growing stuff, you know, so they couldn't enlist." All Vivian had ever been told about her father's people was that they had worked a large cotton plantation in South Carolina before the war, and had come to New Orleans during Reconstruction.

"Maybe."

Willie now had access to the town library's collection of war memoirs through Masie, who, with her grown-up's library card, was allowed into this inner sanctum. He had been recently reading about South Carolina mulattos. Many of them had gone to New Orleans after the war. Willie watched his friend tearing rose petals from their stem. Her curly black hair fell forward as she concentrated, for she was playing He Loves Me, He Loves Me Not; and if she had anything to do with it, which she most certainly did, it would turn out right.

_ℓℓ_

Antoinette's luck held until the last night they were in New Orleans. They'd been out dancing. Antoinette was an amazing dancer, which John found all the more wonderful because it was so out of character. Her slender figure twisted lissomely at the waist, she set her tiny feet surely, she could have followed a whirling dervish and still the dreamy, pleasant expression she wore would have remained undisturbed. When she danced, she was the music pure.

It was the only time she did not think of how she looked or about other people watching her. In fact, she looked beautiful, and nearly everyone watched her. While dancing she was completely unself-conscious, and owing to the establishment's watered drinks, John Washington was, for once, sober enough to notice the general admiration Antoinette was attracting.

So it was then that what Antoinette had dreaded since her marriage came to pass. At three-twenty in the morning, in room 333 of the Roosevelt Hotel, she conceived a child.

Chapter 7

When they arrived back from New Orleans, John was disappointed in the results of his recent venture into the art of landscaping. Unreasonably, he'd expected to find his new plants flourishing, perhaps even flowering, and his young trees grown visibly larger. Emmy had taken every care, but the weather had turned hot, and despite her best and determined efforts, the new bushes and trees looked in danger of perishing.

While Antoinette went inside the house to take a cool bath, John stood out in his yard growing angrier by the second, looking at the drooping plants and withering saplings, and thinking of the money he'd just pounded down yet another rat hole. Then it occurred to him that he knew the man to work the miracle that needed working: Gilbert.

Gilbert, after all, had been the one to coax John's mother's garden into its glory and to keep it in order—and he still was. John had been unable to bring himself to sell his mother's house, nor could he tolerate the idea of strangers living in it. It stood empty, with Gilbert maintaining the grounds and Cassie coming in to keep the house swept and dusted once a week. John decided to drive out that very minute to the settlement where Gilbert and Cassie now lived and talk to him about attending upon this new venture.

John didn't like Gilbert; he was, in John's opinion, a surly son of a bitch by nature. He was borderline insolent to nearly every-one, and to John Washington in particular, but he had come with Cassie—without whom his mother would have been virtually helpless. It had been the Great War and France that had ruined Gilbert, John thought. When he'd returned, he gave himself airs. He'd got above himself.

When John drove up into their yard, just to establish who was who and to signify his true feelings, he purposefully ran over a bed of zinnias before braking hard and leaning on his horn.

After a minute Gilbert came out and walked over to the car. He looked from his ruined flower bed to John Washington, his face and voice unreadable. "Mr. Washington."

"I need you to tend to the yard over at my new house. What day do you and Cassie go over to my mother's place?"

"Wednesdays."

"I want you to come to the new place when you come Wednesday, then. I think you might have to come every day for a while. I had Cochran's come out and do some landscaping, but I just got back from New Orleans, and it looks like the goddamned Gobi desert. I don't think they know what they're doing. Everything's trying to die off on me."

Gilbert had lost the thumb and two fingers of his right hand in an accident in France; it was this disability that had caused him to become Mrs. Washington's yardman. He'd assiduously retrained himself to use his left hand. The only thing he still did with his right hand was to hold his cigarette—between his pinkie and his ring finger. This he did now. It was a calculated insult to John Washington, in the etiquette of that day and that place. And Gilbert did it in the same spirit as John had run over Gilbert's zinnias.

Taking a drag off his cigarette and very nearly looking John Washington in the eye, Gilbert said, "I can't give you every day. I'm working over at Mr. Callahan's now. Where Cassie's working at."

"I'll take what you got left over," John Washington said, starting up the motor. "Just be there Wednesday." He slammed the car into reverse and backed back over the zinnias, and to the road, where he turned around and tore off back for town.

Cassie had come out on the porch. She was standing there with her arms crossed watching John Washington's car rocket down the dirt road, throwing dust on people walking home from work and forcing them into the ditch. "What did he want?"

Gilbert tossed his cigarette and ground it out in his destroyed flower bed. "Wants me to tend his new place. Come over next Wednesday and look at it with him."

"What did you say?"

"I didn't say nothing, 'cause he never *asked* me nothing. When did he ever ask anybody anything?"

Cassie sat down on the steps, and Gilbert sat down beside her.

"Did you hear what happened to that woman that's working for them?"

"Uh-uh."

"That new wife locked her out of the house in the middle of the night in the rain. She come down with the pneumonia and nearly died."

"That the harelip we see at The Lucky Pig?"

"Emmy. I think she might could be simpleminded, too. It's hard to tell, 'cause when you try and talk to her she can't get the words out of her mouth." Cassie imitated Emmy trying to order The Lucky Pig's special. "L-l-l-let m-m-m-m-meee have the, the, the nu-nu-numb-b-ber t-t-two."

Cassie and Gilbert had never given any quarter, and they expected none.

～❦～

That night at supper John Washington mentioned that he'd hired Gilbert to take care of the yard. Vivian looked up from her plate. "You mean *here*?"

"Of course, here. That's what I just said, isn't it?"

"Yes, but . . ."

"But nothing! I just spend a goddamned fortune on this yard, and it's dying all around me from criminal neglect."

Vivian returned her attention to her plate; now she had a new worry. What would Gilbert think when he found she'd given his name to her dog? Gilbert who was always mad, would be madder than ever when he found that out. And it was too late to change the dog's name. She would just have to be careful not to call him by name when Gilbert was around. When she'd named him, she'd thought that Gilbert was out of her life for good. Now here he was coming back.

Antoinette was not happy about Gilbert either. Not because she knew him, but because she did not want another particular black face for her dreams. And, too, if she were home alone, and Emmy and Gilbert were both there, why she'd be outnumbered two to one! But she could see that John had made his decision, so she made no protest. Since the fight they'd had about the dogs, she hadn't confronted John directly. She said, "Well, that's just a wonderful idea, John. Of course we've needed a yardman right along, but because you've been gone so much there's been no chance to do anything about it. I'm glad you're getting to it."

"He'll be here Wednesday," John said.

It felt good to make a pronouncement. He had been right to spend some extra time with Antoinette. They'd had fun in New Orleans. She'd seemed happy, she had been cheerful, and hadn't had one headache the whole time they were there. He'd seen her again in the light he'd first seen her when they'd been courting, before Vivian and Clara had come home. He was hoping this would last. A happy home life, his life on the road, and of course, his life with Odessa in Sylvan—from these separate worlds, John Washington felt he could fashion a life fit to live.

When Della was alive, before she got sick, he had not required worlds. Oh, he'd fallen in love with Odessa when she was only a child, but he might not have done anything about it if his world hadn't been dissolving like ribbon candy in a bowl of water. Before Della's illness he saw his own life as he saw the physical world—a vista stretching out into a future he wanted to live into. That had disappeared altogether with Della's death, and later it had become bifurcated into two worlds, Odessa and Sylvan, and home and Antoinette. He was about trying to unify it again. He sensed that if he were very, very careful, he might do it.

Odessa had mastered two of the arias from *Madame Butterfly*. John had said he would be gone two weeks, which had now turned into three. She was anxious for him to come and to bring her the props she needed for the songs. Of course, she had a fan, but it wasn't the right sort of fan. It was left over from Mama's funeral and had this verse written in bold letters: BLESSED ARE THOSE THAT MOURN. Odessa got mad every time she read it! Maybe blessed compared to those who *were* mourned, but it wasn't much of a choice by any reckoning, and surely nothing to stir up any elation. Anyway, a big old ugly cardboard fan with that dismal verse printed in a bad purple color was most certainly not a fan the Butterfly could use.

When John had been there last she hadn't made any real progress; she'd meant to start him down the path to his decision. Odessa did not aim to go on being anybody's second choice forever. Her mother had not raised her to that. John could talk all he wanted about his "marriage" to Antoinette, but Odessa did not recognize it. *She'd* been John's only real wife once Della died.

Her mother had preached making things happen by intention of will and perseverance. Of course, she'd also gone on about something called Grace, but Odessa had seen this as a tricked-up, sanctified way of talking about luck, and she didn't intend to place herself at the mercy of that. Just about everybody in Sylvan relied on luck, and look where it had gotten them.

She'd tried to talk to John about all this last time he'd come, but he'd succeeded in putting her off; he'd romanced her, and when that hadn't worked, he'd made her feel sorry for him. John was very good at that. But who would feel sorry for Odessa? Nobody, unless she wasted her own time doing it, which she was way too smart to do.

On John's account she'd put herself outside her own community, not that it had ever exactly clasped her to its bosom. To begin with, Cassandra's fierce religiosity had not been conducive to easy dealings with folk in Sylvan. She had been harshly critical of people for understandable and natural failings, such as drinking and card playing and dancing and what she'd always insisted on calling "fornication." So much so, that Odessa's precocious affair with the white drummer had been soul-satisfying to just about everyone in Sylvan.

Watching Cassandra get her comeuppance from her own child that she'd treated like a princess—too good to play with their children, too special to work in the fields that their own children had already been working for years—this was the best present they could have had, and they made the most of it.

When Cassandra died, people didn't talk about the Christian life she'd led, how she'd single-handedly kept their little clapboard church cleaned and scrubbed, or the years she'd spent teaching Bible lessons to children (managing in the process to teach at least three of them, besides Odessa, to read) and trying to raise up their morals. No. They talked about Cassandra's daughter, and how she'd run to the bad, and in so doing had made a laughingstock of her sanctimonious mama.

Had she known this, Cassandra would not have been unduly surprised, or even dismayed. She'd chosen to walk with her Lord, knowing the path to be narrow, knowing she might have to walk it alone. And she'd had no wild expectations, unless you counted Life Everlasting. But that was a promise, wasn't it? Yes. That was a covenant.

Odessa, who'd fought her mother every day of her life, was nonetheless both frightened and angry when the very people her mother had tried to serve and to love in her own peculiar, pinched way, did not have the simple decency to mourn her. They had shared the same hard life; Odessa thought they should have felt *something* for Cassandra when she was consigned to the pitiless ground everybody had spent their lives scraping at.

Nor had what Odessa told John been entirely true. Everyone in Sylvan did not know John was as black as many of them. Though some people doubtless suspected it, it was by no means common knowledge, and prudence demanded that those who did think it keep the notion to themselves, lest word of their suspicions reach John himself, who, white or black, was a man to be reckoned with.

John was right about people seeing what they expected to see. John made a convincing white man. And because he was not only (in their sight) white, but also eccentric, people never knew exactly what to expect from him. Hence, his peculiarities were put down to his florid style. Children adored him; women eyed him with interest—whatever else he was or wasn't, he was devil-handsome. Men sensed an air of suddenness and danger about John Washington. It was common knowledge that he carried a pistol in his suit jacket pocket, as carelessly as if it were a pack of gum. He used his unusual height to look down on everyone, black and white, but this seemed a natural result of his build rather than a calculated technique to intimidate. It was, Odessa knew, both.

While she waited for John Washington to return, Odessa, hot and sweating in her little shack, practiced her arias. She sang "but now beloved, you are the world." And she tried to imagine John singing "Oh Night of Rapture." Well, they had at least had that. Many nights of rapture. And John had been since she could remember, her "beloved" and also her "world." And though he did not seem to know it, since Della died she had been his.

Irene Stewart was back from Vernon, and the unusually hot spring had forced her to begin her canning season early. She sent word to Odessa that she needed her help. Though she didn't pay Odessa in cash for slaving in the hot kitchen with her, she did pay her in the jars of vegetables and fruit they were putting up. Odessa could never have afforded this food, even had it been available to purchase, which it wasn't. And the work was no harder and easier than most in Sylvan.

"I was afraid to death I wouldn't get back in time to do this first round of canning. I knew with this early hot spell we've had we'd have to start right in, and I was right. But seemed like my sister was determined to keep me there till Christmas!" Irene told

Odessa as they began sterilizing the glass jars they were going to fill with early English peas.

Odessa believed Irene had been born talking. Irene was famous for talking; why, she talked to her chickens if there wasn't a person handy. When you went into Dixie Home to buy so much as a Coca-Cola, and Mrs. Stewart was behind the counter, she'd keep you there talking at you until she ran herself down. She'd talked at Hank for so many years, he no longer heard a word she said. He'd perfected various techniques of indicating that he was listening, but he'd stopped years ago.

Right now she was saying, "I said to Vera, 'Vera, I got me a life to get back to, I can't be staying here until the end of time just because your stitches got infected.' Well, I couldn't, could I?"

"No, ma'am," Odessa said, putting on another kettle of water to boil.

"I told her, I said, 'I got me a husband home alone on crutches! Don't that signify to you?'"

"Umm," Odessa replied.

"But of course it don't. Vera thinks she's the only person alive on this earth. Always has. Selfish as the day is long, always was. Absolutely no regard for another living human soul. Just what do you think she'd do if I said I needed her help and for her to come out here and put her back into something?"

Odessa lined up the glass jars on the counter. "What would she say, Mrs. Stewart?"

"Well, I'll tell you, she'd say she had to stay there in town on account of her little girl's piano recital, or some book club she belongs to or something like that. Oh, I know just exactly what to expect from Vera!"

Irene stopped and mopped at her face with a tea towel. It was probably a hundred degrees in the kitchen, and not that much cooler outside; the boiling water was causing the windowpanes to weep. Frankly, Irene felt like weeping herself, what with all this work—that she knew nobody would ever notice or remark. Certainly Hank never would. Did he really think English peas just appeared on his plate the year around? Probably. But she didn't say any of this to Odessa. Somehow she felt it was all right to complain about her family in Vernon, but not about her husband. Hank, after all, had to have these niggers' respect to get anything accomplished. She couldn't go to undermining that. But then, she'd always felt Odessa was a special case. She wasn't like the others, which was the reason Irene called on her when she needed help.

Odessa's mother, old Cassandra, had raised the girl up right. Taught her her Bible and right from wrong. Taught her to keep up her personal appearance, too. The girl had morals, and she was extremely talented. Why she could sing like a mockingbird! She'd been singing an opera song when Irene came into this very kitchen, singing so true that at first Irene had thought it was Sunday, and the Texaco Opera show was on the radio. That's how good she was. It was a shame that Odessa was colored and stuck out in the middle of nowhere. A white person with her voice, now she could have got somewhere.

"I heard John Washington was here while I was gone to my sister's."

"Yes, ma'am, he was."

"How did he seem?"

"Ma'am?"

"How did he *seem*, Odessa—for heaven's sake, pay attention! Was he in good spirits? Was he drinking a whole lot or just a little? Do you reckon he's happy with that new wife of his? Do you think he's going to be *okay*?"

Odessa began rinsing out the colanders with boiling water.

"Mr. John, he seem almost cheerful these days, to me, Mrs. Stewart. Yes, I'd say he going to be fine."

"I surely to God hope so," Irene said. She was seated at the table now, shelling peas, her fingers a blur. "That man has suffered more than his share of tragedy. For a person so young, I mean." Irene's eyes flicked up to meet Odessa's. "I know he's particularly fond of you, child, on account of how much he respected the kind of woman your mama was. Of course, we all appreciated her. I hope you know *that*."

And where was you when I buried her all alone? Odessa thought. "Yes ma'am, thank you. Mama was a righteous woman."

"Amen to that," Irene said. "I just hope you keep her memory green and never do anything to scandalize it. She worked so hard to set an example for all your people here in Sylvan, you especially." The colored girl was standing now with her back to her at the sink. Irene's fingers stopped their automatic motion, and she rested them a moment in her lap. She was fighting back tears. She lived right on the brink of tears all the time. At her sister's she'd twice had to go into the bathroom and run the taps so she could cry without Vera demanding to know what was the matter. What was the matter was that she had recently had to face the fact that the daughter she'd longed for all her life could never be a reality.

Nobody could know how much she had wanted a child, and particularly a daughter. Another female to keep her company. Her bottom bureau drawers were stuffed with patterns she'd cut from magazines over the years for matching mother and daughter dresses she'd never now have occasion to sew. In the end, the good Lord had not seen fit to send her even one child, whereas he'd sent Vera three. He'd just left *her* out here in the middle of nowhere with only Hank and niggers for company.

And the niggers didn't even *like* her, and Irene flat didn't understand that, because she tried to be fair, and treat them decent. Not everybody would. It wasn't her fault they'd been put on earth to hew wood and draw water. Irene Stewart hadn't written the book. You could believe if she had, more than a few things would be different!

And it wasn't her fault that they all lived and worked—herself and Hank included—in Sylvan, at the beck and call and sufferance of Catreirs who'd owned the land and every living thing that grew from it as far as you could see, ever since God invented trees. One reason she liked to go to Vernon and see her sister, as much as Vera irritated her, was that at least while she was there she wasn't treading Catreir ground. It wasn't like she and Hank had made up the rules that kept everybody in Sylvan in debt and scraping. But since the Catreirs rarely showed their faces, everybody naturally blamed her and Hank for everything.

And who were *they* supposed to blame, she'd like to know? So here she was, with nobody but Odessa to talk to. Well, Irene thought, going back to shelling peas, we can't know what God's plan for us is. Stand ready, and be of pure heart, isn't that what the Book said? She took a deep breath and wiped the tears and sweat from her face with a dishcloth.

"Gracious, I'm about to perish in this heat. I think we should take us a break, don't you, Odessa?"

"Yes, ma'am, that would be welcome."

"Why don't you pour three glasses of iced tea. I'll take one in to Mr. Stewart and visit with him a few minutes, and you can take yours out back, and we'll both rest a bit."

Odessa poured the tea and handed two glasses to Irene. The white woman looked ready to topple. Her face was red except for a white mask around her eyes; her once ginger, now sandy, hair was matted to her head with sweat. All this work, Odessa thought, just so Hank Stewart can eat fruit and vegetables out of season and get even fatter than he is.

Odessa walked out in the yard and sat down on the bench built around the trunk of the walnut to drink her tea. She heard Cecelia Jefferson's boys giggling and whispering from the direction of Mrs. Stewart's chicken house. When she looked around from behind the tree, she saw Billy Jefferson drawing in the dirt with a stick while the twins sneaked up on one of Mrs. Stewart's pet chickens, Henrietta, with a two-by-four.

Poor old Henrietta was running fast as she could, which was not very fast—she was so petted and overfed, she could scarcely walk, much less run—but she was leaning forward into her strut, giving it all she had.

"Hey," Odessa shouted. "What are you all doing back here? Put that board down, Tom Jefferson, and leave Mrs. Stewart's chickens be. You *hear* me?"

The boys tossed their weapon in the dust and stood still, waiting to see what Odessa would do next. Little Billy dropped his stick, too. He was too young to know if he was included in Odessa's command. None of them wanted to get on the wrong side of Odessa of all people, for they knew she had John Washington's ear, and a bad report from Odessa to John Washington could separate them—in order of magnitude—from the Essex, the Coca-Colas, and the gingersnaps.

"Them's Mrs. Stewart's *pets*. Muss a feather on their heads, and you going to answer to John Washington when he get back. He mighty partial to them chickens. You all didn't know that?" Odessa asked, raising an eyebrow. "Oh, yeah, he bring 'em special food all the way from Memphis; he named that chicken you all was trying to murder, Henrietta, after an old auntie of his. You'd have been mighty sorry if you'd killed her, 'cause if Hank Stewart hadn't of beat you to death, John Washington might have shot you down with his gun when he got back here and found his Henrietta in somebody's old stewpot."

The older boys kicked the board farther away, as if by doing this they could further distance themselves from their crime. Billy began to cry. Fat tears plopped into the dust and on his bare feet. "You ain't going to tell him, is you Miss Odessa?" the twins pleaded.

Odessa, arms folded, chin down, studied the ground and said, "Why wouldn't I?"

The boys did not know this answer, so they waited in silence.

"I don't suppose it ever going to happen again?"

"No!" they chorused.

"Well, then, I won't say anything. Was there to be another time, there'll be no talking. Now, get on away. You know you ain't supposed to even be back here, much less here persecuting Petey and Henrietta."

The twins took off, and Odessa called Billy to her. She wiped his tearstained face with her apron. "I didn't mean you, Billy. You weren't doing nothing." She took his small hand in her own, and they walked back toward the house.

Billy loved John Washington with all his heart, and not just for his Coca-Colas or his gingersnaps or his car. These he valued only because they belonged to John Washington. Billy loved the tall man. He loved his smell and his red-gold shoes and his voice.

"Would you like a grape soda?" Odessa asked the forlorn child, who gulped and nodded. "Okay, you wait for me here on the steps."

Odessa went into the store and bought a grape soda and paid with a nickel from her pocket. "This here's for little Billy Jefferson," she explained to the Stewarts. "Those brothers of his so mean, they got him to crying. I'm just trying to put a smile back on that little face."

Which she did.

Back in the kitchen, looking out the window, she could see

that Henrietta had gone back to pecking at the dirt, and Petey had come around from behind the chicken house where he'd been ingloriously hiding. Billy sat peaceably on the bench drinking his grape. After every sip he held the bottle up to the sunlight to admire its wonderful purple color.

How come, Odessa wondered, those Jefferson twins was so murderous, anyway? Of course, they could never know how Irene Stewart would have grieved for them chickens. They didn't even imagine for a minute that Mrs. Stewart was a human being like themselves. But, then, they'd never been encouraged in that line of thinking. Not by Mrs. Stewart most certainly, who, on the other side of the coin, could no more imagine Cecelia's boys being boys she might have had. To put this thorny subject from her mind, Odessa went back to singing her aria.

At first she'd identified with the Butterfly completely, but as she worked her way through the opera, she was losing patience with her. She should, Odessa thought, be taking a more active role in working out her own fate. She ought not to trust that Pinkerton to do the right thing on his own. You couldn't do like that with men. They needed some help along the way, some poking and prodding to bring them to the right thing.

And also, in Odessa's mind, the Butterfly had been a big fool to lumber herself with that child. If a man won't pay attention to a woman, is he going to pay attention to a baby? Odessa knew better. But for all the Butterfly's mistakes, Odessa still found the purity of her faith beautiful. If anybody could love a man into line, the Butterfly could.

Chapter 8

School was out, and the heat settled in like an unwelcome house-guest. Gilbert came part of every day to work in the yard. John was gone. Antoinette stayed in her bedroom, where the venetian blinds and drapes kept out the worst of the heat and blinding sun—which pierced her head like a knife—and where she could hear neither Vivian's loud voice nor the dogs barking quite so plainly. She had a bell by her bed, which she rang for Emmy when she needed something else cool to drink.

She'd been afflicted with an unquenchable thirst for a week, and the heat had put her off food. She lay in bed in the dark and drank iced tea and nibbled at soda crackers. Something, she knew, was wrong, but just what she did not imagine. She could not tolerate the idea of Dr. Knox, her mother's doctor, coming to stare and to poke at her, and she did not want her mother to know that she was ill, so she had resolved to stay in her room until she felt better. But this was proving difficult, for there was nothing to do but read, and when she tried to read she fell asleep. But when she fell asleep she dreamed, and so spent most of each day staving off an army of colored people who clamored for every last thing she had. And now this army had itself a new general—just as she'd known it would: Gilbert.

Gilbert was unpleasant enough in person, but to have him stalking around in her dreams was really too much.

She was interested to see that she was not the only one who disliked Gilbert. Vivian didn't like him either, and Emmy, though she never said anything about him one way or another, was wary of him. When she carried out his dinner in the middle of the afternoon, she placed it on a tree stump and left without speaking.

Gilbert had actually had the colossal gall to complain of the dogs—asking Emmy to keep them penned up while he was working. Antoinette, who had been in the kitchen looking for something cool and refreshing, reaching for some grapes at the back of the refrigerator, had overheard this and been so infuriated by the man's insolence, she had marched right into the backyard and taken him to task.

"These dogs are for our protection," she'd told Gilbert, who stood leaning easy on a rake. "They are to remain free to roam the yard and keep an eye on things." (*You*, she meant.) "I think you must have forgotten who is working for whom. When Mr. Washington comes home, I promise you he will set you straight."

Gilbert had removed his hat when Mrs. Washington had come out to speak to him, but he returned it to his head when she came to the end of this indignant speech. Gilbert had no intention of kowtowing to the little Irishwoman—who was, according to Cassie, mad as a hatter and twice as hateful. He made no answer.

"Did you hear me?" Antoinette demanded to know, her little voice going all high and screechy.

"Yes, ma'am, I heard. You say let the dogs run loose to undo everything you paying me to do fast as I do it. That what you want done, that exactly what I going to do. Mr. Washington's mother never let dogs run in her garden, but you different, and if you want to set goats loose in it, I ain't supposed to say nothing about that either, on account of I working for you."

Antoinette was so infuriated by Gilbert's smug face and his sass, and the white light of the hot afternoon was so bright that she retreated indoors, banging the kitchen door to and leaning weakly up against it.

Who was this nigger, and how dare he talk to her like that? Goats, indeed. When John came home they would talk about this. First he saddled her with pets he wasn't home to care for, and then he saddled her with an insolent and now, she suspected, dangerous yardman. What next?

Next, Gilbert began mowing the grass directly outside Antoinette's bedroom window. It felt like the blades were whirring around inside her head. She pulled the coverlet over her head and wept.

Because Antoinette was staying in bed, and Gilbert was stalking about in the yard like somebody had died and made him king, Vivian and Clara, with Emmy's knowledge and permission, decamped to the Malones'. When Antoinette asked where the girls were, Emmy simply and quite ably lied. She said they were in their room or in the sunroom or playing in the front. She now had Mrs. Malone's permission to lie to her daughter.

Antoinette thought herself safe from her mother's watchful eye in her bedroom. What she didn't know was that since "the incident," Emmy was serving as Mrs. Malone's special agent. And as such, Mrs. Malone's orders took precedence over Mrs. Washington's. Emmy called Mrs. Malone on the phone twice a day and gave an account of Mrs. Washington's condition, and received instructions. For the moment, Mrs. Malone was keeping to a very conservative plan of action. "Let the poor child rest," she always said. "Please see that she rests."

"Yes, ma'am," Emmy would reply, and wondered just how she could have stopped Mrs. Washington from "resting," had she wanted to. Though, for a woman who slept so much, seemed like poor Mrs. Washington never did get any less tired.

Clara had a crush on Maureen, and she spent all her time watching this exquisite creature. She watched her practice the piano; she watched her wash her fairy hair and fluff it dry in the sun; she even watched her not-eat. Clara and Snow-Ball never strayed far from their new ideal. Most of the time Maureen seemed scarcely to notice, but Clara expected this. She knew she was not yet accomplished enough for Maureen to see her as an equal. She was willing to serve an apprenticeship.

Willie and Vivian spent the hot afternoons with Willie's tin soldiers playing out battles inside the rose bower. The roses had withered in the heat, but the bower itself had grown into a veritable thicket. Green and cool, it was like the briar castle of the Sleeping Beauty. Normally Willie was afraid to be outside for any length of time on account of bees and sun, but with the blooms gone, the bees had moved on to the oleanders beside the garage, and also Vivian had declared herself Vivian the Bee Killer, and sworn on a biography of Robert E. Lee to defend Willie from the flying assassins, even unto death. Willie felt almost safe with his fierce and vigilant friend so near, and beneath the rose's branches there was ample shade.

Mrs. Malone, watching out the kitchen window, enjoyed seeing the two children together. Now in summer they made even a more striking contrast to one another than usual—for Vivian had turned quite remarkably brown in the sun, and of course, Willie stayed as white as his white mouse, Longstreet. Mrs. Malone had always taken great pleasure seeing her children at play. She herself had had no opportunity to play, having been prematurely cast in the role of mother by her own mother's long sojourn in bed. Papa had, in fact, used to call her "little mother." And though at the time she'd been too busy to feel sorry for herself, now she took justifiable pride that she and her husband had lived in such a way as to give their own children the privileges of an American-style childhood. This was the real reason she turned a blind eye to Masie's Indexed reading material. Each of her children had done something quite different with their leisure, but Mrs. Malone was certain they all profited from it. So the sound of Maureen practicing at the upright, and the sight of Willie and Vivian hunkered in the rose bower, even the knowledge that Masie was in her room reading Karl Marx, God save us, pleased her equally.

Papa Maguire was sitting at the kitchen table, stirring a cup of hot tea, having first shoveled in several spoons of sugar. It was an article of faith with him that drinking hot liquids on a hot day cooled the blood.

"Isn't it nice to have little Vivian back with us, though," he said now, saucering and blowing his tea. Vivian had breakfasted with him that very morning, pouring the milk for the cats and scattering toast crumbs for the birds.

"It is, though I only wish the reason for her visits was happier."

"What exactly ails our Antoinette?" Papa asked.

"Fatigue and headache, it seems, Papa."

"Your poor mother, God rest her soul, suffered so much from that. Perhaps it's in the blood."

Mrs. Malone, who secretly had wondered the same, nodded. She was polishing silver, for she never sat idle. Sitting itself was rest enough for her.

"And when will John be coming home?"

"Another week," Mrs. Malone said, rubbing at the garlands of roses that fretted the teaspoons she was polishing.

"She married a man like her own papa," Papa Maguire said.

"Not exactly," Mrs. Malone heard herself say, and was surprised to hear her own frosty tone. "That is, they both are away from home for long periods, but there, I believe, is where any resemblance ends."

"Ah," Papa said, looking more closely at his daughter and seeing the two little vertical lines between her eyes—lines he was unaccustomed to seeing on her round, smooth face—though these same lines had been etched permanently upon his late wife's face.

"Papa, I very much hate to say this, but I cannot think of anyone else I might say it to. I believe that John Washington is not a faithful husband."

Papa, who knew that faithful husbands (and indeed, faithful wives) were always in shorter supply than is generally supposed, nodded. He himself could not imagine being faithful to such a woman as Antoinette had turned into, and did not blame John Washington, but he did not say this.

He did not care all that much for his granddaughter's sake, but he did care for Kathleen's. He wanted her happiness in all things, for she'd earned it in a thousand ways.

"Daughter, most likely John Washington is exactly what he seems, a traveling man, and—as I'm sure you know with your lifetime of experience with your old father—something of a drinker. I would doubt he has time to be carrying on with a woman, too. Traveling and drinking, they both take up a man's time and strength. Particularly with this vile Prohibition. I myself have only enough strength left to drink."

"Papa, I shouldn't know what I'd do without you to talk to." Mrs. Malone smiled at her father, and when she did the lines from between her eyes disappeared without a trace.

"You'd do without," Papa said, and finished off his tea, savoring the sweet slush of sugar at the bottom of the cup. "I've been meaning to ask *you* something—also of a confidential nature. Have you been noticing that channel of cold air which travels with little Clara?"

"Whatever do you mean, Papa?"

"I mean literally, there is a coldness around the child. Like a cold current in a stream when you wade into it. It generally sets low, near her feet. I happen to know because she sits across from me at table, and I have to move my own feet away and put them on the rungs of my chair."

"Papa I *thought* I was talking to a sober man. You didn't let me confide in you when you're already into the bottle!"

"No, no, little girl. I'm sober as a judge. I speak of a chilly area around that girl Clara's feet. Surely to God you've noticed!"

"I've not. Merciful saints!" Mrs. Malone replied, and got up to put the silver in the sink to wash it in hot water. "I hate to be saying this to you, Papa, but if you came to the table sober, these things wouldn't happen."

Papa nodded his head somberly and appeared to take his daughter's rebuke to heart. "Where's Masie?" he asked, to change the subject.

"She's reading, bless her."

"Ah," Papa said. "That one's the smartest of us all."

"Well she thinks she is, which should count for something," her mother said, smiling.

∗

"Goddamn it, Willie! I've been doing what you want for days. I'm sick to death of this yard. I feel like I'm growing into the ground like this damn bush. And I'm tired of the War and the maps and playing out battles that always turn out the same way."

Willie had known it would be only a matter of time before Vivian ran out of patience with his notion of fun. "What do you want to do instead?"

"We could go down to my camp. Swim or fish or anything we wanted. There's nobody looking out a kitchen window at you there." To sweeten the pot she added, "I've never shown it to anybody, not even Clara."

"What about snakes and alligators? What about bees?"

"How can you worship at the shrine of Stonewall Jackson and still be afraid of practically *everything*?"

"I'm not afraid of battle—I'm only afraid of nature." Willie said. "And anyway, I can't swim."

"You know, Willie, all these battles"—Vivian knocked over a line of riflemen with an angry sweep of her hand—"were held *out of doors*. Soldiers had to swim their horses across rivers. They had to take their chances with bees *and* bullets."

Willie put this unpleasant version of his beloved war directly from his mind. "What will we tell Mama?"

"Tell her we're going downtown. Jesus H.! The great General Malone can't think of a lie good enough to cover his butt with his own mother! Even if you're afraid of bugs and water, I would think you could handle administrative detail."

≪

That afternoon, Clara asked Maureen if she could play Chopin's F Minor Nocturne; Maureen said indeed she could, but she didn't have the music at home.

"Oh, we've got it at our house. My grandmother used to play it, and I have always adored it," Clara said. That summer she "adored" everything that she did not, in turn, "despise." Numbered among the things she adored were Snow-Ball, Chopin Nocturnes, Saint Teresa of Avila, forsythia, and most of all, Maureen Malone. The list of things she despised is too long to reproduce here. Though one was the Snow Dream, and another, sadly—for Clara felt almost guilty about it—was Vivian.

"We could walk to our house and get the music," Clara suggested. "We could just go to the back door and ask Emmy to fetch it for us. We wouldn't have to disturb Candy. I mean, Antoinette."

"Oh, yes, let's! I'd love to play that piece for you. *You*, I know, would actually appreciate it. So often—" Maureen brushed a tendril of hair back over her shoulder and sighed. "—well, so often, I feel I'm only playing for myself. Mama really has no discrimination. She's as happy if I play 'Pop Goes the Weasel' as when I play Chopin. And the rest of them . . ." She raised her eyebrows in an expressive gesture.

"I know," Clara said. "I know all too well."

The girls exchanged a deep gaze of commiseration.

≪

It was a long walk across town, and Willie walked slowly. "Come *on*, Willie. It'll be dark by the time we get there at this rate! Think of Stonewall marching his troops."

"The general was, I believe," Willie said, stopping to lean against a tree and wheeze, "on horseback."

Vivian tore off an overhanging bough from a tree and impatiently slapped her own leg with it.

But when they finally arrived at Vivian's "lodge"—skirting Vivian's house and approaching it from a pasture—Willie admitted the beauty of it. "It's perfect, Viv. Really. It's beautiful. And nobody knows? Really nobody?"

Vivian beamed proudly, and in so doing, looked exactly like her father. "Nobody but us. I've been saving it, because I wanted it to be just ours."

"Thank you," Willie said sincerely and humbly. He sat down on the bank and took off his shoes and socks and then waded into the water. It was very shallow where he stood, and he could see and feel minnows swimming over his white toes. Vivian, who had left her shoes back in the rose bower, came and stood beside him. It was quiet except for birds, the almost inaudible chortle of the water, and in the distance, a train whistle.

"Look," Vivian whispered, pointing across to the other bank. "Do you see that egret?"

Willie settled his glasses more securely on his nose and peered hopefully—sighting along Vivian's arm. "Oh. Yes, I think I do," he said. He couldn't see across the water at all. Everything beyond three feet from his nose was a green blur, but he wanted to show his gratitude to his friend for singling him out to share this private place.

"Do you want to come in swimming? I'll hold you up. We won't go where it's deep."

"Maybe later," Willie said, and sat down with his feet in the water.

Vivian stripped off her pants and shirt and ran into the water in her underwear. She flailed at the surface of the water in what she believed to be the Australian crawl. Willie, shielding his eyeglasses from the splashing, called, "What about gators, Vivian?"

"What about them? They'd better stay out of my way if they know what's good for them," she proclaimed, and took an inadvertent drink of bayou water and came back up coughing and sputtering. Willie thoughtfully looked up into the canopy of the trees behind him until the coughing subsided. He was on the lookout for bees and snakes. Mercifully his shortsightedness prevented him from seeing either—though they were all around him—in well-camouflaged abundance.

"There are books in the lodge, Willie, and a jar of water, and some saltines. Make yourself at home." Saying this, Vivian dived to the bottom, showing her heels to Willie. She was just so pleased to have finally gotten him here, she felt like she was flying under water.

Willie went back to Vivian's makeshift shelter and helped himself to some water and a cracker. He sat in the shade; it would serve no purpose to get sunburn. Then Mama would know he'd lied to her. It was, from his point of view, very regrettable that he'd had to lie to her, but on the other hand, he was no longer a baby, even if he had the skin and hair of a baby, and always would, he could not live out his whole life in the Malone house and yard and Saint Clare's—the only places his mother seemed to consider safe.

He did not understand how Vivian could enjoy swimming in the murky waters of the bayou. Once you got past the edge, the water was filled with vegetation and branches, and he just knew that the bottom, if indeed there *were* a bottom, would be squishy. How, he thought to himself, did Vivian become my best friend? And why is she the wild one, instead of me? It didn't seem quite right, but at the same time it seemed perfectly natural, and always had, even though boys were supposed to be wild, and girls were supposed to be afraid of bees and snakes.

He almost wished his constitution permitted him to take the role boys took in books. Though he knew even if he could, it would not turn Vivian into a storybook girl—like Maureen or Clara, who would have stood on the bank, making gratifying little squeaking noises, while he, Willie, swam about like Tarzan in the movies, perhaps wrestling an alligator for their enjoyment. But he was Willie Malone, not Bomba the Jungle Boy; he had a fate quite different from that of Saturday movie serial heroes. There would come a day when his talents would be valued. This he knew.

"Willie," Vivian shouted, "Bring me my towel! It's hanging there beside you."

Willie obligingly brought a white towel with Antoinette Washington's monogram stitched on it in silver thread and handed it to Vivian as she waded toward him.

"Are you sure you don't want to come in?"

"Perfectly sure, but thank you."

⚜

They were sitting in the shade of the lodge swilling water and eating crackers when they heard the shot.

"What the hell was *that*?" Vivian asked.

"A pistol shot would be my guess," Willie said.

"But it came from my house," Vivian said. "Come on."

Vivian ran up the path with Willie following the best he could. The grass was high in the pecan grove, and they ran low until they could see the house and the yard, and then dropped down in the grass where they could not be seen.

Vivian, as she looked at the scene before her, felt like she felt when she came into a darkened theater in the middle of a movie.

To the side of the house, by the garage, Emmy stood with an

arm around Clara and another around Maureen. They, too, had heard the shot, but Emmy had not let them around back, and they could not see the tableaux in the backyard—for a new lattice fence, which supported a morning glory vine, blocked their view.

What Willie and Vivian saw was this: Standing with her back to the back door was Antoinette, one hand was held up to her head, her neck was bent like a broken flower stalk, and in her other hand—which had dropped to her side—was a black pistol. On the grass, about eight feet in front of her, was Snow-Ball, on his side, his white fur rapidly turning bright red with the blood that still gushed from his wound. And beyond the dog stood Gilbert, holding a pair of pruning shears, staring at the white woman with the gun who was dressed in a white silk robe with white feathers at the neck and the hem and a pair of white-feathered mules—one of which had come off and was lying like a dead dove in the grass.

Nobody moved for the longest time. A cardinal sang. Cicadas droned. Vivian listened to Willie wheezing next to her.

Then Antoinette screamed.

Emmy ran around the side of the house to her; Maureen and Clara followed. When Clara saw Snow-Ball, she threw herself to the ground beside him. Maureen stood apart from this scene, looking from Antoinette to Gilbert—who still had not moved.

Then Emmy began coaxing Antoinette into the house, holding her up on one side. The gun still dangled from Antoinette's hand. Maureen approached and gently removed the gun from her sister's limp fingers. She stood holding it a minute. Then she took it inside the house.

Willie and Vivian had not given themselves away. The scene was over, whatever it had begun as, it was over. Snow-Ball was dead. Maureen had come back outside and now knelt to comfort Clara.

"Vivian?" Willie whispered. "Let's go home. Nobody knows we were here."

Vivian was watching Gilbert, who had walked to the toolshed, replaced the pruning shears, and was now walking away from the house toward the road.

"She missed," Vivian said.

"She didn't miss, Vivian, look at him. He's not even twitching. That is one dead dog."

"She wasn't aiming at Snow-Ball. She was aiming at Gilbert."

"No, she wasn't," Willie said automatically, though the moment that Vivian had said it, he knew it was true. "What were Clara and Maureen doing here, do you think?"

"I don't know, maybe Clara came to get something. Poor Snow-Ball."

"Poor Clara," Willie said. For now Clara was the only one left in the backyard. She sat on the grass holding her dead dog; there was blood all over her yellow dress.

Vivian and Willie looked at one another. "Yes. But lucky Gilbert," Vivian said. "Let's get out of here."

⚜

Inside the house, Emmy had helped Antoinette into bed. Emmy did not begin to understand what had happened, but she knew it did not fit with her instructions from Mrs. Malone to see that Mrs. Washington get plenty of rest. Shooting off guns and killing things in the backyard wasn't any part of restful.

Antoinette was shivering. Maureen sat down beside her on the edge of the bed. "Antoinette, tell us what happened," she pleaded.

"It went off," Antoinette said.

"Yes, we know that, but why did you have it? Where did you even get it?"

"John bought it for me because I get so scared when he's gone. What if somebody were to try to get in here? We're just a house of women out here almost in the wilderness, for heaven's sake. I need it. Where is it?"

"In the kitchen," Maureen said. I put it out of sight, and out of reach. But why did you shoot poor Snow-Ball?"

"He was barking and barking and my headache was so bad, and I don't know, I only meant to scare him."

Emmy stood at the foot of the bed. She could watch out the window at poor little Clara grieving over her dog. One thing was sure, crazy women shouldn't be having guns! It was one thing for crazy women to lie up in their beds all day out of everybody's way, but it was a whole other thing having them parading around out in the yard in their nightclothes shooting off loaded pistols!

And no matter what Mrs. Washington said, Emmy didn't believe for a minute that John Washington had bought his wife a gun. It wouldn't be like him. He was the one with the gun. And, Emmy suspected, he would not fancy the notion of being out-gunned in his own house.

Emmy left Antoinette with her little sister and went outside to deal with Clara. And just where had that gardener—that Gilbert, who was always laughing at everybody—where had he got off to? Who exactly was going to bury this dog?

When she got to Clara she knelt down beside her and tried to put her arms around the girl. But she was stiff as a rod. She tried talking to the child. "Clara? Baby? I so sorry about this awful thing that happened to the sweet little Snow-Ball. I ain't never known a nicer dog. Now that's the truth. That dog always be so well-mannered and sweet-tempered, why, he always just like his mistress was what."

Clara looked up at Emmy. "Why did she shoot my dog?" Her voice was clear and sure.

"I don't know, baby. She say the gun went off by itself, that she never meant it to happen. She told Miss Maureen that just now. Clara, honey, let me help you clean yourself up now. Won't you?"

Clara looked down at her blood-drenched clothes and then back at Snow-Ball's open, shocked eyes. Then she began to cry.

In the end, Emmy had to half carry Clara into the house—big as she was—lug her to her room and then start her a bath. As she adjusted the bath temperature, Emmy realized that she'd never seen either of the Washington girls cry before. She'd seen their daddy cry. He was the cryingest man she'd ever seen, white or black—and her grandpa had cried like a woman when the mood was on him. Mrs. Washington worked herself up into a froth regular, but neither of the little girls, until that moment, had ever shed a visible tear.

❧

"I wonder where Gilbert the dog is?" Willie said as they sneaked into the Malone backyard through the alley and back under the rosebush.

"I don't know, but thank God he wasn't with Clara and Snow-Ball." Vivian whistled for Gilbert, three shrill trills, like an angry whippoorwill. The kitchen door opened, and Gilbert trotted out.

Papa Maguire stood in the door and called out, "Gilbert was taking a nap with me," he said. "Where did you children get off to? You worried Mama. She just got a call over the telephone that something had happened out to your house, Vivian. Antoinette killed a dog or some such. Some sort of unholy accident or other, and then Mama looked all around for you, and she was worried near to death. She had to call Jim to come and get her and take her out to Antoinette's. I don't appreciate you children worrying Mama. She has enough to worry about."

"We're sorry, Papa," Willie said. "We told Mama we were going downtown to the library, though. And we just got back. How come Antoinette had to shoot a dog?"

Papa closed the door most of the way, and then said, "Took some kind of a notion would be my bet." The door slammed.

❧

Gilbert—the man, not the dog—walked home nearly five miles at a slow and shambling pace. He longed to run; he longed to be inside his dark little house, but he was afraid to attract attention to himself. As he walked he went over and over in his mind what had happened.

He'd been in the Washingtons' yard working on a flower bed behind the house. He'd been thinking about Cassie. If you could call that thinking. Mainly he was concentrating on the job at hand. He'd heard Emmy's voice at the side door, and Clara's voice. Then the white dog had run around the side of the house, which had irritated him, but then he'd thought, Never mind, I'm working for *them*, they're not working for *me*, and he'd laughed to himself, and gone on with what he was doing. A minute after that the back door opened, and Mrs. Washington came out, like she'd done that other time. She was in her nightclothes, and he thought, Oh-oh, what now?

He'd looked up at her, and he'd remembered to take his damn hat off, because like Cassie had said, when he'd told her about that other time Mrs. Washington had come after him, "You just black, damn it, Gilbert, you not stupid!"

So there he was, kneeling in the dirt, surrounded by the

marigolds he was laying out, garden shears to one side, because he'd been cutting the bedding plants out of their cans with them. Hat in hand, and looking up at her in what he hoped was a respectful sort of way. He'd not had much experience with having to *appear* respectful. Old Mrs. Washington had *commanded* respect, like the officers in the U.S. Army had; he'd never had to think about it.) He saw Antoinette's eyes and realized she wasn't really seeing anything at all.

He'd thought, this woman got to be sleepwalking. His grandpa had been a sleepwalker, and his mama had told him how they'd had to tie him up to his bed every night of the world or else Night Riders would have found him out wandering the woods in his nightshirt. So, Gilbert, real careful-like, stood up just as slow as he could so as not to startle her. That's what Mama had said you had to watch with sleepwalkers—startling them.

"Mrs. Washington," he said real low.

That's when he'd seen the pistol in her right hand; it had been hidden in the folds of the robe she was wearing—the one that had all the feathers on it. She was already raising the gun, and she took true aim at him.

He hit the dirt.

The dog, seeing Gilbert drop to the ground, thought the man wanted to play, and ran at him. Mrs. Washington fired, hitting the dog, who gave one surprised yowl as the shot propelled it three feet toward Gilbert. Then, except for the reverberation of the pistol shot, everything went dead quiet.

Mrs. Washington went into shock. Gilbert recognized it from the War. When he stood up, he realized he had grabbed the shears and was holding them like a weapon. He stood stock-still and waited. The moment went on a long time. Suddenly Mrs. Washington screamed, and Emmy and Clara and another girl ran around from the side of the house. The girl Gilbert didn't know worked the gun out of Antoinette's fingers. And then all but Clara moved indoors.

Gilbert looked down at Clara and her dog. The dog's back was broken. Slowly Gilbert backed away. Clara didn't seem to notice him. He returned the shears to the shed, and he kept walking out of the yard and into the road. That woman meant to kill me, he thought as he walked. He was still thinking the same thing two miles down the road, and he was still surprised.

Worse, he pictured in his mind, as he walked, what the others had seen. A tall black man holding garden shears at shoulder level and a tiny, half-dressed white woman leaning up against the door to her house with a discharged pistol dangling from her fingers. He could find nothing in this scenario to lighten his step, though it quickened it some.

Mrs. Washington had gone back to sleep when Emmy called Mrs. Malone, but it wasn't a natural sleep, even for her; and poor little Clara, once begun crying, couldn't stop. Emmy flat had not known *what* to do. She was afraid to leave Mrs. Washington alone with Maureen, who wasn't but a young girl herself, but she could hear Clara weeping in her room, which fairly broke Emmy's heart, so she'd run back and forth from one room to the other. Everytime she passed by a window she could see poor Snow-Ball's body lying where it had fallen in the yard. The crimson blood had turned brown, and crows had begun lighting on the clothesline. Merciful Jesus, Emmy thought, send somebody to *help* me!

That's when Emmy heard a car in the drive. Her prayer answered, she opened the front door to Mrs. Malone and Jim; Mrs. Malone went straight into her daughter's room.

Jim went outside, got a shovel from the toolshed, lugged

Snow-Ball into the pecan grove, and commenced to bury him. And he was glad to do it. It was, anybody could see, the only straightforward job on the premises.

~~

Mrs. Malone sat in a chair beside her daughter's bed. She had questioned her, but Antoinette had gotten out only a few incomplete sentences before she began weeping again. The weeping had exhausted her, and she had gone back to sleep. Now Mrs. Malone waited for Dr. Knox. Antoinette looked terrible. She was thinner than ever. She'd been (Mrs. Malone knew because Emmy had told her) sleeping around the clock, but her face looked ravaged, and now this! Mrs. Malone did not want, however, to try to locate John Washington yet. She waited on the doctor, whom she'd called from her house; this situation had gone beyond her power of understanding, and she knew it. As she sat by Antoinette's side, she prayed to the Blessed Virgin. "Please," she beseeched her, "Help your humble servants. Have mercy on us."

~~

It had been the noise of the gun firing that had wakened Antoinette. She came to herself out in the yard, to see the dreaded and horrible Gilbert standing just feet from her with the garden shears raised up in his hand. He must have already killed the dog—who lay on the grass in front of him, all bloodied. He will kill me next, she thought. That was when she had screamed, and then fainted. In the dream that she'd still not quite awakened from, Gilbert had been taunting her:

"Who's working for who now?" he'd asked in the dream.

He'd had hold of her arm, she could smell him, he smelled hot. He had smelled like blood. And then he had kissed her. She had struggled in his arms, but he held her so tightly she could not get away. She had begun to kiss him back. Well, she'd had to, hadn't she? Otherwise she couldn't have breathed. Anybody would know that. But as it went on, she began to enjoy the kiss, and this sensation had been more frightening to her than her plight. She'd gone limp, and he had dragged her back to the toolshed, where it was blessedly cool and dark and her head didn't hurt her as bad. She hadn't struggled. She'd let him, the same as she let John Washington.

His face inches from her own, he'd said, "Now you're no better than me. All your babies will be black like me, and everyone will know what you've done and who you done it with."

In the dream the yard was suddenly filled with newborn goats, all of them black. They were struggling to their feet; they were wandering across the grass like drunken things. Antoinette had run through them—they had butted up against her legs, and bleated after her—but she'd kept running for the house, and her gun.

The gun she'd bought in New Orleans in the pawnshop, when John thought she was shopping for a silver evening bag. The gun she'd been keeping in her pocketbook. And she'd returned with it to shoot Gilbert before he could tell anyone what she'd done. That's when she'd woke up.

She could not understand why Emmy and Maureen were there, but she'd let them bring her inside and put her back to bed. They asked what had happened, but she didn't tell them. She wasn't that stupid. They seemed to think it had to do with the dog. She let them think that. She was so sick with horror and fear that she felt as if she might fly into a million pieces. She pulled up the covers to keep the pieces of herself from getting loose and flying around the room. She willed herself back to sleep. Sleep, was no longer a safe place, but at least others could not follow you there.

Then Mama woke her up asking questions. Asking her why she'd shot Clara's dog! She hadn't shot Clara's dog, for heaven's sake! But she didn't want them to know about the other, so she said she had; and then they wanted to know why, why would she shoot a dog? She said it was on account of her headache. Then she fell back asleep. Mercifully, in this sleep she didn't even exist. She was a lump of coal on a grate. She burned; she turned blue and orange. It was the best dream she'd had in a very long time.

Dr. Knox took Antoinette's blood pressure three times; he'd never seen a reading so low. She was hot to the touch, but she had no fever. Her heart rate was that of a songbird. She was dehydrated. She was undernourished. He also thought that there was a good chance she might be pregnant.

He prescribed bed rest, nourishing food, and forcing fluids. He told Mrs. Malone, "She will be all right for now. But in a day or two, when she's feeling stronger, bring her to my office and let me take a closer look at her. She needs a lot of building up."

"I think she's been dieting," Mrs. Malone whispered.

"It's a scourge," the doctor said, "Young women are destroying their constitutions right and left with all this 'slimming.'"

Mrs. Malone agreed. "Should I call her husband to come home, do you think?"

"I wouldn't think that's necessary. She's got help here?"

"Yes."

"Then take the girls to your house so they don't disturb her. Let her rest a couple of days."

Mrs. Malone wanted to say she'd done that. She wanted to say that Antoinette had already had more than her share of bed rest, and nourishing food *and* liquids, but she didn't like to appear to be arguing with Dr. Knox. Still, she did say, "She has been resting, but she never seems to get *rested*."

"I'll prescribe something. So she can get some real sleep. It's difficult to sleep in this heat. I mean restful sleep that does a body any good."

This was so, Mrs. Malone knew herself. "Thank you, Doctor," she said.

❧

Gilbert did not reach the safety of his house until late. Cassie was already there, waiting. Worried. "What happened?"

Gilbert stumbled past her, pulling her along behind him into the dimness of the house. "Come inside," he said urgently. "Shut the door."

Cassie did as he said. Reluctantly closing the door on the only breeze, the only coolness that could reach them.

Gilbert collapsed on the bed. "Get me some water."

He was inside. He was home. Cassie was there. For the moment they were all right. He gulped the water she brought him in the dipper from the cistern.

Cassie put her hand to his forehead. Was he feverish? Was he sick? She knew better than to speak. She held her tongue and made herself breathe normally.

Gilbert unlaced his boots. "It was that woman," he said, hurling one boot across the room.

"Mrs. Washington?"

"Yeah. She crazy as you said. Crazier."

"What she do?"

"She tried to kill me, is what. She took a gun and tried to shoot me down."

Cassie did not say anything. She took a sharp breath and waited for him to speak and tell her more. Her legs were shaking and she sat down next to him on the bed.

"I swear to God, Cassie, that woman come out in the broad

daylight of the afternoon in nothing but her nightdress all covered over with feathers, and she pulled out a pistol," Gilbert raised an imaginary pistol and took aim at the wall. "She leveled it at me, and she pulled the trigger."

"But you *here*. You ain't hit. What happened?"

"I dropped. Like they always saying to us in the war, hit the dirt, that what the sergeant always said. Well, I hit it, and the dog, it was running at me, one of the little girls' dogs, you know, it was running at me like I said, and it took the bullet. I swear to God, Cassie, she was *asleep*! Asleep the whole time. Like my grandma used to tell about Grandpa. She didn't know what she was doing, not in the regular way, but in a different way, I think, she did!"

"What way was that?"

"Her eyes. She wasn't seeing me in the ordinary way, but she was seeing *me*. Seeing me some kind of way I don't know about. Get me some more water."

When Cassie returned with the water she asked, "Who all saw this?"

"That's the worst part, see. Nobody saw it happen; we was alone then. But then three people see us after. And what they saw was me holding garden shears up like this—" He raised his arm. "—and Mrs. Washington leaning up against the door to her house in a fainting spell. They saw the dog dead in the grass. I been thinking and thinking what they could make of that, and seem like to me they might think she was defending herself from me. Like I was coming at her or something. That's why I walked home so slow. The whole time I been afraid the sheriff was going to pull up 'longside me. 'Cause I don't know what she went to telling people afterwards."

"Who all saw this?"

"Emmy, and the girl Clara, and one of her friends. I guess, I didn't know her."

"How come you decided to light out? It look so bad, Gilbert."

"Nobody talked to me. Nobody say stay; so I left. I'll tell the truth, my feet left before I did. I mean, I was walking down the road for home before I ever thought what I was doing." He pulled off his shirt, wiped his chest dry with it, and then flung it in a corner.

"And when did all this happen?"

"Around three o'clock."

"She couldn't have said anything to accuse you, Gilbert. It been too long. They'd been out here by now. She must be keeping quiet for reasons of her own. She going to ignore it. So we going to ignore it. You show up for work tomorrow like always. Like nothing happened. That's how to do."

"You think?"

"Yes," Cassie said. There were not so many choices, though neither of them cared to say so. Stay and act normal, or run. Running would only call attention to them, and could give Antoinette ideas, and in any event they couldn't afford to run far enough to be safe. "I got a feeling," Cassie said, "this going to be just like a bad dream in a couple of days. But when John Washington get back, you going to quit. Don't tell him nothing about this. Tell him you full-time now with the Callahans and can't help him no more. He'll cut up some, but he ain't going to pull his gun. That woman's showed herself way too dangerous to mess with. You the second person she almost killed—first Emmy, now you."

"Don't forget the dog," Gilbert said. "She killed that, sure. It's a lot of money," he said, starting to roll a cigarette. "To give up on, I mean." He was calm enough now to reflect on that. But he couldn't stop seeing Mrs. Washington standing in front of him, aiming that gun. She'd looked at him like she knew him. Like only a woman you'd been with can look at you.

"Dead men is all broke, don't matter how much or how little

they stored up," Cassie said, and she got up from the bed to serve Gilbert his supper that she'd been keeping hot on the back of the stove. There'd been a little space of time when she had wondered had she cooked it for a dead man.

Chapter 9

When John Washington left Myrtle, he'd driven first to New Orleans to confer with the Kraemer Brothers about the route. John and Otto, the younger Kraemer brother, were good friends. It was Otto, the more personable of the brothers, the Kraemer bon vivant, who manned the phones to their suppliers, keeping contacts fresh, making new ones, keeping their good salesmen happy, getting rid of lackluster ones, and finding fresh men. Even the best traveling salesmen burned out on these long rural routes. A man who was a go-getter at twenty-two was often a liability at thirty, and Otto was always on the lookout for younger ones. John was one of his best. John was a man Otto enjoyed spending time with; Otto hated to think about the day he'd have to replace John Washington, though he knew it would come eventually. It always did. He worried some about John's drinking, but so far John was skating it. Otto figured there were quite a few good miles left in John Washington.

Stephen, the older brother, put in long days going over the company's books and keeping a sharp eye on the warehouse employees. He rarely left his cagelike office, to the point of having his meals sent in—and sorry meals they were, too. He might have still been living in Hamburg, for all the advantage he took of the city of New Orleans. He took a taxi from his apartment to work and back. His whole world was laid out in grids on ledger paper. He had a bad stomach.

After the three men had taken a long look at John Washington's route in Otto's ledger, after John had recommended they drop three country stores in south Arkansas that were so far from everything that they'd begun costing more to service than they'd turned since the Depression had hit, Otto took John out to lunch at Tujaques.

Afterwards they'd said good-bye on the sidewalk, and John wandered around the Quarter and the department stores on Canal Street looking for a copy of *Madame Butterfly* that would play on Odessa's Victrola. After he found that, he went shopping for a kimono and a suitable fan. He did not bother pretending to himself that any of this was a chore. He always delighted in pleasing Odessa. Insofar as pleasing her did not involve displeasing himself.

He found a shop with hundreds of fans and spent the better part of an hour choosing just the right one for Odessa's Madame Butterfly. It had a yellow background, and red poppies flourished at its edges. A bridge arched across a pool of lilies. Willows wept on both sides of the bridge. And it was a good size. Odessa hadn't wanted what she'd called a "puny" fan. She wanted a big one like in the pictures. The right kimono was harder to find. John had despaired of finding one that day until he saw a red one displayed in the window of a small shop. An absolutely glorious red kimono. John did not know what the exact color might be called. And on this fabric was embroidered in metallic thread, butterflies—big and little, all of them different. He had the shop girl gift wrap it.

"Your wife is going to love this," she said as she labored over the bows.

"Do you think so?" John said, smiling at the image of Antoinette, swallowed in the red kimono.

"Oh, certainly. You've beautiful taste."

"Yes, I do," John said. "And, thank you for noticing."

Antoinette could not have been any more surprised to learn she was pregnant if she had been a certified virgin. Though she'd worried about this eventuality constantly, now that it had happened she could not bring herself to believe it. Dr. Knox seemed to think it was the best news Antoinette would ever get. She pretended to think so, too. The doctor said it explained her sleepiness and possibly even some of her headaches. He said she'd probably start feeling better soon. He said the worst was over.

That's how much he knows, Antoinette thought bitterly. She had watched her mother going round like a breed sow for years of her life; Antoinette knew the worst was not over. When she left the doctor's office she did not want to go home. She let Jim, who had driven her to her appointment, take her to Mama's house instead.

Mama met them on the front porch. "Well," she called out. "What did he say?"

Antoinette ignored her and went into the house, all the way down the hall to the kitchen, where she sat down at the table. Mama followed her. "What did he say?" she asked again.

Antoinette sat back in her chair and looked around the room. She had always hated it. "I'm fine," she said. "He gave me some pills. Could we have some lunch? I'm hungry."

Mrs. Malone, delighted Antoinette had an appetite, made her a thick roast beef sandwich. Willie and Vivian were gone downtown, and Clara and Maureen were at the piano. Papa was still asleep, having come in only hours before.

"These pills, what are they for?" Mama said over her shoulder as her hands went on making sandwiches.

"They're for my blood. He says I have iron-poor blood." Antoinette had heard this phrase on the radio.

Masie came into the kitchen from the back stairs. She was carrying a book and was followed by Rufus and Lucy.

Antoinette didn't like Masie. Margaret and Maureen and she could find things to talk about, but Masie was like a character in a play that Antoinette would never have gone to see. Always pretending to be so smart. Thinking that no rules applied to her. Neglecting her appearance.

Masie plunked herself down across the table from her sister. "Hi," she said. "How are you feeling?"

"I'm perfectly fine, thank you, Masie. And you?"

"Fine. Mama can I have one of those sandwiches you're fixing?"

"But you had lunch with me."

"I know, but I've been reading about starving people, and it's made me want to eat up the whole house."

Mrs. Malone sliced more bread from the loaf.

"Can you imagine yourself starving?" Masie asked, leaning on her elbows. Then, looking at Antoinette's pinched face and stick arms, she said, "I don't know why I'm asking you. You starve *yourself*."

Antoinette did not imagine anything. She never knew what people meant when they said, "Can you imagine?" Usually they were about to say something ridiculous. Mama put a plate down in front of her, and she picked up the sandwich and began eating it at once. She didn't feel even a little sick anymore.

Masie watched Antoinette wolf the sandwich with some surprise. "What are you," she said, "pregnant or something?"

Whenever Mrs. Malone had been pregnant, she ate all the time. With Willie she'd gotten up in the middle of the night and cooked herself entire meals, then sat down to the table, said grace, and eaten them alone.

Antoinette put down what was left of her sandwich. "What gave you such a repellent notion?"

Mama turned from the counter and looked at Antoinette appraisingly.

"Just how you were eating, is all," Masie said, and took a bite of her sandwich.

"What's your excuse?" Antoinette said.

"I don't need excuses. I'm not here to fulfill anybody else's idea of what I should look like. I eat when I'm hungry, and I drink when I'm dry."

"Masie," their mother said.

"I didn't mean *whiskey*, Mama."

"I know what you meant, but when you talk that way, some people could get a wrong impression."

"You're too sensitive on this subject. Just because Papa Maguire is a drunkard, nobody assumes the rest of us are."

"You are not to talk that way about Papa."

"I'm sorry. I don't mean any disrespect. *He* doesn't mind me saying it."

Antoinette sat back in her chair, relieved that the subject of conversation had shifted from herself, and with it, her mother's attention. She wouldn't tell anyone what the doctor said. He couldn't tell anyone else. It was against the law or something. Anyway, she was sure he was wrong. He'd been wrong about everything Willie ever had. He was always saying that Willie was dying of this or that, but he never had. She would know if it were true; she would feel it if something so big and important had happened to her. And she didn't feel anything. She put her hand to her concave stomach. No. She felt nothing at all. Except hungry.

꙳

When Antoinette got home she went into her own kitchen, so unlike the one at home. Hers was bright, and painted white. Why Mama had that dark hunter wallpaper in the *kitchen* she would never know. She wanted to tell Emmy what to prepare for supper, and she wanted a glass of iced tea, but she had forgotten it was Emmy's afternoon off. While she stood at the kitchen counter, putting ice in a glass, her eyes flicked to the window over the sink, and she saw Gilbert. He was fussing with the bamboo John had put in. Really, people would think they were *Chinese*. Antoinette poured the tea into the glass and watched Gilbert narrowly. As she did her blood suddenly ran as cold as the glass in her hand. Everything came back to her. The smell of him. The smell of blood, the heat, and the sound of the shot in the dead quiet of that afternoon. His saying that the babies would be black and everybody would know what she'd done. The baby *was* real. But it wasn't John's; it was Gilbert's. Now she did feel something. Something heavy. Something the exact shape and size of a brick. She felt sick. She poured the tea down the sink.

꙳

John Washington drove into Sylvan at twilight. When he turned off the engine he sat for a moment, to enjoy the peace of that place. The boys weren't there; they'd not been expecting him, though John knew it wouldn't be two whole minutes before they appeared. John got out and stretched. The evening was warm and the sky cloudless, the moon and Venus already risen; the crickets had already commenced sawing at the night with their silvery bows. Then he heard Odessa's voice from across the road, from into the pines, raised in one of the butterfly's songs of pure hope. It wrenched his heart in his breast.

There was a skitter of bare feet on the worn boards of Dixie Home's porch, and John Washington's fan club belatedly appeared, as he'd known it would. "Boys," he said, removing his hat. "Where you been? You all has about hurt my feelings. I thought nobody cared about old John Washington anymore."

The smaller of the boys came and stood next to him, brushing his trousers with their bodies. John Washington pressed Blackjack chewing gum into their open palms, and smiled into their eyes. It was like being in a corral with young horses. It was close to dark, and in the quietness of the night, and with Odessa's voice rising into the tops of the breathing pines, John was overcome with a tenderness for these young lives. He would have liked to bend and clutch them to him, as he had used to hold Vivian when she was younger, but he contented himself with touching Billy Jefferson's springy hair. They could hear the ticking of the motor as it cooled.

Hank came out on the porch. He was using only one crutch, and he used it more as a prop now than to take his weight. "Is that you, John?"

"None other," John replied, and walked toward him. The boys stayed with the car, touching its hot hood experimentally.

"Well, hell, we wasn't expecting *you* this night."

"What I've done is to rearrange the route some. Cut off two laggards in south Arkansas, which put me ahead of time. Hell, I didn't know I needed a damn engraved invitation."

John stepped up on the porch and leaned against the inside post across from Hank. Yellow light spilled out from inside the store, Irene's voice, talking and talking, with it.

"You don't need no invite. Irene will be glad to see you; she was real sorry to miss you last time. Been asking me all sorts of questions she thought I should know the answers to about what you was up to, how your kids was, and all like that. I told her you and me don't get out our sewing and talk about our families when we get together, but she don't understand that."

John shook out a cigarette and held the pack out to Hank, who took one. John lit his own and then Hank's. "I was just standing there listening to Odessa sing," John said.

Hank turned his head and glanced in the direction of Odessa's voice; it was completely dark now. "Hell, if you lived here, you could listen to it about eighteen hours a day. I wanted to tell her to cut it out, but Irene, she likes hearing it. Keeps telling me that gal could be on the radio. And I tell Irene, I wish she was, 'cause then I could turn her off."

"Well, I don't hear it often enough for it to get on my nerve," John said, putting one foot behind him against the post and exhaling smoke. "I have to say I'm with Irene on this one."

Two black men came out the door and stopped to tip their hats to John and Hank. John nodded to them. They'd been the ones Irene had trapped at the counter, for now her voice was stilled, and in a moment she came out on the porch, looking to see where Hank had got to.

"John Washington," she said when she saw him. "As I live and breathe, I was just this *moment* talking about you. You been on my *mind*."

"Was that what was on it?" Hank said. "I thought you looked kind of top-heavy."

Irene slapped at her husband's arm. John embraced her briefly. "Sorry to bust in on you, Irene, but I got thinking, why stay in a tourist court and eat bad food when I could drive on to Sylvan and enjoy Irene Stewart's famous hospitality."

"Well I should hope *so*," Irene said, taking John's arm. "Come on in this house this minute and let me get you something. Hank and me already had our supper, but there's plenty left, and I can cook you up something else if it ain't what you want."

John paused at the door to hear the last note of what Odessa had been singing. It spun in the air like a turning oak leaf.

"You're listening to Odessa, ain't you?"

"Yes ma'am."

"She sings like an angel. An absolute angel. How I know is this old devil,"—she poked at Hank—"can't hardly stand it."

They went inside. The boys sat on the Essex's running boards and leaned up against its hood; they talked quietly. The night took over from the day in a faultless changing of the guard. Sylvan, except for the lights from Dixie Home and a few kerosene lanterns gleaming in the tenant shacks, was black. The quarter moon and the stars seemed a very long way away.

❧

In the kitchen Irene and Hank drank coffee and watched John Washington eat his supper. John, normally not a big eater, dug in determinedly. You could stay on some women's good side with words of endearment and presents, others with little, secret touchings, but with Irene there was only the one way, and that was to eat the food she put in front of you. It was good—but Lord, it was plentiful! There were never less than five serving dishes on Irene's table, and Irene never made corn bread that she didn't make biscuits, too. John worked away with his fork like he was digging out of a mine cave-in, his eye on a sliver of light in the distance—the coffeepot setting on the stove.

Hank knew the effort his friend was making. Irene watched with deep pleasure. John, so tall and so thin, was her greatest challenge. And it seemed to her nobody enjoyed her food the way John Washington did. He absolutely attacked it! She stayed alert so that when he finished anything on his plate she was ready with a serving spoon to replenish it.

John, finishing his serving of creamed peas, sat back from the table a moment and watched in horror as Irene filled the empty place he'd made on his plate back up. John raised his eyes to Hank's in an appeal for help.

"He's had enough, for Christ's sake, Irene! Leave the man be. John's got a delicate constitution. He ain't like me—you can't just keep tamping it down him. Besides, one of us should be out front, and since my foot's killing me, I elect you."

"I've had a gracious plenty, Irene," John said. "I never eat so well as I do at your table."

"Oh, I'm sure your wife's a fine cook," Irene said.

John laughed. "My wife can cook macaroni. That's her whole repertoire. Cheese is extra, she hasn't got that down yet. If it weren't for the colored gal we have at home, I'd starve to death."

"Well is *she* a good cook?"

"Why, yes, she is. Not in your league, but then you can't hire this kind of cooking. This here is the cuisine of the heart," John said.

"Well," Irene said, deeply pleased. "It's the only way I got to show old Hank or anyone else how I feel about them."

"Well, you showed me tonight that maybe we ought to run away to Mexico," John said.

"You're talking like a traveling salesman, for sure now," Irene said. She got up, laughing, and went toward the store. "There's coffee on the stove, and there's a blackberry cobbler in the oven if you all can't wait till I close up."

John and Hank exchanged glances, and as soon as she was out of the room, John picked up his plate and scraped it into the pail for table scraps under the sink.

"Great God Almighty," John said to Hank. "That woman was trying to kill me, I do believe."

"Oh, it takes a lot more than that. I'm still on my feet, more or less. I thought your eyes was going to pop out your head every time she put another helping on your plate. I felt sorry for you, now, I honestly did, but I couldn't see a way to save you till you'd done that plate some justice."

"You want coffee?" John asked as he was pouring himself a cup.

"Yeah. Let's take it out on the back porch."

"What about a little dish of this here cobbler?" John said, imitating Irene's inflections and smiling Irene's smile.

"Jesus God!" Hank screamed. "You got her to a tee."

"Let's adjourn," John said.

Outside they sat with their feet up on the rail and breathed in the night awhile, both of the men content to be quiet and sip their coffee. Every once in a while they heard the store bell ring, and Irene's chirrupy voice raised up.

"Now I know a nigger's born to suffer," Hank said contemplatively, "but it don't seem right he should have to stand on one foot and listen to my wife talk for thirty minutes just to get himself a hunk of overpriced bologna. Seems like that's pushing it."

Every time John Washington heard the word "nigger" on his friend's lips, and he heard it often, something cinched a little tighter in his chest. It's nothing but a word, he told himself. But he knew a word carries its own world inside it, like dandelion fluff carries its seed. And that word being loosed changed the very texture of the night John was trying to enjoy.

"Seems like Irene's the one ought to be on the radio. So we could shut *her* off," John said, and his voice was colder than he'd meant it to be.

Hank spit out the doorway, whose screen door was ajar for the purpose. "She can't help it," he said. "She's lonesome. She's one of those people *born* lonesome. Even when I was still trying to do something about it, I couldn't make a dent in it. Not the kind of lonesomeness Irene's got. So now I just clean my plate. But I do that religiously."

John was sorry he'd said anything.

"You got any whiskey with you?" Hank asked, lowering his voice. "I mean that I could buy off you. My bootlegger had himself a accident."

"What kind of accident?"

"He accidentally sold some homemade to the sheriff's boy, who got drunk as a hoot owl and wrapped his daddy's car around a tree, and now he's in jail up in Shreveport."

"You both have my deepest sympathies. I think I can let loose of something for you to get you by till justice is served."

"Don't be calling justice down on anybody's head!"

John pulled out his pocket flask and splashed some whiskey into their coffee cups. "Just in case Irene should bound in to see if we're ready for that cobbler yet," he said.

Hank sipped it appreciatively. John tossed his back.

"Women," Hank said dispiritedly.

"Bless them and keep them out of the way, like my daddy used to say," John said, lifting his cup in a toast.

"How you going to work seeing Odessa? Irene just finished cleaning the parlor yesterday for when you was coming. She's going to expect you to sleep in it."

"And I will," John said. "That's just exactly where I'm going to do *all* my sleeping."

"Be quiet coming back in—she'll hear you. Used to be that woman could sleep through a twister; now she wakes up every hour and wants to know do I *hear* something? She's got it in her mind that robbers in Shreveport and Little Rock and Dallas are sitting up nights planning raids on The Dixie Home."

"Jesus H. Christ!" John said. "What's in it for them?"

"A tail full of buckshot," Hank said. "And forty dollars if they're lucky."

They laughed softly.

❦

When Irene came back, everybody had to eat a dish of blackberry cobbler swimming in heavy cream. "My Lord, Irene, I'm going to be awake all night with this setting in me."

"Of course you aren't. That's just the thing to put you to sleep and give you sweet dreams. Sweet as what you're eating." She licked her spoon. "Did you bring me any of that special feed for my Henrietta and Petey?"

"Why, I certainly did. It's in my trunk. What are those two up to, anyway?"

"Most four pounds each," Hank said.

"Hold on, mister. You're talking about my *pets*."

"Mine, too," John added. "Those chickens are the king and queen of the chicken world, ain't they, Irene?"

"Yes, indeed," she said. "Anybody would know that."

"Anybody," John repeated to Hank, grinning.

"I'm going to bed," Hank said, getting up. "This is at the point I can't follow you all's conversation: when you two go to coronating chickens and giving them human names."

Irene rose, too. "Let me make you comfortable in the parlor, John."

"I know my way, Irene," he said. "But thank you. I'm going to take a walk down to the river before I turn in. Lay on my back in the moss and watch the moon and stars float around up in the sky.

You know, my muscles get so stiff driving, if I don't stretch them out some, I won't never get to sleep."

"You watch yourself out there, John," Irene said. "Hank, he heard a panther not long ago."

"Is that right?" John asked Hank, interested.

Hank nodded his head. "Found tracks."

"And the niggers, they been saying they've heard what they think's a bear back in the woods."

"What you got going here, Noah's damn ark?" John asked, slipping his cigarettes in his pocket and moving for the porch steps. "Don't you worry, Irene, I got my boon companion here." He patted the pocket that held his pistol.

"That won't do you no good with a bear or a panther," Hank said. "When you come in, lock up, you hear?"

John nodded. The Stewarts bade him good night and retired. John stood a moment on the porch, listening to their voices, hearing them stir around in their room; when their light went off, he left.

The boys had gone. The Essex stood alone. John got into the trunk for Odessa's presents. He'd bought something else, too, in Memphis. Carrying the packages, he crossed the road. He didn't go the shortest way, through the yards. He went up a path that ran from the road up into the pines and skirted Odessa's. He could see her lamp burning. She would know he was here. People would have told her John Washington was over at Dixie Home. For once, she didn't have that damn phonograph on. He could hear voices drifting from porches, and saw the scattered glowing embers of cigarettes. A lot of folks were still up. Irene always went to bed with the chickens, and Hank had gone with her, John knew, just to accommodate him.

When he was even with Odessa's, he cut across through the

trees. Twice he tripped over roots and nearly dropped the packages. The second time he had to stop and rearrange them, cursing quietly in the darkness.

"Is that you, Mr. Destiny?" Odessa called to him from her steps.

John could see her outline, she was wearing a light-colored dress, she shimmered in his sight like a ghost. "The same," he answered, moving toward her more quickly now. "But I might have been that bear I heard tell about, you ought to be more careful."

He crossed the swept yard she kept around her shack and sat down on the step beneath her, putting the packages down beside him. He could smell her perfume, Blue Roses, which she had insisted he buy her after seeing an advertisement for it in one of Irene Stewart's magazines. It fascinated John that the perfume smelled one way in the bottle and quite another way on Odessa. Odessa even improved attar of roses. He put one arm around her legs and leaned up against her knees.

Odessa took his head in her arms and tilted it up to kiss him. "You been gone too long. I hope you got a good excuse," she whispered.

John stiffened. "Excuse? No I don't have any excuse, and if I did, I wouldn't proffer it."

"I see," Odessa said. "What's in them packages?"

"Presents. Sacrifices. Let's go inside and you can find out."

≈

The kerosene lantern lit the room like a theater set. The bed was in shadow. The mirror fractured the lantern light, sending it darting into corners and pooling on the ceiling. They sat at the rickety table.

"Open this one," John said, handing her the package that contained the fan. He wanted to save the kimono for later. He'd left the records in the car. Odessa would want to play them right away, and he did not intend to sit up all night listening to opera.

Odessa tore open the box and pulled out the long fan. The light shone on her face. John watched, savoring her delighted expression as she opened the fan. She held it first away from her to study its design and colors; then she held it to her face, and peeked over it. The lantern light danced in her eyes.

"It's perfect," John said.

Odessa went over to the mirror and studied herself. She held the fan in different positions and posed in the attitudes she'd learned from the libretto's illustrations. John might as well not have been in the room; she had moved completely into the reality of the Butterfly.

John took the fan out of her hand. "You can open the other ones later."

꘏

Later John got out of bed to fetch the flask from his jacket, which hung on a chair at the table. Odessa sat cross-legged on the bed. The quarter moon was centered in the high window over the bed, like a painting in a frame. The lantern had been turned way down. Its light flickered in the mirror like a fire in a hearth. John reached into the jacket pocket and got his flask and then picked up the big, gold foil package, which held the kimono, and brought it back to the bed. John took a long swallow from the flask and then held it out to Odessa. She tipped it up, inclining her head backwards, arching her long throat. John watched her swallow. He thought if he could keep only one picture in his mind, this was the one he would keep.

The shop girl had twined ribbons all around the box, and now Odessa went to untying them. She had a superstitious dread of bringing bad luck by breaking any of them. She bent over the package, the tip of her tongue caught between her front teeth, her breathing careful and steady. John leaned up against the headboard and lit a cigarette. Smoke swirled in the lantern light like mares' tails.

Shortly becoming impatient, he leaned over and yanked the last remaining ribbon. It broke with a loud pop.

Odessa looked up. "John Washington, you are a reckless fool."

"Washington men only live to sixty; I got just so much time to waste."

Odessa stared at him. She took a long breath and then let it out.

"Open it, damn it, Odessa." John, too impatient to wait any longer pried open the box and pulled out the shimmering kimono and held it up. He heard her intake of breath, and he looked, over the top of the kimono to see her face. She looked dazed. "Well? Is this what you had in mind?"

She nodded, her eyes still wide.

"Put it on," John said. "You know, at least two hundred little Japanese women went blind making this just for you. And were glad to do it."

Odessa climbed down from the bed and took the kimono to the lantern, where she could study the embroidered butterflies, each one different. It was difficult to believe that human hands had performed this feat. John got up and came over to her. He guided her by her shoulders to the mirror, and he slipped the kimono over her bare arms and settled it on her shoulders. The fit was perfect. The butterflies shone colored light onto Odessa's face. She gazed intently into the mirror. John put his arms around her waist from behind. He nuzzled her neck. "Madame Butterfly, I presume," he said.

"The same," Odessa replied, smiling at last.

John slipped the kimono from her, and it slid to the floor.

"No," Odessa said urgently. "Pick it up."

"It's not the damn flag," John said, but he bent and picked up the kimono and draped it over the chair with his jacket before he led her back to bed. The moon had moved from its frame in the window.

❧

John did not leave Odessa's until three-thirty that morning. Before he left, Odessa saw there were still two packages on the table. "What are these?"

"That's the what else you told me you wanted."

John was pulling on his jacket.

"What else did I say? I don't remember."

Odessa was already opening the larger package. John was leaning against the door. Odessa opened the box and saw the dull glint of gunmetal. She looked up at John.

"What did you say? You said you wanted a gun. So now you got one. Be careful with it."

Odessa took a step back from it. She did not pick it up. "What's in the other one?"

"Bullets. One's no good without the other."

"I only said that to provoke you, John. I don't want this."

The air had turned cool. Odessa pulled the kimono tighter around her. John looked tired in the predawn light.

"A gun's nothing to joke about, girl. And maybe you don't want it, but I got to thinking about it, and it started making sense. You're out here by yourself. The sheriff sure as hell isn't going to come out here to look after you. Hank's asleep most half the time—you need some protection. Keep it. I'll feel better."

John picked up the gun and the ammunition and took it across the room to the Victrola and tossed it in the record cabinet. "Just leave it in there. I don't want you messing with it until I get a chance to teach you how to use it, anyway. You understand?"

Odessa nodded. It was a relief to her just to have it out of sight.

"I got to get back. God only knows what time Irene gets up of a morning. I'll see you tomorrow."

At the bottom of the stairs John nearly stumbled over Billy Jefferson, who was curled up asleep on the bottom step.

"Jesus H. Christ! Odessa, come out here."

Odessa opened the door she was just shutting and looked out. John was holding Billy. "What's he doing out here in the middle of the night? Which is the Jeffersons' house?"

Odessa came down the steps. Billy had not wakened when John picked him up. Odessa glanced toward the Jeffersons'. There were no lights showing. "Let me have him. He can sleep with me, and I'll take him home in the morning. Them Jeffersons is so no-account, they won't have missed him, and if they did, it wouldn't worry 'em none."

"But why was he *here*?" John asked.

"He got a crush on you, John. You ain't noticed?"

Odessa took the sleeping child from John's arms. John peered down into his face.

"No," he said honestly. "Good God, I can't believe people let their children wander around in the night with bears and panthers. Somebody ought to take their daddy out and whip him."

"Too late for that," Odessa said. "He took off two weeks past. We don't look to see him back."

"What about Cecelia?"

Odessa shook her head. "Cecelia give herself over to the cough syrup. She don't got time for none of her children. Them twins of hers run wild."

"Well, you watch him, then," John said. "He's just a damn baby, for Christ's sake."

"I know," Odessa said. "Go on. Sneak back into that parlor before it get too late."

John took off, and Odessa took the sleeping child inside and laid him in the bed. She hung her kimono over the window to keep out the morning's light and so she could see it first thing when she woke, and got into bed with the boy. He smelled of Grape Nehi. She put an arm around Billy Jefferson's little hollow chest, matched her breathing to his, and went fast asleep.

In her dream she was in a glade near the river. Butterflies coursed through the air, all different colors and sizes, flying high and low and resting on the grass and on twigs, beating their wings. Someone stood just out of the picture, blasting away at them with a pistol. Odessa knew this was a dream.

Chapter 10

Vivian and Willie went nearly every day to the bayou. They had become appalling little liars, one or the other of them came up with a new lie every day for Mama or Emmy (or both). They had become so accustomed to lying, they no longer even felt remorse. They spent a lot of time down in the tall grass in the pecan grove, spying on the house and conjecturing about what they had seen the day that Antoinette shot Snow-Ball. But they'd not seen anything interesting since. Gilbert worked in the yard as if nothing had ever happened. Every noon Emmy took his lunch out to him and put it on the tree stump.

"She doesn't like him," Willie said.

"I know. Nobody really likes him except for Cassie. He's always in a bad mood. I think he was born in a bad mood." Vivian lay on her back and watched the clouds.

"Why do you think Antoinette shot at him?"

"She's crazy."

"That's not a reason. Even crazy people have reasons for what they do. Their reasons might not make sense to us, but they make sense to them."

Vivian rolled over on her stomach and pretended she was as small as an ant and that the grass was a jungle. She watched a doodlebug scurrying for someplace. "I really don't know," she said. "Sometimes I think she gets up before she's awake and does stuff that is going on in her dreams."

"You mean she's sleepwalking?"

"I guess. Sort of. Then she wakes up—she's confused and doesn't want anybody to know, so she goes on doing whatever she was doing like it was on purpose."

Vivian poked a stick in front of the doodlebug and watched it try to figure out which way to go.

⁂

Antoinette remained closeted in the house, alone with her terrible secrets. She had not been able to keep the pregnancy a secret from her mother, however. Knox had told her. Just told her. Without a by your leave! Antoinette had been beside herself. But nobody knew the other part. Except for Gilbert, of course. Antoinette had not set eyes on *him* since that terrible day she'd seen him from the kitchen window and realized what had happened. She'd asked her mother to tell John about her pregnancy when he should come home. She said she didn't know how to tell him. She was too embarrassed, she said.

"But he's your *husband*. He's the baby's daddy; there's nothing to be embarrassed about, darling."

But Antoinette had pleaded with her, and it occurred to Mrs. Malone that it might be the "other woman," whose existence she was increasingly certain of, that was complicating poor Antoinette's response to expecting a child. So she'd agreed to tell John.

⁂

John reached home late in the evening. To his surprise, his mother-in-law opened the door. John immediately assumed the worst, that Antoinette was sick or dead, but Mrs. Malone hurried to reassure him that his wife was only tired, and since she hadn't known what time he would get in, she'd gone to bed and would greet him in the morning. The girls were spending the night at the Malones' house, and it was Emmy's evening off.

John sat down at the kitchen table, where Mrs. Malone had been sitting while she waited for him. She poured him a cup of coffee and served him a wedge of lemon meringue pie.

The kitchen door was open, and John was seated facing it. As he ate his pie, he watched the fireflies floating over the grass; it was restful to watch their aimless flight after staring all day at the unyielding center line. John, who had scarcely seen the road before him for the persistence of the image of Odessa—in her kimono, bathed in the yellow light of the lantern—floating always just a little above the hood of the Essex, was in reality glad Antoinette was asleep. The problems occasioned by living two distinct lives in two very separate worlds, lay, John had found, mostly in the exiting and the entering.

His mother-in-law had something on her mind. He could tell by her fluttery movements and her hectic conversation. But he would have to wait, he knew, for her to come to the point. She was circling in on it. He stirred at his coffee.

"And how is your business, John?" Mrs. Malone asked suddenly, sitting down herself. "In these hard times?" she added, sympathetically.

"I lost two of my accounts in Arkansas this trip. And I'll lose more. But I'll replace them. I'll have to." John pushed his chair back and picked up his coffee cup.

"But you'll be okay?"

"Yes, I think so."

"The reason I ask is Antoinette has some news that she's asked me to relate to you. I would have thought she would want to tell you herself, but she was always my shy one."

John Washington brought his gaze from the open door and looked into his mother-in-law's shockingly blue eyes. "Antoinette?"

"Yes, well, she was shy when she was a girl. At home." Mrs. Malone folded her hands on the table and stared intently at her red knuckles and her wedding band, now worn thin. "Well, I don't really know another way to say this, except straight-out. Antoinette is expecting. That is to say, *you* and Antoinette are expecting. A Christmas baby. She only found out while you were gone. She'd been sick, and I had been worried about her, so I finally got her to Dr. Knox, and it turns out she wasn't sick at all, like I told you. She's expecting."

John followed his mother-in-law's eyes down to her hands. "Well," John said, taking in a breath of the cool evening to steady himself. "I *am* surprised, and like you, I'm even more surprised that she asked you to tell me."

Mrs. Malone clasped and unclasped her hands. "Well, Antoinette's been unwell. The heat and her condition, you know. I am afraid we had a very unfortunate incident here while you were away. For which, I regret to say, John, in great part, I blame you."

"Another 'incident'? Can I know what I am being blamed for?"

"The gun, John! Whatever were you thinking of when you bought Antoinette that gun? She's much too high-strung. I really blame you altogether."

John Washington put his fork down and looked levelly at his mother-in-law. "What's happened?"

"Antoinette shot Clara's dog. By accident."

"How do you accidentally shoot a dog?"

"She didn't mean for the gun to go *off*." As she said this aloud, Mrs. Malone heard again the paltriness of the explanation, but she had no other; she was stuck with it.

"I see." John lit a cigarette. He returned his gaze to the fireflies. What could he have expected? While he had been gone, life here had run completely off its track. He was unhappy, but scarcely surprised. And if Antoinette had told her mother that he had given her a gun, he would not say otherwise before he could talk to her and to the girls and find out what in holy living hell had been going on.

Mrs. Malone, sipping at her coffee, looked so miserable, so unlike her usual cheerful self that John reached for her hand. "I'm sorry we're so much trouble," he said. "Quite obviously we're incapable of living our own lives in an orderly fashion. But we'll get better at it. We're bound to, we couldn't get much worse. You know I'm grateful for all your help and concern."

Mrs. Malone looked into John's brown eyes. There were flecks of gold and green in the irises, so that looking into them she saw the same colors she had seen peering down her papa's well on summer days. John's long fingers closed over her own. She was abruptly and completely ashamed of the suspicions she had harbored in recent weeks.

When he drove back into his driveway after taking Mrs. Malone home, John turned the motor off and got out, but instead of going inside the house, he leaned up against the front fender and lit a cigarette. He stayed outside, in the night, smoking and watching his home as if its occupants were all unknown to him and he himself was a disinterested stranger.

The house was dark except for a light above the stove in the kitchen, and the night-light that Antoinette always kept lit in the bedroom. Above it, the moon looked to be sailing. Clouds were rushing across it in a great hurry to rain on Mississippi. John looked at the outlines of his new trees, whose shadows lay across the lawn. In the dark they looked nearly substantial. He had been right to hire Gilbert.

And what, he thought, as his eyes swept past the bedroom window, was Antoinette doing with a gun? Where had she gotten it? And *why*?

John was an expert liar and judge of liars. The Washingtons' entire family history, resting precariously, as it did, upon the pinnacle of one huge lie, had necessitated a thousand lesser ones. He had not known, however, that Antoinette was one, too. John had to admire the workmanship of Antoinette's lie. It was clear to him from her lie about the gun that she was a liar, and a practiced one. The gun story, John knew instinctively, was too good to be accounted for by beginner's luck.

He ground his cigarette out with the pointed toe of his narrow shoe. What else didn't he know about Antoinette? He would never have guessed, for instance, even if he had known of the gun, that she could hit the broad side of a barn—much less a moving target like a dog. She had killed it with one shot, he'd just been told. In the "accident."

John smiled to himself. His Antoinette had been keeping secrets from him right along. And now she was keeping John's baby inside her like a secret. Mrs. Malone, in an effort to make John feel better, had told him that Antoinette had not even told *her* about the baby, that she had learned of it from Dr. Knox.

John sensed that if Antoinette had had a choice in the matter, the baby would still be a secret. And this did not please him. His wife was welcome to her own little secrets, but not to secrets concerning something belonging to *him*.

He wandered around the yard in the moonlight, checking on his new plants as he thought about these things. The morning glories and the bamboo had shot up in the recent hot spell. He walked through the backyard and saw the new beds of marigolds, one of his mother's favorites—because, as she had remarked so often, they were sacred to the Blessed Virgin. He could see into his own bedroom window, lit by the night-light.

He stepped closer and stood there watching his wife sleep. Now she was no longer just his wife. Like as not, she carried the son he had both wanted and been afraid of all his life. The son to carry on the Washington name, the son who would move up another rung on that ladder that his grandfather had set up against the white man's bastion. And unless a dread and rare genetic joke was played upon him, this would be the whitest Washington ever born—for its mother, except for her black Irish hair, was fair as buttermilk.

Antoinette was sleeping on her side, facing the window, and while John watched, a moonbeam shone across her face. John hurried to go into the house and draw the drapes; moonlight shining on a sleeper's face was known to be the worst sort of luck.

Returning from a night spent at The Lucky Pig, Emmy was walking toward the back door just before John turned from his own bedroom window to go inside. At first she did not recognize him, and she stepped behind the trellis. But when he walked she knew him. His long legs moving in his characteristic lope were plain even in silhouette. Why, she wondered, had he been watching his wife like a Peeping Tom? It purely gave her the creeps to see him tiptoeing around his own yard. She stood still in the shadow of the trellis and waited until he went inside. The morning glories were all furled up tight like little closed umbrellas. Waiting for the sun. Emmy waited five minutes more before she slipped in the kitchen door and into her room. One thing she knew—if the times were not so hard, and if nice old Mrs. Malone were not counting on her better nature, she would be gone out of this crazy house in seconds flat. That was an absolute fact.

⸎

In the morning Antoinette awoke to see John sitting in the little armchair by the window. When she opened her eyes, he got up and sat down on the bed.

"Good morning, darling."

"You startled me so! I never know when you are coming home." Antoinette pushed herself up and rested her back against the ivory pillow. She lifted one hand to check her hair.

John took the hand and kissed it. "You look perfectly lovely, as you always do," he told her. He smoothed the coverlet. "Your mother told me."

"Oh," Antoinette said, and pulled her hand away from him. She reached for her cigarettes on the nightstand. "Ring for Emmy to bring the coffee in. I can't discuss this before coffee."

"I'll get it," John said.

When he returned he carried the breakfast tray that Emmy had already prepared and a pot of coffee and two cups.

Antoinette had combed her hair and put on an embroidered bed jacket. John set the tray across her lap, and sat down in a chair to drink his coffee.

His wife ate like a ravening beast. He had never seen a person eat with equal speed or ferocity, not even the dockworkers at the po'boy stands in New Orleans ate like this. He was used to seeing

Antoinette pick at the food on her plate—never so much eating as rearranging the food she found there into new patterns.

He watched while she wiped her plate clean with the last of the four pieces of toast. Then she pushed the tray away and picked up her coffee cup. She took a dainty sip.

"If Mother talked to you, then you know why I didn't stay up waiting for you. I get so terribly tired."

"And so terribly hungry," John remarked.

Antoinette looked down at the empty plate. "Yes," she said. "I'm either terribly tired or terribly hungry—it's not much to choose from."

"Why didn't you tell me about the baby yourself?"

"Because I didn't want to have to pretend to be happy about it. I've been thinking back, and it must have happened when we were in New Orleans."

"Probably so."

"When you were drunk," Antoinette accused.

"In all likelihood," John said agreeably.

"It's fine for you to be happy, but I'm the one who has to carry it and have it." She had decided to stay with this perfectly sensible story. She could not very well say she didn't want the baby because it wasn't John's and it would be black as the ace of spades and look exactly like Gilbert Jackson. Could she?

"Did you never want a child of your own?"

"Frankly, no. I thought if I married you, since you already had two, I wouldn't have to have any."

"I see. Well, I am sorry."

Antoinette was surprised John was being so agreeable. But she remembered that her older sisters' husbands had acted nicer than they really were when her sisters were pregnant. She supposed that men felt guilty about putting women in such an untenable position, and therefore tried to be a little nice to them. She wouldn't mind John being nicer than he was for a few months. Because, of course, once the baby was born, no one would ever be nice to her again. Not even Mama. This thought brought tears to her eyes. No matter what she had done, no matter how angry anyone had ever been with her, even when she'd killed that kitten, which *had* been an accident, Mama had gone on loving her. She could not begin to imagine what her life would be like when everyone, even Mama, stopped being nice to her.

But they would. And soon. She would kill herself, but that would just put her in Hell faster. No matter how bad things got in this world, at least you were not in Hell. There was always a slim chance of redemption so long as you were breathing in and out. Dead by her own hand, the last word would be written and could never be erased.

John was untouched by the tears that shone in Antoinette's eyes. "We need to talk about the *gun* that you've lied to everyone under the sun about, and you *are* going to tell me just what in the hell you thought you were up to when you shot my daughter's dog."

Antoinette stared at John over the lip of her coffee cup. His face was set.

"Oh, *that*," Antoinette said. And then she began to cry in earnest. Not out of remorse for lying and shooting dogs, but because she was Hell-bound, and she knew it.

"Yes, *that*." John got up from his chair and began to pace in tight circles around the rug.

"It was an accident."

"It wasn't an accident that you had a gun. Where did you get it?"

"New Orleans."

"Why?"

"I wanted it!" Antoinette shouted, surprising even herself, but why lie now? All the lies in the world wouldn't save her now. "I always wanted one," she added. Then in a burst of indignation—"*You've* got a gun. I'm a grown woman, so why shouldn't I have one? What business is it of yours or anyone else's if I have one? Or why I want it?"

John stopped a moment in his pacing. He had not expected this parry. Quite honestly, he hadn't thought Antoinette capable of parry. He'd just given Odessa a gun she hadn't wanted, while Antoinette, to hear her tell it, had been asking Santa Claus to bring her a gun since she was three. He had given the right gift to the wrong woman. This, he thought, is the story of my life.

"And what I told Mama about being afraid out here by myself with just the girls and Emmy, it isn't why I *bought* the gun, but it's still true."

"All right. Forget the gun. For the moment. Tell me why you shot Clara's dog? I know you were unhappy I bought the girls the dogs, but I can't believe you'd go out and buy a gun to shoot them."

"Of course not. I told everyone I never meant to shoot that damn dog," Antoinette said. Again she'd told the truth.

"I want you to tell me where this gun is. I'm getting rid of it today. Your mother is worried sick there might be another 'accident.'" John looked at her hard.

Antoinette poured another cup of coffee. She could give up the gun, and John might stop harping on it, or she could refuse and God knows what he and Mother would do. "It's in the kitchen," she said. "On the top shelf, behind the molasses."

Without a word, John got up and left the room.

※

Later that morning the girls came home—along with that canny survivor, Gilbert the dog. John was sitting in the living room, reading the papers. He continued to follow, with a certain morbid relish, the decline of his stocks. When the Crash had come he had decided to sit tight. The Washingtons had never been financially reckless. His investments were basically sound, sooner or later they would come back up, and when they did John was damned if some sharp, Yankee son of a bitch was going to make his fortune on John Washington's bad luck. It was later now, but still nothing was budging.

"Daddy," Vivian yelled and ran toward him.

John Washington was appalled to see his youngest child the color of a hickory nut. "Jesus H. Christ," he roared, "What have you been doing?"

"Nothing." Could he know about her camp on the bayou? "I've haven't been doing *anything,* Daddy." Vivian said, afraid.

"You're black as the inside of Toby's damn hat."

Vivian didn't know who Toby was. She looked down at her arm. "I'm not *black,* Daddy. I have a suntan; Willie almost has one, too. We've been playing outside a lot." Vivian came up closer to her father.

John laid aside his paper and forced himself to smile. All children tanned in the summer. Then he looked at Clara, who stood by the piano, waiting her turn to greet her father. Clara was not tanned. She held the hat she always wore when out of doors in front of her, twisting its ribbons. More and more, John thought, she looks like Della.

"I've missed you, Daddy," Vivian said.

"And I've missed you," John said.

He hadn't, of course. A successful traveling man lived by the adage, Out of sight, out of mind. But had he been the kind of person who missed people, he would certainly have missed his girls. "I've got presents for you," he said, getting up from his chair and putting one long arm around Vivian. "Emmy!" he shouted. "Get my alligator valise from the bedroom and fetch it out here."

"Yes, sir," Emmy called back.

"Clara," John said. "Come here to me, sugar. Let me look at you."

Clara approached her father, leaving her hat on the piano bench.

"You will be the most beautiful woman in Myrtle when you finish growing. Do you know that?"

Clara smiled, as she knew she was meant to, but her heart wasn't in it. Since Candy shot Snow-Ball, her heart had not completely been in anything. At home she had spent whole days in her room, and even at the Malones', in the presence of the divine Maureen, she was subdued. The change in her was so noticeable that Vivian had actually tried to be nice to her. She had grandiosely offered to kill Antoinette to revenge Snow-Ball's death. More realistically she had offered to share Gilbert. Had gone so far as to say that he could be *their* dog, and Clara had known how difficult this was for Vivian—who had always hated sharing. But Gilbert was no Snow-Ball, he would not follow at her heel, or lie at her feet when she slept, keeping them warm. And he was not beautiful.

It had been a pure pleasure just to regard Snow-Ball lying on the rug in a patch of sun, and to brush his long, silky white fur. (Unlike Gilbert—who had grown a wiry coat when his puppy fur fell out that even the steel curry comb could not be forced through.)

When Emmy came back with John Washington's valise, he unlatched it and brought out two identical packages containing Japanese fans for the girls. They were smaller than Odessa's, but still they were hand-painted on silk.

"It's great, Daddy," Vivian exclaimed when she shook hers open. "What are these flowers?"

"Lotus," John Washington said. "They grow in the water."

"Would they grow here?" Vivian asked, thinking of how she might transform the bayou.

"I don't know. Do you like yours, Clara?"

"Yes, thank you, Daddy. It's very pretty." But though she smiled and opened her fan and fanned herself expertly, she did not look particularly happy.

Vivian came close to her father and whispered, "Did anybody tell you about Snow-Ball?"

John nodded.

"That's why Clara is sad." Vivian said.

"Clara, baby," John said. "I'm going to buy you another dog. Before this day is out."

"I don't want another dog, Daddy."

"I don't *care* what you do or do not want, goddamn it!" John shouted. "You're getting another dog." Then he lowered his voice, because even he knew better than to shout words of solace. But though it was disguised as such, solace was not John Washington's motivating force. "Never roll over and play dead, Clara," he went on in a softer but still urgent voice. "It's not smart, darling. If Fate takes something away from you, grab something else. If it sees you crying, it will come back for more. It will take everything you've got and leave you sitting on a curb."

Clara did not say so, but she thought Daddy was talking like a crazy man. But Vivian knew exactly what he was talking about.

"You mean like after it took Mother, and you sat around crying for a year, and it snatched Grandmother! So did you marry Candy to get rid of it?"

John Washington regretted speaking so frankly; he would have to be more careful what he said around Vivian, but he said, "If I hadn't, it might have come looking for more."

Well, Vivian thought, so this is how he looks at things. It occurred to her that Daddy's "it" sounded very much like the extremely bad thing in her recurring dream.

Chapter 11

Billy Jefferson now regularly slept at Odessa's, as well as followed her everywhere she went, to the fields and to Irene Stewart's and to the woods—where Odessa went to practice the Butterfly's songs. Wherever she was, he was—like a shadow sewn to her heels.

Despite John's injunction to take care of him, Odessa had had no intention of watching Billy Jefferson; she'd taken him back home the morning after John had stumbled over him on the steps, but Cecelia seemed too far gone to understand what Odessa was saying. The woman's eyes swam in their sockets, and she'd had to hold on to the porch railing to keep her feet. She told Odessa she was sick. Which, after a fashion, Odessa understood, she was. So Odessa said she'd keep Billy with her till Cecelia was feeling some better.

At first, the way the boy dogged her made Odessa about crazy.

He kept so close to her she could hear his breathing; at first the sound scraped at her nerves, but over time she got used to it. When she walked he stayed three steps behind her. When she stopped in her tracks he stopped short, like a well-trained dog; when she stood still he crept up behind her and sometimes took hold of the hem of her dress.

He didn't talk much. Nobody had ever talked to him, so he'd never got the habit. His older brothers, whom he'd followed around before he hooked on to Odessa, had ignored him, as had his parents. Except for John Washington and now Odessa, nobody had ever taken much notice of him.

It was picking season. Odessa was in the cotton all day. Billy trailed her up and down the long rows. He never seemed to get hot, he sat on his heels, he wore only a patched pair of overalls, one strap sliding down his arm, while he poked at the ground with a piece of stick that he clutched in one hand. He listened to Odessa's singing. Sometimes he hummed along.

Odessa found herself, tired as she was at the end of the day, cooking little treats for the boy. After supper they sat on the steps and listened to the new records of *Madame Butterfly* that John had brought.

When Odessa had discovered that Madame Butterfly killed herself at the end of the opera she'd been fit to spit. She wished then she'd never asked John for the new set of records, wished she'd just left the story where the old record set had, before the lieutenant left for good.

So far as Odessa could see, if anybody needed killing, it was Lieutenant Pinkerton and his nasty, white wife. That's how the opera *should* have ended.

Odessa purposefully did not learn Madame Butterfly's dying aria. She did not want it in her head or in her mouth. Maybe that's how women were brought up to do in Japan, but Odessa had no truck with it.

✤

John bought a dog for Clara before the week was out. He got on the phone to Otto Kraemer and had him call around until he located a chow chow breeder. John had to drive to Texas for it, but he was determined to show Antoinette that what she could do he could undo. He also wanted the satisfaction of seeing Clara smile again.

The night he got home with the new dog, it was late; the house was asleep. Gilbert the dog, who generally announced all arrivals, was with Vivian, who was spending the night with Willie. Emmy heard the car and got up. "Mr. Washington?" she said at the door. For a moment, there in the half light, the tall man had looked like the Bible picture of Jesus carrying the lost lamb. "What you toting, Mr. Washington?"

"Somebody's heart's desire," he'd said, and gone directly into his girls' bedroom, where he turned on the overhead light and called out, "Clara!"

Clara sat up, startled awake, and John Washington dropped the confused pup on her bed. "For your information," he said, "That's what a real, goddamn chow chow dog looks like. And don't even ask me what one costs or how far you have to drive to get one." He sailed his hat onto Vivian's empty bed and stood in the middle of the room, beaming, enormously proud of himself.

The dog nuzzled up to Clara; slowly her arms encircled it. It licked Clara's face with its marvelous black tongue. Clara looked into its slanted yellow eyes, and John Washington finally got the smile he'd driven so far and paid so much to see. Though the dog was red, Clara named it Snow White.

The next day, John told Antoinette how much he'd paid to replace the dog she'd shot "by accident" and that he was taking it out of her household allowance. John did not think Antoinette would be shooting any more dogs.

_-ℓℓ_

"When is he coming?" Billy asked Odessa when they were eating supper, same as he asked every night.

"John?"

"John *Washington*."

Billy was eating a piece of cold corn bread. Odessa didn't have a cookstove of her own, but Mrs. Stewart was letting her use hers to cook meals for the boy. Sometimes Mrs. Stewart cooked something for him, too. A little sweet potato pie or a little cobbler. Always something just child-sized.

Mrs. Stewart purely pitied Billy Jefferson. Seemed like to her he was worse off than if he'd been orphaned. How his mama could shunt him off the way she'd done, Irene couldn't begin to imagine. But she admired the way Odessa had stepped in. It was just the kind of thing her mother would have done.

Odessa was staring out the front door at the last light. "It won't be much longer, Billy."

"After supper?"

"No."

Billy had no sense of time at all—not even the day before the day before Sylvan variety. He asked Odessa every night was John Washington coming, and by that he meant *that* night. Odessa had to tell him no over and over—to the point that it was beginning to depress *her*. He never asked was John coming tomorrow. Nights were long and dark, and one fell between each day, and these long nights kept the concept of tomorrow too unreliable for Billy to latch on to.

"Are we going to play the music?"

"You want to?"

Billy mopped at some molasses on his plate with his finger. He smiled and nodded his head shyly.

⚘

Gilbert knocked on the kitchen door. He had come to tell John Washington he was quitting, in accordance with Cassie's plan. When Emmy answered, he asked could he talk to him. Emmy disappeared and John came to the door.

"What is it, Gilbert?"

"I need to talk to you, Mr. Washington."

"Talk."

Gilbert could see only John's silhouette through the screen. He didn't want to talk without being able to see the other man's expression, but he couldn't ask a white man to step out into the light. So Gilbert said. "I need you to look at a tree that's doing poorly."

This got John out of the house; he'd paid a fortune for those goddamn trees!

Gilbert led him out to the back, where there was a fig tree that wasn't thriving, but actually so he could talk to John Washington on the closest to equal footing available.

John stood and regarded the tree a moment in silence; then he said, "Goddamn it all to Hell, Gilbert! What am I paying you for?"

"That's what I need to talk to you about, Mr. Washington. You paying me *part*-time. The Callahans that Cassie works for, they wants a couple. Her, and me, not part-time like I've been. Permanent and full-time like we was for your mother. And Cassie and me, we talked about it, and told them yes. So I'm quitting you."

John stared at the man. He could not believe his ears. He stood with his hands in his pockets, looking down at the ground and jingling his change, fighting a powerful urge to knock Gilbert down. "You treacherous son of a bitch," he finally said.

Gilbert didn't say anything. He thought he saw the curtain in Mrs. Washington's bedroom twitch. Was she watching him? John Washington commenced into raving about ingratitude—a subject he considered himself an expert on—while Gilbert studied the grass. How John Washington had got the notion that he, Gilbert, owed him *any* goddamn thing, Gilbert would have liked to know. But it was like Cassie said, all he had to do was stand still and hold his hat, eventually the man would run down; he'd throw him off the place and *then* he and Cassie'd be done with the Washingtons for good and all. That was the plan. Gilbert didn't listen to a word John Washington was saying.

John was outraged that Gilbert, of all people, was quitting *him.* He was so furious he couldn't see straight. He tried to provoke the man every which way into saying or doing something incautious so he could at least have the satisfaction of calling the sheriff on him, but Gilbert just stood there, still and mute as a statue on a courthouse lawn.

In frustration John took hold of the trunk of the ailing fig tree and gave it such a yank he pulled it right out of the ground. This was more like it, John thought, as he hurled the tree overhand across the lawn. Both men stood regarding the uprooted tree, which lay now up against the side of the toolshed, its roots and sparse withered leaves quivering.

"Oh, to hell with it," John said then. He was feeling calmer. "I hope you weren't counting on me for a reference to the Callahans, because if you were, you can put it out of your mind."

"I wasn't going to ask you for no reference," Gilbert said.

"Get off of my property. If I see you on it again, I'll consider you a trespasser."

Gilbert nodded and turned away and began walking for the

road. He wondered if Mrs. Washington was watching him leaving. He carried his hat in his hand. He didn't put it back on his head until he was off John Washington's property; then he set it firmly on his head and gave it a firm little congratulatory pat.

John stood in the sun and watched him go. He'd always hated that black bastard. Now that it was over, he was glad he'd quit—he was! By the time he went back in the house, he almost had it in his mind that he had fired him. By suppertime he believed it.

"I fired Gilbert," he pronounced at the table.

"Fired Gilbert?" Antoinette asked, looking up from her plate—which she'd cleaned once and was now beginning in on again. "Why, John?"

"For criminal damn negligence," John said. "I don't know what he's been doing these last weeks, but it sure as hell wasn't gardening."

Antoinette held her breath.

Vivian was relieved, but she said nothing because her mouth was full.

Clara was surreptitiously feeding Snow White under the tablecloth.

Antoinette saw this and ignored it. John had said he was going to make the announcement that she was expecting. Antoinette was sure the girls knew already; after all, they spent so much time at Mama's—no respecter of a person's privacy! But John wanted to make a formal announcement, so fine. She was concentrating on her food, anyway. She'd never had a real appetite before. But now, ugly and hateful as the woman was, Antoinette was blessing Emmy's name every night, because where would she be with this huge appetite and nobody to cater to it? She'd begun timidly trying to make up to Emmy for all the mean things she'd done and said, because if Emmy took a notion to leave, Antoinette was afraid she might starve to death.

In fact, Emmy had had to shift down several gears in the kitchen, and about double every recipe she used to keep the platters and serving bowls on the Washingtons' table filled since Mrs. Washington had given up sleeping and taken up eating.

"Girls," John said in his listen-up-and-listen-fast voice, which they both recognized instantly. Their heads snapped up from their plates. "Candy and I have some very happy news we'd like to share with you tonight."

Vivian looked at Clara, but Clara didn't meet her eyes, for she had her head inclined at Daddy and she was wearing her little social smile. Vivian decided for once to follow suit.

"Come Christmas, you will have a baby brother. Or," John added grudgingly, "maybe a sister."

Antoinette went right on eating while the girls looked over and stared at her like she'd just turned purple. Even Clara's smile faded for a minute, but she rallied quickly.

"How wonderful, Daddy!" Great, she thought. If he gets a boy, Vivian and I may as well hang ourselves.

Vivian was confused. Why was God sending Daddy and Antoinette a baby now? Why hadn't he sent it before if he was going to? She could tell Clara didn't like it. Antoinette didn't seem too happy about it either. Daddy was smiling, but he'd spent the afternoon in the garage, so it might not mean anything. What would they do with a baby? Antoinette didn't even like dogs.

Daddy stood. "A toast to the new baby."

The girls scrambled to their feet, raised their glasses, and drank to the new baby. Antoinette used this occasion to reach the platter of corn bread closer to her plate.

⸙

Over the course of the summer, Willie had learned to dog-paddle. He paddled around with his glasses on, and he had to wear a long-sleeved shirt even in the water or he would have turned as red as a beet and Mama would have known what he was up to.

The day after Daddy's toast to the new baby, they were in the water splashing and talking.

"She is expecting. Did you know that?"

"Yes," Willie said.

"Then why didn't you tell me?"

Willie tried to shrug, and his head went under and he came up sputtering.

"Do you think I should tell him what really happened? About Gilbert and Antoinette, I mean?"

"No," Willie said. It was his policy to listen to adults at every opportunity, but to tell them nothing. It had served him well thus far.

"Don't you think he has the right to know what kind of person he's married to?"

"I suppose he already knows."

Vivian had never thought of this.

"Daddy fired Gilbert, you know."

"How come?"

"He *said* because he hadn't worked hard enough while he was away, but I don't think that was it. Maybe Antoinette told him what she'd done, and he wanted Gilbert gone."

"I think Gilbert probably quit, and your father just told everybody he fired him."

For Vivian this had the ring of truth. Daddy wouldn't stand for anybody quitting. Daddy would fire a dead man.

⁂

John Washington was glad enough to drive away from Myrtle at the end of that week. To drive away from the tiny town and from all the complications of his family life, which seemed to double and triple every time he left. God only knew what would be waiting for him *next* time he got home!

When he drove into Sylvan a week later, at the tail end of a lackluster sales trip through north Mississippi and south Arkansas, he was in no mood for more complications. But there was a complication, and it was of his own making: Billy Jefferson.

"Jesus H. Christ, Odessa," John said that night. "I didn't tell you to take him to *raise!*"

"Yes, you did. You told me to do exactly that. You said, '*You* look after him, then.' Do you remember that?"

"I meant for a couple of days. I didn't mean move him in lock, stock, and barrel, damn it. The last thing I need in my life now is another damn child."

What lock, what stock, what barrel? Odessa had been about to say, but she picked up on that word "another." "What *other* one?"

"Damnation. I wasn't even going to tell you, I just found out myself, but Antoinette's pregnant."

Odessa's body stiffened. Her face turned into a mask. She and John had been sitting at the table drinking. Billy was asleep in the middle of the bed, which is what had occasioned John's outburst when he'd arrived late expecting to get into that selfsame bed with Odessa. In the silence Odessa listened to the hiss of the lantern and the snuffling noises Billy made in his sleep.

She had been confident right along that in her war for John's affections with Antoinette, she would, eventually, win. But Antoinette had played the one card that had never been in Odessa's hand. She was going to bear John Washington a legitimate child. With her Irish luck, likely the son he'd always wanted. The boy to carry on his name. Whereas, even if Odessa were to have John Washington's child it could only be another black bastard.

"Well?" John demanded. "I'm sure you have something to say

on the subject, so *say* it. You've got my full attention, and there's nothing we can do anyway but talk." He poured more whiskey into a thick white cup. He looked very sorry for himself—which he was.

"What would I have to say about it?" Odessa asked him. "It's not my business. It's not even my *problem*. I seem to have accumulated myself a child, too." She glanced over at Billy to assure herself he was really asleep. Though why she bothered, she didn't know, for Billy had no guile. He couldn't pretend to be sleeping; he didn't even know what pretending was.

"I didn't *plan* this, you know," John said. "I wasn't expecting it. After all this time." He lifted his eyes to Odessa's in an appeal to her, but she was staring off into a dark corner of the room and did not return his gaze. "It's not my goddamn fault!"

Odessa returned her eyes to his. "No, John. When has anything been your fault? Why even say it? Your wife's pregnant, but naturally you had nothing to do with it. Anybody would see the sense of that." Odessa took a cigarette from John's pack on the table and lit it. She shook the match out with a snap of her wrist.

"You want things to be my fault?" John demanded, his voice rising. "Is that what would make you happy? Okay. Heap everything on me. I'll stand real still while you do it. Every last damn thing's my fault; I admit it freely. I am the son of a bitch who's ruined your life. *And* Della's—hell, I killed *her*—and my mother's and my children's and now Antoinette's. She's none too happy about this baby, I don't mind telling you." He paused to light a cigarette. "In fact, I got the feeling that if she thought she could have gotten by with it she would have gotten rid of it and I'd never have been the wiser. But her mama got onto it, so she couldn't. Do you know what she did while I was here last?"

Odessa exhaled smoke at the lamp chimney and watched the smoke swirl furiously. "What?" Her voice was flat.

"She shot Clara's little dog."

"She shot your daughter's dog?"

"Killed him on the spot. Said it was an accident, said the gun just 'went off.' Like she could have killed a dog with one shot by accident. Then she told everybody I gave her the gun."

Odessa was interested in this story in spite of herself. She'd never imagined Antoinette had the gumption to kill anything. It raised her up some in Odessa's estimation. Not that she shot a little girl's dog, but that she had some hidden depth to her character, even if it was turning out to be a bad character. From Antoinette's picture and from the things John had told her, she had seemed as bland and as predictable as grits. "Where she get a gun?"

"Bought it. At a pawnshop in New Orleans, for Christ's sake!"

"It don't sound like her," Odessa ventured.

"I think she's been keeping more than one secret from me," John said darkly. He'd been thinking about this, as a matter of fact, the whole road trip.

Odessa said nothing. She let John think along these lines by himself awhile. She shaped her cigarette ash.

"Hell, how do I even know this baby is *mine*? I hardly ever get close to that woman, what with her damn headaches and her hair appointments and God knows what all other excuses she comes up with."

"Ummh," Odessa said. "Well if it ain't yours, whose could it be?"

"Damned if I know," John said. "But likely it's got to be mine, because lately she's been holed up in that house. Nobody comes around but her family. It's just us and Emmy and Gilbert."

"Gilbert?"

John just looked at her; he'd had a lot to drink sitting out back with Hank before he made his way to Odessa's.

"Don't think I don't see what you're up to. Gilbert is"—he corrected himself—"*was,* my yardman, and before that he was my mother's yardman. Are you implying right to my face that my wife is sleeping with a nigger?"

Odessa laughed and ground out the cigarette. "Oh, why not? *You* are. Niggers is good enough for you but not for her, is that what I'm expected to believe?"

"Hells bells, Odessa, that's not what I meant."

"I hate to be the one to remind you, John," Odessa said in a quieter voice. "But Antoinette never slept with anyone *but* a nigger. There's no difference between Antoinette sleeping with you or your nigger yardman."

John drew in a long breath. Afraid she'd gone too far, Odessa moved her chair back a few inches. Then John put his head in his hands and swung it side to side. They sat awhile in silence again until John finally said in a low voice, still staring at the chipped tabletop, "I cannot believe we're talking to one another this way."

He got up and stepped behind Odessa's chair and put his arms around her shoulders. "Damnation, but I *hate* that word, and still it flew out of my mouth like a bat from a cave. And I know you hate it, but you spit it right back in my face like it could kill me. Which for all intents and purposes, let's face it, it could."

He was rocking Odessa in her chair with his arms, and he had his face in her hair that smelled like first rain on dust. "Please let's stop this. That word doesn't have anything to do with us. We're going to wake up that poor exhausted child yonder. It would have been better to wake him rolling around in the bed with him than sitting here shouting 'nigger' at each other."

Odessa bent her head and nodded. "Let's go to bed. I'll move Billy down to the foot. I don't think he'll even wake up."

And he didn't.

In bed John asked, "You don't really think Antoinette is sleeping with Gilbert, do you?"

And Odessa smiled in the dark and said, "Well, I never *seen* Gilbert . . ."

John raised up on one elbow.

She relented. "No, John," she whispered. "Why would she?"

In the morning Billy Jefferson awoke to find John Washington sleeping in the same bed with him. For Billy this was the biggest thing since the Christmas Mr. Stewart had dressed up as Santa Claus and distributed gifts off the front porch of Dixie Home. Odessa was already up; she was just leaving to get water from the spigot in the yard to make coffee. She was wearing her Butterfly kimono.

"Don't wake him up, Billy," she said. "I'll be right back."

Billy nodded. When Odessa left he crept up to the top of the bed next to John's head. He was sleeping on his side, his face to the wall. At first Billy just sat there and watched John Washington breathe in and out, but when he didn't stir, Billy—remembering that time that John Washington had put his hand on his hair, that time right at dusk by the car—placed his small hand tentatively on John's hair. John Washington's hair was thick and black, and it smelled like the wild violets that grew far back in the woods.

John's right hand was outside the cotton blanket, and next Billy examined this carefully, memorizing it for later when John would be gone. Billy had memorized everyone he had ever known, and when they were gone, which they mostly were, he sat with his bit of stick drawing in the dirt, and he called up every inch of them from his memory. John's fingers were long, and his nails were manicured and buffed. He wore a gold ring with a black stone on one finger. There was some kind of writing on the gold of that ring.

When Odessa came back in with the water, she said, "When this coffee is ready, you can wake him up."

Billy left the bed and attached himself to Odessa. While she poured the water into the coffeepot he traced one of the butterflies on the back of her robe. He liked the big blue ones best. While the coffee dripped, Odessa grabbed the cups they'd been drinking whiskey from the night before, took them out on the porch, and rinsed them. Then she set them back on the table. Looking around the room, she said to Billy, "Okay, now!"

Once when he felt sick in the night and his mama wouldn't wake up, Billy had tried to wake his daddy. But he'd done it wrong, and his daddy had woke up mad and hit at him. Next day he'd seemed sorry, but Billy's nose still looked like a summer squash. "No," Billy said to Odessa, looking down at the scuffed floor. "*You* do it."

So she did, leaning over the bed and kissing John Washington's cheek, brushing her face into his wild-violet hair that Billy himself had just been touching. John's hand with the gold and black ring came up then and caught Odessa's neck and pulled her head down.

"John," Odessa said, "Lookie who's here." She motioned with one hand for Billy.

John sat up and saw him and said, "Why if it's not Billy Jefferson his *own* self! Come here to me, boy!"

And Billy, thus encouraged beyond his wildest dreams, ran at the bed and flung himself on John, who picked him up and held him out in front of him, shaking him gently side to side like a rag doll, all the time saying, "Is this really Billy Jefferson? Why, I believe it *is*!"

Billy, laughing helplessly, felt like he was flying through the blue, blue sky, above the green tops of the pines the way the crows did. When John pulled him to his chest and clasped him tight, he nearly swooned.

Hank, who'd given up his crutch, but had taken to carrying a stout stick to lean on and flourish when he spoke, stumped up to Odessa's about ten that morning. Irene had sent him to find out why Odessa hadn't shown up at eight for work. Irene was looking at putting up twelve quarts of tomatoes, and time was a-wasting. Hank had already lied to his wife once that day when he'd told her John had gone fishing. He was damned if he'd lie for John's nigger girlfriend, too. When he got to Odessa's, he found the two missing persons sitting on the steps, watching Billy Jefferson fly a paper airplane John had made from a shirt cardboard. They looked like fond parents in the park on a Sunday afternoon. The only problem with this, to Hank's way of thinking, was that they weren't Billy's parents and this wasn't no park, and it wasn't Sunday.

"Odessa," he called, stopping and planting his feet apart, leaning on his stick. He was breathing heavily from coming up the slight incline. "My wife's unhappy, and when my wife's unhappy, I'm unhappy. She been waiting on you two hours."

Odessa scrambled to her feet. "It went clean out of my head. I'm gone right now."

As Odessa rushed into the house to dress, Billy retreated to the steps to stand between John's legs. John looped an arm around him.

"I told Irene *you'd* gone fishing," Hank said when he got up closer.

"Time got away, Hank, by the time I caught up with it, I reckoned it was too late to bother with."

"You're spending too much time with niggers, John. You starting to tell time like they do. You know that?"

"You could be right," John said; he kept smiling.

Odessa ran out the door dressed for work and started for Dixie Home. "You coming, Billy?"

Billy looked up at John Washington's face. John said, "He can follow me around today, I reckon."

Odessa nodded and headed down the path. It felt strange to be walking without Billy coming behind her like a caboose. She hadn't realized until now how much she'd slowed her pace to accommodate his short legs. She quickened it, and she was nearly flying when she came in at Mrs. Stewart's kitchen door.

"Where have you been?" Irene was flushed and mad as a hornet.

It's going to be a real long day, Odessa thought. "I'm sorry, Mrs. Stewart. I had to stay awhile with Billy, he took sick in the night."

"Is he all right? Where is he? You didn't leave a sick child alone, did you?"

"No ma'am. He fine now—it was just a touch of the summer complaint, and Mr. Washington he just walking past when Mr. Stewart come up, he said Billy could trail along with him today."

"Well, I wish you'd thought to send me *word*."

"Yes, ma'am, I ought to done that."

"I parboiled a kettle of these tomatoes, so you can get to skinning them while I put in a new batch.

The two women went to work. One thing about Mrs. Stewart, Odessa thought, she always work as hard as I do.

❧

Hank and John sat smoking on Odessa's steps while Billy played with his airplane. Hank understood John sleeping with Odessa—hell, he'd do it himself in a minute if John was out of the picture. What he didn't understand was John playing house with her—a nigger and all. He could have understood maybe if John were a single man, but he had a family. Hank didn't like it. He didn't think it was quite nice.

"You getting mighty careless," he said. "Irene's not as dumb as you seem to think. You keep dropping all these clues and she will figure out what's going on. And I got to tell you, John, it wouldn't set well."

John knew the warning was well meant, but it made him mad that Irene Stewart was in a position to monitor his behavior. "I overslept, for Christ's sake."

"Don't matter to me," Hank said. "But my wife's a Christian woman, and Odessa's a pet of hers. Why she loves her near as much as Petey and Henrietta. If she were to find out the real skinny on this, like as not she'd insist we change wholesalers. Kraemer Brothers ain't the only suppliers I could go with. And something else to think about, John, she'd send Odessa off the place. Why, she'd be honor-bound! So if Dixie Home ain't exactly the jewel in your crown, you still ought to be thinking of Odessa. What would become of her if she was forced out of her home?"

John kept his eyes on Billy, who was tossing the plane up into the pines while Hank talked. John's blood had come up to a boil when Hank began to tell him his business. It took every measure of self-control to keep sitting there being told by Hank Stewart how to conduct himself. He turned his head and took a look at Odessa's shack—what Hank was right then calling Odessa's "home." If he'd opened his mouth to reply to any of this, he knew he'd say something he'd later regret. He lit another cigarette.

Hank, having delivered himself of a warning he felt he owed John, stared bleakly out at Sylvan. He'd felt John tense up. But, damn it, John Washington was his closest friend, and many other things, good and bad, but he wasn't much at seeing out into the future. The man had no eye for consequences. Never had.

"Tell you what," Hank said, breaking the silence, "why don't we go down to the river, do a little fishing, take the curse off the lie I told at breakfast?"

"Fine with me." Billy would enjoy it; John could teach him some things about fishing. Soon he might have a boy of his own to teach; he could use the practice. Though, John knew, the things he would be required to teach his boy would prove more complicated, more difficult, than fishing.

✧

Snow White was like Snow-Ball, only more so, Clara decided. It was as if Snow-Ball had been a pale preview of coming attractions. Clara, without knowing she did so, incorporated the first dog into the skin of the second.

Maureen had been terribly impressed that John Washington bought Clara a real chow chow. Snow-Ball was the only chow chow in Myrtle, and one of only five dogs in town, not counting bird dogs, that had pedigrees of any sort. The girls took the dog with them everywhere they went.

"Oh, he's a chow chow," Maureen would say when one of her friends stopped them. "They're ancient, ancient Chinese dogs, bred to guard the gods." Whenever she saw friends up ahead, Maureen asked Clara if she could hold the leash. That's how Clara knew that parity had been achieved with the Adored One. And she'd thought she would have to master a Chopin Nocturne!

As summer ebbed, Antoinette's appetite fell off. She stopped worrying about starving to death and started worrying about worse things. The birth to begin with. It was so unfair she should suffer to bring forth the very thing that would seal her fate. But she couldn't do anything about that. For now, people were nice to her. Nicer than they'd ever been. They gave up their seats to her; they hurried to get stools so she could put up her feet; they inquired how she was.

How, Antoinette wondered, could people like someone who wasn't even *born* yet better than they'd ever liked *her*? For these same people had never cared, much less *asked* how she felt before. Except for Mama, of course. It was a very confusing business. And would have been even if Antoinette did not know what she thought she knew about the baby she carried inside her.

❧

Vivian and Willie had had a falling out. Mrs. Malone had seen it coming. Why, they spent more time together than an old married couple, and like an old married couple, they'd very little but each other in common. She'd tried to head it off; she'd suggested to Willie he spend a little time by himself or with his family, but he'd become more willful over the course of the summer than ever. She had at last stepped back and let events take their course. Which they did almost at once.

Mid-August Willie slammed into the kitchen from outside in a rage. His face was red, his mouth set, his pinkish eyes brimmed with tears, and his white hair stood nearly on end. He was carrying something under his arm, which he threw into the corner, knocking over Lucy and Rufus's water dish.

"Willie! What's happened?" Mrs. Malone asked, turning from the sink, where she was washing dishes.

"That horrible girl," he said. "That vicious, vicious Vivian is what has happened."

"What now?" His mother asked, sighing and drying her hands.

"She's so stupid!"

Mrs. Malone waited.

"Look at it!" Willie marched over to the corner and picked up the thrown object—a library book titled *Johnny Reb: My Life as a Confederate Soldier* by Joel Ranier Laughlin. He held it up for his mother to see. "I let her read it, and she left it out in the rain.

Look at it! It's ruined. Mrs. Parkinson will have me arrested and thrown in jail." Mrs. Parkinson was the town librarian.

"Maybe not," Mrs. Malone said, taking the book from Willie's hands. "Let me see." The book's spine was broken, and its covers warped and mildewed. She opened it. Some of the pages were stuck together; a few had come loose altogether. Mrs. Malone smiled to herself as she pictured Sheriff Schulberg dragging Willie to the Black Maria, but she kept her eyes sad and assessing. "This *is* terrible," she said. Looking up, she saw that Willie had thrown himself into Papa's usual chair and had put his head down on his arms.

"I know it," he wailed. "She'll send the sheriff after me. Mama, this is the only copy of that book in the world, except for the one Mrs. Joel Ranier Laughlin's got or left to her descendants! It was a private printing. Masie got it out on her card for me from the Special Collection. Even if the sheriff *doesn't* get me, Masie will kill me."

Masie, Mrs. Malone knew, was a lot more likely to kill Willie than Mrs. Parkinson was to call the sheriff. "Oh, my," she said, sitting down next to her son and patting his back. "Oh, dear," she added.

Long ago she'd learned there was no sense in trying to underplay an event that upset Willie. The only way to go was right along *with* him. Only when he saw she understood the true extent of his misfortune would he listen to her advice. Anyway, Mrs. Malone was by nature a very sympathetic person. It was all too easy for her to see things from other points of view. In fact, she was so sympathetic she scarcely had a point of view of her own left; she slipped instead from one to another of her big family's viewpoints and thus was constantly seeing the world through different eyes.

"I think we might be able to have the printer put a new bind-
ing and a new cover on this, Willie. I don't believe it would cost so
very much. For just one book. He makes albums, photo albums,
wedding albums, autograph books. He makes the covers for those.
It can't be much harder to make a cover for a regular book. I will
tell Mrs. Parkinson the book was left on the porch by accident,
and how sorry we are, and we'll give it back to her good as new.
Better in a way, as I believe this spine may have been damaged
from the start. And I'll personally stop Masie killing you."

"Vivian wouldn't even say she was sorry," Willie said tearfully,
but he lifted his head up from the table.

"Well, she may later."

"She told me to take my lousy goddamn book and get out of
her *sight*."

"She was upset," Mrs. Malone said.

"I hope I never see her again so long as I live."

"Well, maybe not quite so long as that," Mrs. Malone said, getting up and returning to the sink. "I'll call Jim and have him take
this book to Mr. Almon. I believe Jim knows him quite well.
Don't cry, Willie, you know how your eyes puff up."

"But what if she won't play with me anymore?"

"She will. Give her a little time. Didn't I say the two of you
needed a little vacation from one another?"

"Yes, but when Vivian gets mad, she stays mad."

"Even Vivian cannot stay mad forever," Mrs. Malone said.

"But I *love* her!" Willie said this in the tone of voice someone
says, "You're on my *foot*!"

"They say love conquers all," Mrs. Malone said complacently.

"Don't you *ever* get upset?" Willie asked his mother crossly. He
was feeling a little better. Really, this woman very nearly drove
him mad!

"When I've cause," she said quietly, and she began drying the dishes.

⁓

Vivian had stormed home after the big fight, as well. She pushed past Emmy at the door, Gilbert the dog at her heels, and rushed into her room, where she threw herself across her bed. She wanted to cry, but as usual, the effort only made her hot. She lay there breathing furiously with one arm around Gilbert's neck and the other thrown over her dry eyes. She was very worried that people thought she was a monster because she couldn't cry. Daddy, for instance, and the Malones. Particularly the Malones, who cried practically for the fun of it, it seemed to Vivian. She was thinking she might have to move to Hollywood and become an actress so she could learn how to *look* like she was crying.

She'd told Willie she never wanted to see him again; she'd said she didn't care about his damned book. But she did. She did care about the book, and she would surely die if she didn't see Willie again.

But he was so *fussy*. He was fussier than Grandmother had been, for heaven's sake. He should have known she was as upset as he was that the book got ruined—what did he expect her to do about it? Cast a magic spell? Gilbert was panting his hot breath in her face. Vivian pushed him off her; he hopped up on Clara's bed and lay down on her pillow.

Clara was off with Maureen. They were swanking around town with that dumb dog. Snow White. He wasn't even a girl; he wasn't even white! Just because he had papers didn't mean he was a better dog than Gilbert—something Clara managed to insinu-ate almost daily. And anyway, Vivian thought Snow White's black tongue purely disgusting, and she hated his devil eyes. But Clara had bought a collar and leash with fake rubies and emeralds pasted on it at Woolworth's, and she and Maureen walked that dog all over town. In Vivian's opinion, they were making big fools of themselves.

You would have thought Clara would feel guilty about abandoning Snow-Ball's memory and giving herself over to a new dog so soon. She was always after Vivian for forgetting Mother. Didn't a dog have a right to be remembered, too? But Clara didn't seem to think about Snow-Ball or even what had happened to him anymore. Vivian wished she could forget it.

She hardly closed her eyes without the weird scene she and Willie had witnessed from the pecan grove playing itself out on the backs of her eyelids. She still thought she should tell Daddy what had really happened that day. Or *almost* really happened. But Willie was so against it, she hadn't. She'd seen Gilbert downtown once. He had seen her, too, she was pretty sure.

Gilbert the dog went down to the foot of Clara's bed and began digging at the bedspread, like he was digging out a gopher from its hole.

"Stop that, you dumb dog!"

Gilbert looked up from between his paws and whined.

"Come here." Gilbert was interested in the place where the cold, white thing slept, but he reluctantly obeyed.

At least now that Candy was expecting she'd stopped caring what Vivian and Clara did or where they were. She thought only about herself. Vivian had watched in fascination as Antoinette went from compulsive sleeping to compulsive eating, and she wondered what her stepmother would compulsively do next. But for now, Antoinette seemed almost normal. She spent her days sitting in the living room or sunroom, reading magazines, or she went to the movies with her sister Margaret, or she shopped for maternity clothes, though she hadn't worn any of them yet. Vivian had never lived with anybody who was expecting, so she didn't know what was next. She guessed all that was left was for Antoinette to get fat.

✿

John pulled himself out of his mood. He would have had to work at it to stay in so black a mood on such an unusually fine day. Warm but not hot, and a fresh breeze blowing all afternoon. And then Billy's wonderment when he caught his first fish ever. Both Hank and he had been tickled near to death by the child's unadulterated delight. They brought his fish, along with their own, back to Irene, who made much of it. She even let Billy "cook" it.

Irene stood him on a kitchen chair at the stove and let him turn his fish with a fork in the frying pan. Odessa, who had stayed on to help with the meal and wash up afterwards, leaned against the counter and watched. She and John exchanged a fond glance over Hank and Irene's heads.

When the meal was ready, Odessa and Billy ate in the kitchen, and John and the Stewarts ate at the table on the back porch. Irene said she'd been locked in the kitchen all day and wanted to sit out where she could enjoy the breeze.

Where did she think *I* was, Odessa thought, sitting and sweating at the kitchen table with Billy.

There were hush puppies and coleslaw to go with the fried fish, and fresh sliced tomatoes and green onions from the garden. John passed the plate of tomatoes to Irene, who let out a little scream. "No thank *you*," she said. "I've spent the day elbow-deep in those. I can't look one in the face."

After supper, while Odessa did the dishes, Billy came trailing out on the porch. He leaned against John's chair and drew invisible lines on the floor with his stick.

Irene called for Odessa to bring them more coffee.

"What that girl's done for this little fellow—why, it's just wonderful," she pronounced. "I only wish Cassandra was still here to see how her daughter's turned out. She'd be so proud."

Odessa was pouring fresh coffee into John's cup. He nodded his head solemnly. "Yes, indeed," he said, glancing up at Odessa and twitching away a smile. Not a day went by, he wasn't *still* glad that old woman was dead!

"By their fruits ye shall know them," Irene quoted, but her voice choked, and her face was suddenly sad.

"Apple don't fall far from the tree," Hank said, trying to help out.

Suddenly Irene bolted from the porch and ran to her bedroom. John remained standing, not sure if she was coming right back.

Hank waved his hand. "Sit down. She'll be back in a little bit. And don't say nothing when she does."

The crickets seemed louder in the sudden silence. Every place Irene had ever left endured a sudden and comparative moment of silence. Odessa went back in the kitchen.

"Children's a sore subject nowadays with Irene. But hell *she's* the one brought it up," Hank said, scraping his chair back from the table.

John nodded and stirred sugar into his coffee.

Antoinette was home waiting on a baby she already hated, sight unseen. Irene was pining for one she'd never had. Billy's parents didn't know or care if theirs was alive or dead. And there are people, John thought, who believe in a just and merciful God! Irene among them. John encircled Billy's little waist with a long arm.

Odessa was washing up; she began singing, but still Irene didn't come back.

"Irene!" Hank finally shouted. "Damn it! Where's my dessert? Are you going to leave us out here on the porch like a couple of old bird dogs, all alone and hungry?"

Irene came out then, stung by the suggestion she was neglecting her duty. "For heaven's sake, Hank! You don't *need* any dessert!"

"Don't matter if I do or if I don't," Hank said. "It's my due. Anyway, John needs his."

Irene thrashed into the kitchen and came back with a peach pie. Odessa followed with the plates and forks.

"Was that song you was singing from *Madame Butterfly,* Odessa?" Irene asked as she cut the pie into thick wedges.

"Yes, ma'am."

"Well, it's so beautiful, it made me cry, is all." She dashed at her eyes with the back of her hand. "I wish you'd learn a more cheerful opera next time."

"I wish she'd learn 'Oh Susannah' or 'Camptown Races.' Something perky," Hank said. "Something with a beat, something a normal person could sing along to."

Without thinking about it, Irene handed Billy a plate. "Don't show off your ignorance, Hank," she said.

"How else people going to know how deep and wide it really is?" Hank said.

Chapter 12

Emmy was sitting alone at one of the back tables in The Lucky Pig. The jukebox had been unplugged, and Lester Gray and a stranger were playing guitars. They sat knee-to-knee. They were having some kind of a contest, who was the best player, Emmy guessed. Or maybe just who was the loudest. In Emmy's opinion, loudness was all they could shoot for. Grandpa, now *that* sweet man could play a guitar. Friendly, old-time music that made a person feel happy. Not like this that Lester and the other man were playing, which sounded mean and low-down like the men that were playing it and the others that were listening to it. She was half listening to a drunken conversation from a table behind her when she recognized one of the voices as belonging to Gilbert.

"He never fired me," he was saying in a loud, arguing tone to somebody, "I quit that bastard."

"That ain't what I heard at Cochrans'," the other man said. "I heard you was disrespectful to his wife, and he fired you."

"Do I look *insane*? I quit him flat."

Though The Lucky Pig could not sell liquor, many of its patrons brought in wine and beer or moonshine they'd purchased elsewhere, which they drank from containers shrouded in paper sacks. Gilbert sounded like he'd been drinking a good long while. Emmy had been taking a little fruit wine for her stomach's sake herself. She had to think Gilbert was talking about Mr. Washington. And the next thing she heard confirmed this.

"That second wife of his be crazy as a tick. She'd say anything." Then before Emmy could turn around, he said, "She took a shot at me."

"Man, she never did!"

"She surely did. Reason she didn't hit me was I dove for the dirt, like I learned over in France. She hit one of her own dogs, though. Killed it."

Emmy took another sip of her wine. Was that what had really happened? She didn't think she could tell Mrs. Malone this. If it was even true. Which she was afraid it was. True or not, it was too late to be telling anyone. It was over and done with—except in Gilbert's mind. He was talking like it had happened yesterday. But he was still talking that way about the war he'd gone to over in Europe, and look how long ago *that* was.

Little Snow-Ball was dead and buried, and already replaced by that ugly devil-dog Mr. Washington had brought back from Texas. Emmy's notion of Texas had been formed at the picture show, and from an evil boyfriend who was always talking about going home to Texas—she'd been especially glad when he had— so she knew it to be a rough place. Mrs. Washington had stopped her sleeping *and* her crying, and she was acting almost normal. The last time Emmy had called Mrs. Malone she'd been relieved and pleased to tell her that everything out to her daughter's house was okay, and for her not to worry herself anymore about it.

Emmy decided then and there not to tell her this she'd learned listening to people's private conversations in what really amounted to a barroom. She sipped her wine until her stomach felt some settled.

When Gilbert left, he bumped into Emmy's chair, but he never looked at her or bothered excusing himself. He was headed for his bootlegger. Ever since Mrs. Washington had shot at him, his nerves had been all tore up. Seemed like only way he could handle how he felt nowadays was to stay lit.

"But she missed you, and nothing happened," Cassie was all the time saying. But Gilbert didn't think it *was* over. He was waiting, as he'd told Cassie until she was sick to death of hearing it, for the other shoe to drop. It had got to where he thought about Mrs. Washington all the time—when he was weeding Mrs. Callahan's lady lily bed, when he was pruning her rose of Sharon—he was thinking about how Mrs. Washington looked standing out on the grass in her white nightgown, the way she'd looked at him, like he was somebody she had some kind of history with. Cassie had not looked into Mrs. Washington's eyes the way Gilbert had in that long moment while she took her aim. He guessed if she had, she'd understand better. He guessed she might worry a little if the shoe were on the other foot.

✤

Now without Willie, Vivian's camp seemed empty. A stray cat was hanging around, and was all she had for company. Vivian named him Harvey. He was black and had long fur, all matted and full of burrs. Because he was fat, at first she'd thought he belonged to somebody, but he'd been there three days and nights, and he showed no signs of leaving. Every morning before Emmy got up to bring the bottles in, Vivian stole the cream off the milk for Harvey's breakfast. As she watched him lap it up, she thought about what Papa Malone had said about milk taming beasties. She missed Papa. Since she'd been boycotting Willie, she hadn't seen Papa either. She wanted to tell Willie about the cat, but she couldn't because she wasn't speaking to him. Finally toward the end of the week, she decided Willie had suffered enough. She would be big about it. She would forgive him.

❦

The library book had been repaired, Mrs. Parkinson had not called the sheriff, and Masie had not killed him (though she wouldn't check out books for him anymore), so when Vivian showed up, Willie was glad to see her. He had been reduced to reading a biography of General Lee he'd read before; he was bored to tears and felt himself on the verge of going mad for sure. He'd missed, much to his surprise, the outdoor life he'd been living all summer with Vivian. Even the swimming.

So the very afternoon Vivian and he made up, they were back at their camp, divvying up parts and acting out a Bomba the Jungle Boy book—a great favorite of theirs called *The Hidden Temple*. Just as though nothing had ever happened.

They needed Harvey to play the part of the man-eating panther. Harvey, however, had disappeared.

"Maybe he went home," Willie said.

"This *is* his home," Vivian said, and she began thrashing around the underbrush with a stick, calling for the cat. Gilbert the dog was looking, too, and it was he who found Harvey, in a little burrow he'd clawed out for himself under a cypress root.

"Oh, no! Something's wrong," Vivian said, pulling the dog back from the cat.

Willie hunkered down for a closer look, and then stood up, dusting his hands on his knees. "This cat's right in the middle of having kittens. There's nothing really *wrong* with it," he added, because Vivian looked so horrified. Willie had seen many kittens born at home, and though of course it *was* disgusting, it was scarcely impressive.

Vivian, who'd not seen the process before, was both disgusted and impressed. She insisted on watching. All told, five kittens emerged—wet, little eyes glued shut, mewing in faint voices.

"Will they be okay?"

"Usually one or two die," Willie allowed. He sat facing the water and throwing little pieces of bark into it.

"What kills them?"

"Nothing *kills* them. It's just how it works. That's why cats have so many babies. Because some of them always die."

"I won't let any of these die."

"*You* won't have anything to do with it, actually," Willie said. "You're the big Nature fan, Vivian. Well, this is how Nature works—who would have thought I'd be the one to tell you. Now maybe you see why I'm not a big Nature lover."

Vivian ignored him. The kittens were attaching themselves to Harvey's teats—previously hidden by her long, matted fur.

"Come on, let's play. We can *pretend* there's a man-eating panther."

Vivian took a last look over her shoulder at Harvey and her babies. She would have liked to stay with the cat and watch the babies eat, but she didn't want Willie mad at her again so soon, so she said, "Gilbert can be the panther."

The next morning Vivian got up very early, before it was hot, to take Harvey and her babies cream. As she walked through the pecan grove, the wet grass whipped at her bare legs. Here under the trees it was already autumn. It had been lurking here in the shadows for almost a week, but as soon as the sun was high, it hid itself again and turned back into summer. Still, this morning it served to remind Vivian that school would start soon. And before she knew it, it would be Christmas, and Candy would have her baby, and, Vivian could only imagine, her life would be changed completely. Again.

When Vivian got to Harvey's lair, it turned out that Nature was even crueler than Willie had said. All the kittens were alive; it was the misnamed Harvey herself who was dead. The kittens were crying and blindly seeking milk, which had dried up. Vivian sat looking at this pitiful sight for some time. Surely, she thought, I should cry *now*. But she didn't. She tried to feed the kittens the cream she'd brought, but they didn't know how to drink. "I can't believe you're so stupid!" She told them. She would have to take Harvey's kittens home; maybe she could feed them with a baby bottle that had come with one of her old dolls. Vivian took a towel and put the kittens in the middle of it. Then she filled in the hole under the root where Harvey lay. She had put her hand out to pet Harvey before she'd known she was dead, and she couldn't forget how it had felt. She did not want to touch the dead cat again.

Emmy, who had been rolling out biscuit dough and watching out the window, saw the girl coming through the grove. She knew about Vivian's camp by the bayou, though she'd never said anything to her about it. What was that child carrying? When she opened the door to let her in, the kittens were crying, their voices surprisingly loud. Vivian folded the towel back and showed them to Emmy.

"Where's their mama at?"

"She's dead," Vivian said. "They're starving, I think. I have a doll's baby bottle, I could feed them with. Watch them while I hunt for it, will you?"

Emmy nodded. So, Vivian was the one who'd been taking the

cream; this had mystified Emmy for days. The kittens were still searching for milk, their voices insistent.

"Hold on," she told them. "We going to come up with something for you all in a short minute."

The kittens looked like ink spots on the towel. What were they going to do with five cats? Mrs. Washington wasn't going to like it.

Vivian returned with the miniature baby bottle. They filled it with milk and sugar water. Vivian sat at the kitchen table trying to get one of the kittens to try it. It moved its head from side to side and ducked the rubber nipple. "Come on, damn it!" Vivian entreated.

"Do this way," Emmy said, handing her an eyedropper she'd fetched from the bathroom, and she showed her how. The kitten squirmed, but then it swallowed. It raised its head in surprise, its mouth searching again for the dropper.

"It worked," Vivian said. "How did you know that?"

"I raised a baby bird this way once. My grandpa showed me."

"What kind was it?" Vivian asked.

"A jaybird."

Emmy took another dropper, and soon they were both feeding the kittens and talking about Emmy's bird, whose name had been Squawk. They both looked up in surprise when Antoinette walked into the kitchen.

Antoinette had not been awake long. She had been dreaming about the baby, and she was in no mood to see her stepdaughter and her maid sitting at the kitchen table feeding kittens with eyedroppers.

"What is this?"

Emmy stood up, putting one of the kittens on the table. "Vivian found these kittens in the grove, Mrs. Washington. Their mother dead, so we trying to get some milk down them."

"Get those filthy creatures off my kitchen table. What are you thinking of?"

Emmy scooped the towel off the table and held it to her chest. The kittens began crawling up her shirtfront.

"I cannot believe what I'm seeing," Antoinette said. "Do you think you could find time to get me a cup of coffee, Emmy? Is that one of my monogrammed towels, Vivian?"

Emmy handed the kittens to Vivian and turned to get Mrs. Washington her coffee. "You want some toast with that?"

Antoinette took her cigarettes from her pocket. "No," she said. "I want coffee, and I want it sometime before sundown." She lit her cigarette. Vivian began backing toward the hall door with the kittens.

"Where do you think you're taking those, little miss?"

"To my room?"

"No, indeed. You will put them in a sack with a brick and take them down to the bayou and drown them."

"I won't," Vivian said.

"You will. Or I'll know the reason why. And bring that towel back. I've told you a million times not to take towels from my bathroom."

Vivian ran out the kitchen door. She took the kittens to the toolshed, where she managed to get them all fed; then she hid them in the fabric sling on the lawn mower. They fit perfectly; it was as snug and dark as Harvey's lair.

"There," Vivian said to the sleeping cats. She would smuggle them to the Malones' that afternoon. Papa Maguire, she knew, would feed them.

At supper that night Antoinette said, "Vivian, what about those cats?"

"They're gone," Vivian said.

Antoinette stared at her hard. "Did you do what I said?"

"Yes, ma'am."

Vivian wanted to say no she hadn't, but Candy was already in such an evil mood, she didn't think it would be safe to provoke her. When they'd sat down to the table, she'd taken the lid off the rice and pitched a fit because it was sticky.

"My God in heaven," she'd screamed at Emmy, "Can't you even cook *rice*?" Then she'd carried the rice back into the kitchen and dumped it in the sink. "Make a new pot."

Emmy hadn't said anything; she just started boiling water. Everyone had had to sit at the table in silence while they waited for the rice to cook. Vivian could tell by her face that Antoinette was still on the hunt for things to be mad about.

"If I find out you didn't, you're going to be a very sorry young lady."

"I *did*, Candy."

Antoinette supposed the girl thought she was some kind of a monster—well, let her think it. The kittens were better off. Most, if not all of them, would have died anyway. She really could not be expected to take in five cats! Not on top of everything else.

❧

Sylvan's cotton was picked and gone to the gin. Odessa had memorized all the Butterfly's arias—except the one she had decided against learning. The weather was turning cool; she kept a quilt folded at the foot of the bed now. As fall started coming on, Odessa tried repeatedly to return Billy to his mother, but since Cecelia paid the child no more attention, maybe less, than before, he kept drifting back to Odessa's house like smoke. Odessa would come home at night to find him sitting on her bottom step, drawing with his stick in the dirt. She and John were Billy Jefferson's family now.

In September, John brought Billy new clothes—his overalls were past patching and was all he seemed to own—and every time he came, John brought Odessa boxes of groceries: potted meat, canned vegetables, food that needed no preparation or that Odessa could heat on her kerosene burner. Finally, he'd brought an iron cot and a mattress. They put it in the corner next to the Victrola. "I'm damned if he's going to sleep in the bed with us," John said, like he was mad, but how mad could he be? Because he never came back that he didn't bring Billy some little play-pretty—a yo-yo, a model airplane, a box of Crayolas, something. Fact was, John was crazy about Billy. Bringing him presents, letting him sit on his lap, fetching quarters out of his ears, producing boxes of Cracker Jack from his jacket pocket. So maybe the Butterfly had been right, after all, Odessa thought, about men and children. Maybe she'd better hang on to Billy, so when Antoinette had that baby, she'd have one, too. Not a little baby, of course, but a child. 'Cause facts was facts: now Billy lived permanent there at her house, John acted nicer in a lot of ways when he came. He didn't swear every minute, for one thing. He wasn't so nervous either. Sometimes his cigarette went out in its ashtray and he never noticed.

※

The week before Thanksgiving John and Antoinette were in New Orleans. Antoinette had wanted to make a trip to the city before the baby was born. "To lift my spirits," she'd said, and John had no difficulty believing that indeed *those* needed lifting, and were probably the only thing Antoinette had that *could* still be lifted. At this stage of pregnancy, Antoinette, with her slight frame and short stature, looked like a ball with an attached head. Unable to wear stylish clothes, too dispirited to go to the beauty salon, she looked like a great, hugely pregnant child. It was a pitiful spectacle. Everybody, even strangers on the street and in shops and hotel lobbies, looked stricken when they saw her. Even John had become sorry for her.

What Antoinette had actually had in mind when she asked John to take her to New Orleans was to go to confession at the cathedral. She'd put it off too long as it was. Because, what if she were to die having this nigger baby? And perhaps worse, what if she didn't? There was the basic sin that had been worrying her so long: her disbelief in the forgiveness of sins itself, and then all her lying to Father Ryan—under oath, so to speak. And she supposed she would have to confess to a sin against charity having to do with when she'd locked Emmy out. Oh, there were too many old lies to even go into; she'd just say she'd lied and leave it at that. Then, of course, there was the other. Gilbert. She had steeled herself to confess to adultery. Since the church made no specifications about the race of one's partner in adultery, she could leave that part out. At least inside the Church, unlike in the world, sin was uncomplicated by skin color.

"Behold me at thy feet," Antoinette began, kneeling to pray in the side aisle near a line of confessionals in the cathedral, and she tried very hard to mean every word. "Pardon me as thou didst the penitent thief . . ." She prayed until a fat, middle-aged woman left the confessional and knelt behind her. Antoinette struggled to her feet and went into the vacated confessional box.

John Washington sat on a bench in Jackson Square and waited for his wife. It was a pleasant day, with a brisk breeze off the river. John was wearing a new charcoal gray suit. He'd spent the morning at Kraemer Brothers, talking to Otto. Otto and Stephen had invited John and Antoinette to dinner that evening at Antoine's. To celebrate in advance the new baby. After leaving the Kraemer

brothers, John had his shoes shined and a shave in the hotel's bar-
ber shop, and then driven Antoinette to the cathedral.

"Why come to New Orleans just to spend your time in
church?" he had asked.

"I only want to go in a moment to light a candle and say a
prayer. If you were in my position, I dare say you'd be praying."

Glancing sideways at Antoinette, he supposed he might.

John was unaccustomed to waiting on people. Waiting involved
being in one place, with no one to talk to and nothing in particular
to do. Eventually, even for John, it culminated in reflection—an
activity he successfully avoided in the normal course of events. He
smoked two cigarettes, but that didn't take long, so he turned his
mind to Sylvan and to Odessa and Billy, and thought about how
amazingly and completely happy they were. Of course, at first,
Billy had disturbed the natural balance. Sylvan had never been
about family. Family belonged in Myrtle. But that was all different
now. Though he did not himself understand why. His Sylvan family bore no resemblance to any family he'd known. Certainly not
the family he had grown up in. And not the family he had patched
together since Della died. Though it did put him in mind some-
what of his life with Della when Clara had been little—before
Vivian was born. He was still thinking about this when Antoinette
finally returned and sat down beside him on the bench.

"Prayed out?" John asked.

Antoinette nodded. She was reluctant to speak and inadver-
tently say anything problematical. She'd been right to come. She
felt almost light, which under the circumstances was a miracle in
itself.

"What would you like to do now, little bit?" John asked. He
felt guilty about being so happy when poor Antoinette was so
miserable—and would be even more miserable if she knew the
cause of his happiness.

"I'd like to go back to the hotel and take a nap."

While Antoinette had been saying the rosary, the first of ten to be said on consecutive days, which constituted her penance, she had decided to spend as much time asleep as possible from now until the baby was born. Asleep she couldn't commit any new sins for which she could be held accountable.

⁓

There was only end of the season work left in Sylvan; soon that would run out, and come Christmas, lay-by would start. Then folk had to find other work to make it through to early spring when the cotton year would begin again.

Odessa went to ask Mrs. Stewart if she could give her enough work to get by on. Odessa usually went into Acacia and worked as a dishwasher at the high school cafeteria, but she couldn't do that now that she had Billy. They wouldn't let her bring a child with her there.

Odessa found Mrs. Stewart on her back porch shelling black walnuts and stated her business.

"Find you work? All I'd have to do is give you but a third of mine for you to drop in your tracks," Mrs. Stewart said triumphantly, stopping to push her hair back from her damp forehead. "But I couldn't pay you much. I can afford to *feed* you. I could probably work out something with Mr. Stewart on your rent. Then what I could pay you might see you through. Unless, of course, you got debts I don't know about."

"No, ma'am, I ain't ever owed to nobody but the Dixie Home. That arrangement work fine for me."

"Here, Billy," Mrs. Stewart said, handing him a brick, "*You* pound some of these nuts awhile. Odessa, come in the kitchen with me—I need to look at the pineapple upside-down cake I got in my oven."

Mrs. Stewart pulled her cake from the oven and poked a broom straw in it. "It's got a while to go," she announced, sucking the batter off the straw. "Sit down; I need to talk to you, and I don't want Billy hearing this."

The two women sat across from one another. Irene Stewart knitted her hands together on the table. "I'm real glad you aim to keep looking after Billy," Irene said. "But I got to warn you, Mr. Stewart's going to put Cecelia and the twins off the place. She ain't hit a lick in months. I kept hoping she'd get herself back together, and I spoke up for her, on account of her children, but like Buddy Catreir says, they ain't running no poor farm out here. Buddy was out Sunday to look at the books, and he wants Cecelia off. He's got another family picked out he wants moved in before Christmas."

Odessa nodded. She was ticking off the weeks to Christmas on her fingers. Four.

Mrs. Stewart went on, "Do you think *you* could talk to Cecelia? Find out if she's got any relations that might take her in? Because like I told Hank, we have to find someplace to send her *to*. If we just put her out, the state she's in, she's likely to lay down in the middle of the road. Then where would we be?"

Odessa smoothed an eyebrow. "I think she say once she from Mississippi. I can try and talk to her. But if you scare up relatives to take in her and the twins, they going to want Billy, too." Odessa had been secretly worrying about this since September. She'd been more than a little surprised that Cecelia had been allowed to lay-up in one of the Catreir shacks doing nothing so long. And she wouldn't have been either, she was sure now, except for Mrs. Stewart had spoke on her behalf.

"Sure they'll want him—who wouldn't want our Billy?—but I doubt very sincerely if anybody's going to fight for the right to take on a fourth extra mouth. In these times. Not once they see somebody that's Christian and decent is prepared to. Nobody's going to take our Billy away from us," Mrs. Stewart said firmly. "Put it out of your mind. Why, John Washington wouldn't let them! Believe you me. I never *saw* a man so crazy about any child. You'd think Billy Jefferson was white. You'd think he was his own, the way he dotes on that child."

Chapter 13

John Washington had done most of his Christmas shopping in New Orleans. But he did his Christmas shopping for Sylvan in Memphis. He bought Irene a lace tablecloth, with matching lace napkins, and four sterling silver napkin rings, which he had her monogram engraved upon—having asked Hank his wife's middle name and discovering to his surprise and amusement that it was the same as his mother's. Althea. And for Hank, he'd bought a new pair of felt slippers and a box of shotgun shells. He spent the most time and had the most fun in a toy store, where he bought Billy a circus wagon, carved in Germany, with twelve hand-painted animals to pull it and ride in it. He already had Odessa's gift and was carrying it in his pocket; he was giving her a ring that had belonged to his mother. He'd taken it out of his safe-deposit box in New Orleans. A flat, gold ring, that his mother had used to wear upon her right hand. He hoped the ring, being so like a wed-ding band, might make Odessa feel as good as married. Hell, they *were* as good as married. He didn't know what more she thought he could do about that. And now with Billy, they were a family.

It was still ten days until Christmas, but since he would not be back to Sylvan until sometime in January, he and Odessa were going to have their Christmas early—just the two of them, and Billy.

When John arrived in Sylvan it was dark. Smoke was rising from the chimney of the Stewart's house, but there was no greeting party out front. Originally he'd thought he would be longer in Memphis, and had planned to spend the night in Arkansas and drive into Sylvan the next morning, so he wasn't expected. Getting out of the Essex, he shrugged into his jacket and then stopped a moment to look up at the black sky to sight the North Star. He looked every night of his life to see it, automatically, like touching wood. This one, simple act was John Washington's only foray into prayer. When he walked into Dixie Home, there was no one behind the counter. He stuck his head through the serge curtain that divided the Stewart's place of business from their living quarters and called out, "Hank? Irene?"

There was no answer.

He wandered back out to the porch and looked to see if Hank's truck was there. It was. Along with a late-model Packard that John had never seen before. He walked around the building to the back porch. The walnut's now bare limbs stretched toward the sky, and a quarter moon hung above it, small and hard-looking, like a coin. It was quiet but for an owl in the woods.

John struck out then for Odessa's to find out what the hell was going on. When he'd crossed the road and was starting up the path that skirted the houses, he could hear the murmur of voices. As he came out of the trees, he saw lanterns bobbing in Odessa's yard.

"Hank?" John called out, running now, stumbling over roots, toward the lights.

Hank Stewart, who had been standing in the yard, turned, and seeing his friend, strode to meet him. He put his arms out straight on John Washington's shoulders, stopping him in his tracks and said, "Wait, John. Something's happened."

John looked from Hank's somber face to Odessa's shack. There were people standing out front, and lantern light shone from inside it. "What's happened, man, goddamn it!"

Hank Stewart kept hold of John's shoulders and said, "Billy's dead."

John Washington looked into Hank's face a moment and saw what he said was true. He slumped a little. Hank took him by the arm and guided him to a tree to lean up against. "He found a pistol Odessa had in there somewheres. He must have been playing with it and it went off."

"Where's Odessa?"

"In the house. Doc Corbin's with her. I called him and he come out, but it was too late for Billy long before he got here. I'll tell you the truth, it was too late when I *called* him, but Irene didn't want to believe that, so I called him just the same."

Hank lit two cigarettes and handed one to John, who was still leaning up against the tree.

"I gave her that gun," John said when he could speak. "She didn't want it, she told me to take it back, but I said, no, I'd feel better if you kept it. On account of her being so isolated out here and all." He looked down at the cigarette in his fingers.

Hank nodded. "I give Irene one, too, when she got so worried about robbers. It wasn't nobody's fault, John," he said. And goddamn it, Hank thought, it wasn't. Life was big, and it moved fast. Something was always taking an unexpected turn, veering out at you just when you thought the coast was clear. He'd never seen the sense of people taking on blame for all the things that happened. What people didn't seem to realize was if one thing hadn't happened, another would, and would likely be just as bad. He exhaled smoke. "What we got to worry about now is Odessa. She's taking this real hard. It's about knocked her flat. She's blaming *herself,* so no sense you even getting started down that road, John 'cause she's got a head start on you."

"When did it happen?"

"Most two hours ago now, I guess."

Two hours ago, John thought, I was driving down Highway 1, singing every verse of "The Animal Fair." I was never happier in my goddamned life.

"We was eating supper when I heard the shot," Hank went on. "I got up right away, 'cause unless *you're* here, I'm accustomed to thinking I'm the only one in Sylvan with a pistol. I never thought about it being Odessa's. I thought one of these bucks had bought himself a firearm over in Texas, and I meant to confiscate it. Then Odessa, I had her minding the store while we ate, she suddenly call out, "No!" Just like that. And Irene, she thought the robbers from Little Rock was finally come, and she near faints, and I run out to the store prepared to fend them off Odessa, but I see her streaking for home, calling Billy's name. But he don't answer."

No, John thought, drawing on the last of his cigarette, he don't answer.

"So I followed Odessa, 'bout broke my neck running up here, damn near fell into the cistern—it was dark as the inside of Toby's hat, the moon wasn't risen yet, you understand—and I didn't even know what I was following her for, 'cept when she'd screamed no, well, I knew something awful must have happened."

Something awful happened, John thought. Yes. Continue.

"She'd already got into the house when I come up on the porch steps. That's when she screamed, liked to turn my hair white, John. So I come in, and she was over in the corner by that Victrola you give her—which was going like sixty, loud as hell, and she was holding Billy up against her, so right away, I didn't see what had happened, but then she held him out like she was offering him to me. And I seen his head was about half blown off."

"Ahh."

"Well, I'm telling you, right away, I seen he was dead. So I took him from Odessa and laid him on his little bed, I took the pillowcase off his pillow and I tied it round the side of his head. Just so it wouldn't look so bad, you know. And I felt for his pulse to be doing something, and 'course he didn't have one. About that time Irene showed up. She'd got her courage up to come in and help me fight the robbers off, and seen me running after Odessa, so she followed. She was the one turned off that damn screeching. Then it was so quiet I wished it was back on.

"Certainly," John said. "May I have another cigarette?"

Hank lit two more and handed one to John, who took his with a steady hand and drew on it languidly. Everything had slowed way down. It seemed likely to him now that this night would last the rest of his life, and continue at his death on into eternity. Every second was a universe of time. The trees, the lighted house, his friend's face, all appeared very small and far away, as though he were viewing them through the wrong end of binoculars. "So," he said, exhaling. "Irene turned off the Victrola, you say . . ." He would help Hank tell his story. Hank needed to tell it. John supposed he needed to hear it, though he couldn't say why.

Hank studied John's face a moment in the dark. "Yeah, well then Irene screamed. It was an awful shock to her, seeing something like that. A child and all. Irene, she went over to Odessa, where she was sitting on the floor. Irene puts her arms around Odessa, and the two of them hug and cry on each other. Then they both stopped. Just all of a sudden. Irene got up then and got on me to call Doc—I still don't know why, 'cause she could see Billy was dead plain as I could, but I knew not to argue with her right then, so I went back to the store and telephoned."

John nodded. "He come out?"

"I told you already he did. He's still here."

"Is that his Packard over at Dixie Home?"

"Yeah."

"Nice cars, Packards," John said, and flicked his ash.

"John, man, I see I'm losing you. I got to do something about you. You got your flask on you?"

John looked down at Hank. "Why, yes, I do." But he made no move to get it. He was busy smoking.

Hank reached into John Washington's pocket and took out the flask himself. He shook it to see if there was enough in it to do any good, and discerning there was, he unscrewed the cap. "I want you to take a long drink of this here, John. Right now. Do it."

John accepted the flask from Hank's hands. "Thank you," he said automatically, and did as he had been told. Then he handed the flask back to Hank, who looked at John's blank face and took a long pull of his own.

"John, we going to go in there now. I told you what you need to know. See if you can't be some kind of comfort to Odessa. I didn't know where to start. You the one got to do that. Hear me?" Hank shook John by the shoulder. "Hear me, now?" He asked again.

John nodded.

"Good."

Hank took John's arm, and they walked up to the house. Odessa's neighbors stepped away from the steps as they approached, and cast their eyes down. Nobody wanted to see John Washington's face at this moment.

Irene and the doctor had put Odessa in bed. Irene sat on its edge; she was holding Odessa's hand, which lay outside the quilt—more like something belonging to Odessa than any living part of Odessa. The doctor was sitting at the table writing something. Odessa lay staring out the window over the bed at the moon. Next to the Victrola, Billy and Odessa had put up a Christmas tree. It was decorated with paper garlands and tinfoil stars. Billy's body lay on his cot—someone had covered it with Odessa's kimono. John turned first to Billy. He knelt by the boy's body and pulled back the cloth from his face. The kimono was exactly the same color as the blood that had seeped through it; the cloth was drenched. "Blood red," John said. "I *asked* that shop girl what color this was; she said she didn't know, but it turns out that it's *blood* red. I should of known *that*."

"I reckon," Hank said. He had no idea what John was talking about.

"Why, hell," John said incredulously, looking up at Hank, "Half his damn head's blown away."

Hank hushed him and pulled him to his feet. "I told you that already, John. Hush."

"Who's this?" the doctor asked, looking up.

"My supplier from New Orleans, and a good friend of me and Irene's. John Washington. The boy was real attached to John. John, this here's Doc Corbin."

The doctor put out his hand, but John was staring across the room at Odessa and didn't see it. Dr. Corbin put his hand in his pocket and said to Hank, "I gave her a sedative. She'll be out like a light once it takes hold. And stay that way awhile. It's not much, but it's the best I can do for a person that's had this kind of a shock."

Hank nodded and said, "We've *all* had a shock, and I think maybe it's time the rest of us should take a little something for ours. Why don't you finish writing up that report over at our place where you got electric light."

The doctor began gathering his papers and his bag. "I have to give this to the coroner; he'll decide if he wants to hold an inquest. But I don't believe he will. Generally he doesn't bother if the deceased is colored. Unless it's a homicide, of course." He snapped his bag closed and walked out onto the porch to light his pipe.

Irene came over to John and put an arm around him. "Oh, John," she whispered. "This is the worst thing yet. I'm so sorry."

John looked down at her tear-stained face and rallied for a moment. "I know, Irene. I know you are." He patted her shoulder. "I have his Christmas present out in my car," he blurted out suddenly.

"Oh!" Irene cried.

"Let's clear out," Hank said, taking his wife's arm.

"What about Billy?"

"Leave him be. I'll call when we get back to the house to get a coffin out here in the morning, and then, I say, bury him next to Cassandra. There ain't no sense in sending the body to Mississippi that I can see. Nobody knew him there—this was his home. I don't reckon poor Cecelia is going to know or care at this point. I never expected to hear from them people again anyway."

"I suppose," Irene said. When Cecelia's family had come for her, they had not thought twice about leaving Billy. And Cecelia herself had not seemed to understand any of it.

"I'm going to stay awhile," John said to Hank.

Hank nodded shortly and guided Irene outside.

"John will be along in a minute," Hank said out on the porch, to the doctor. "He wants to pay his respects to the mother."

One thing Hank did *not* want to get into with the doctor was Billy not being Odessa's natural-born child. And there was no reason in the world he should have to. These people didn't keep records. Few if any of the people living and working in Sylvan could have produced birth certificates, and when they died, their people buried them and that was that. It was the one aspect of the niggers' lives that Hank frankly envied.

_ℓℓ_

John Washington lay down next to Odessa on the top of the quilt, like a stone. Neither of them spoke until the Stewarts and the doctor's voices and footfalls had faded away. Odessa's neighbors had gone back to their homes after they'd seen John Washington go into the house, and in all the Sylvan houses, Odessa's light was the only one left burning.

"Did you look at him?" Odessa asked then.

"Yes."

The moon had moved out of the window frame, and she was staring straight up at the ceiling now. She was keeping her eyes fixed on a point so they couldn't stray to where Billy lay.

"How come that gun to be loaded?" John asked at last; he couldn't stop himself asking that.

Odessa sighed. "It had to have been the twins. The week before their grandpa come for them, they got in here when I was gone and got into all my belongings. They played the records. They must have fooled with the gun."

John folded his hands over his chest.

They fell silent again. Their bodies lay not quite touching.

"Did you see the Christmas tree? This morning, we went way back in the woods and Billy picked it out. Did you see it?"

Of course he had seen the Christmas tree. Over the head of Billy's bed like the angel of goddamned death. How could he have missed *that* recurring symbol in his life? "Yes," John said.

"He saw the Stewart's tree and wanted to know when was we getting *ours*. I never fooled with no tree, but he bent on it, so this morning, we go. He pick it out. It had to be big as him, he say. And it has to be the right shape he have already in his mind, and he want it to have little cones on it. Finally he find the one he want, and I hack it down, but he carry it most all the way back himself. You couldn't barely see him. It tickled me so to see that tree walking and singing. 'Cause Mrs. Stewart, she teach Billy how to sing a little Christmas song about a Christmas tree, and Billy singing that song all the way home."

Odessa turned her head to look at John. Tears were welling from his closed eyes. Odessa put a finger to one of these tears and placed John's tear on her tongue and tasted of the salt.

The shot Dr. Corbin had given her made her feel like she was floating. Normally she would have been cold, she'd always been the first one in a room to feel the cold, but for now she was floating inches above the bed, and she was as warm as if she'd woken late on a summer morning. She knew that Billy was across the room, dead, on his cot, beside his Christmas tree. And she knew John lay beside her stiff with grief and cold, and, she suspected, anger—anger that would find its way to her. She reckoned that inside himself he might already be moving away from her at the speed of light. She knew all this, but she did not feel any of it, and mercifully, at that moment, did not suspect she would ever feel anything again. She continued to tell John what had happened. So he would know.

"Tonight we was fixing up Billy's tree. Mrs. Stewart, this morning, she give Billy that colored paper and paste and showed him how to make the garlands, and she give him some tinfoil to cut out stars with. We was making the decorations and hanging them on the tree. He kept saying, 'This here's John Washington's tree.' Did you know he thought you lived in your car when you was gone? I try to explain to him you got another house and another family even, but he don't understand. Course, I never understand *that*, so I give up talking to him about it. He thought whenever you weren't here, you was driving the car."

He was mostly right, John thought.

"About six-thirty, Mr. Stewart sent a boy over here, ask me to come mind the store so Mr. Stewart could eat his supper along with Mrs. Stewart. Naturally, I told the boy we be right along. But Billy, he really don't want to go. He don't want to leave his tree; he got a little crush on a tree. Ain't that precious?

"I only going to be gone an hour. So—" Odessa stretched her arms in front of her and stared with interest at her fingers, which seemed so very far away. "So," she repeated, and she let her arms fall back to the bed. "I say he can stay. I warn him not to touch the lantern, because *that* the thing I always worry about.

"But when I hear the shot, I know. Right at the counter, I see everything that's happened. Same as when all of a sudden you remember a dream. Only I was remembering something that hadn't happened. Until then. But I knew it already, knew it was true."

"When something is terrible enough," John said, opening his eyes, "we always recognize it for our own."

"What that doctor give me making me feel all floaty."

"It's supposed to put you to sleep."

"I don't want to sleep." Odessa struggled up on her elbows. "What if when I wake up I don't remember what happened. And have to find it out over again."

"It doesn't work that way. Nothing is so easy as that. If it was," John gazed up at the ceiling, where the light danced, "people would be sleeping every minute. Towns would be empty, there wouldn't be a soul on the street, everybody would be home in bed, forgetting their lives."

"I don't want to forget my life. Not even this *night*." But she lay back down. "I don't ever want to forget a minute of Billy's life, so short as it turned out to be."

"No," John said. And he thought, You'll never forget it not in a thousand years—but he did not say it.

When at last Odessa closed her eyes and slept, John leaned over her to study her face. The drug had temporarily erased the marks of her life from her features, but it was plain even so that Death had touched her, leaving its thumbprints scrolled in the hollows beside her eyes. And that same, scarring touch, John knew, would have run through straight to her heart.

He got up, and bringing a chair to Billy's bed, sat down beside him. He did not lift the kimono. Because the dead, John already knew, bear no resemblance to their living selves, but have instead an uncanny resemblance to one another. He stared at the Christmas tree. John Washington's tree. He sat there all night.

The lantern cast shadows on the ceiling and reflected in the mirror. Just before dawn, when the light outside was bleakest, but after the birds had begun to sing, John extinguished it.

And John was proved right. Long before she was actually awake, before she opened her eyes the events of the night before came rushing into Odessa's mind like floodwaters overflowing an earthen dam. She lay still until the terrible images stopped broiling, until all had attained an even, icy, smooth surface. Then, slowly, carefully, she pictured Billy's cot and the barely perceptible bump of Billy's body beneath the butterfly kimono. She brought this picture into finer and finer focus until she could see each butterfly, before she opened her eyes. She'd thought, only the *exact* truth can help me now. So when she sat up in bed, prepared for what she expected to see, she was shocked instead to see the cot empty and bare even of bedclothes, the kimono gone, too. At this moment Irene Stewart came in the door carrying a tray. It was evidence of their grief and distraction that neither of the women even noted the reversal of their roles. Not with distress or even irony.

"I brought you something. I wish you'd try and get it down," Irene said, putting the tray on the bed and sitting down beside her.

"Where is he?"

Irene put her hands to her face and rubbed her temples before she spoke. She hadn't slept a wink, and she scarcely knew what she was doing. "Hank and John Washington came and got him this morning while you was sleeping. You probably think it's morning, but it's past noon."

Irene poured out a cup of coffee and handed it to Odessa, who took the cup and held it. It was restaurant ware, heavy and brown. "But where is Billy?"

"He's in my parlor, Odessa. They brought out a coffin from Carroll's Undertaking, and old Mr. Carroll come out and took care of everything. It was what John wanted. He paid in cash from out of his pocket."

"They didn't call Ezekiel?" Ezekiel was the colored undertaker.

"John called the one he knew the name of, which was Carroll's, 'cause it's the one he drives past all the time. I don't think it even came in John's mind about Billy being colored. You should have seen the old man's face when he got out here and saw we'd called him for a nig . . . for a colored boy.

"Well, he started to tell John to call Ezekiel, but John took out his pistol and put it on the counter; then he spun it like a bottle and said how he was so bereaved and beside himself, he was just praying for an occasion to shoot somebody! Well, that's when Mr. Carroll quit explaining his policy on coloreds. I'm glad you slept through that. I sure, Lord, wish I had."

Irene took up a biscuit from Odessa's plate and nibbled at it with her front teeth, her pale eyes drifting wide. "I wish you'd eat one of these, 'cause I'm sure you going to need it."

"Where's John now?"

"Asleep on the couch in the parlor, or was when I left. Me and Hank are the only ones that hasn't been to sleep yet."

Odessa drank her coffee. She couldn't taste it, but she could feel it going down her gullet, which she found reassuring. "I'll get dressed," she said.

The other woman nodded. "I wish you would. We're burying him in three hours."

⬿

It was the oddest funeral ever held in Sylvan. Three white people, four counting the white undertaker, and Odessa, burying a black child—and not one member of his real family in attendance or even notified. No preacher either, though Mr. Carroll, in an effort to mend fence with John Washington had found a black preacher from Vernon willing to read a service. But John Washington declared he'd shoot the black son of a bitch if he showed up. He didn't want, he said, to hear some sanctimonious bastard go on about the will of God, or his goddamned mysterious ways. Irene Stewart had been shocked, but she'd been too tired and too grieved to say anything. She'd always put John Washington's reluctance to speak about religion down to his being a Catholic. Now she saw that wasn't exactly all there was to it. But when it was time to go to the little graveyard by Sylvan's black church, she brought along her white leather Bible, never mind *what* John Washington thought about it. And as she stood at the graveside, with her feet together, her legs bowed, she clutched that good book in her hands, like it might could save her—which she firmly believed it could.

So the four adults stood around the tiny coffin with Mr. Carroll standing to the back, hardly knowing where to look, still wondering, now that John Washington had put away his pistol, how he, of all people, had gotten involved with such as these. And Tom Anderson, Mr. Stewart's right-hand man, stood behind all of them leaning on a shovel. He'd been the one to dig the grave, and waited now for the service to be over so he could fill it in and go home.

The day was cold and clear. Crows had assembled in the trees surrounding the small, weathered building, and they called back and forth to one another over the people's heads imperiously.

With no preacher to begin things, everyone simply stood and regarded the coffin. The crows cawed. Finally, because someone had to, Hank stepped forward.

"We're here to say good-bye to our little friend, Billy Jefferson. I want to say how much we're going to miss him," Hank said, and then could think of nothing else to offer. He looked at Irene and cleared his throat several times over. She stepped forward and opened her Bible to Psalms. Then she looked over her shoulder at John to see if he would raise an objection, but he was looking down at his shoes and seemed a million miles away, so Irene read in a trembling voice: "I will lift up mine eyes unto the hills from whence cometh my help . . ." It was her favorite psalm; she'd found it went down well in most all circumstances.

"Amen," Hank offered when his wife stopped reading.

Neither Odessa nor John had looked up or said anything. Their silence was thick in the air around them, isolating them from the others and from each other; not even the crows had been able to penetrate it, and Hank could see that neither of them was yet willing to break it. He nodded to Mr. Carroll, and the two of them let the coffin down on the ropes. After Mr. Carroll stepped back, Hank took a handful of dirt and dropped it on the coffin.

"Dust to dust," he said. He didn't remember the rest, but as a farmer, he felt that about said it.

Irene spoke up then in a reedy voice, and recited the Lord's Prayer. In the middle of the prayer, John walked away; Odessa hesitated for a minute and then followed after him. When Irene said Amen, Hank motioned for Tom Anderson to come forward.

Mr. Carroll left then. More indignant, and madder by the step, back to his nearly new, Cadillac hearse. Nobody must know, he thought—he was already imagining what might happen to his business if anyone were to find out that the Carroll hearse had borne a nigger boy to a country church. Well, he'd be ruined, that's all.

Hank watched him leave and spat on the ground; then he sighed. "Let's go, Irene."

She took her husband's proffered arm. "I wish John would have let us have the preacher."

"We did the best we could," he said.

As Odessa hurried after John, she kept stumbling in the soft dirt. She still felt half in and half out of her body. No part of her seemed connected to any other part. John had walked off in his long strides past the church to the edge of the woods, and there he had stopped. When Odessa caught up, he was leaning against a tree and looking out at an empty field. As she approached, he struck a match on the sole of his shoe and lit a cigarette.

"John," she said. They had not spoken face-to-face all day.
"Yes?"

He did not reach for her hand. He did not touch her shoulder, as she had hoped, thought, he might. So she sat down on the ground to catch her breath—which was snagged up somewhere inside her chest. "Nothing," she said.

The grass was dead. The first hard frost had been two weeks ago. Under the trees where the long grass and the wild sweet peas had flourished, where she and Billy had come from the field to eat their lunch in the shade, there was only yellow stubble. She broke off a straw and watched an ant march from one end of it to the other. Then she followed John's gaze and stared off across the field, a field she'd picked her way up and down—Billy, with his little piece of stick, drawing in the dirt behind her, humming to the *Madame Butterfly* arias she'd sung. Looking at the field now, she could almost see herself and the boy moving down the long rows. She could not imagine what John Washington was seeing as he looked out at it.

He finally said, "I want you to know I don't blame you. Or even myself. Not for the gun. If it hadn't been the gun, it would have been something else; he would have got sick, or been run over. Something. It would have ended the same—right there. In the cemetery."

Odessa exhaled. The temperature was dropping; she could see her breath. "John, don't . . ." Ever since his mother had died, John maintained something was hunting him down to strip him of every last person he loved. For a while, Odessa thought she'd shown him he'd been wrong.

"I'd got to thinking I'd shook it off. It took Billy dying to show me it's still here. Still here, and still hungry."

"You ain't the only person seen bad luck. You ain't the only man that lost a wife or a mother or a child, or even all three, John."

"I'd gotten to thinking I was safe from it here. And when Billy came to live with us, it seemed like a sign to me that I was finally meant to be happy."

"We all *meant* to be happy—it just don't always work out," Odessa said. "But there is no 'it.'"

John, who was not listening, turned and looking down at her, said, "You see, I thought if I made my real home in a shack, on the far side of yonder, and if you and Billy didn't even carry my name, I thought then we'd be safe."

He sat down then on the ground beside her.

Odessa took his hand. "Ain't nobody safe, John. It ain't a safe world. You no different from anybody else. Look at me. I loved Billy, too. But you won't comfort me; you won't even let me comfort you. What we need to be doing now is comforting each other. That's the way to do. That the way other people get up the courage to go on after a thing like this."

"I can't," John said. "I don't know what to say to you. What can I say to you?"

"Say how sorry you is that my little shadow-boy dead. Say you love me. Say sorrow won't last always. Say it going to be better by and by. Say *anything*, John."

"Christ Almighty," John said with genuine contempt, no wonder the woman didn't have anything, she didn't even *want* anything. "Is that all you can want?"

"It's more than I got; it wouldn't be so little to *have*," Odessa said.

John still could not pronounce aloud any word of comfort; but he did take her in his arms. Which, Odessa thought, feeling John Washington's heart thud against her breast, was a start, and probably the most she could hope for.

Chapter 14

He came home from the road late Tuesday night, four days before Christmas. Everyone was asleep but Vivian, who had been waiting up for him in the kitchen. She heard the Essex turn into the driveway and waited to hear the car door slam and for her father's steps on the shell drive. But the engine cut off, and all was quiet again. She put on her coat over her pajamas and went outside under a sky brilliant with stars, and so cold that her lungs hurt when she took a regular breath.

"Daddy?" she called, standing just outside the garage. She heard a funny noise from inside the car; he was probably listening to the radio.

John Washington rolled down the window. "What are you doing up?" The radio wasn't on. He was blowing his nose into one of his big white handkerchiefs.

"I was waiting up for you," Vivian said, stepping up on the running board and hooking her arms around the window posts.

"It's cold as a witch's tit out here—get in the house."

"I've got my coat on. Aren't you coming in?"

"Of course I'm coming in. Did you think I was going to sleep in the car?" He wiped again at his face with the handkerchief and tucked it back in his pocket.

"Do you have a cold, Daddy?"

John Washington opened the door and stepped out. He put an arm around his daughter. "No, I don't have a cold. Christ Almighty, but it's freezing! It was actually snowing up around Pineville."

"Really?" Vivian didn't know where Pineville was, and she had never seen snow. "Snowing really? Like in the movies?"

"No, baby, not like in the movies like in real life: cars going in ditches right and left, an accident every five goddamn miles." John reached across the seat to pick up his alligator valise. "How are things here?" They began walking toward the house. Gilbert the dog, who had been waiting in the yard, fell in behind them.

"We've been waiting. For you to come home, and for it to be Christmas, and for the baby. That's all that's been going on around here. Damnable waiting."

John opened the kitchen door, and Vivian slipped under his arm and into the warm room.

"I made some coffee for you," Vivian said, getting out a cup and saucer from the cupboard. "It's still hot." Gilbert the dog lay down in front of the door.

John hung up his overcoat and his hat on the coatrack behind the door. "Why, thank you, Vivian." He sat down and ran his fingers through his hair. The events in Sylvan had taken place in a sort of agonizing slow motion so that now John felt he'd been away a lifetime. He had lost a child. As dear to him as any of his own, and he could not even speak of it. Myrtle would expect him to be in good spirits. Because it was Christmas, and because he was about to be a father again. He could not tell them that he had just come from burying a son.

"Daddy, Mama Malone is in the guestroom. She's been staying here. Because Dr. Knox said that Candy has to stay in bed until the baby gets here."

"I'm glad she's here," John Washington said. And he was. He took off his jacket, hung it on the back of his chair, and lit a cigarette. He watched his daughter carefully pouring coffee into a cup.

"I wanted to warn you, Daddy, she's put up a Christmas tree. It's in the living room."

A goddamned tree! But he only said, "It won't bite."

Vivian sat down across from her father. She thought if he didn't have a cold, and he'd said that he didn't, he must have been crying. His eyes were red and his face was blotchy. She wondered what had made him cry. Was he still crying about Mother? She knew better than to ask. "Are you excited about the baby?"

"Right now I'm just everlastingly tired, darling. I have been driving since this morning. I'll be excited about the baby later."

"How long will you be home?"

"As long as I need to be. Until after the baby comes, anyway." John stirred at his coffee. He was tired and he could no longer keep the last image of Billy from his mind; he was afraid that he might begin to weep again. He had scarcely been able to see to drive the last fifty miles for tears—that had come late, but once begun had been unstoppable. "You'd better get in bed; it's very late. Too late for little girls. But I thank you for waiting up for me, and for the coffee."

"You're welcome. Is it good?"

John Washington smiled. "Why, yes, it is good."

"I'm glad because I've never made it before. I used to make tea for Papa Maguire, but I'd never made coffee. And Daddy, I'm not a little girl, you know. Not anymore."

John Washington looked up. "No," he said. "I see that now."

When Vivian had gone to her room, John started for bed. He turned off the kitchen light and locked the door, but then instead of going to the bedroom, he sat back down in the dark and smoked another cigarette. He slept in the living room on the sofa. He had, at that moment, rather lie down next to a Christmas tree than next to his wife.

Osceola John Washington Jr. was born late on Christmas night. John Washington spent most of the day in the waiting room at the hospital with Mrs. Malone. He came home around noon, at Mrs. Malone's urging, to give Vivian and Clara their presents (Vivian was very surprised to get besides the identical gifts that she and Clara always received, a circus wagon—did Daddy think she was *four*?) and have Christmas dinner with them, and then went back to the hospital. His son was born at eleven o'clock that night. When he went in to see Antoinette, she was just coming out from under an anesthetic. John didn't think she even knew he was there. She was muttering to herself. Something about Gilbert. John leaned closer to hear her.

Vivian's dog had chewed up a pair of bedroom slippers of Antoinette's the night before, Christmas Eve. The ones with the feathers. The dog had thought he'd found a bird. Antoinette, whose nerves were in shreds, had flown into a rage. Vivian had rushed to the dog's defense. John had had to step in and make peace. John supposed that now in her mind Antoinette was back home, chastising the dog. "Hush," he said to her. "It's all right."

"I tried to stop him, you know," Antoinette said, her eyes flying open.

"Yes, I know you did. He's an evil-tempered brute altogether," John said. "I've locked him out of the house."

"Did you?" Antoinette asked, and then shut her eyes and fell silent, for she was suddenly awake and desperately trying to make sense of the conversation she found herself in the middle of. Afraid of what she might already have said.

"Yes," John said. "Did you see our baby?"

Antoinette shifted her head on the pillow. She answered carefully: "I don't quite remember. Because of the ether. Have you seen him?" He hadn't, she knew, or he wouldn't be smiling.

"Not yet. Everyone has been saying how brave you've been. I wanted to see you first to thank you."

"I think really you should go home to the girls, John. It's terribly late. You can see the baby in the morning."

"Emmy's with them. I don't want to wait."

Antoinette reached out for his hand. "Couldn't we see him together? They won't let me see him until tomorrow. Please wait. For my sake." She began to cry. "It's really not fair—I'm his *mother*! But they hide him away from me and they let other people see him."

John was annoyed, but in the circumstances he did not want to press the matter. "I'm not exactly other people. I'm his father— but if it's this important to you, I guess we can both wait until morning."

"Yes," Antoinette said. "It's important."

"Don't cry anymore, then," John said. And he kissed Antoinette's white forehead. "Go to sleep, little bit. I'll see you and Osceola John Washington Junior in the morning."

When John walked out and the door shut behind him, Antoinette closed her eyes and drew a ragged breath. She had seen the baby. Maybe, she thought, he will look different in the morning.

He didn't.

-- ❧ --

When John first saw his son, he was afraid Antoinette would hear his heart beating from across the room. Jesus H. Christ, but the boy was blacker than the inside of Toby's hat! Nestled in the snowy bassinet the baby was at least a shade darker than Billy was. Had been. Thank God his eyes were green like Antoinette's. And his hair plentiful, straight and long. God bless the Seminoles; they had come through once again.

He said, "He's beautiful." And trying to plant a seed, he added, "He looks so like you."

Antoinette, who'd been holding her breath, let it out in a rush. "Yes," she said.

For God's sake! Were they all blind? No one, not Dr. Knox, or the nurses or even Mama and now John, had said anything about the baby being so dark. And of course, he looked nothing like her! What was John thinking of? He looked nothing like any of them. She had studied the baby's face while he slept beside her bed. He looked exactly as she had known he would. Like the loathsome Gilbert. But Mama always said that people saw the likenesses they expected or needed to see. And *that* was turning out to be truer than scripture.

When Mama and Papa Maguire came up later to see the baby, John went on and on about his great-great-grandfather, the Seminole chief. "They've never surrendered, you know," John said to Papa, who had smiled gravely and replied, "Ah, nor have I, John."

-- ❧ --

Immediately there was confusion as to what people could and couldn't call the baby. Holding him for the first time, Mama had called him her Johnny-Boy, but John Washington spoke up to say that under no circumstances was a son of his going to be called Johnny. John's father had forbidden the use of all diminutives. "Make them say your right name," he'd said. "Or make up your own name. But never let them call you by some torn-off corner of it." John acknowledged that a junior needs a name distinct to himself, but John would be the one to choose it, not his mother-in-law.

"Well, what then?" Mama had reasonably demanded, for Antoinette had so far referred to the unfortunate-looking child only as "the Baby" and "It."

John called him Chief.

⁊

Two weeks later, Mrs. Malone said to Antoinette, "We can't call a little boy Chief, for heaven's sake. Chief is a dog's name."

"Call him whatever you like, then," Antoinette said, pushing up in the bed and lighting a cigarette.

She was almost sanguine. She was back home, the baby was born; she hadn't died and gone to hell, and no one, hard as it was to believe, obvious as it *should* have been, had guessed her secret.

She was only sorry now that she'd confessed all those sins to that priest in New Orleans. But he didn't know who she was, and she'd certainly never go back *there*. Not in a million years. Antoinette watched her mother feed the baby its bottle. "John's home so rarely he'll never know what you call him."

"Well, he rather does look like a little Indian brave," Mama said, smiling, watching Chief gulp the formula. He had an excellent appetite. "I can see what John means."

Antoinette didn't say anything. She picked up a magazine and began flipping through it back to front. Right now she was glad

enough of John Washington's Indian blood. It was certainly coming in *handy*, but even so, she thought John was a little *too* proud
of it. She would have thought he'd have the grace to be embarrassed. He certainly hadn't talked about being a quarter Indian
when he came courting! She had noticed his dark complexion,
certainly, but she had always assumed it was sunburn.

"What do you call him, darling?"

Antoinette looked up from her magazine. "What?"

"What do you call the baby when you're alone with him?"

"Chief. I call him Chief, too. Why not? I can't very well call
him Osceola John Washington Junior, can I?" Antoinette herself
did not care what the baby was called. John could call it by what
Mama thought was a dog name if he wanted.

"I was thinking we could call him Osceola."

"No. If we call him Chief, it's a sort of a joke we're telling on
ourselves. But if we call him Osceola, people could think we are
real Indians."

"Oh. You may be right. Should I put him down, or would you
like to hold him awhile?"

"Put him down." Why did Mama think she wanted to hold
him? Why ever would she want to *hold* him?

"You know, Antoinette, I'm going home tomorrow. It isn't fair
to Papa and Willie and the others to stay any longer. Now you're
well again."

"I don't *feel* well. Do you have to?"

"I have to." Mama placed Chief on his stomach in the bassinet,
and then stood a moment stroking his hair—so black, and so long
and, thank a merciful God, under the circumstances, so straight!
None of Mrs. Malone's babies had had any hair to speak of when
they were born, Antoinette included, and poor Willie had been
practically bald.

"Could you take him in the other room so I can sleep a little? I'm still so tired. I think I'll be tired the rest of my life."

"You won't have time." Mrs. Malone said briskly, and picked up the magazines from Antoinette's bed and stacked them neatly on her bedside table.

"I wish you could stay longer."

"I know."

Antoinette was asleep in seconds. Mrs. Malone lingered a minute, looking from her daughter's face to her baby's. From the Irish rose to the Indian chief. Really, she thought, no one would credit it! She was just a little worried about what outsiders might say. Hurtful comments some might make. Soon people would begin calling to see the baby. There wasn't a way in the world to stop them! Perhaps if they were to dress the baby in darker colors so there would be less contrast . . . he looked *so* very dark against the white linens.

Mrs. Malone remembered Vivian talking about her Indian ancestors. Mrs. Malone had not thought much about it at the time. Children exaggerated so. Vivian particularly! But the Washington Indian blood was a subject on which, it seemed now, Vivian had not hyperbolized.

Really, Mrs. Malone thought, carrying her grandchild into the living room, if you didn't know better, if you didn't know about the Washington's Indian blood, if you were, say, to see Chief in a baby buggy outside a store, it was *just* possible you would think he was a little colored baby. So perhaps it was as well to call him Chief, Mrs. Malone decided. Maybe John had known exactly what he was doing when he chose the child's nickname.

Vivian, to her own and everyone else's surprise, was absolutely crazy about Chief. She spent the whole of her Christmas vacation lurking around the house, waiting for opportunities to hold him, or even just to sit near him and watch him sleep.

She liked to place her hand on Chief's back so she could feel it rise and fall, and to rest her chin on the edge of his bassinet so she could inhale his odd, new smell. Sometimes, to her delight, he made little snuffling noises just like a puppy's. She thought him quite the prettiest baby she'd ever seen. But Vivian was alone in her enthusiasm. The grown-ups, all of them, seemed nervous around the baby. Even Mama Malone. And Vivian did not think Antoinette liked him at all. She was always asking Mama to take him out of her room—where he supposedly slept. And when she did have the baby with her in the bed, she propped him against a pillow like a stuffed toy and then went back to looking at her magazines until he began to cry—then she rang for Emmy or Mama to take him away.

Daddy *talked* about him like he liked him. And he'd thought up his cute nickname. But, Vivian had noticed, he avoided touching him. As soon as Mama brought Chief out to the living room, Daddy found some excuse to leave. And at night Daddy slept in a guestroom, not with Antoinette and Chief.

"So as not to wake them," he'd said.

Vivian tried to talk to Clara about this. Clara said she didn't like Chief or not like him, he was an *infant,* for heaven's sake; what was there to like or not like?

"But he's so cute," Vivian persisted.

"He's hardly 'cute,' Vivian!" Clara burst out in exasperation. She had been sitting at her dressing table putting up her hair. She put down her brush and turned to look at Vivian, who was lounging across her bed, Gilbert the dog beside her. "Just between us, that baby looks but *exactly* like a pickaninny."

"No, he doesn't," Vivian said, shocked. But he did. Sort of. "He looks, he looks like a papoose, like Daddy said."

"Same difference," Clara sniffed.

"It's not the same at all. He's our brother. You shouldn't *say* that."

"I can say anything I want. Anyway, Maureen was the first to say it—that I *know* about. She remarked on the resemblance to me the first time she saw him. And *she's* Antoinette's sister! I'm not claiming him; they can't make me. In any event, by the time he's old enough to count, I'll be grown-up and moved away. You will be, too, you know. It would be a waste of your time to go getting attached to him."

Vivian had not thought of this. But Willie's older brothers and sisters were grown and moved away, and Willie was still their little brother. So she didn't think that in a real family, a regular family, this should matter. "We'll maybe be more like aunts than sisters to him later, but he'll still be our brother."

"Have you thought what other people are going to say when they see him? Do you really think that Maureen and I are the only people who are going to notice what he looks like?"

"They are only going to notice how cute he is." But would they? She knew not even Mama thought Chief was cute. Not really cute. Whenever Mama changed him, she talked to him and she always said, "Well, you'll just have to *do*, won't you?"

"How do we really know Daddy is his daddy?"

"I don't know what you are even talking about."

"Nothing," Clara said. "Forget it."

"What do you mean, Clara? How could anybody else be his daddy? Antoinette and Daddy are *married*."

Clara bestowed upon her younger sister a pitying look. She

checked her hair and picked up her bag. She and Maureen were going to a King's Night party at Odelle Morrison's. She had to wonder if she would have received an invitation if anyone outside of family had seen her new baby brother yet. Very likely, she reflected bitterly, *not*.

꧁

It was mid-January, and the first time that John Washington had driven into Sylvan since the night Billy died. The usual boys were waiting for him on the porch of Dixie Home. The cold snap that brought snow to the northern part of the state at Christmas was past, but it was a raw day, and dark clouds that held a cold rain were moving in rapidly from the west. Hank came out on the porch to greet him.

"Well?" he shouted.

"A boy, Hank. A son and heir."

"There you go. We been wondering how you all had made out. Come on in."

Every boy in Sylvan, except one, was already at work on the Essex. John flipped a fifty-cent piece in the air to the oldest boy, but he could not bring himself to his usual banter with them.

Irene and Odessa were taking first of the year inventory. Odessa was atop a stepladder, dusting and counting items on the high shelves, while Irene wrote down the information in a ledger. They both turned to him at the same moment. "John Washington!" Irene cried. "We have been talking about you all day. Tell us your news."

"What news is that, Irene? Hello, Odessa."

Odessa nodded. She had never looked down on John before. She rather enjoyed the vantage.

"You know exactly what we want to know—just tell us and be quick about it."

"Okay, I already told Hank outside, it's a boy. And his name is Osceola John Washington Junior."

"Well, that's wonderful. And how's your wife?"

"She's fine, thank you, Irene."

"Well you can't call a baby all *that*. What are you all going to call him for him to answer to?"

"We're calling him Chief," John said. "On account of the fact he looks like a red Indian." John caught Odessa's eye.

"You can't call a human baby Chief!"

"Already did. How have you all been?"

"Tolerable. Come back to the kitchen—let me get you something to eat," Irene said, coming out from behind the counter. "Watch the store, Odessa."

"Yes, ma'am." Odessa came down from the ladder.

John was still leaning on the counter. "How you holding up, Odessa?"

She pushed her hair back. "I'm fine, thank you. Congratulations on that new Indian baby of yours."

"Thank you." John turned toward the others. "I wish you all could see him. Looks like Geronimo if he looks like anybody. About to broke his mother's heart when she saw him."

"Don't talk like that about your own child," Hank said. "If you ain't prepared to lie and say how cute he is, ain't nobody else going to either. That's what happened to me. My mama never stood up for me." Hank said.

"Well damn," John laughed, "I got to say my boy's beautiful, then. I surely don't want what's happened to you happening to a child of mine."

⁂

That night before bed John excused himself, saying he needed to walk off his dinner. Hank asked if he wanted company, but John said no. He needed out of the Stewart's hot kitchen and away from Irene's voice—which sawed at his nerves worse than usual that night—away from the coffee cups and the cakes and the everlasting pies.

He went out through the store, turned left, and walked along the verge of the road. He turned up the collar of his coat; it was late and no cars passed. When he came to the wagon ruts that led down to the cemetery by the little church, he turned again. The ground was hard, and his leather soles rang on rocks. When he reached Billy's grave, he stopped there and regarded it for a long time. It was already sunk down a little from the rain and snow of late December and early January. There were flowers stuck in jars, and someone had placed seashells around its edges. There was no marker, but John Washington would do something about that tomorrow. He'd brought one up from New Orleans; it was wrapped in burlap, in the trunk of the Essex.

The night was quiet but for the wind sighing in the tops of the pines and a solitary killdeer crying in the field. Not once during the evening at the Stewarts', John realized now, had anyone said Billy's name. Though John was pretty sure that everyone had been thinking about him. Perhaps this was why he had felt he needed to visit the grave tonight. Alone. To see it with his eyes, to learn the truth of it again, deep inside himself where all John Washington's painful truths had to be rehearsed over and over before his mind could hold them. He had picked up a stick as he walked along the highway; now he laid it down. "Billy," he whispered, "here's a good stick."

The wind was picking up, John Washington turned back to the road, but he didn't go back to Dixie Home, he crossed the road and turned up a path that would bring him to Odessa's with the fewest people seeing him. Sylvan was even smaller and lonelier in the winter than it was in the summer, when people sat out and

their children played amongst the houses until late. Now all the
doors were closed, and the windows shuttered. When John
knocked at Odessa's, there was no one to see him do it and no one
to see her answer, or to see the two of them standing on the tiny
porch, holding on to one another as if for dear life while an icy
rain began to fall from the sky, like a judgment.

⁂

Irene was locking up the store for the night. Against the Little
Rock and Dallas burglars who peopled her dreams. She stepped
for a moment out onto the porch, crossing her bare arms against
the cold, to look at the rain spout at the edge of the porch eaves to
see if Hank had mended it like she'd told him to. He hadn't. The
water was pouring onto the steps like somebody was standing on
the porch roof emptying a bucket. Well, if he'd rather replace a
whole set of rotting steps than wire up a rain gutter, she guessed it
was his business. She peered down the highway looking for John
Washington. She was pretty sure she knew where he'd been going.
To the churchyard. She'd gone many a day.

She'd brought out some mason jars and set them there for the
flowers that people had begun bringing and leaving at the grave.
It was really the strangest thing. People that hadn't ever said his
name out of their mouths when he was alive, now were bringing
little things, marbles, and cigar bands, and such, and leaving
them on his grave. He was being invoked to intercede on people's
behalf. Sometimes they left notes on little scraps of notebook
paper, names mostly: "Leroy R." or just "Little Mary." Irene herself stood there and talked to him like he was alive. She could
only hope nobody else had seen or heard her. Standing there like
a big old fool, talking to a little dead colored boy. But you could
really talk to Billy. You could tell him things you hadn't told a living soul. Certainly things Irene would never have told the real

Billy, had he been alive. After all, he was colored, and barely five, ignorant as dirt—why, she'd just began teaching him his ABCs when he died. But there had been something in his eyes. When he looked at you, you stayed looked at. He really saw you. Saw a you that even you, peering into the peeling, streaked mirror in your bedroom in the dusty, yellow light of a late, hot August afternoon, had never seen. Saw you and forgave you. And loved you still. Because somehow he understood. It was a crazy feeling, she knew that because one night she'd tried to explain it to Hank, and he'd *told* her it was crazy. Flat out. Not meaning anything unkind, she knew—because he'd kept his voice low, and he'd called her sug. And probably it *was* crazy, and she didn't care. She would go ahead talking to Billy as long as he went on listening.

As she slipped the bolt across the door to the store, she saw a lantern bobbing through the settlement. Someone was coming toward her; she opened the door a few inches and looked out through the curtain of rain. The someone was whistling "Bye-Bye Blackbird." It's just John, Irene thought. She gently closed the door. She would pretend not to have seen him. As she always had.

It was the next day. Tom Anderson and Hank Stewart were struggling to lift the marker for Billy's grave from out of John's car trunk. John Washington had backed the Essex almost to the gravesite, but could bring it no farther because of the mud from the heavy rain of the night before. The memorial was still shrouded in burlap, and the men had no idea what they were straining to lift and carry, but they knew because John had told them, that it was made of concrete, and they knew that it was the heaviest thing they'd lifted in their lives—and both men's lives had been full of heavy lifting.

John Washington, for reasons, as always, unquestioned, was directing their movements, but carried no part of the burden. Even so, he contrived to appear the most aggrieved of the three.

"No, goddamn it, Tom, swing it up on this side. This side. *This* side! Jesus H. Christ, man! Watch my paint, could you?" John Washington took out a handkerchief and wiped the back of his neck. Irene and Odessa were standing under some pines out of the way.

"Why, I can't wait to see it," Irene said. "Did he tell you what it was?"

"No, ma'am. He told me he was getting something for Billy's grave, but he don't say what it is."

"It's bound to be nice, John has such beautiful taste. I guess he must have been born with it."

"Yes, ma'am." Odessa was being careful to keep her hands in her apron pockets, for she was wearing the ring John had given her, and she did not want Mrs. Stewart to see it and ask its significance. Well, it didn't *have* a significance, did it? Not really. It couldn't. The world had conspired to rob Odessa of ever having anything with *that*.

John had taken his jacket off and hung it on the car door. While Hank and Tom maneuvered the monument to the head of the grave, slipping up to their ankles in the mud, John frowned fiercely and rolled up his sleeves. Watching him, Odessa couldn't stop a smile. She took her right hand out of her pocket and covered her mouth, pretending to cough.

"Which side up?" Hank gasped.

John rushed up to them to say, "The other way, damn it."

When the men finally had it standing up, John beckoned at Irene and Odessa. "Come on over closer. I want you all to see this."

Hank and Tom stepped away, wiping their palms on their

trouser legs, their eyes still wild, their mouths open gulping air. John took a silver penknife from his watch pocket and began sawing ineffectually at the rope that held the burlap.

"For heaven's sake," Irene called, "*Help* him, Hank!"

Hank wondered as he fumbled in his overall pocket for his jackknife, how in the world John did it. Here he'd likely herniated himself, his clothes were ruint, and the whole time John had stood around not doing thing one but shifting his weight from one expensive shoe to another, and rolling up his sleeves! Like he might be going to do something! Lord. And then Irene has to holler at *him* to help John Washington.

"That's all right, Hank," John said magnanimously. "I think I've got it."

He stepped back, and the burlap fell away. "There," he said.

It was a statue of a small boy, seated on a tuft of marsh grass, holding a fishing pole. It was not a funerary statuary at all, but a decoration for a backyard fishpond.

"Don't that look *exactly* like Billy, though?" Hank exclaimed joyously, coming closer and bending down to look it. He wore a wide and wondering smile.

"That day he caught his first fish?" John said to him, and they both stood there looking from each other to the statue.

"That's right," Hank said, remembering. "That's his very expression! To a tee."

Irene, who had been expecting to see a figure of her Redeemer, or at the very least a lamb, didn't know what to think. Odessa said nothing; she was busy marveling at the boy's white face with its painted-on freckles and rosebud-pink lips.

"Of course, I know it's not what you all were expecting," John said. "To tell the truth, it isn't what I went to get. Not at all! I intended to get a lamb. Maybe an angel. But I looked at all those sad statues they had, and I didn't like them. I didn't want one of them setting on Billy's grave for all eternity, making us all even sadder than we already are. And then as I was leaving around to the side the man had these yard statues, and I saw this one and I thought why not get something that would remind us of Billy like he was when he was alive."

"White?" Odessa asked.

"What? No. Christ Almighty, I couldn't choose the *color*, Odessa," John said, and thought, When could you ever *choose* the color? He kept finding that out. "This is the only one of these Little Fisherman he had."

Irene spoke up in John's defense: "Well, John, it kind of startled me at first 'cause I was expecting something so different, you know, but what you say makes sense." After all, it wasn't like John Washington was a religious man. And poor little Billy'd probably never even been baptized. "And I never seen Billy happier than he was that day he caught that big old fish. Did you, Odessa?"

"No, ma'am," Odessa said. "I never did."

"And see here—" John Washington bent to the base of the statue. "—I had a brass plate engraved with his name and his dates."

Irene and Odessa approached nearer to read the brass plate: BILLY JEFFERSON. DIED DECEMBER 16, 1932. BELOVED OF ODESSA POWELL AND JOHN WASHINGTON.

Irene supposed that John, being a man, had no idea how the pairing of the two names that way looked. But poor John, he was so pleased about it, and he'd meant so well. She was sure it must have cost a great deal of money.

Odessa reached her hand out of her pocket again, this time to brush at a tear. There was now one place in this world where her name appeared linked with John's. A cemetery.

*

By the next day when Irene stole away to talk to Billy, somebody had already placed a frayed straw hat on the statue's head. And the next there was a necklace of acorns around its neck. Every day it was something different. Everybody, seemed like, wanted to give it something—a blue-jay feather, a button, a piece of broken mirror. Because of the fishing motif, people began leaving cans of sardines and Jack Mackerel at its base.

"I'll tell you what," Irene said some months later when she was talking to Billy, "Some of these people that come to see you got to be crazy as spotted pups! Like you'd pay any more attention to somebody that brought you a can of tuna fish than you would to somebody come empty-handed with an open heart. You're more patient with them than I'd be, Billy. I don't mind telling you."

Over time, as the weather stripped the Little Fisherman's paint, it came to look more and more like Billy Jefferson.

⸎

"Black as the inside of Toby's goddamn hat." John said again, splashing more whiskey in their glasses. It was later that night.

"Who is this Toby you always quoting at me? That's what I need to know," Odessa said, picking up her glass. They were sitting at Odessa's table, and they were both a little drunk.

"This is serious, goddamn it, Odessa. Nobody outside the family's gotten a good look at him, except for the doctor. When they do, there could be hell to pay."

"What do Antoinette say?"

"Not a damn thing."

"She must say something, John."

"I'll tell you what she does: She sleeps. She hasn't really talked to me since I took her to New Orleans in November. For a while I thought she was getting religious on me, now since the baby's come that seems to have passed off. But she's closemouthed."

"Then nobody's straight-out said it?"

"Did you really think somebody was going to stand up in my living room and yell, 'Look out, your baby's a nigger!' Jesus Christ Almighty!" John put the flask back in his pocket. "I do believe you've had enough of this. No, it's what they *don't* say that's worrying me. You know how people normally act around a new baby, how they can't say enough about it. They fall all over themselves to say how cute he is, how he looks like you or his mother, what a cute nose it's got . . ."

Odessa nodded.

"Well, we haven't had any of that. Antoinette's mother brings Chief in the living room to rock him and people hold books up in front of their faces, or they fiddle with the radio—nobody says word one about poor little Chief. Me included. Because of what they're afraid of saying, you understand, they don't say anything."

"Maybe nobody *going* to say anything, then. How dark is he? Really."

"Look in a mirror," John said shortly.

"Somebody going to say something."

"Isn't that what I just said?" John lit a cigarette. "Actually, Vivian treats the baby sweet. But I'm damned if I know why, up to now the only thing that girl ever thought was cute was a dog."

Chapter 15

The baby was crying and crying. Antoinette did not think she could stand it much longer. Why had Mama gone home and left her alone? She rang the bell by her bed vigorously. She'd sent Emmy to the drugstore, but she should have been back hours ago. Where was she? She was probably right here in the house. Hiding. She must hear the baby crying. People downtown, inside offices, inside shops, must hear him. When he had started crying, he had sounded merely plaintive, but now he was making a noise like yellow jackets in a jar.

Antoinette got out of bed and walked across the room to the bassinet. She peered down at him. The crying was making him even darker. She hurried to pick him up and tried to hold him up to her shoulder the way Mama did. But the baby arched his back and screamed all the louder. A high-pitched, furious scream. She seemed to be making things worse. She laid the baby back down. "Wait," she told him. "Stay here," she added, panicked, looking over her shoulder at the baby as if she expected it to rise up and follow her.

Antoinette padded out into the living room looking for Emmy, but the room was empty save for Vivian's dog, asleep in a patch of sun across the rug near the piano. Gilbert the dog raised his head briefly and then settled his chin back on his paws. He kept his half-closed eyes warily trained on Antoinette.

The baby's crying seemed to fill every square inch of space in the house. It was as loud in the living room as it had been in the bedroom. Antoinette trailed a finger over the dining table as she passed it. Really, she didn't think that woman had turned a hand since the baby was born. Why she hadn't even dusted! It was really too much. Antoinette absolutely hated her. Really she did. She had hated her on sight, and would *never* have hired her if Mama hadn't made her do it. It had been a mistake to let Mama override her judgment—a mistake Antoinette was now more than ready to remedy. She wouldn't be surprised if Emmy knew about Gilbert. She might have been hiding *that* day, too. In fact, Antoinette was nearly certain that she had been.

She burst through the swinging door into the kitchen. Antoinette turned around in the middle of the room, her pink rosebud gown flaring out around her ankles. The door to the broom closet was ajar. Was she hiding in there? Antoinette flung it open. Mops and a bucket fell out on the floor with a clatter. The baby's crying got louder. How *could* it? Thinking about how she'd been so cruelly abandoned by all the people who were supposed to love her, Antoinette began to cry, too. The girls were at school. John was gone; John was *always* gone. Mama had gone home to be with her precious Willie and her disgraceful old papa. Wasn't it Emmy's *job* to be here? Antoinette reflected bitterly that she had been unable to even *pay* anybody to love her. She would have to fix the baby's bottle herself. Her head was splitting. Where was

Emmy with her pills? The screaming was doing something to the inside of her head. Antoinette put her hand up to her temple. It felt as if a little spring inside her head had broken loose; she'd *heard* it, even over the baby's crying. She couldn't seem to think; not really think. The blue light that lit her dreams bathed everything. The baby cried and cried and cried.

❦

Not very far away, just across the bayou from Vivian and Willie's camp, at the Callahan's, Gilbert sat drinking under a magnolia whose boughs swept the lawn. Gilbert hadn't been able to stop thinking about Mrs. Washington since what Cassie always called "the incident." He'd expected something else to happen ever since Mrs. Washington shot at him, for the other shoe to drop. The way it seemed to Gilbert, Mrs. Washington trying to kill him like she'd done was a kind of a story. A story he'd been in. A story in which he'd been every bit as important as Mrs. Washington. But the story still didn't have an ending. Beside him sat Emmy Clegern.

"Little darling, have another sip of this here," Gilbert said, and passed the bottle back to Emmy. "Maybe it could settle your thinking."

Emmy knew she needed *something* to settle her thinking. She was probably already in the worst kind of trouble. Mrs. Washington had sent her downtown after her headache pills at the drugstore 'cause she didn't want to wait on the delivery man.

"Just walk fast," she said. "It's not but about a mile. And hurry straight back."

So Emmy had got the pills, but then she'd stopped off at The Lucky Pig to get herself an RC to drink on the walk home.

Gilbert had been there, and he'd come up to her like they was old friends. He'd asked her all kind of questions about what was going on at the Washington house. Some about the new baby but mostly about Mrs. Washington.

"Girl, I been wanting to talk to you for the longest time," he'd said.

Emmy never remembered hearing that sentence before. "What you been wanting to talk to me about?"

"Well, one thing, when I quit your place I stepped out of there so quick, I left some belongings in the toolshed. Some good leather work gloves and a lunch bucket, too. I been afraid to go back for them on account Mr. Washington say he see me there, he going to shoot me for a trespasser."

The whole time he was talking, Gilbert had been pouring liquor from a jar into Emmy's RC—just a little at a time. She'd said to stop it, but he'd done it anyhow, and laughed, and the man behind the counter, Jake, he'd laughed too. Like it was a good joke they was playing, so she'd drunk it, so they would know she wasn't one of those people you couldn't joke with. Grandpa always said he couldn't abide folk who couldn't take a joke on themselves.

"You know I always wanted to get to know you, but you always too busy to talk to the yardman," Gilbert said, real sorrowful like.

"I got to get back."

"Here," Gilbert said, and took Emmy's elbow, "You going back to the house now? I just working across the way from you all now, at the Callahan's. I'll walk you."

But walking home, the liquor went to Emmy's head, and Gilbert said, "You better come rest a minute. You don't want to go back like this."

And that's how she wound up under the magnolia with Gilbert.

_ℓℓ_

"Now," Gilbert said, looking off across the bayou and talking real soft, "I *thought* I remembered you talking funny, but I must have been remembering wrong, on account of you ain't talking funny *now*."

"I ain't?"

"Uh-uh. Maybe you just needed a little drink to relax. Probably you was just nervous them other times."

"Give that here to me a minute," Emmy said, and reached for Gilbert's bottle. But it was empty.

"You going to get them things for me?" Gilbert said.

"Come for them tomorrow night when Mrs. Washington in bed. I got to get back now. Mrs. Washington, she ain't feeling good yet, and she alone with the baby."

"It don't matter," Gilbert said in a soothing voice. "She ain't going to hurt her own baby."

"No," Emmy said. But Emmy knew if she was walking in her sleep, there wasn't nothing that woman wouldn't do.

_ℓℓ_

Even before Vivian opened the door, she could hear Chief crying. She found him alone in Antoinette's bedroom. He had rucked up his sheets and his blankets and was lying with his face pressed into the side of the bassinet. The poor little baby's cheek was marked with wicker stripes.

"Poor little Chief," she said, rocking him in her arms. "It's okay. You're all right. I'm here." Where in hell *was* everybody?

Carrying Chief on her shoulder, patting his back, Vivian went into the kitchen looking for Emmy. There were some mops and brooms on the floor, and a baby bottle lay broken in the empty sink. Chief was starting to calm down. He'd stopped crying and was hiccoughing.

"Emmy?" Vivian called. But there was no answer. There was blood in the sink and on the floor, and Vivian followed it to Emmy's room at the very back of the house, where instead of Emmy, she found Antoinette—curled up on Emmy's little iron cot. Her hand was wrapped in a bloodstained bath towel.

"Candy?" Vivian whispered.

Antoinette did not stir.

Vivian closed the door and went back to the kitchen just as Emmy came in the back door. "Where have you *been*?" Vivian asked.

"I had to go out," Emmy said vaguely. "Who broke the baby's bottle?"

"Candy, and she's cut herself; we should call Dr. Knox. I think she's fainted or something. She's back in your room. Chief was all by himself, screaming the house down when I got home. This is getting to be a goddamn madhouse."

Emmy still stood with her back to the kitchen counter. She doesn't look right, Vivian thought. "What's wrong with you?"

"Ain't nothing wrong," the woman said. But her eyes were wide and staring, and her hand, when she reached up to remove her hat, shook ever so slightly.

"Then call Mama Malone and tell her Candy hurt herself and to please, please come over here," Vivian said.

Emmy burped, and put her hand up to her lips in a dainty gesture. "'Scuse me," she said. She heard her own voice, and she hadn't tripped over either syllable; maybe there was something to this relaxing.

"Jesus H. Christ," Vivian said then, and she went to call Mama herself.

Emmy sat down at the kitchen table, put her head on her arms, and passed out.

❧

It took fourteen stitches to close the gash in Antoinette's hand. It looked like the Hand of the Mummy. Mama had taken the girls and the baby back to her house. *And* the girls' wretched dogs. Antoinette had tried to tell Mama how Emmy had caused the whole thing, but she hadn't believed her. Mama had made a pet of Emmy. Like she had of Willie. Probably because of her harelip. Mama only loved the lame and the halt. It didn't seem like she could really love a *normal* person.

Her right hand throbbed painfully, but she didn't mind; she would willingly gash open her own hand every night of the world if it meant that someone would take that baby out of her sight. The house felt big and airy with the baby gone. And so blessedly quiet.

Antoinette finished her soup and rang for Emmy.

"Take this away," Antoinette said.

Emmy had a headache, too. But worse, she was heartsick over letting Mrs. Malone down. "Can I bring you something else, Mrs. Washington?"

"Not now, Emmy."

Antoinette picked up a decorating magazine and held it open in front of her.

Later, Emmy came in to help Mrs. Washington get ready for sleep. Because Dr. Knox had said that Mrs. Washington couldn't get her bandage wet. Antoinette stood by the washbasin while Emmy washed her face with a warm washcloth. Emmy had to bend her knees a little on account of Mrs. Washington being so short. She rinsed out the cloth and went over her face again. She never got used to how white a person Mrs. Washington was. She was white as paper. White as flour. The whitest person in the world, probably. A person had to wonder how it was her baby was most dark as Emmy herself.

"Emmy, do you ever see Gilbert when you go uptown?"

"That dog?"

"Not the dog. You know who I mean."

"No. I never seen him," Emmy lied.

"You've *never* seen him? That's funny, because *I've* seen him. Uptown when I've gone to the picture show."

"Oh," Emmy said. "I maybe seen him like that. Yes, I remember, I seen him once. Uptown. Like you said. But I ain't seen him to *talk* to." Emmy had a hard time getting this out. There was likely something to what Gilbert had said about being relaxed and talking straight, because right now each word was sticking to the top of her mouth like it was rolled in molasses and pinfeathers. She wondered how Mrs. Washington could have found out so soon about her seeing Gilbert. She prayed she didn't know nothing about the whiskey. She'd have to be real careful Mrs. Washington didn't see Gilbert when he came for his things.

"He wasn't much of a yardman," Mrs. Washington said. She'd picked up her hairbrush and was brushing her black hair back from her forehead with her left hand.

After Emmy had gone, Antoinette opened the drawer in her bedside table and took out a black velvet box. She opened it and stared at the yellow-pink, pear-shaped diamond pendant inside. John had given it to her on Christmas Eve. It had been his grandmother's. Looking at it made Antoinette feel better. Her breathing slowed, and her head felt clearer. She regarded it several moments before she closed the box and put it back in the drawer. When she closed her eyes to sleep, she could still see it.

Mrs. Malone decided the baby should sleep in Emmy's room at night, so Antoinette could get what Mrs. Malone called "good sleep," and recover her strength faster. So it was Emmy who got up with Chief in the night, Emmy who fed and rocked him, and Emmy who got up early to feed him again, before starting the family breakfast. Under this new regime, Antoinette, not surprisingly, did begin to feel a little stronger. Emmy, however, was soon exhausted.

John Washington came home from the road, but stayed hardly any time at all. He no sooner got home than he had to go down to New Orleans to confer with the Kraemer brothers about changes they wanted to make in his route. The few days he was home he seemed distracted and, Vivian noticed, spent most of his time out in the garage, and the rest of it listening to radio programs he normally made fun of or turned straight off. Vivian was sad to see him go away again so soon. Clara did not seem to care, and both Antoinette and Emmy, for reasons of their own, were relieved.

Antoinette would have been as happy if John Washington were to stay on the road for the rest of his life. She was very worried about getting pregnant again—she had no intention of repeating *that*—and although John hadn't approached her since before Chief was born, she felt safer when he was gone altogether.

Emmy was glad to see him go on account of Gilbert didn't come to the house when Mr. Washington was home. Of late, Gilbert had been coming over most every night, after Mrs. Washington was asleep. He said he didn't sleep good anymore. He said Cassie was mad at him. He and Emmy would sit out in the garage in the little chauffeur's room where Mr. Washington went to drink when he was home. At first, this made Emmy nervous, but she'd never had a man come calling on her before, and even if he was not exactly a young man, and was missing fingers, and always wanting to talk about Mrs. Washington, he was still company. And he brought along that special liquor of his that Emmy was beginning to think *did* make her talk better.

~

In mid-February, after John Washington had gone back to the road, it turned bitterly cold. On the fourth night of the cold snap, the gas grates in the living and dining rooms went out. Right before supper. Antoinette got on the phone and demanded that the installer come out and fix them that very night. But despite pleas and finally threats, no one would come out until morning.

Banging down the phone, Antoinette said, "What am I supposed to *do*?"

"We could go to Mama Malone's," Vivian suggested. They were all in the kitchen for warmth, where Emmy was cooking supper.

"Pack everything and troop all the way over there for just one night? No thank you."

Antoinette sat down in the breakfast nook and lit a cigarette.

"Shouldn't we bring Chief's bassinet in here where it's warmer?"

"You want my baby to sleep in a *kitchen*?"

"Well, it's the only really warm room right now."

So when Vivian and Clara and Antoinette sat down to their supper, Chief's bassinet stood beside the stove. Emmy sat on a kitchen stool and ate her supper from the breadboard.

"It's cozy eating in here instead of the dining room. It's like we're in a log cabin or a wigwam or something," Vivian said.

"It's a *night*mare," Antoinette said. "Cooped up in this tiny room with all of you." The room *was* small and there *were* too many people in it, but by Antoinette's lights, any room with more than one person besides herself was crowded-up.

Clara ate silently.

"If your father were ever home, this wouldn't be happening. I cannot do everything myself."

"*Your* father's never home either," Vivian said, without thinking.

Antoinette put her fork down and looked hard at the girl. "Isn't it enough that we are packed into this kitchen like sardines? Must you provoke me?"

"No, ma'am," Vivian said. "I'm sorry. I only meant I thought you'd have expected it. That's all." Vivian went back to eating. Mama Malone had no trouble running *her* house, and Papa Malone was away longer and more often than Daddy was. Vivian was reminded of the first night that she and Clara had spent in this house—when the gas grates had gone out too, and they had huddled here in the kitchen for warmth, while Daddy went through the house relighting them. Only then Emmy wasn't there yet, and Chief was not even born.

How did people come from nowhere to be born? Where had Chief been before he was here—in the wigwam-kitchen, or the nightmare, however you looked at it. Where did God keep all those babies before he sent them to married people? In a big room up in heaven? And while Vivian was thinking about this, Chief woke up and began to fuss. Emmy picked him up and hushed him while the others finished their meal. In the kitchen light, much stronger and brighter than the pink-shaded light of Antoinette's bedroom, or the yellow lamp light of the living room, Vivian noticed that Chief was almost the same color as Emmy. She was glad that Clara's back was to him.

◦

Everyone except Emmy went to bed early. It would be, Antoinette decided, warmer in bed, and warmest asleep. But Emmy stayed up to scrub down the kitchen floor. Antoinette had said that if the baby was going to be in there it had to be clean. Really clean.

"Yes, ma'am," Emmy said. She didn't mind. The kitchen was warm, and anyway, she was expecting Gilbert.

◦

In their room, the girls were getting ready for bed. Vivian let her dog right under the covers.

"How can you *do* that?" Clara said.

"It's easy."

"Oh, I'm sure it is." Clara was sitting on the side of her bed, brushing her hair. "For *you*."

"Do you still think about Mother, Clara?"

Clara went on brushing and counting.

"Do you?"

"No," Clara said finally. Putting down the brush. "Not anymore. And now, I suppose, *you* do."

"I do. Because of Chief, I think. I never knew a baby before, because I was the baby, so I never got to see one—the way you did me. Anyway, now when I hold Chief, I think about Mother, because I think I know sort of how she felt. She must have loved me."

"Of course she loved you. She loved both of us."

"I know. I am saying I didn't *used* to know. Because by the time I could remember anything she was sick and I hardly ever saw her."

"We saw her every night."

"But I can't remember that. So anyway, now I think about her is all I was saying."

"Well, better late than never, I guess. I'm glad you remember her. Finally." Clara turned over on her stomach.

"I'm sorry I didn't believe you when you used to tell me how she loved us. I'm sure she meant for me to remember it. I just hope I haven't hurt her feelings too bad, is all."

"Even *you* can't hurt a *dead* person's feelings, Vivian."

"I think anybody can," Vivian said. "But you can make it up to them, too."

"And how do you think you are making it up to our mother?"

"By loving Chief, and holding him and telling him how cute he is, by paying him attention. Then she'll know that I know how she felt way back then, when I was a baby."

"I don't see what Chief has to do with any of this. You have a silly crush on that baby. Like you had a crush on your stupid dog. Like you have a crush on Willie Malone. You're just at that *age*."

"I'm not. Anyway, *you* have a crush on Maureen Malone, and you think *you're* so terribly old."

"Maureen is a close friend. We have a million things in common. There is a difference between a friendship and a crush."

"Fine," Vivian said. "But Clara, do you ever get the feeling that Mother is still watching us?"

"No."

"Really?"

Vivian was watching her sister. Or the back of her sister's head, which was all that she could see of her.

"Really," Clara said, and turned to look at Vivian. "*Why* would I think *that*?"

Vivian's eyes went to the bottom of Clara's bed. Where the white wispy thing still slept. Next to Clara's dog. "No reason," Vivian said. "Just sometimes I get this feeling, you know?"

"No I don't know, and I don't want to hear about it. I'm cold, and I'm going to go to sleep. If you have to keep talking, talk to your smelly old dog."

Clara always said that, and Gilbert wasn't smelly at all, but there was no point in saying anything, because Clara had already made up her mind about that. Clara was almost asleep, Vivian could tell by her breathing. She really didn't seem to know about the ghost. Why don't you sleep with me? Vivian whispered to it. Even if I can't remember what you looked like, I'm the one who thinks about you *now*. Clara's stopped even *missing* you, on account of Maureen.

She put her arm around Gilbert and put her nose under the covers where the air was warmer. The house was quiet. Vivian pushed her face into Gilbert's ruff. Daddy would be home tomorrow. She wondered what he was doing. She wondered if he was sleeping. She wondered if he missed them.

Chapter 16

Gilbert was walking through the tall grass of the pecan grove toward the Washington house. He stopped awhile, under a tree near the fence, and watched Emmy through the window over the sink. She was washing dishes, her face as bland as a boiled egg. Next, Gilbert came through the gate and into the yard and along the side of the house and took up his post at Mrs. Washington's window. Emmy had opened the drapes so he could see inside. He stood in the shadows for almost an hour, intently watching Mrs. Washington sleep and fingering a river stone in his pocket. A stone he'd been given by Madame Shebat; holding the stone in his hand, he was to keep his gaze on Mrs. Washington's face until his eyes wore out her face like the river had worn out the rock. When her face was as smooth as the stone in his pocket, he was to take it in the dark of the moon and drop it into still water. When the water closed over the stone, Antoinette Washington would fly out of his head and leave him in peace. Madame Shebat had warned Gilbert this could take a long time, but already Gilbert had worn away the two little lines between Mrs. Washington's eyes.

It was cold, and a strong wind was coming up; Gilbert moved away from Mrs. Washington's window and tapped at the kitchen window. Emmy smiled to see him.

In Antoinette's dream, she was asleep but not in bed. She wore the white chambray nightgown that Mama had embroidered with tiny pansies for her trousseau. She was banked by white flowers. The same flowers that she'd carried on her wedding day. Narcissi, lilies of the valley, and white roses. It was very cold. She was lying on some kind of platform; people were coming up and gazing at her. As always in Antoinette's dreams, all the people were black. And, as always, she supposed, they would want something. But what? What did they want *now*? She was really very, very tired. She tried to sit up, but she was too tired. She was holding in her hands, looped through her fingers, the diamond pendant that John had given her. She hoped no one would see it. They would be sure to want that.

Emmy came toward her; she was holding Chief in her arms. He was crying, but for once Antoinette couldn't hear him. She couldn't hear anything. Emmy sat down with Chief, who stopped crying and put his tiny balled fists up to his eyes. Gilbert stood at a distance, dressed all in white. He even wore white shoes and white gloves. Who did he think he was?

The people were sitting in pews, Antoinette realized now. They must be in some kind of a church. But it wasn't Saint Clare's. And it wasn't the cathedral. This church was little, its walls were white-washed, and there were open, rough-hewn beams above her head. Really, this is too far-fetched, Antoinette thought. What would she be doing in a church like this? She wouldn't be caught dead in a church like this one. It was probably out in the country somewhere; there certainly wasn't a church anything like this in town. Then she thought, Oh, no, I must be in a *colored* church. Then she saw John. He was coming toward her. But it couldn't be John. There were never any white people in her dreams not even Mama. It was, Antoinette thought, a kind of rule or something. But it was John, and he came straight up to her and laid a white lily on her breast. He was saying something. She watched his lips moving. He was saying, "I am sorry, little bit. Truly. Very, very sorry."

Sorry for *what*? What did he mean?

In the very cold heart of the night, a spark leapt up. It might have been from Gilbert's cigarette-end on the floor of the garage, probably it was, but it doesn't matter. The spark recognized no progenitor. It was a spark, no different from the first or the last spark, and it, in its turn, breathed upon a wood shaving, which curled over to a bundle of newspapers tied with twine. The tiny flame traveled on the twine, as on a wick—tied four times around the newspapers—and the papers began to smolder. And then went out. Or seemed to go out.

From over the grove and beyond Vivian and Willie's camp, and across the narrow arm of the bayou, the Callahans' dog was barking. The dog, a decrepit collie with a crippled back leg, had a sharp bark, like a fox. It barked three times and, there being no response, sniffed the wind, which was cold and rising, and then threw himself back down on the worn, cypress boards of the front porch, and closed his cloudy eyes to dream again of summer, and of squirrels playing carelessly in a leafy tree.

Emmy stirred. The barking dog had penetrated just far enough into her sleep that she raised her head a fraction of an inch above her pillow to listen for Chief. But the baby slept on, and the dog did not bark a fourth time, and Emmy, who was dead-drunk, did not quite wake. Later she would remember that she'd had a dream in which she'd heard Mrs. Roosevelt call out her name.

The newspapers were damp and were packed densely; the spark, which was on its third life, moved at a snail's pace, zigging and zagging through the shipping news and the obituaries and the Maison Blanche After-Christmas-Sale advertisements. Had you yourself been standing there looking at the bundle of newspapers on the Washington's garage floor, you would have seen . . . nothing at all.

Vivian could hear Mother calling.

"Vivian," the voice said, "I need you."

But Vivian, who was in the bamboo thicket by Grandmother's fishpond, bit her lip and did not answer. For she was not sure that the voice was Mother's. It sounded like Mother's voice, as best she could remember it—which was not at all—but it could be a trick. She waited in the bamboo.

Clara was deep in the Snow Dream. Under drifts and drifts of cold, cold snow. So far away that had the very sun in the sky exploded, the light and heat would not have reached her for hundreds of years.

⤆

In Sylvan, John Washington woke suddenly from a sleep that should have carried him safely up on the shores of morning. He sat up in the dark, his heart thudding so in his breast that his rib cage shook. Except for the sound of his own heart, the room was perfectly quiet. He looked down at Odessa; she was sleeping peacefully on her side. John put on his trousers and shirt and went out onto the porch, closing the door silently behind him.

The moon was just going down, and the stars beginning to blink out one by one. The wind was sighing. Miles down the road, a pair of headlamps swept a curve and then disappeared. He heard the high-pitched whine of tires on wet pavement, and then it was quiet again. John Washington took in a breath of the cold air. Had he been dreaming? And if so, what had he dreamed that jolted him awake so abruptly? He reached into his shirt pocket, pulled a Chesterfield from a crumpled pack, and lit it. In the flame of the match, he saw his shaking hand, saw the half-moons of his nails. Exhaling smoke, he leaned on the railing and gradually he felt a little steadier. If he could recall even a snatch of the dream, he might feel better. Anything that would explain the way he felt when he first bolted up out of sleep. Somewhere, in one of his worlds, John Washington knew, something was very wrong. But so much was wrong in so many of them. He didn't know how to begin to think about it. He brought more strong smoke deep into his lungs.

"John?" Odessa had slipped outside; he had not heard her. "What's wrong?"

"I don't know," John said. "Something, I think."

Odessa put her arms around his waist. She laid her face against his back. "Come inside," she whispered. "Ain't nothing you can do now. Not here in the dead of the night."

She was right. There was nothing he could do. There never *had* been anything he could do; he had only thought that there was.

But an hour later just at false dawn, John Washington was in his car, driving south, toward Myrtle.

~

In their bedroom, the Stewarts heard the Essex's engine turning over, and then they heard gravel scattering.

"That's John's car," Irene whispered, getting up and looking out the window. She was in time to see the lights sweep the front of Dixie Home as he turned back up toward the highway. "What time is it?"

Hank squinted at the Big Ben alarm clock, which he'd never once heard go off because he always woke exactly eight minutes before the time he'd set it for. "Four o'clock," he read.

"Did John say anything to you about leaving this early?"

"Didn't say nothing to me about nothing." Hank pulled a blanket over his bare shoulder. "Come to bed, Irene. It's cold, damn it."

"I'm coming. Do you think he's all right?"

"John's all right," Hank said. He had to get up in half an hour. "Don't worry about old John."

Irene got back in bed. She put her feet up against Hank's legs.

"Man! You walk to the window or to Alaska on them feet?"

Irene said, "Go back to sleep."

A rooster crowed.

"Goddamn it," Hank said, sitting up. "He went and woke up Petey! It's sure as hell morning *now*."

~

Driving south, despite the cold, John Washington had all the car's windows rolled down. He liked to hear the singing of his tires on the road, he had always liked being connected fleetingly to the landscapes he drove through by their sounds and smells. He'd been going to leave for home today anyway. He had told Odessa, and himself, that he was only starting a little earlier than usual.

"You could call home from the Stewarts, you know, John, if you so worried," Odessa had said from bed while she was watching John Washington dress. "That's the thing to do."

"Damn it. I don't want to call and wake people up, I want to get on my way. Get about my business. Hell, it's not like I *live* here."

"And you don't live there. Where *do* you live, John?" Odessa asked.

John ignored her. He picked up his change and his comb and his cigarettes and matches from the table and dispersed them in his pockets. "I live in my car," he said, turning around to face her. "Like Billy said. Damnation, Odessa, don't crawl me. I don't owe you or anybody else an explanation for when and where I go."

"I only asked where you lived."

"And I told you," John said. "In my goddamn car."

John banged out the door.

Odessa didn't go back to sleep. She put on the *Butterfly* records and played them straight through. Even the last one. The music was so bright and so red, it warmed the cold room. It was, Odessa thought, about as good as a stove.

❧

The stack of newspapers was in the corner of the garage near the door to John's little room—beside the red cans of gasoline lined up against the inside wall. So that when the gasoline cans did explode, they engulfed the garage in flames instantly.

Gilbert the dog and Snow White leapt down from the girls' beds, barking, their toenails skittered on the floor as they ran in frantic circles. The garage, visible from the bedroom windows, was a solid bank of fire. For the first moment the room was lit up bright as the sky outside.

Vivian was out of bed and on her feet before she was fully awake. Clara, who had burrowed beneath the pillows and blankets in a vain effort to keep warm in the snow dream, had to be dragged out of the bed by her sister.

"Clara! Get up. Hurry. Fire!"

Both dogs now scratched furiously at the bedroom door and barked.

"Where?" Clara said, looking up uncomprehendingly from her snowbank.

"Everywhere," Vivian said.

There was another explosion from the garage as another gas can went up. The bedroom window shattered.

"Jesus H. Christ," Vivian said. She grabbed Clara's wrist and pulled her along into the hall. The dogs streaked ahead for the kitchen, and the girls followed. There was smoke in the kitchen, and Vivian threw open the door and dragged Clara with her out on to the back lawn.

The wind, which had been blowing all night, now blew harder. While the girls stood there on the grass, not quite understanding how they'd gotten there, the dogs at their bare feet, the flames jumped from the garage to the morning-glory trellis, and from the trellis to the roof of the house. It took no time at all. The fire then began, invisibly, to eat through the attic.

Though neither Clara nor Vivian were aware of it, they were holding hands. The sky was black, and the flames so red and so bright it hurt to look at them. The dogs whimpered.

"Vivian," Clara whispered, "Where are the others?" Her teeth were chattering. The wind fanned the flames, which now ran across the roof and began licking at the back of the house. The girls moved back, toward the fence between the lawn and the grove. "Why aren't they here?"

"Chief," Vivian cried. "He can't run or anything. He can't do *anything* but cry."

"Maybe they went out the front," Clara said. "They could be looking for *us*." She tugged at Vivian's hand and they ran around the far side of the house, past Daddy's magnolia, to the front. But there was no one there. The white house was backlit by the fire, and in the eerie light the lawn glowed, and looked like a field of shimmering, melting emeralds. There were no flames at the front of the house. Vivian shook Clara's hand from her arm and ran to the front door.

"Don't go in," Clara called.

"I'm going to get Chief," Vivian called back, and she opened the door.

The most surprising thing was that the living room looked perfectly ordinary. It looked the way it always looked if you went in it at night when everyone else was sleeping. The clock ticked on the mantel. The piano keys shone ghostly white. But in the dining room it was warm and the air was smoky. Vivian pushed through the swinging door into the kitchen now filling with thick smoke, and leaned by the door a moment, coughing. She could hear a noise like cellophane crackling, and a fretful sighing sound. Vivian got down on the floor because it was cooler and not as smoky there, and crawled to the stove. Where Chief's bassinet had been at supper. But it was gone. He would be in Emmy's room then, Emmy would have taken him with her when she went to bed. But why hadn't she run out, like they had? Vivian opened the door from the kitchen to the back hall, which led back to Emmy's room and the utility room at the back corner of the house. But the fire was roaring inside the hall, and Vivian had to slam the door shut again. Even on the kitchen side, the door was so hot it burned the palms of her hands.

-ℓℓ-

At the Callahans', the noise of the first explosion woke Gilbert. He'd been asleep only an hour. He thought he'd been having one of his dreams about the war, and automatically reached for the bottle under his bed; then, through the window, he saw the glow in the sky.

"Cassie," he said, shaking her shoulder, "The Washington house." Gilbert was up at the window now. "It's on fire. The son of a bitch is burning down."

Cassie did not move. She was sick to *death* of hearing about the Washingtons. "What would you like me to do about *that*?" she asked.

-ℓℓ-

Antoinette's dream was so cold, so white, that it took the fire a long time to reach its way into it. When it did it first took the form of candles in the people's hands. Everyone was suddenly holding lit candles, which heated the air until it became so warm that the scent of all the white flowers became overpowering. It actually was the flowers, not the flames, that woke Antoinette. When she opened her eyes the room was light. It's late, Antoinette thought. It's probably after noon.

In the bedroom with the drapes drawn and the shades pulled, the light from the fire did look like late-afternoon summer light. But then Antoinette smelled the smoke. She ran to the windows and pulled back the curtains. She could see a solid block of fire where the garage had been, and cinders rained down from the roof right in front of the window.

Had she died? Was she in Hell then, after all? She stared out the window at the scene disbelievingly for a long moment, then, half-understanding, she ran for the door. Jesus, Mary, and Joseph, the house was on fire! She tried to get into the kitchen to go out the back door, but the kitchen was burning furiously. She ran instead through the dining room, which was only just going up, and into the living room—still untouched—and out the front door on to the front lawn.

Someone, in the dark and the confusion, Antoinette did not at first know who, ran up to her and pulled her away from the door. Antoinette was now uncertain *which* was the dream—the white cold church with the flowers, or the house fire. Both were horrible, and neither made the slightest sense. Strong arms encircled her. She let her weight rest against her rescuer.

His arms tightened. Then he spoke, "Mrs. Washington? Where's the baby at?"

Antoinette's head came up, her eyes opened wider, and she saw Gilbert.

"The baby, Mrs. Washington. Where's it at? Which room?"

He'd come for the baby. She'd wondered all along if he would.

"You can't have him," she said. "He's not even yours like you think. He's an Indian," she said, "Really!" And she laughed, and tried to push Gilbert away. Then she thought of a plan. "I have something else for you. I have something better than the baby." She was thinking of the diamond pendant. "I'll get it for you if you will stay here."

It's like before, Gilbert thought. She's sleepwalking, and she don't even know her house is on fire! He let go of her, afraid of frightening her worse; Grandma had said don't startle 'em, 'cause if you do, no telling *what* they could do next. He stood looking at her. She was so *little*. Standing there, barefoot, in her white nightgown, she wasn't as big as either of her stepchildren.

"I'll just go get it," Antoinette said, and turned back toward the door.

"No!" Gilbert shouted, and lunged at her, catching hold of her nightgown. "You can't go in there, Mrs. Washington. It's on fire! Listen to me. You got to *wake up*, Mrs. Washington."

But Antoinette pulled away, and the skirt of her gown tore away in Gilbert's hand. Antoinette ran back inside the house and slammed and locked the door against him. Gilbert beat on the door and called her name.

The living room, though smoky, was still untouched. Antoinette was having trouble breathing; she sat down on her chaise. She really did not know which was worse, the fire or the church, nor was there, she knew, any way for her to discover which was real. The only thing she knew for certain was that the very worst *possible* thing was Gilbert. Look! She held her nightgown out from her and examined the rent; he'd tried to tear her *clothes* off. But the door was locked now. She'd locked both locks. He couldn't get in. And she *wasn't* going to give him the baby. She might not give him the diamond pendant either. She would trick him. While he waited for her to come back with the pendant, she would sneak out the back and run to Mama's. She would do it in just a moment. When she caught her breath. Why was she so *cold*? She pulled up the shawl from the bottom of the chaise and covered herself. She would rest here a few moments more. What was that banging? He was trying to break the door down. But she'd had the builders put in a solid oak door with good Yale locks. John had complained of the expense, but see? She'd been right to do it. Because now she was safe. Completely safe. She pulled the shawl over her head to muffle the sound of the banging.

Antoinette did not hear the rafters give way, and she had already slipped back away into the white dream when they crashed into the living room—raining the fire down on top of her.

❧

Mr. Callahan had called the fire department, and at his wife's urging, he had called Mrs. Malone, too. John Washington was out of
town. Antoinette, the Callahans thought, would need her own
people around her. After they called, they got in their car and
raced to the fire.

At the same time that Antoinette had been feeling her way out
of the house by the front, Vivian was trying to flee at the back.
When she had seen the fire in the hall that led to Emmy's room,
when she had shut the door on it—knowing that she was shutting
it on Chief and Emmy forever—she had known herself to be
trapped. She was going to burn up. Vivian had only been surprised
that she was not more afraid. She thought briefly of how sad Daddy
was going to be, but reflected that like everything else that had
made Daddy sad, this simply couldn't be helped. Then, suddenly,
she felt all around her, something wonderfully, and surprisingly
cool. Cold, really. It was too smoky to see anything. She wondered
if a pipe had burst, maybe the room was filling up with cold water.

But it was not a burst pipe. It was the white thing that slept at
the bottom of Clara's bed, and had, in happier times, ridden on
the back of Snow-Ball. And this thing enveloped Vivian completely, finally curling like a cat around her neck and keeping the
heat and the smoke from the girl's face long enough that she was
able to stumble out the kitchen door to the backyard and safety.

Once outside, Vivian lay gasping on the grass; she could hear
voices and cars at the front of the house, and from town she heard
the three urgent blasts of Myrtle's fire whistle.

❧

The fire had been burning nearly three hours. Long enough for
Clara and Vivian to escape once, and for Vivian to escape twice.

And long enough for Antoinette to waken and run out blindly into the arms of, all people, Gilbert, and to choose the fire. Long enough for Gilbert and Mr. Callahan, together, to chop a hole with axes from the toolshed, in the windowless wall of the maid's room, where Emmy lay overcome by smoke on her cot. Long enough to pull out the insensible Emmy and the screaming Chief. Long enough for Mrs. Malone and her children and Papa Maguire to arrive and cluster in horror to watch Antoinette Washington's house burning to the ground. With Antoinette in it. Long enough for Myrtle's volunteer fire department to arrive, and after playing what water they had in the truck's tank, stand by helplessly—there being no fire hydrants (a detail sadly over-looked in all Antoinette's architecture and design and decoration magazines) and thus nothing left for them to do but watch the house burn.

It was a miracle, they said later, that Vivian had escaped with the minor burns on her hands and her curly hair and eyebrows singed. They were of the opinion that she had been confused and only thought that she had been in the kitchen. They explained to Mrs. Malone that nobody could have been in that kitchen. Not and lived.

Clara and Maureen stood off from the rest of the family on the front lawn, with their arms around one another's waists; Snow White sat beside them, the fire reflected orange in his yellow eyes. The girls murmured quietly from time to time. They were sharing yet another moment. Sadder even than a Chopin nocturne. Form-ing another bond—that was to last the rest of their lives.

Willie stood next to Vivian, who held Chief. Mrs. Malone had placed him in the girl's arms, knowing from experience the great solace it was in time of bad trouble to hold a child in your arms.

Vivian looked from the still burning house to Mama Malone. Papa Maguire and Jim stood to either side of her, supporting her.

Gilbert had been the last one to see Antoinette. He'd told Mama that she'd come out the front door, and been safe, but then she'd turned and gone back in when she'd learned that her baby was still inside.

"She sacrificed her life," Mama said, weeping. "For her baby. And I'd thought, God forgive me, that she wasn't a good mother."

And so in the dark and the smoke and the cold, the Malones acquired their very own martyred mother. A lately living saint, who gave up her young life to save the life of a child. Knowing the Malones' great regard for mothers, and their proclivity for tears, Vivian could only imagine the oceans of Malone tears that would be shed down the generations whenever Antoinette's name fell from anyone's lips. And the interesting part of this to Vivian, was that Antoinette hadn't even liked Chief. She really hadn't. So perhaps the Malones *were* right to pay this homage to mother-love.

When the others left, a little before dawn, Papa Maguire stayed. He sat in a lawn chair, wrapped in a blanket, drinking whiskey against the cold, until morning. Someone had to stay because Antoinette's body was in the rubble of the house, beneath the rafters, which still glowed red-hot, and it could not be safely removed until morning. Papa would stay until it was done. It would also be his sad duty to be there when John Washington arrived. For John was already gone from Sylvan when Mr. Callahan telephoned to the Stewarts. John Washington, Papa thought, would drive up expecting to see his house and his wife and his children just as he had left them. But nothing, Papa knew, stays as you've left it forever. He himself had come home one day, to the wife who had dependably laid abed for ten years, to find that good woman dead.

✿

Antoinette's requiem Mass was attended by nearly everyone in Myrtle. A young mother who has died trying to save her baby from flames is generally acknowledged and much honored, after all. And this is as it should be. The friends of the various members of the Malone family were every one present, and the Malones themselves, all of them, even the ones sojourning in Texas and Tennessee, formed a solid phalanx at the front of Saint Clare's. John Washington and his girls sat in the first pew. Emmy sat with them, holding Chief. Behind them, the Malones and Papa Maguire. And at the very back of the church, near the door, stood Gilbert, who'd delivered the flowers. He was dressed in white coveralls.

The coffin on its bier at the bottom of the main altar, was banked with white flowers. All the same flowers that Antoinette had carried at her wedding. Mrs. Malone had been adamant about this. John Washington had had the Kraemer brothers arrange for the flowers that were out of season and rush them to Myrtle. John himself went forward before the Mass began to kneel a moment in prayer and to lay a white lady lily on his wife's closed coffin.

"O Lord Jesus Christ, King of glory, deliver the souls of all the faithful departed from the pains of hell and from the bottomless pit; deliver them from the lion's mouth, that hell swallow them not up . . ." Father Ryan intoned.

Really. What, wondered Vivian, would Antoinette be doing in a *lion's* mouth, anyway? She took Chief from Emmy's lap and held him to her tightly, much as she might have held Gilbert the dog. She sat next to Daddy. Clara sat on his other side. Clara kept having to nudge him so he would know when to stand and sit and kneel. Maybe because he was too upset to pay attention, or maybe

Daddy really *didn't* know what to do. He'd almost never come to church with them. He sat perfectly still, his eyes on Antoinette's child-size coffin. He didn't look so much sad as he looked tired. Everlastingly tired, as he would have said. And to Vivian's surprise, he wasn't crying. He hadn't cried once since he'd come home and found his wife dead and his house burned down. I hope, Vivian thought, he hasn't been saving it up; I really hope he isn't going to start crying now, with everybody in creation *watching* us.

But it was not John Washington who cried; it was Vivian. Who was more surprised than anyone. Daddy gave her his big white handkerchief and patted her shoulder. Clara leaned across to look at her. "What *is* it?" she hissed.

Vivian shook her head. The smell of all the white flowers was overwhelming. She saw the old nun from the convent garden sitting just across the aisle—the old woman's head was bowed, her crippled hands in her lap; the air around her was dense and fretted with fervent prayer. Vivian could smell the yellow smell of tuberoses, but there were none in the church. Daddy took her hand.

"Little Vivian's the softhearted one," Mrs. Malone whispered to Papa Maguire.

"Aye, she always was," he said.

Vivian was still crying when it was time to go up for Communion. And though she'd worried for years, all her life, almost, about not being able to cry, already she was worrying about what she'd do if she couldn't stop.

Coda

John Washington, twice widowed, and still young, never married again. There was not a woman in Myrtle who over the years did not grieve to watch John Washington's good looks and youth slip away.

Nor did he rebuild Antoinette's house. Instead he moved with his children back to his mother's house on La Salle Avenue. And he brought Gilbert back to live above the garage to care for it. Gilbert—who had risked his life, going twice into the burning house after Antoinette, and who along with Mr. Callahan had rescued John's infant son. Though John had never liked him, and though Gilbert had what seemed to John, who should have known, a worsening drinking habit, John Washington felt honor-bound to do what he could for him. Cassie, however, did not return; she left Gilbert and moved in with a sister in New Orleans, having washed her hands of Gilbert and all the Washingtons, living and dead.

But the house, being so large, needed a full-time housekeeper, and so John Washington sent to north Louisiana for a light-skinned colored woman named Odessa, to run the house. As Cassie had done in his mother's time.

Nobody in town knew who she was, or why John Washington should have sent for her. Or how it was that he knew her at all. And it was not explained to them. It was generally thought that this Odessa woman was peculiar and high-handed. She wore jewelry and somebody claimed to have seen her sitting out by the fishpond in a red kimono. Tradesmen who worked in the Washington house said she spent more time singing than working and that she acted like she thought she was white, and the mistress of the house instead of its housekeeper. But poor John, the ladies of Myrtle exclaimed, and Bless his heart, they often remarked. If that peculiar colored woman made his life any easier, and it seemed that she did, well, they would keep their own counsel. For *his* sake.

In time, people in Myrtle took to calling anyone who put on airs or had a high opinion of themselves Miss Odessa. A child who wouldn't eat what was put in front of her was so addressed: "You think you're too good to eat rice and gravy? Well go hungry, then, Miss Odessa." This is, in fact, the only context in which her name is remembered there today.

Emmy stayed on as Chief's nurse. And later, as the years passed, and Chief grew up, Gilbert's drinking companion. Her liver suffered, but her stutter disappeared entirely.

John Washington's girls, it was said, were nothing alike, and grew every year less so. Clara and her good friend Maureen Malone's double piano recitals became occasions so exalted they eventually rivaled Myrtle's DAR History Pageant.

It was agreed that Clara was the picture of her poor dead mother, Della. Della's aunts were the prime source of this information, as few other people in Myrtle by this time actually remembered what Della had looked like. "I see her on the street," Leticia would say to anyone who would listen, "And my heart fairly stops. She's Della, all over." And it was true that Clara was beautiful and in time had many suitable beaux, though she was somehow to end up living most of her life with her good friend, Maureen Malone. (Neither of them ever married.)

Vivian, on the other hand, did not look like her mother. She did look a great deal like her father, but this went largely unnoticed by everyone but Odessa. Vivian didn't play the piano—except for "Chopsticks," which she had the habit of pounding out aggressively on other people's pianos. Nor did she acquire any suitable beaux. She always had her nose in a book, and the only boy except for her brother, the beloved and notorious Chief, anybody ever saw her with was Willie Malone—and Willie, the Malones' smart albino with the Coke-bottle glasses, wasn't anybody in Myrtle's notion of a suitable beau. As it turned out, Vivian and Willie were the only ones ever to mistake one another for their hearts' desire.

The Chief, as he was known, always with the definite article, became Myrtle's pet. If his mother had died for him, the least the town could do, it seemed to have concluded, was to love him. And they *did* love him. With a vengeance. Without question. No matter what. Even, years later, when he came home from a stint in the penitentiary, they loved him. (They tried never to think what he had been in there for.) Sometimes when he was still a child, strangers asked whose he was, some even remarked the boy was two shades darker than the inside of Toby's hat. If they'd made this remark to a man, it would be met with a silence so cold and so solid that the visitor dropped the subject immediately. Didn't even think it to himself again when alone. If the remark was made to a woman, she answered so volubly and in such detail about the darling, darling Chief, and his sainted, dead mother and his poor, poor daddy that the visitor (if only in self-defense) never raised the topic again. Wouldn't have dreamt of it.

And so the threads of the Washingtons' history, like those of Myrtle's other families, were spun into whole cloth. Theirs was one of the finest families in the South, people said. Did you know that John Washington's people had fought in the Revolutionary War? His grandfather, it was now belatedly, and quite mysteriously, remembered, had led a regiment from South Carolina in the War Between the States. He'd been wounded. He'd lost an eye.

John Washington's two beautiful dead wives became every year more beautiful in memory, until their own proud mothers would have hesitated to claim them. Their sufferings and their heroism became epic and legend. As, of course, did John Washington's twice-broken heart, which the ladies enshrined, and found ever more touching as John aged and his crow-black hair turned finally white.

Clara and Maureen, and Vivian and Willie, like most of Myrtle's young people, grew up and moved away—far beyond the rings of green towns that John Washington had spent his life driving away from and back to. And eventually there came the day that John Washington parked his car in the garage next to the old red Essex—long off the road, too beloved to junk—and without a backwards glance, went into the house.

Walking into the bedroom, tired, and, John knew, old—too old to live on the road anymore—he threw his hat on the bed.

"Odessa," he announced, "I'm home."

"You moving in out of your car now, John?" she asked him softly.

"Darling," John Washington said, "I thought maybe I would."